The Twins of

Narvik

Part I

A Historical Novel by

David Trawinski

Drawn From the Case Files of

Sterling Investigations International

The Twins of Narvik, Part I

Published by DAMTE Associates

Front Cover Original Image Created by Kellen Churchill
Front & Back Cover Photos Copyright 2020 by Elizabeth Marie Trawinski
Front & Back Cover Layouts Arranged by David Trawinski
Editing and Original Photographs by Elizabeth Marie Trawinski
All Interior Image Attributions Listed on Page 348
Proofed by Paul Catterton, Jim Sprouse, and Jack Coffman

The author wishes to gratefully acknowledge the following sources:
> The International Churchill Society
> The Polish Institute and Sikorski Museum of London
> The War Museum (Narvik, Norway)
> The Ofoten Railway of Norway
> The Witchery at Castle Gate Restaurant, Castle Hill, Edinburgh
> McNaughtan's Bookshop, Edinburgh

And Special Thanks to Allan Foster, Author of Book Lovers' Edinburgh
> for allowing the use of his impressive tome in assisting my
> description of the literary wonderland that is Edinburgh.
All efforts to capture the Scottish burr are shamefully mine alone.

Historical Novels
by David Trawinski

The Chopin Trilogy:
    The Willow's Bend   (2016)
    Chasing the Winter's Wind   (2017)
    War of the Nocturne's Widow. (2018)

Ever Blooms the Rose   (2019)
    (Co-authored with Marie Trawinski)

The Life of Marek Zaczek Volume 1:
    Under the Wings of Eagles   (2020)

The Twins of Narvik, Parts I & II   (2021)

This Volume is Dedicated to All Those
Devastated by the Silent Cruelty of
Alzheimer's Disease and
All Forms of Dementia.

These Cold Hearted Afflictions Have
Robbed My Own Family of the Woman
Who Brought Us All Into this World,
Mildred Trawinski.

Thank God They Have Not Stolen Away
Those Most Cherished Memories
of Our Hard-Working
and Even Harder-Loving Mother.

Air view of Narvik from the north-west

Norsk Telegrambyraa

Figure 1: The Battles of the Arctic Port of Narvik
The Forgotten Early Engagements of World War II

A Chronology of Events in this Volume

1902   The Ofoten Railway connects Narvik, Norway to Sweden (11/15/02)

1909   SIS (Later MI6) established under Capt. Mansfield Smith-Cumming

1914   Austrian Archduke Franz Ferdinand Assassinated in Sarajevo (6/28/1914)

           Germany invades Belgium as fighting begins in Europe (8/3/1914)

           Mansfield Cumming's leg amputated after his son dies in car accident

1915   Allied Naval incursion into the Dardanelles Strait (3/18/1915)

           Gallipoli Landings by British and ANZAC Troops (4/25/1914)

1918   End of Fighting in Europe; Poland re-established as a Nation (11/11/1918)

1919   Treaty of Versailles formally ends World War I (6/28/1919)

1920   Prohibition introduced the United States by the 18th Amendment

           Polish-Soviet War concludes after the *Miracle at the Vistula*

1923   Ofoten Railway electrified

           Mansfield Cumming dies of heart attack

           Admiral Hugh "Quex" Sinclair named 2nd Chief of SIS

           Munich *Beer Hall Putsch* fails, Hitler imprisoned

1929   US Stock Market Crash begins the Great Depression (10/24/1929)

1932   Hitler loses German Presidential Election to Hindenburg

           Polish Cryptographers break the German Enigma Code

1933   President Hindenburg appoints Hitler German Chancellor (1/30/1933)

           Prohibition repealed in the United States by the 21st Amendment

           Reichstag Fire (2/27/1933); Book Burnings Begin

1934   *Night of Long Knives* (SA decimated by SS and the Gestapo) (6/30/1934)

1936   Nazi Troops re-enter the Rhineland violating the Versailles Treaty

           Germany Hosts Olympic Games in Berlin

1938   *Anschluss* of Austria into the German Reich (3/12/1938)

           Munich Conference awards Czech *Sudetenland* to Germany (9/30/1938)

           German *Kristallnacht - Night of Broken Glass* (November 9-10, 1938)

1939   Launch of Battleships *Bismarck* (2/14/1939) and *Tirpitz* (4/1/1939)

           Hitler Invades remainder of Czechoslovakia (3/15/1939)

           Germany invades Poland beginning World War II (9/1/1939)

           SIS Chief Hugh "Quex" Sinclair dies; Stewart Menzies named 3rd SIS Chief

Author's Note:

Let the prospective reader be forewarned that this volume constitutes only one half of the historical saga that is "The Twins of Narvik". I chose to break this story which encompasses over 800 pages into two volumes, Parts I & II.

This volume's story is told in alternating chapters covering Sterling International Investigations' search for the truth in the modern day, and the exact nature of that truth which actually occurred in the period from 1912 to 1939.

"The Twins of Narvik, Part II" is similarly structured, with the storyline covering the time period of 1939 - 1945 during World War II.

I am a devout lover of history, and occasionally my recanting of the historical elements surrounding the timeline of my story may not be of interest to the casual reader who may be eager to continue the story itself. For the consideration of those readers, I have marked such chapters clearly on its title pages and headers as *"Historical Reference"* so that the reader may skip these without affecting the overall flow of the storyline. Of the 37 chapters in this volume, 8 are so marked.

I hope you enjoy this tale of adventure, courage, dedication, interdependent identities, and above all else, brotherly and familial love.

David Trawinski

The Life of Winston Churchill

This novel references the life of Winston Spencer Churchill after becoming the First Lord of the Admiralty at age 40. However, his exploits before that age were themselves enough to fill volumes. He was born in Blenheim Palace, the home awarded to his ancestor, John Churchill, the First Duke of Marlborough for his victory at the Battle of Blenheim in 1704. Winston was born in 1874 to a politician father and an American socialite mother. His mother was reportedly very promiscuous among the men of the English upper strata, often with liaisons intended to further young Winston's career. His father, a prominent Member of Parliament himself, failed to reach his goal of becoming Prime Minister, and sadly eventually died from complications of syphilis.

Young Winston graduated from the Royal Military Academy Sandhurst, and soon found himself in Africa, and later India. He served in the British armed forces while concurrently reporting as a journalist for England's newspapers. His reporting skills led him to write several books, including _"The Story of the Malakand Field Force"_ (1898), _"The River War"_ (1899), _"From London to Ladysmith Via Pretoria"_ (1900) and _"Ian Hamilton's March"_ (1900). The last two volumes documented his being taken prisoner during the Boer War in South Africa, his escape, and the victorious march back into Pretoria to free the prisoners with whom he had been held. He even penned the political novel, "Savrola" in 1900.

By the time Winston Churchill became the First Lord of the Admiralty in 1914, he was already an extremely popular figure in Britain. That would change with the great disgrace that beset him following the Dardanelles and Gallipoli campaigns during World War I. He would lose his position atop the Admiralty, only to regain that stature, albeit briefly, in the opening months of World War II. He then transcended it by becoming Prime Minister of the United Kingdom at the age of sixty-five. He led the country through its serpentine path to the war's victory, at which point he was voted out of office. Despite this indignity, Churchill returned as Prime Minister only six years later in 1951.

His writings on the histories of the World Wars, along with the remarkable gravitas of his other works, had earned Churchill the Nobel Prize for Literature. He died of a stroke in 1965 at the age of ninety. His memory remains inseparable from British perseverance, and in this way he will never be forgotten.

WARMONGER, PEACEMAKER   SOLDIER, PRISONER OF WAR
SCAPEGOAT, GLORY HOG   BRITON, AMERICAN'S SON
WRITER, PAINTER   CHARISMATIC, REPUGNANT
HISTORIAN   MAKER OF HISTORY
LIBERAL   CONSERVATIVE
VICTOR   VANQUISHED

FIGURE 2: THE CHANGING FACES OF WINSTON CHURCHILL

1 The Client's Conundrum

*"The longer you can look back,
the farther you can look forward."*

Winston Spencer Churchill

"Truth is not a procurable commodity. It is nothing more than a virgin pearl dropped in the all-consuming sea of time. It sinks into the obscured depths of the ages. Time, like the sea, offers just enough clues to intrigue us, so that we keep searching her murky depths. She even offers false truths, misconceptions hardened by the aging of her hand that she desires for us to accept as 'real'. In this way, time demonstrates her dominion over the poorest wretched souls and even those affluent beyond all measure. We will all one day come to realize that no matter the bounds of our personal resources, be they of largesse or of want, we shall all be consumed by the eternal tide. Only then, will time yield her ultimate secrets, those of the unobstructed truth."

Diane Sterling was unsure where this elaborate oratory came from within her. Perhaps from her two recent brushes with death, or perhaps from their result, which was her own uncertain questioning of life's very meaning. She did however know for certain that the assignment she was being asked to undertake was a nearly impossible task.

In any case, *"The Huntress,"* as she had been known during her years at the Central Intelligence Agency, was being asked to investigate a situation from over eighty years ago, and she was not sure if enough relevant information existed to lead her to "the truth".

"That's about the biggest crock of shit I think I may have ever heard," said the man standing next to her, looking penetratingly into her eyes. He then replaced his ear protection, and Diane followed, putting on her own.

"Pull," yelled the man, who had raised his Silver Pigeon Beretta over/under shotgun, and was soon tracking an orange clay target that had been launched upon his command.

The target glided gracefully over the manicured lawn that sloped gently down and away from the two figures. The Brazos River flowed sedately at the bottom of the landscape, but well beyond the flight path of the orange disc, or the exploding shot that soon pursued it.

The man raised his shotgun, coming up and behind the target, which was still ascending to its apogee. His gun shuddered as his finger pulled the trigger, with an explosion from its upper barrel. The clay disc shattered, with fragments flying in multiple directions. The barrel of the shooter's gun had never stopped moving, following through the target's path as Diane herself had long ago also been instructed.

Wade Conley's face creased with the slightest smile of satisfaction. He was a man who had long ago wrestled with pride and had learned to wear it with dignity. It was a trait that Diane had come to know in the ultra-wealthy. The greatest pleasure of wealth was in allowing it to show itself in an understated manner. No need to be flamboyant. Just let the simplicity of confidence tell the world you have mastered its tasking. You are one of the few, the self-select. You are one of the most deserving of its inhabitants. You are, quite simply, in a word, *"Special"*.

The scene repeated itself until Wade Conley had taken aim and fired at four more flying clay disks. Wade's volleys hit solidly upon each of these four targets from his position behind and to the left of the trap house, from which the decoy disks were launched. On his face, Diane could see the imprint of satisfaction, stamped with the unyielding force of pride.

Wade then removed the ear protection, stuffing the plugs into the pocket of his shooting jacket. He had told Diane that he preferred the earplugs over the headphone-styled protection because the latter interfered when he brought his chin to rest against the shotgun's stock to line up his eye with the barrel's bead.

"Nice shooting, Wade," Diane congratulated him.

Wade Conley looked at her hollowly, as if she had not said a word. It was another trait of the rich to treat compliments with disdain, as if they were mere useless flattery, unless they came from someone richer than themselves. And there were few richer than Wade, or more correctly said, than his father.

Diane could see that Wade was focused now, and not only on the flying clay disks that he had so effectively dropped from the sky into shattered fragments onto the manicured lawn.

Wade was intent on passing his views along to Diane, while he could do so unfiltered before the dinner meeting in a few hours with his father, Jake.

"Damn it, Diane," Wade said, as he ignored her compliment, "what good is having all the money in the world if you can't buy what you want with it?"

"I suppose not of much use at all," she responded, not missing a beat, "if what you want is for sale."

"Everything's for sale, Diane," Wade continued. "We all know that the truth is just another thing to buy, just that it may cost a little more, mind you. Now, in this case, I told Daddy to save his money. We've already had his Mama's claims looked into. Not once, mind you, but twice. Both investigators came back and reported that there was nothing to them. But when he saw that piece on the news show about how you had taken on the CIA and won, and then used the settlement to start your own agency focused on international investigations, he demanded I call you to do one last inquiry. I told him no, that this thing had already been settled, but that man sure can be a hard-headed son of a bitch. I guess you don't get to being one of the richest men in America being anything else, do you?"

Wade opened the breech of his shotgun and the last empty shell ejected out over his shoulder. The look on his face was one of steely determination.

"Wade, am I to infer that you just want the same answer a third time so your father can have some peace of mind?" asked Diane, reading the man's intention.

By that point, she felt she knew this man, although she had just met him earlier that day. She knew the type.

"Diane," Wade Conley responded, "my father is eighty-seven years old and his doctors say he has only a couple years left at best. I want him to be able to relax with a clear mind so he can really enjoy the little time he has remaining."

Diane was reading Wade well by that point. *He just wants the status quo, no competition when it comes to inheriting his father's estate*, she thought.

"Surely your father must have some reason to believe your grandmother's claims," reasoned Diane, "or he wouldn't have called in my firm."

"Daddy's Mama passed twenty years ago," interrupted Wade. "She was as crazy as a loon before she left us. Why can't Daddy see this? Well, I guess his own mind hasn't been so clear over the past several years."

"Well, Wade, given the length of time since your grandmother's passing, and the nature of her claims," said Diane, "I am only saying that this is likely to be quite an expensive investigation."

"Not for Daddy," added Wade, "not with the fortune that he's stockpiled. My view is it's a waste of good money, but he so wants to believe in his Mama's rantings. She was bat shit crazy at the end, you know. If you want to know the full truth, she was pretty loony even before the dementia crept in."

Diane opened the breech of her shotgun and loaded a shell in the upper barrel. She noted it was the second time that Wade had questioned his grandmother's mental acuity in such a coarse manner.

"Today we understand her condition a bit better, Wade," she said. "It's a process, a debilitating and heartbreaking process. Your grandmother had dementia, possibly Alzheimer's Disease. That was twenty years ago, and even then it was not as well understood as it is today. Give her a break. For someone who had lived past the century mark herself, I think she deserves a little consideration."

Wade looked at her with mild contempt that seemed to Diane to say, *Don't you even begin to judge me, woman.*

Wade Conley smiled softly, almost smirking at her. "Don't get me wrong, Diane. I'm not insulting her," he said, "I loved the woman, for God's sake. I'm just stating a fact. Even when she was young, Cassandra was unpredictable at best. She could go from the highest highs to the lowest lows in the flash of a summer's lightning storm. She loved a good time, that was for sure, but her joy never seemed to last long. The names of the diagnoses given to her severe mood swings kept changing: social anxiety disorder, chemical imbalances, manic-depressive disorder. Even given all that, she never came by her strangest claims until the last ten years of her life. The fact was that Cassandra was plum loco by the time she was making all this shit up."

Diane noticed how Wade, a man in his late fifties, with his neatly trimmed gray hair and a matching pencil mustache, refused to acknowledge his father's mother as his grandmother.

He referred to her by her name, Cassandra, or as his father's Mama. There was a perceptible lack of intimacy in his relationship to her. Was this because her "mad ravings" were a direct threat to his claim at a sole inheritance?

Diane replaced her ear protection, snapped the breech of her shotgun closed and walked over to the marked position from which Wade had just finished shooting. It was her last round of five targets. She had been intentionally letting her client win, but thought she would go out strong. She brought the gun up to her shoulder and shifted her weight forward onto her left leg. Her right foot was at ninety degrees as she lifted its heel.

"Pull," she yelled. The clay flew from the trap house. She tracked it with the bead at the end of her barrel.

She followed the target, and passed through its path of flight before she gently squeezed the trigger. The clay exploded upon impact into the tiniest of fragments. She quickly cracked open the gun's breech and as the empty shell was ejected over her shoulder, she rapidly reloaded the upper barrel, snapped the breech closed, raised the gun back to its shooting position, released the safety and again yelled "pull". She swiftly repeated this sequence three more times.

The last four pigeons each exploded into scattered fragments of clay confetti. The consecutive hits were impressive, but it was the pace at which this all occurred that surprised Wade.

"That last five was some damned good shooting, Diane," offered Wade, once she had removed her ear protection and had breeched her gun after her final shot.

"Thanks, Wade," she said. Diane smiled at him, with a look that she hoped would further say what she cared not to. *That's the way I always shoot when I am not letting a client feel good about himself. Or more correctly, the client's son.*

"I think that's enough trap for today, Diane," said Wade. "You must be feeling that twelve gauge after fifty rounds?" asked Wade

Diane's shoulder was pulsing, despite the finely padded and fitted woman's shooting jacket that Wade Conley had supplied to her upon arrival earlier that day. She thought it strange, at first, that he would have such a collection of sizes for his visiting lady shooters, then she formed an image of Wade as a man who liked his ladies. Diane imagined that Wade liked to bring his women here to show off his prowess with the shotgun.

Thinks it makes him look like more of man than he is?

"Yes, Wade," answered Diane, "I think I have had enough of you schooling me on proper technique. Sorry I didn't give you much competition."

I could have beat him outright if I was not holding back.

"Don't fret one bit, Diane," Wade responded, "you surprised me with your handling of that gun. Hitting thirty-two of fifty is nice work for someone who doesn't do it all the time. Now that the shooting's over, let's have that drink."

Diane had counted. Wade did not mention that he had hit forty of his fifty targets. He just allowed that fact to linger unstated between them. They walked away from the trap house, each with their barrels breeched.

"Just give that gun to Kellen, here," Wade instructed her, "he'll take care of both of these for us. Take your shooting jacket back to your room. If you don't care to take it home as a souvenir, then lay it on the bed and Lucita will retrieve it while we're having dinner with Daddy."

Diane had not yet met "Daddy". He was resting when she and Wade had arrived earlier that day. Jake Conley, Wade's father, the billionaire fracking king, was resting. Diane looked forward to meeting him later that night.

Diane and Wade both handed their guns to Kellen, who slung them over the padded shoulder of his khaki shooting sweater. He handled the weapons like second nature. Diane had tagged him as ex-special ops earlier as he was demonstrating the trap and skeet range for her. He had not missed any of the ten clays he took aim upon.

Jake and Wade likely had hired him for security. Perhaps only a driver/personal bodyguard, but something told Diane it was much more likely that he was the head of their entire security program. It was the way he hovered patiently, with the spare weapon. Just in case…

Diane and Wade walked over to the black wrought iron table and chairs that were elevated just behind their shooting positions. Waiting for them on a silver tray was a Balcones Texas Single Malt Whisky in an oversized rock glass for him, and a tall, cold Belvedere Vodka with grapefruit juice for her.

It had become Diane's signature drink in honor of her former mentor, the late Stanley Wisniewski, from her long career within the CIA. Diane had taken up drinking only Polish vodka as a simple tribute to her departed friend.

The CIA's Deputy Director of Operations (DDO), Jack Trellis, had tasked her to hunt down Stanley, who then was on the run across Europe. Little did she know that Jack Trellis used her to track her friend and mentor only so the DDO could hide his own corrupt secrets.

When Trellis subsequently turned on Diane, the British Secret Service, MI6, helped her take refuge and lay low. Ultimately, her own life was threatened by Trellis and the Agency, not once but twice.

Diane resigned her position and brought suit against her former employer in a case that made headlines worldwide. No one had ever successfully sued an intelligence agency before, and much sensitive material was declassified on the order of the judge who appeared to favor her claim. Just before the case went to jury, the agency granted her a windfall settlement, which she then used to open her own agency, *Sterling Investigations International, or SII.*

In establishing *SII,* she was able to convince her two young colleagues from the Agency, Emory Hauptmann and Sophie Czystowska, to join her firm. Over the past three years, they had created a burgeoning agency of top-shelf clientele, with small but very respectable offices in New York, London and Berlin. It was when her story had been highlighted on a prominent TV news magazine that she had been contacted by Wade on behalf of his dad, Jake.

Diane seated herself and removed her protective eyewear, tossing the gear onto the table. Wade did the same. He then raised his drink to offer a toast to his guest.

Diane raised her glass in return as Wade toasted, "Diane, may you always be in the pink, even if it won't always be under the pink skies of a Texas sunset over the Brazos!"

Before them, beyond the river and the trees that lined the hills climbing its far banks, the skies were painted with the most incredible palette of salmon and coral shades ranging to crimson. A few clouds' undersides were illuminated by a tender hues of softened magenta. Splashes of aqua and indigo traced through the sky as highlights. It was truly spectacular, thought Diane.

"Yessiree," Wade professed, stretching each syllable, "the good Lord certainly paints upon one very impressive canvas, doesn't He?"

"He most certainly does," agreed Diane, truly impressed by the spectral elegance of sky framing the setting orange sun.

She could see that Wade had this all timed out perfectly and had likely made a habit of shooting at this time of day to impress his partners. It would make him feel manly, feel virile. She imagined, despite his mentioning to her that he was married, that he brought his women here to watch him shoot. *He's too cocky of a son of a bitch not to have some women on the side.*

"Cheers," said Diane, gently clinking glasses with her host. She drank from her cool libation, which was perhaps the best drink she had in some time. Did she detect a trace of St. Germain liqueur? In her mind, she could hear her young friend and now employee, Sophie, saying, *I hope you are enjoying your Pomeranian.*

It was an inside joke. Vodka and grapefruit juice is known in bars throughout the world as a "Greyhound". Variations are known as Salty Dogs, Dirty Dogs, and so on. Sophie, or *Zosia*, as Diane preferred to call her, dubbed her vodka and grapefruit as a Polish Dog, or Pomeranian, because Diane had come to demand only Polish vodka.

If Emory, her American born specialist in German culture and history were there, he would begin a good natured discourse that the area known as Pomerania, while it was inside the borders of Poland today, historically was a German province. Hell, even the Swedes possessed it at one point. He would argue it was anything but Polish. How those two could squabble, she thought. Diane laughed to herself thinking of the good natured ribbing that would ensue between Emory and Sophie.

"Cheers," replied Wade as he pulled from his Balcones. "So, Diane, you must have a thousand questions by this point. What can I fill you in on before dinner with Jake tonight?"

"Well, to tell you the truth, Wade, I did my research on your father and his firm before I came down," she admitted.

"I would expect no less," Wade replied, "for someone of your background. I just thought you might still have a few questions about Cassandra. The old girl was a real Hell-raiser all her life. Even throughout her eighties. Wasn't until her mid-nineties when she lost it all, poor girl. Most people say she's where my father got his spark, his drive from. His own dad was much more reserved, but damn if Grandpa Lucas didn't love him some Cassandra."

Wade's father, Jake, had inherited a small fortune years ago from his own father, who had been a second tier Texas oilman for his entire life. His father had ridden out the boom/bust cycles of the industry and had passed from this world with a modest fortune that was left entirely to his only son. And now Wade's father, Jake, would go on to turn that modest fortune into a truly indecent one. One that Wade had waited his entire life to inherit.

Jake had taken that comfortable sum left to him and invested it in the latest technology, going all-in on the most modern extraction method of hydraulically fracturing the massive underground shale formations to release trapped reserves of oil and natural gas. The so-called "fracking" approach became somewhat of a craze in Texas. Jake Conley had become one of the first who learned how to extract the enormous wealth hiding within the massive shale formations that ran under the state.

Jake Conley had intuitively bought up mineral rights, for fractions of a penny on each dollar, from landowners who never suspected the great wealth that was within the shale deposits which lay beneath their ranches, farms, and even larger homesteads. Fracking would go on to make Jake a multi-billionaire over the next forty years.

Now, like his father before him, Jake found himself facing death with a fortune that stubbornly refused to cross that last great divide with him. Also, like his father, he had but a single son to inherit his fortune. However, it was an even more massive wealth that death would strip from Jake Conley.

Jake's son was the man sitting beside Diane. Wade Conley was a man in his late-fifties. His age was not far from Diane's own. He had an outdoorsman's features, but even these were softened with the trappings of his own wealth. His face was tan, but not weathered. His hands were strong, but not calloused. His fingers knew work, but their manicured nails suggested that work was directing the on-goings of his father's firm, but certainly not undertaking any of its manual labors.

"Cassandra passed away twenty years ago, right?" asked Diane. "She was how old?"

"The glorious age of one hundred and four, and it was only in the last ten years or so that the old bird totally lost her marbles, God rest her soul." Wade lowered his head in mock respect.

"She claimed that she had two other sons than Jake?"

"So she claimed, after she went stark raving mad," said Wade. He washed down the bitter words with a pull of Balcones.

"Dad was always an only child, just like me. There were never any other children, just Jake."

"In her last years she claimed to have been born in Norway?" Diane asked, although she knew it via her client prep.

"Like I said, not until she went off the deep end," clarified Wade. "She claimed her two boys, identical twin boys, mind you, were war heroes. Both gave their lives for their country during the war."

"Which war?" Diane was in full business mode by then.

"She never clearly stated," answered Wade, "but if it were true, which it most certainly is not, it would most likely have had to have been World War II. Hell, my grandfather knew her since the twenties, when they met in a New York City speakeasy. He brought her back to Texas and they married in 1922. She had as much Norwegian blood in her as I do Comanche, not a single red drop."

"How old was she when she met your grandfather?" asked Diane.

"In her early twenties, from what our other investigators found. She was born in England, came to New York City just after the First World War."

"It is possible she may have had children before she met your grandfather, isn't it?" asked Diane.

"No, Diane, it is not. There is no such record here in America nor over in Britain. Our earlier investigators checked that out quite thoroughly. Dad has no brothers, period, end! Now, I am sorry you had to come all the way down to Texas just to keep Daddy happy, but I'm afraid this is all about the ravings of a mad old woman who died twenty years ago. Jake will fill you in on the rest at dinner."

It was clear to Diane that Wade saw even the remote possibility of his father having unknown brothers as a threat to his pending inheritance. Even if these twins did indeed exist and it was true that they had perished in the war, they might have produced offspring who could arise suddenly and make a claim. This uncertainty gnawed at the man like a chronic irritation.

It was just easier for Wade to say that Cassandra's claims had been debunked, not once but twice, case closed!

Unfortunately, his father, Jake, still wanted it desperately to be true. And Diane knew it was Jake who had brought her to Texas, not Wade. It would be Jake that would be paying her fees should she agree to take on this case.

"I am sorry I didn't get the chance to meet your father earlier when I arrived. I must admit, I was quite eager to do so, Jake certainly is a well respected man in these parts...."

"In all parts..." Wade corrected her.

Wade had met her at the DFW Airport when her plane touched down and Wade had his driver take them over to the nearby helicopter facility. There they boarded his father's private chopper for the short flight to the Texas Hill Country. Wade made a great tour guide, pointing out the branches of the Trinity River, as they flew over Fort Worth. To points west and then south, Wade had the chopper follow the route of the meandering Brazos.

After they had arrived at his father's compound (it was too secure to merely be called a home, a ranch or even a mansion), After learning that she was proficient with shotguns, Wade had insisted that they shoot trap together. Along the way, Diane had pegged Wade as being tired of his role as second-in-command, waiting for the bulk of his father's wealth to become his own.

Wade Conley, in the setting Texas sunlight, drew another pull from his Balcones and addressed Diane's last comment.

"Well, Diane, Jake is just as eager to meet you, but he needed to rest this afternoon. He wants you to take on this project very badly. After we wash up, we'll go in and have dinner with him. However, don't be surprised if he doesn't eat much at his age. He always loved his meals, but at eighty-seven, he finds less joy in them. I'm just glad he's still at the table, if you know what I mean..."

"I can understand that, Wade. I lost my own father at a much younger age, so consider yourself blessed."

"Well, that is a blessing, of course, but at times can be somewhat of a minor curse, also," added Conley. He again raised his Balcones, drawing strongly from it.

"Really? A minor curse? How so?" she asked Wade.

"Daddy is clearly getting ready to cash in his chips. He won't say so outright, but you can tell it from being around him. Telling the estate manager what is to go to whom, and so on. I'm told many older folks get that way, that somehow directing the distribution of even their smallest possessions gives them a sense of accepting their own mortality. I'm not saying he's given up on living, not at all. He's just adjusted his outlook on life to accept it."

"What exactly do you mean by *it?*" asked Diane. She could see he had waited a long time for his father's pending physical demise. It was near now, perhaps only a year or two away, and Wade could taste it - the inheritance, that is.

"Well, Diane, Daddy's come to realize that life is a finite arc of time and travel. His wealth may have protected him from being blasted out of his destined flight, sort of like one of these clay pigeons, but no mountain made of money is going to stop his life from ultimately shattering to the ground."

Diane thought to herself, *Now Wade, that was a much bigger crock of shit than what I said.*

"Naturally, I stand to inherit the bulk of his estate, but…" Wade hesitated for the first time since she had met him earlier that afternoon.

"But what, Wade?" asked Diane.

"…this whole business with Cassandra seems to have become all he has been able to focus on for the past several years. I have been running the family business for the last dozen years or so, and a good thing too, cause Daddy can't get his Mama's ramblings off his mind."

And you, Wade, can't get the thought of having to share his inheritance off your mind, Diane thought.

"Well, that's understandable," she said. "Don't you think so? His mother lived much longer than his Dad, didn't she? Only natural that he would dwell on her. Any man who had been a single child all his life would surely want to know for sure if he ever had brothers."

"Diane, I know you must be a special talent, but remember that you are the third firm to investigate this for Jake. I brought in two other agencies, both top notch, mind you, over the past several years to look into Cassandra's ravings."

"What exactly did my colleagues uncover?" she asked.

"Just the truth, plain and simple, that's all. Both found no basis whatsoever for her warbled recollections, but the old fella just won't accept it." An anger, or was it merely frustration, simmered in Wade's eyes.

"Perhaps the third time will be the charm," she quipped.

"Well, Diane, as charming as you are, I certainly hope your team will not work too hard trying to prove Cassandra prophetic," replied Wade Conley, raising his palpably resentful eyes to Diane's own. "She was as crazy as a loon. Terrible what that disease does to *these people.*"

It's not prophetic if she was talking about the past, Diane thought. She was aghast about how callously Wade could speak of his own grandmother, whether her claims were potentially complicating his life or not. For sure, Wade wanted everyone to agree she was talking nonsense. That there were no relatives, living or imagined, for which Wade was to share his father's mountain ranges of wealth. Let the present be as it is, and let the past rest like a sleeping dog.

They finished their drinks and walked along the lighted, flagstone paved path back to the house as the fringe of darkness called out the metallic songs of the cicadas. That is, if one would even dare call this structure simply a house. It was a mansion in every respect of the word, with more wings than some homes have bedrooms. And in all its imposing elegance, done up in a very expensive western decor, Diane felt already that this structure lacked most what would make it a true home - love.

Diane washed up and rested for thirty minutes before dressing for dinner. She was called upon at the appointed time by a house servant's polite, but crisp, knock on the door. A young, beautiful Hispanic girl then led Diane to the central cascading staircase, which was carved from mahogany, the grains of its wood polished bright like ripples upon a stream.

That staircase descended - no, more like it flowed, she thought - from the upper floor down a grandiose, straight balustraded flight of stairs to an intermediate gray granite landing, upon which stood a table with a fragrant bloom of exquisite, fresh-cut flowers. In front of the table, inlaid in a most attractive red granite, was the unique shape of the state of Texas.

Why was this shape so prominent somewhere in the home of every Texan I have ever visited? she wondered. She immediately answered her own query. *For every man born here wants to be as independent in life as the shape of this state is to nature. Texas is like no other, whether by shape, by topography, or by attitude. True men not only respected her independence, but saw beauty in her symbol, and welcomed her unique presence into their homes.*

From this intermediate landing, there extended two curved matching mahogany staircases hugging the contoured paneled walls descending to the marble tiled floor of the entrance hall below. Overall, the staircase was like a waterfall crafted in wood, a single flow splashing upon a granite outcropping before separating into mirrored streams of mahogany, Diane thought.

As she descended one of the lower curved staircases, she sighted Wade Conley waiting beneath her. In front of her shooting partner was an aged man in his wheelchair, with a plaid woolen blanket draped over his legs.

It was Diane's first sighting of her new client, but Jake Conley looked anything but old. His face still looked chiseled, silvered-haired with a trimmed matching mustache. He looked vibrant for his eighty.

"Well, here comes our little lady house guest," said Jake as Diane approached the bottom of staircase.

"Come on, Daddy, you can't call her a little lady! That's disrespectful and is stereotypical of us Texans. Like we don't have any couth!"

"Wade, why don't you just shut the hell up!"

"No, no, it's fine, Jake," Diane said, extending her arm to take Jake's hand. "I rather like it coming from you, Mr. Conley. I find it quite cordial."

Jake shook her hand with a firm, authoritative grip. He then turned his head to address his son, Wade.

"See, Wade, she finds my distain for political correctness cordial. Besides, I am not apologizing for my life of privilege, after working my ass off my whole life to obtain it."

Jake turned back to Diane.

"He treats me like I'm feeble, which I most certainly am not. Come on, Diane, let's get on down to the dining hall. I don't get to use it much anymore, so I am looking forward to showing it off a little. We can talk over dinner."

"Lead the way, Jake," said Diane, "I am all yours."

"You better be, for what I am getting ready to pay you…" responded Jake with a half-hearted smirk.

They managed their way down the hall to the great dining room. Jake explained he had it installed after visiting the Biltmore Mansion in Asheville in North Carolina's Blue Ridge Mountains. He described how he had to tear out several rooms over the existing dining room to make way for the cathedral ceiling.

Jake had the trophy heads of his greatest game conquests stuffed and mounted on the walls surrounding the imposingly long dining room table, which he explained could seat forty in a pinch. Diane thought to herself that these animal heads could easily be replaced by the heads of all the business partners and competitors he must have taken down over the years.

"Truth be told, Missy, everything on the walls here was bagged by me on safari in Africa. I could have saved a lot of money by just going to one of the Game Hunt Reserve ranches not too far from here. Could have shot them all there. Yup, I could have, but that would have taken all the fun out of it, now wouldn't it? Besides, I held many a business dinner in here, and it wouldn't impress my guests much to find out these magnificent creatures were taken on a *pay-to-slay* hunt."

The meal of smoked quail and pheasant was served with asparagus, fresh roasted corn tamales and whole grain brown rice. The wine served was a Bordeaux that Diane found to be little drier than suited her taste, but she did not fail to partake of it. Jake explained that a pairing with a nice Chilean Merlot had been recommended by his house chef, Juan Sebastián, who also served as the wine steward. Jake, however, decided he wanted his beloved Bordeaux.

"Imagine that, I actually get to save on a staff position. Well, not really though, given what I am paying him. Besides, I figure if I am not going to drink what a sommelier recommends, why bother having a full-time one? I do love my Bordeaux, but if you prefer a Merlot or even a white, I can have someone fetch it for you."

"No, Jake, I am enjoying this wine very much, and whatever you are paying Juan Sebastián is money well spent. This food is incredible." Diane's last statement was sincere.

"Thank you. You know, I thought it only fitting to dine on this game amongst these trophy heads, Diane. From what I have been able to gather, you are quite the hunter yourself."

Diane blushed, as she knew that Jake was referring to her old CIA nickname, "*The Huntress*".

"I am not surprised, Dad," Wade interjected, "you should have seen her on the trap range this afternoon. Knows her way around a shotgun, that's for sure."

Turning to Diane, Wade then continued, "Dad was ever so impressed by that business of you taking on that corrupt group inside the CIA. He couldn't get enough of that in the press. It was after he saw you profiled on that TV news magazine that he had me call you to come down."

Jake, perturbed, interrupted his son. "Wade, don't go on talking about me like I wasn't here, damn it. Besides, we're not talking about your little game of winging clay pigeons in the sunset. Diane here is a life and death huntress. A hunter of men."

Jake then turned to speak directly to his guest. "You know, my boy uses that damn trap range of his as foreplay for his women. Knows his own pretty little wife can't get through the gates without calling ahead. So, Wade brings these women over here to my home, teaches them how to fire a shotgun, shows off the house and has been known to take a few of them upstairs for a toss. Disgusting, I tell you. Absolutely disgusting."

"Come on, Dad," Wade objected, "Diane doesn't want to hear all this."

"And nothing is more repulsive," Jake continued, "than the fact that he lets them shoot with a damn 28-gauge Beretta shotgun. Damn waste of a Silver Pigeon, if you ask me. He didn't get saucy with ya' out there, did he? I'll bust his britches. The boy is still not too old for that!"

Diane was embarrassed as she watched Wade lower his head as his father reprimanded him. "No, Wade was the perfect gentleman. And a remarkable shot, Jake."

"Only cause everything he shoots at doesn't fight back. That rhino over there, I shot that bastard dead on the run as he was charging our group. I was a lot younger back then, but that gray bastard would have stomped my ass had I misplaced that shot. Only thing that ever charged Wade here was a Texas highway patrol officer with a DUI. I got his ass out of that, too."

The dynamic between the father and son was unusual to say the least. It appeared Jake had no respect for his only son, and Wade was willing to put up with his father's sharp barbs so long as the inheritance was waiting on the wind.

"Well, Jake, you certainly know how to get things done, that's for sure. Wade tells me you had brought in two other firms before mine to investigate your mother's claims."

"Fact is, Diane, Wade brought those amateurs in. They didn't tell me anything I didn't already know. It was a waste of good money, nothing more."

"Maybe there isn't anything further to be told," suggested Diane.

"That is always possible. If you have finished eating, let's move on into the library. I always liked saying that, sounds like something from one of those old movies, doesn't it?"

Jake, Wade and Diane moved into the library. The room was absolutely massive, two stories with only a laddered walkway surrounding the second story of shelves. The books were all custom bound in volumes of black, brown, green, blue and red leather. Each was set ablaze with gold lettering. Those that had not been purchased in their original bindings were rebound in leather embossed with the line declaring, *"The Personal Library of Jacob Barrett Conley"*. It was as if the books were nothing more than a herd of cattle, their leather hides embossed with the brand of the Conley Ranch.

"Amazing, Jake. Did you see this at the Biltmore, too?" asked Diane.

"No, at some chateau in the Loire Valley, if I recall. Was there years before I could afford this place. Good thing, too, because unlike the Great Dining Hall, I don't think I could have had my architect retrofit this library. I am not sure who I paid more money to, my architect for this room, or the bookbinders for all these customized volumes in it."

"Well, it is magnificent. What's your favorite book, Jake?" asked Diane.

"Well, the most expensive book I have is an eight hundred-thousand dollar volume of James Joyce's Ulysses. Signed by Joyce, special print on Dutch paper, limited run, or some such horseshit. Ridiculous money to pay for a book. But I got it for two-hundred-grand from a collector who was down on his luck and needed fast cash. Most everything else are collectibles. I had them all bound in Chelsea, in London – your neck of the woods, I understand. But my favorite book of all is one of the few I actually took the time to read: "True Grit" by Charles Portis. I like the way it portrays the Old West."

"Even though it was written in 1968?" asked Diane. "Is it a true portrayal?"

"Diane, as you get older," Jake said with a laugh, "you get a certain clarity on the things you have come to respect in life. For me, it's the grit and honesty of the Old West, and certainly as immortalized by none other than the Duke, John Wayne. I loved that son of a bitch. Whether it's all true or not, I defer to one of my other favorite men, Winston Churchill. He once said of the lore of King Arthur, '*some things are either true or they should be...*' I loved that old bulldog."

"Yes, I saw you had some very nicely bound autographed editions of Churchill's works over there on the shelf. That man was also not much for political correctness, now was he?" offered Diane. "I guess that ability to say what was on his mind, whether the others wanted to hear it or not, was what got Britain through the war."

"Gotta love a man," responded Jake, "who said, '*I like pigs. Dogs look up to us, cats look down on us, but pigs treat us as equals.*' Wade, fix me a Drambuie off the cart over there. What would you like, Diane?"

"If you have a Scotch neat, that would make me happy…"

"Blended, Johnny Walker Black perhaps?" Jake offered.

"Oh, Jake, I'm sure you must have some single malts stashed away over there somewhere," she countered.

"Attagirl! Woman after my own heart, or liver, maybe," said Jake, gently slapping his thigh in delight. "I can't drink much of the good stuff anymore, but the Drambuie opens up my sinuses and helps me sleep. Tastes like horse piss, but I do like to bag a few z's every chance I get anymore."

Wade brought over the drinks. "Eighteen year-old Oban?" He offered the drink to Diane.

"Delightful, Wade. Thank you. Cheers. Here's to old Winston." The three of them raised their glasses. Wade's was once again full of Balcones Texas Single Malt.

Diane and Wade settled into a matching pair of western calfskin wing chairs, the only elements in this library that tied in with the upscale Western motif throughout the rest of the mansion. All elegantly done, and Western through and through. Jake faced them in his wheelchair.

"Well, Jake, I am sure you didn't bring me all this way to just impress me with your home, your cuisine and your literary collection. I think it's time to get down to brass tacks. Wade tells me you are concerned about some claims your mother made before she passed away some twenty years ago."

"Yes, let's get down to business. I like that about you, Diane. Well, I am afraid my boy here, Wade, really doesn't want to get down to the truth when it comes to my mother, now does he? Especially, given her ramblings after she had been diagnosed with Alzheimer's. Truth is, Missy, I am a might closer to the end of my own trail than the beginning of it, and old Wade is deathly afraid of having to share all of my estate that will be left behind with anyone else."

"I am sure I do not understand," Diane played along.

"Sure, Grandmother made some odd claims," Wade said, "but as I have already told you, we had her ramblings looked into, but there was nothing to them. Both investigators hit a brick wall, and I am not sure your firm won't do any differently."

Diane noted that only in the presence of his father had Wade referred to Cassandra Conley as "Grandmother" for the first time.

"Wade, if you're not going to let me tell my damn story, then get the hell out of my house!" Jake Conley began to choke on his own anger, beginning to cough hoarsely. He regained his breath after a few seconds. It was the first time he appeared frail to Diane.

"Back in the late 1980s, we had to have a full-time nurse companion brought in to live with my mother. Cassandra had just come up on ninety-years-old by that time. I wanted to bring her over here to live, but she refused to leave her and Daddy's old home up in Colleyville, close to DFW. She loved that house, called it her sanctuary, even though Dad was long gone. Soon enough, word got back to us that she kept telling Miss Andrews, her live-in nurse and companion, the same story over and over."

"And what was that, Jake?" asked Diane.

"My mother told Miss Andrews that she was from a small fishing village inside the Arctic Circle in Norway. She claimed she had two boys, a pair of identical twins, who fought for their country during the war. Kept telling that same story for the rest of her life, at least until just before the end. No more details than that. I never thought much about it, as I was still too busy making and enjoying my fortune at the time. But I am at a point in what's left of my life where I now realize I spent too much time chasing money and not enough trying to find out the truth."

"Dad, you've had a great life. Why do you continue to trouble yourself over this?"

"First of all, Wade, I ain't dead yet. So what if my doctors are telling me I may only have a couple years left. I still got plenty enough time to rewrite my Last Will and Testament, and if you keep dogging me over this, I may just do that. I guarantee you that you'll be kicking yourself in the ass if I do…"

Jake's voice had grown taut and stressed. Once again, the strain between father and son became evident to Diane. The discourse between he and Wade seemed to wear on Jake, yet he seemed to do nothing to alleviate it. Instead, he exasperated it further each time he spoke harshly to his son.

"Dad, I am only worried as to why you continue to agitate yourself over all this," replied Wade. "Grandmother Cassandra had dementia - this was all just the disease talking."

"Wade, damn it, I want to know the truth. Did I or did I not have two brothers out there that I never knew about? Or was, as you never fail to say, old Cassandra just plain out of her mind? And if she was not, I would just like to die knowing what happened to them. Is that too much for an old man to ..."

The old man began to cough again. It was a deep hacking cough, as if he was trying to expel every vile thing his body had ever done. Diane waited until he regained his composure to speak.

"Okay, Jake. So, Wade told me this has been investigated and there was no merit to her claims. A simple DNA test could clear this right up."

With her mention of the DNA test, Wade rose to his feet in objection. "I just have to interject at this point. Dad's lawyers have told him repeatedly *NOT* to do this, as it could open up all kind of claims to his estate, especially if Cassandra's ravings were proved to be true."

"What my son is saying, Diane, is that he is scared shitless that there may be other family members out in the world that he will be forced to share my fortune with. Sons of my brothers, maybe even their sons by now. My boy is deathly afraid of allowing anyone even so much as an opportunity to claim against his inheritance." Jake sneered in the direction of Wade at this point, before asking his son directly. "Wade, did Diane sign the Non-Disclosure Agreement?"

It had been the very first thing that Wade had her do upon arriving at the mansion. The NDA papers were beautifully laid out on the elegant round table in the foyer, in the place where she presumed fresh cut flowers in a vase were normally set out. In fact, when they came down for dinner, there were flowers arranged there, as well as those on the granite landing.

"Yes, Dad," Wade responded, "Diane signed as soon as she got here. Nothing we discuss while she is here will be communicated to anyone other than those we approve of in advance, whether she takes the assignment or not. Unless she wishes to run afoul of our army of lawyers."

"Good, now we can all get down to brass tacks," said Jake. A light sparked with his eyes. "Diane, my mother could be a very impulsive woman. Did whatever the hell she wanted. Certainly loved to play hard. Had more lovers than regrets. Her moods swung like a double-edged ax, but she sure as hell was not crazy."

"C'mon, Dad," objected Wade one last time. "Grandmother was battling dementia. She came to this country from England as Cassandra Barrett, married Grandpa during the roaring twenties and came to live with him afterward here in Texas. You were their only son. It's all very simple and straightforward. Why is it that you just can't accept this?"

"Because of Lucita ..." lashed back old Jake.

"Who's Lucita?" asked Diane.

"She's the family house servant, Juan Sebastián's daughter, the young woman we sent up to your room to collect you before dinner," explained Wade. Turning to his father, Wade demanded, "What the hell does Lucita have to do with this? She's only been here a few years."

"Because against the advice of my council of counsellors, I spit in a DNA vial and had Lucita send it off as her own. Paid her five grand to keep it a secret from you and everybody else around here."

Diane looked at Wade, who was fuming that his father had gone around him, but was too timid to confront the old man.

Jake continued on. "Turns out Lucita is half-Norwegian. Her Scandinavian heritage lit up like the Trafalgar Square Christmas tree," scoffed Jake Conley, causing Diane to smirk. Having lived in London for so long, she knew that Norway donated a majestic spruce every year to Trafalgar Square in honor of Britain's defense of their country in World War II.

"Dad, that was absolutely foolish, damn it. Any good lawyer will be able to trace that sample back to you. Why can't you just listen to me once in a while?" yelled Wade at his father.

"Because all you are interested in is my money and how you can squander it, my boy. Besides, you never say anything worth listening to..." blared Jake. "Diane, go find me the truth and you are in no way to take any damn direction from Wade on this. Is that understood?"

Diane liked the old goat. He said what he thought, and it was clear, despite his declining health, Jake still had a lot to say.

"Loud and clear, Jake. Loud and clear," she said. "If there is any truth left to be found, my team will find it."

"Just don't let them take too long," answered Jake, "or there might not be anybody left here who cares to hear it."

Figure 3: The Route of the Vessel "Nordlys"

2 The Seeds of Truth

November 1912

"The truth is incontrovertible.
Malice may attack it,
ignorance may deride it,
but in the end, there it is."

Winston Spencer Churchill

The sea heaved and dropped in a never-ending rhythm of undulation cloaked beneath the frigid, dark night of the northern latitudes. The salted lash of the sprays of foam reached like the fingers of mourning souls threatening to claim their living brethren. He tasted the salinity of the sea in each drop, as his vessel's bow crashed down from the peaks of the swells only to knife into the smoothened recesses before climbing again the next. The man sailing this vessel had left his home port of Dundee, Scotland and had found his way north past the Shetland Islands into the warm waters of the North Atlantic Current that would allow him to take both he and his father home.

Birger Alvorsen had been at sea for several days with a minimal crew taken on in Edinburgh. In his mind, Birger weighed the constant threat of the sea taking them all in a single rogue manifestation of her unbridled and immeasurable strength. Well known of those who plied her unforgiving surface was her capacity, at any time, for snapping in half a wooden sailing vessel like his and casting its shattered remains aside like a hulk of rotted driftwood.

In this case, Birger knew that should a towering swell crash down upon them, and cast himself, his father and the crew into her waters, the Norwegian Sea would devour them all. It would consume them eternally unto its murky depths. He prayed to the Nordic gods of his ancestors, as well as the Christian Lord of his father, to protect them all from the vengeance of the furious rolling waters on which they so arduously climbed and so precipitously fell. Birger prayed as fervently for their delivery from the storm as any invocation that had ever been offered on any soul's sacred pilgrimage.

It was at this point, on the night of the last day, that Birger had first spotted it. The angry undulations of the sea had smoothed somewhat, and the threat of devastation by her hostile hand had begun to recede. The black skies that had loomed so ominously above them for the first time shred back the curtains of mist that had long been drawn closed over them. Then, faintly, he saw the first glowing arcs of *the Nordlys* welcome him. It was none other than these Northern Lights for which the vessel upon which they travelled was named. A name his father had decided upon so that the land of his forefathers would never be forgotten.

The polar lights that are the Aurora Borealis are a phenomenon that Birger had experienced many times at sea. This night, after viewing these illuminations, he left the wheel in the hands of his first mate and stepped outside with his father onto the deck. Above them, the crawl of luminescent ribbons appeared in their finest glory. At first sight they appeared pale to the eye, but the longer Birger watched them, the more vibrant the hues became. Ranging from greenish-yellow to a violet-infused indigo, they traced across an increasingly starry sky like the streaked fingerprints of the Nordic gods upon the firmament. They welcomed the sailors to the Arctic coastal waters of Norway, where Birger's father had been born and raised.

Soon, their ship glided peacefully through the black eternal winter night, plying a more placid section of the Norwegian Sea. The vessel, *Nordlys*, had just completed the thousand mile sailing journey from Scotland to the Lofoten Islands, and its reward was that the ending leg of its passage would be relatively smooth.

They had sailed the North Atlantic Current, one of the warm water flows birthed from the mid-Atlantic's splitting of the Gulf Stream. It flowed northward over the western side of Ireland before bending over the top of the Scottish land mass, between it and its outlying islands, before continuing across the Norwegian Sea. Its warm waters dominated that sea, keeping it ice-free and navigable when other portions of the North Atlantic could threaten to be impassable. The current's warm waters also kept the ports along the northern coast of Norway open throughout winter, when other bodies of water, like the northern portions of the Baltic Sea, would freeze over solid.

This far north, Birger had instructed the mate to navigate as his father had once taught him. The compass would play nasty tricks on any unsuspecting sailor inside the Arctic Circle.

Under the transparent but rhythmic glow of the Northern Lights' spectral veil, Birger had his navigator set course by the stars that appeared in ever thickening quantities. Using the heavenly lights as his guide, the mate steered his father's craft, the fishing ship *Nordlys,* toward the distinctive jagged mountainscape that was Norway's rugged Lofoten Islands.

The craggy peaks of Norway's Arctic coast jutted volcanically from the icy sea, framing the natural gateway to one of Scandinavia's most beautiful and expansive fjords, the *Vestfjorden*. In this westernmost fjord, the sea's angry waters calmed before pressing ever further eastward into the massive cuts that had long-ago been gouged by the unstoppable advancement of glaciers between these chains of ruggedly formed mountains. The undeniable force of the ice age had created an interconnected series of spectacular fjords. As the once frozen sea had penetrated to the east, the *Vestfjorden* would narrow and give way to the smaller *Ofotfjord*. It was in this fjord that the sprawl of smaller fjords would caress the strategic gem that was the port town of Narvik like a pair of cupped palms.

The town of Narvik was situationally invaluable because it was the closest ocean-navigable town to the Norwegian border with Sweden - a border that was defined by imposing snow laden mountain peaks running between the two countries.

This landscape was etched deeply within Birger's mind, fused in an amalgam of coastlines, landmarks, currents and hazards. He knew, as the alpine scent of the Norwegian coast welcomed him in from the open sea, that he would not ply much deeper inland this night. He would cross only the outer Lofoten Islands, and soon reach his destination in the wide open waters of the *Vestfjorden* - the fishing village of Skrova.

This village was nested out in the widest end of this westernmost fjord under the shelter of the Lofoten Archipelago. Skrova was the village that had been his father's birthplace. It was a windswept rock-hewn island seaport village of less than two hundred souls. Actually, as tiny as it was, the village was spread across a number of even smaller islands. The few families that have existed there had long done so subsisting upon the bounty of the waters surrounding them.

In the night under the glow of the *Nordlys* in the overhead sky, Birger had his vessel encircle the islands of Skrova. He steadied his father and sat him upright on the leeward gunnel of the ship, taking every ounce of Birger's resolve.

As the vessel sailed smoothly past the fishing village where his father had been raised, Birger Alvorsen, with all his might, thrust upward the metallic urn, before yanking it back in a violent manner, sending a belch of his father's dry ash into the winds of the Arctic night sky. That cloud of pallid dust was caught in the coastal breeze, and before it could settle back into the sea, was animated to life with the breath of the ocean's wind. The ash danced and flowed away from young Birger, until it was finely dispersed into the Arctic night.

Birger once again heaved the constraining urn, freeing the last remnants of his father's ashes from within it. They clung to the winds that swept across *the Vestfjorden*. The man who had so lovingly cared for him for each of his twenty-four years was this night forever home.

Birger relaxed, knowing he had performed his duty. It was only then that the trembling began deep inside of him. It seemed to shake free a remorse from the deepest recesses of his being that until this moment he had fought to contain. The mourning raised up within his abdomen, before exploding like a seismic upheaval. It forced itself free like the smoke of a raging inferno ignited within him by invisible embers hidden amongst the ash he had just released.

A heaviness befell Birger as the first tears formed in his eyes. These would be the seekers of the path for many more to follow. Soon enough, a deluge would beset itself upon him, and tempted him to hand over control to the demons within him that threatened to overpower their host. Yet Birger would resist their call, and not allow their blackened clouds to lord over him until he was once again alone at his father's home, now solely his own, in Dundee, Scotland.

Birger thought that once he was alone again in Dundee, his tears and heavy sobbing would flow seemingly as unending as the swells of the sea he had just plied for the past many days.

Birger Alvorsen had made this trip many times before with his father, the most recent being only five months ago. It saddened him to think that this was to be their last journey upon the sea together. It was also to be the first of many trips to these islands he would make without his father. What he did not know, until the end of his own life, was that he would never ply the waves of these Northern Seas alone. The spirit of his departed father would always guide and linger within him.

3 The Telecon

"A good speech should be like a woman's skirt: long enough to cover the subject, but short enough to create interest."

Winston Spencer Churchill

Diane opened the video telecon from the New York office, recapping her visit a few days past with Wade and Jake Conley. She had emailed summary notes to each person online – Emory Hauptmann in the Berlin office, Sophie Czystowska in the London office, and the newest member of the team, "Flake" Ferris joining from his home just outside Washington, DC.

Diane had telephoned Sophie the morning after the Conley meeting. On the phone, she addressed this circumspect young blonde woman exactly as the Polish native had always requested when alone with Diane. Not Sophie, nor its Polish equivalent Zofia, but rather the latter's diminutive form, *Zosia*. Diane remembered Sophie once saying, *"It is Polish and pronounced 'Zussia', like Russia but with a Z."* It was a simple intimacy shared between these two very different women that soon deepened into the closest of relationships.

That relationship had been forged by the two attempts upon Diane's life by rogue elements within the CIA. After each attempt, Sophie had stayed loyally by Diane's side, as the older woman healed her physical and psychological wounds from each attack.

Generally, Diane had allowed Sophie to work from her hometown of Poznań in central Poland. There was no office there, but Sophie was quite effective working from her apartment. Occasionally, when matters so dictated, Diane would ask Sophie to take the train to Berlin, a pleasant ride of only a couple of hours, to join Emory in the office there. Diane hated to do so, as she remembered that her *Zosia* had no love for Germany in general, and even less, in particular, for its capital of Berlin. Sophie's feelings about London were nowhere near as hostile, but they still were marred by ambivalence.

That ambivalence stemmed from Britain's long history of following its support for her country with spasms of betrayal. However, given that the mysterious Cassandra Conley was documented as British by birth, Diane thought that there well could be need of her having Sophie working from the UK office. Diane requested her to travel to London, and told Sophie that she could stay at her own vacant Westminster flat while there. Sophie had done this twice before, but this would be the first time she would do so with Diane away on travel.

"Just get the keys from the concierge, Étienne, and make yourself at home," she had told her young Polish friend. And so, Sophie took another trip to London, and took up residence in the luxurious Westminster condominium that belonged to her friend-turned-boss.

At the time of the video call, Sophie was in the large conference room of the London office. It looked out over the green expanses of Hyde Park from six stories above the ground level. Diane, from her own conference room in the New York City office, had wondered if Sophie had been watching the pedestrians and equestrians plying the labyrinth that was the paths of the park. Then Diane remembered the time change, realizing that the twilight of dusk was already feathered into a shroud of darkness over London. And that meant that Berlin was already deeper still into the night.

Emory Hauptmann was joining the videoconference from the Berlin office, not too far off the *"Unter Den Linden"*, near the Brandenburg Gate. Its employees were few, and Diane would not have even kept an office there except it was the singular condition that Emory had set for joining Diane's new enterprise.

Emory had been through Diane's CIA ordeals with her also, though not quite as continuously by her side as Sophie had been. Through it all though, Diane came to understand that the three of them formed a stable and complementary foundation upon which Diane would build her firm, *Sterling Investigations International.*

If Emory had one nagging attribute that had come to Diane's attention over the past few years, it was that he enjoyed fact-checking everyone on company conference calls. Emory was as quick as a lightning flash at the computer keys, but he had become irritatingly obsessed with being correct. Even more annoyingly, he enjoyed correcting those speaking in real time.

Diane set her thoughts of Emory aside to focus on introducing the newest member of their team, at least for this assignment. She had known Flake Ferris for many years, as he had been a genealogy expert that she had known through her years at the CIA.

Unlike her two colleagues, Sophie and Emory, Flake was more of Diane's own age. However, while Diane still was vibrant and youthful in appearance, Flake was somewhat more aged in his. He had worn tweed and herringbone plaid wool sports coats for as long as she had remembered, but now he had the gray curly locks to complete the academic's ensemble. He was the type of man who would never dye his hair or change his style of dress.

"I want to introduce *'Flake'* Ferris to you all," Diane said on the teleconference after having given an overview of the case. "He is a genealogist who I have worked with during my earlier career. He joins us from his home office outside Washington, DC. I am sure we will all benefit from his vast expertise, given the nature of this case. But before I ask Flake to brief us on what he has been able to research in the past few days, I want to remind you all that you have each signed the Conley NDA, and this case is not to be discussed with *anyone* outside of our deliberations. I will also ask Flake to get the 'name thing' out of the way up front. All yours, Mr. Ferris."

The video telecon came alive with the strong energetic voice of the man. Yet despite his exuberant spirit, the screen then switched to a video filled with the bespectacled face and curly gray haired man more than just recently past middle age.

"Okay, I know you all are wondering, 'who in the world could name their kid Flake? What were they thinking?' Right? Well, the short answer is they didn't. They didn't name their child 'Flake' and they weren't thinking at all when they gave him the actual Christian name of Wellesley, either. So, if you want to call me Wellesley, that is just fine. I probably just won't respond to you. Call me 'Flake'. It was a nickname I developed as a defensive mechanism to get through elementary and high school, and it has stuck ever since."

"Just how flakey are you, Mr. Ferris?" asked Emory Hauptmann from Berlin. Diane thought, *here we go*, as Emory seemed to always enjoy being playfully disrespectful.

It was then that Flake paused, removed his glasses, and produced a soft cloth with which he slowly wiped them clean.

He took his time in a passive protest to Emory's intrusion, before returning the glasses to the bridge of his nose. He brushed back the curly fringes of gray tipped hair away from his eyes.

Ferris then spoke slowly and deliberately. "Flakey enough to once have superglued a bully's face to the pages of an unabridged Works of Shakespeare in the seventh grade when he accused me of always having my nose in a book. He never bothered me again after that. Come to think of it, he never fell asleep in class again, either."

Flake heard a few smirks, and decided he had disarmed the group. Having introduced himself so, he moved on to his assignment.

"So, Diane has asked me to look into the lineage of our client, Jake Conley, focusing on his mother, Cassandra *nee* Barrett Conley. Thanks to today's genealogical databases and immediate access to census and municipal records, we are able to construct a lot of knowledge in only a few days. Any questions before I begin in earnest?"

The telecon was silent, until Emory apologetically conceded, "Welcome aboard the team, Flake. We look forward to the expertise you bring with you."

"Thank you, Emory. Now, what do we know of our mysterious Cassandra Conley? It appears to be a quite open and shut case at first glance. Born as Cassandra Barrett in London to a working-class family in 1896, her father was a lieutenant colonel, serving as a military instructor in the British Army. Her mother was a traditional homemaker. She had a younger brother, Ian, who broke her father's heart by joining the Royal Navy over the British Army."

"Ian Barrett was assigned to a destroyer patrolling the English Channel during most of World War II," interrupted Emory somewhat rudely. "It seems that his ship also was deployed at the evacuation of Dunkirk."

Diane glanced at Flake's image on the video screen. She thought she detected a pestered look upon his brow.

"Yes, Emory," Flake said slowly, as if attempting to disguise his irritation. "I read that also on Ian Barrett's obituary in the Times, but I'd rather we focus on his sister, if that's OK by you?"

"Certainly," said Emory. "You brought up Ian Barrett, I was just trying to round out his background. Go on, please."

"Thank you, Emory," said the clearly exasperated Ferris. "Now, back to our client's mother. Cassandra attended the usual prep schools of her day, but no college, excuse me, university, to speak of. She shamed the family by becoming pregnant in 1912, only to have the child delivered stillborn. Whereafter the family resettled from London to Edinburgh for the father's career. Not much record of her from the start of the Great War in 1914 until it was over. Then, just after the war, she came to the United States. She arrived in New York Harbor at Ellis Island in late 1919, traveling from Liverpool on the ocean liner *Mauretania*, sister ship of the *Lusitania*, the ocean liner so infamously sunk by German U-boats in 1915."

Flake Ferris paused for effect. Then, before he could continue Emory energetically interceded.

"Are you sure about that, Flake? The *Mauretania* made her New York departures from Southhampton. You said Cassandra departed from Liverpool."

It was clear to all that Emory, the firm's expert on all things German and all thing's technical, was intent on challenging every detail that Flake was about to put forth. This was despite the warm welcome he had just given to the older man. Diane found Emory's behavior to be uncalled for, but decided not to intercede. Flake could fend for himself.

"OK, Emory, since you appear to be the resident internet fact-checker, please tell me the name of the British coastal carrier Cassandra worked on to make her way from Liverpool to Southhampton," Flake rose to the challenge. "I have it in my records, but if you are just going to heckle the daylights out of me while I am trying to make my summary presentation, we can all stop and wait to see if you are able to find that tidbit. By the way, you won't find it on *Wikipedia*!"

"So," Diane then interceded as the tension had created an ominous silence, "I should have told you all that Flake has a well deserved reputation of hating to be interrupted. So let's all hold our questions until the end. Please continue, Flake."

"OK. So far, so good. Historical records verify everything we have determined to this point," Flake continued. "So, young Cassandra Barrett, who is at this point is only twenty-three years old, works her way through New York City in late 1919 and into 1920 in the garment district. She shows up on the 1920 census, so all is good. It is after this point that things get very interesting indeed."

"How do we know that she worked in the garment district?" asked Diane, breaking her own moratorium on asking questions. "I want to be assured we can answer any questions Jake may throw at us like that…"

"Work permits and International Ladies Garment Workers Union records. New York was run by labor unions even then. LGWU was one of the first. What happens next aligns with the family lore. Young Cassandra gets herself arrested working at a speakeasy in the latter half of '20, not once but twice. Remember that Prohibition had become law of the land that year. After getting out of jail the second time, the next day she gets herself a highly coveted job as hostess in another, more upscale joint. There she meets Lucas Conley, who came to New York regularly on business. Lucas keeps coming back to see her. I can only presume he is *smitten*, as they would have said back then. At some point, Lucas proposes to the young British beauty."

An image of the young Cassandra Barrett in New York then filled the screen.

"She really is beautiful," Sophie could be heard muttering under her breath as she viewed the photo. "Her blonde hair is simply stunning."

"Angelic," added Emory, "If that's not Nordic, I don't know what is…"

"If I may continue…" Flake Ferris said tersely as he was interrupting those who had interrupted him. He proceeded, "In 1922, Lucas Conley took her to Colleyville, Texas where he marries Miss Barrett, transforming her into Cassandra Conley. They have a son, Jacob, better known as our client, Jake, but not until 1933. At this point Cassandra is thirty-seven, but the pregnancy still goes well. Jake grows up and himself marries in 1959, has his own son, Wade, in 1964 and that brings us up to date. All census and other registrar data supports all this."

"What has become of Mr. Jacob's parents, please?" asked Sophie gently. Her question was respectful and asked with the softest of intonations, seemingly the polar opposite of Emory's interjections.

"Well, Lucas Conley died of a heart attack in 1962 at the age of 71. His wife, Cassandra, on the other hand, lived on for another thirty-eight years in generally great physical health, not withstanding bouts of manic depressive disorder and much later Alzheimer's disease. In 2000, she died of its complications at the grand age of 104. Very tidy, everything fits very neatly. All data supports. Case closed."

"Well, Flake, not really," interjected Emory angrily. "Where does the Norwegian DNA come from when Jake has his saliva tested?"

All suspected Emory had been stewing since being shut down so effectively by Flake twice earlier.

"Yes, thank you, once again, Emory, my young purveyor at the altar of the internet oracle," answered Flake. "Well, that is the part that I currently cannot explain. At least not yet. Be thankful, though, for this is the very reason we all have this assignment."

"What about the Barrett family? Any Nordic connections?" asked Diane.

"None that I could find immediately. Just the usual English lineage, with some French, German Saxon and Norman heritage. Certainly not enough to explain Jake's DNA results. No ancestral lineage exists to support Cassandra having any direct Scandinavian heritage, other than the trace amounts that show up in most Brits' bloodlines as a result of the Viking coastal raids and William the Conqueror being from Normandy".

"As in from northern France?" asked Sophie.

"As in from the lands the French Kings gave to the Vikings long ago," said Flake, "to stop them from raiding deeper into their country. Norman, as in '*Norse-men*'. That was where the Normans came from. The same Normans who were victorious across the channel at the Battle of Hastings in 1066."

"So, if there is so much Viking lineage in most British peoples, doesn't that explain Mr. Conley's DNA having some Norwegian elements?" Sophie followed-up. "After all, Cassandra was English. We know that much, do we not?"

"Yes, Cassandra was, but no, it does not explain our situation," snapped Flake, once again agitated, "since the Norman invasion was nearly a thousand years ago. With each generation, that Viking component gets split out, again and again. Until all that's left of that original Scandinavian input is nothing more than a diluted fingerprint of a baseline. Jake's sample turned up 50% Norwegian, meaning one of his parents was 100% Norwegian. Also, with a trace of the *Sámi* mixed in."

"Who are the *Sámi*?" asked Diane, having never before heard the term.

"You would most likely have been taught about them in elementary school," said Flake.

"Never heard of them," professed Diane.

"*Laplanders*," offered Emory.

"Well, well," Flake interjected, "you certainly are fast on that keyboard, hotshot."

"I knew that," Emory said, defending himself. "I went to Tromsø, Norway last year to see the Midnight Sun. Well, I really went to see what's left of the *Tirpitz*, the World War II German battleship. The wreckage is no longer there, but I did get to visit the *Tirpitz* Museum just up the road in the town of Alta. That's as far north as I have been, or am likely to ever be on this planet. And yes, I actually did get to see the Midnight Sun. Very impressive. Our tour guide taught us that the *Sámi* are the indigenous people of the Arctic Circle from Norway all the way over to western Russia. They are the only people still allowed to herd reindeer there. Kind of a perk, like Native Americans owning casinos. Even their *lávvu* tents look like Native American wigwams."

Even though this was only a video conference, everyone could feel the mixed sensations of Emory proudly beaming, and of Flake Ferris cringing.

"Then you should have learned they don't like being called *Laplanders*," Flake said, "it is considered quite a derogatory term to them. I guess the American educational system hasn't quite caught up to that. Congratulations, Mr. Hauptmann, for you just stereotyped the indigenous people of two different continents at once. Any insights into the Mongolian or sub-Saharan peoples?"

"That's enough, you two," scolded Diane. "So, Flake, what is so important about Jake Conley having traces of the *Sámi* in his bloodlines?"

"It means that his dear old Mum, Cassandra, was likely from northern Norway," answered Flake Ferris. "Lets say from the town of Bodø on up. Roughly corresponds to within the Arctic Circle."

"Great, Flake," snapped Emory, "nothing distinctive there. Should we just look for DNA with frostbite on it?"

Ferris had tired of Emory's intrusions. "First, of all, Norway only has about eight million citizens and most of them live in the south, centered around the Oslo-Bergen corridor. So we just ruled out about two-thirds of all Norwegians. Second, the

Sámi did not generally intermingle with the ethnic Norwegians, so somewhere in Cassandra's gene pool, somebody crossed over that taboo line. Maybe spent a cold winter's night in one of those *lávvu* tents, doing whatever it took to stay warm."

"So then, Flake," asked Diane, "how do we get to the bottom of this? How do we figure out where Cassandra got her Norwegian DNA from? With or without the *Sámi* traces. "

"Diane, It is highly unusual to see a *Sámi* match in a Norwegian's DNA, at least one as strong as in Jake's sample. We just need to make sure that Cassandra's DNA is actually the source of Jake's Norwegian/*Sámi* DNA. Certainly, we all believe that this must have been the case, but we must prove it. When we confirm a match, that *Sámi* marker will be the nail in the coffin. When we see it, we'll know we have a solid DNA match."

"Which of the three types of DNA testing methods will we be using, Flake?" probed Emory from Berlin. "Y chromosome, Mitochondrial DNA, or the SNP testing?"

"Very good, Emory," quipped Flake Ferris, "I see you found the NIH Genetics website. I am so very impressed. Now, if you take the time to read it, you will learn that the Y chromosome tests are only good for testing male relative relationships. Remember only us boys have that pesky Y chromosome! Mitochondrial DNA testing, on the other hand, does indeed work on both sexes, as the mitochondrial DNA is passed on from mothers to all their children. This test is excellent for validating mother-child relationships."

"Do we have any samples of Cassandra's DNA?" asked Emory. "Is it still even useable twenty years after her death?"

"We do not," answered Flake, "so strike two."

"She was cremated," added Diane, "and no family members have any keepsakes such as locks of hair we can test."

"However, there is hope," teased Ferris. "There is always the Single Nucleotide Polymorphism DNA test, or as laymen like Emory might call it, the SNP Test. These assess the variations in the SNP's across a single person's complete genome, and compares it to the same distributions in the ethnic databases. This is the type of test that our client took, and it is the type test we will continue to use in our first pass going forward. Thank you for that interruption, Emory. If you find anything else on the internet that you need explained, just let me know…"

"So…" interjected Diane, as she kept this squabble from enflaming. "Just who will we compare Jake's DNA against?"

"Well, on that question there is some good news," said Flake. "We have identified a match of kin in the Barrett family. Cassandra's younger brother whom I mentioned, Ian Barrett, unfortunately passed away in 1980. However, his daughter, Anna, is still alive and living in London."

"Great! That is exactly why I had asked Sophie to travel to our London office," said Diane, "so that she could track down any leads pertaining to the Barrett family. What do you have for her pertaining to Anna Barrett?"

"Sophie, hello?" Flake called out playfully.

"Yes, I am here," responded the reserved accent of the young lovely Polish woman. An accent would not be totally out of place in London, as there were many Poles there. Many young Polish men, but even more so women, came from Poland to work and save their earnings.

"Have you ever seen the Rosetta Stone or the Elgin Marbles?" asked Flake Ferris very seriously.

"I am not sure that I understand your question," answered the Slavic-accented voice as the screen again filled with the image of her beautiful blonde straight lengths of hair framing a confused look on her flawless face.

"Well, if not, you are in great luck. You see, Miss Anna Barrett, never married and lives in a second-story flat above a souvenir shop, just across the street from the British Museum. Miss Anna Barrett, seventy-three years young, is the niece of our Cassandra. She is the daughter of Cassandra's younger brother, Ian. Unfortunately, Ian being long deceased, and apparently not having shared in his sister's genes for longevity, is of no assistance to us. This leaves only Anna to contact. I have emailed her address to you directly. We need to get Miss Barrett to donate a sample of her DNA, so we can compare it to Jake's own. How you do that is your responsibility, but I have a suggestion."

"I will make contact with Miss Anna Barrett immediately," said Sophie.

"I might suggest," the next voice was Emory's in an attempt to preclude Flake's own suggestion, "to tell her that you represent a firm that has a payment to be made to her father."

"Her father who is dead?" asked Sophie.

"Exactly. When she tells you he is deceased, explain that the payment will then be made payable to her upon proof of her being Mr. Ian Barrett's natural born daughter. I would think five hundred pounds or so up front would be enough to get you in the door, with another fifteen hundred to be paid after the DNA sample is analyzed and confirms the relationship."

"Once I am inside Miss Anna's apartment, what exactly do you wish me to do?" asked Sophie.

"Simply get her to spit in a collection vial for analysis," said Flake. "I'll give you the address of a London lab that we can have waiting to process it for us. Better yet, take blood from a finger-prick, but a lot of people, especially of her age, will object to that."

There was a dead silence over the next few seconds.

"I am not comfortable handling anyone's blood," objected Sophie, "not even a few drops worth. How old did you say Miss Anna is?"

"Miss Anna Barrett is seventy-three years old," stated Flake, "and Emory is quite right that the prospect of two thousand pounds, with five hundred up front, will prove itself too appealing to resist. From what we have been able to piece together so far, she appears to be living on a most modest income in that oversized one-room flat."

"And what comes after that?" asked Sophie.

"We simply wait to get the results and compare them to Jake's," answered Flake. "If there is no Norwegian ancestry in Miss Anna's background, then we have a real problem in finding out where Jake got his. Has to have come from Cassandra, doesn't it? If Cassandra was born with Nordic DNA as we suspect, then it reasons that her brother must also have it. And if her brother had Nordic DNA, then it will show up in his daughter, Anna as well. This test should do nothing other than verify that there is a strong Norwegian ancestry in the Barrett family bloodline."

"What was *your* suggestion, Mr. Ferris, as to how to gain Miss Anna's DNA?" asked Sophie.

"Actually, my recommendation will play very well within the framework that Emory has suggested. It turns out that Miss Anna's father, Cassandra's brother, Ian, followed in his father's footsteps regarding a military career."

"He didn't quite follow his old man, did he?" reminded Emory. "Ian was Royal Navy. You said Cassandra's father was in the British Army,"

"Emory, if you would take the time to listen to me, you would remember I said that Ian must have broken the old man's heart when he signed on to the Royal Navy instead of the Army," said Flake. "He became a junior officer, no less. Spent World War II sailing the English Channel. I suggest you tell Miss Anna that her father rescued a Polish flier from the Channel during the Battle of Britain. There were many Poles who flew for the RAF then. More than a few ended up in the Channel. Enough were pulled out by the navy that this story will ring true."

"Of course," Diane added, "in World War II, the Polish airmen shot down more German planes than any other RAF squadron during the Battle of Britain." She had remembered her mentor, Stanley Wisniewski, having so proudly told her so. *Poor Stanley*, she thought, *God rest his soul.*

"Yes, this is true," added Sophie. "and yet after the war was won, they were not even allowed to march in the victory parade through London because the British feared it would anger Stalin, that son of the devil's seed."

"Just tell Miss Anna," Flake added, "that you represent the family of that flier that has made a small fortune in the travel business since the communist regime fell in Poland. His family wishes to repay the daughter of his rescuer with this modest sum. Most likely her father never spoke of the war, and this story will be near impossible for a seventy-three year old woman of modest means to research." Ferris waited for Emory to contradict him.

"I think that's a great idea," Emory chirped in. "We can set up a dummy office number and route it right to our office here in Berlin. I have a young woman who speaks a little Polish for when Miss Anna calls to check out Sophie's tale."

"I have spoken to this woman in your office," protested Sophie, "and her Polish is horrible. Even offensively so."

"It doesn't matter, Soph," Emory responded, "it just has to be good enough to fool an old British woman before they switch over to English."

"Great," Diane said, "it is settled. Sophie will call on Miss Anna Barrett."

Emory then added, "I would also like to add a tail to Miss Barrett afterwards for a few days in case this ploy causes her any unusual activity."

"Like what?" asked Diane. "Why bother to tail her?"

"I don't know," responded Emory, "but if Miss Anna's sample comes back completely free of Norwegian DNA, then for sure somebody's hiding something. My gut tells me that, maybe, Miss Anna might be sharing a secret with somebody else."

4 Shadows of Skrova

1912

"The thousand-mile-long peninsula stretching from the mouth of the Baltic to the Arctic Circle had an immense strategic significance."

Winston Spencer Churchill

Birger awoke early the next day despite the punishing weariness from his journey. Although his aching body yearned for more rest, it was the strain of emotions wrung from his unsettled mind that wore the most upon his very being. The young man forced himself from his hammock in the sparse, narrow confines of his vessel's quarters. His sleep had been shallow and full of the turmoil of a restless soul, as well as clouded heavily with the penetrating angst of despair.

The return of his father's remains to the winds and waters of the *Vestfjorden* the night before had not brought him the closure for which he had hoped. His mind kept returning to the thoughts that it could not suppress: that both his parents were now gone and he was alone upon this Earth. The *Vestfjorden's* waters and her glorious crown of surrounding mountain peaks would scatter and absorb his father's ashes, but Birger himself would never again be cloaked in the warm embrace of the only real family he had ever known.

Then there was the disturbing manner by which his father's life had ended. An expert sailor whose entire life had been spent upon the roiling churn of the seas had been found drowned near his vessel in calm waters. There was an obvious question lingering, not just to Birger, but to all who had ever known his father. *Had the man given in to his inner darkness? Had his father heeded the call of his dead mother to join her?*

Birger's mother had been struck by an automobile, one of the few in Edinburgh at that time. As she crossed Princes Street, she stopped, frozen in fear, when she saw the monstrous machine turning and accelerating from behind a slow moving horse-drawn delivery wagon. The force of the impact threw her cleanly into the air. She laid in the street as a curious and aghast crowd gathered around her twisted, writhing body. Birger's father, who had already crossed the boulevard, had to fight his way back to her through the gathering throng. He then knelt beside his mangled wife's form, promised her that she would be all right, up until the moment she died of her internal injuries. Her last word had been her own son's name, his name, "Birger".

As Birger splashed his face from the cabin's wash basin, he remembered the change that had occurred in his father's demeanor after this tragic event. It was far worse than just mourning his wife's death. It became the total devastation of the man. Without her in his life, his father became hollowed out from within, as if by a constant corrosive dripping of an internal caustic lye. Within that empty shell his father withdrew. Even before his mother's death, his father had already been long known to be prone to his own fits of depression and melancholy. Secretly, Birger had feared his father's drowning might have been his giving in to the hopelessness which had enshrouded him after her loss. Birger had come to suspect that his darkest thoughts had been realized.

A knock came upon the cabin door. "Aye," yelled out Birger.

"Launch coming out to us, Birger," called out the gruff Scottish voice of the mate. "Two locals rowing in a skiff. Should we allow them to board?"

"Those should be my cousins coming to collect me," Birger answered. "No need for them to come aboard. I will be right there."

"Aye, Birger," acknowledged the mate.

Neither the mate nor the rest of the crew would call Birger by the title "Captain" as they had earlier addressed his father. They did not respect him, he thought, even after he had successfully braved the winter seas of the Shetland to Lofoten Island run. Its waters had been punishing on this journey, the seamen had pleaded to turn back, but Birger pressed on. He knew that he had proven himself, but the damn Scotsmen still refused to honor his abilities, as they were blinded by his youth.

Birger had made this run with his father many times, in seas even more turbulent than those of this last crossing. He remembered once when he was a teen, the waters were so rough that his father decided to tie him to the mast until they rode out the storm's fiercest lashings. Birger remembered being overcome with the fear of drowning on that crossing. Yet, somehow he was calmed just enough by watching his father as he battled the elements on behalf of them both. Bravely. Skillfully. Determined. This was the flesh and blood from which he had been drawn forth. After the event, when the bile of fear in his throat had receded, Birger thought that to be taken by the sea alongside his father would have been a very honorable death.

Yet, as he inevitably always did, Birger's father delivered him to safety upon that journey. But now his father was gone, scattered upon the very winds and waters of the fjords, those his father had learned to master as a boy. Those his father had taught him to navigate as a lad. Even returning here to bring his father home could not save Birger from feeling as lost as he had ever been.

Birger stepped out of the cabin into the diffused pre-dawn light of an Arctic winter's morning. The sun would not rise at all, as it was late November. In lieu of sunshine there would only be this amber haze of dim light for the next few hours. It was during this time that Birger would visit upon the island village of Skrova. He would pay his respects to his father's sister and her husband, as he would have wanted his son to do. Birger had never felt a closeness to these distant kin, despite having seen them twice a year since he was ten. Yet he knew that he owed them the honor of a visit, if for no reason than to celebrate the man whose life they had shared.

Birger's Aunt Eydis was kind enough, but her husband, Ørjan, had long regarded his father as a traitor for abandoning his home amongst these islands. He was a Nordic traditionalist and would confront anyone who did not share his passion for the ways of his homeland. Birger was sure that after his father had passed, his uncle's anger would now be transfixed upon him.

As far as his cousins, Eydis and Ørjan's two boys, Hakron and Erik, were by then roughly as old as Birger himself. Birger found them to be oafish and at the same time childish. Always happy to play tricks upon him. He hoped they had matured and would not test him this time, as his heart was heavy, and he feared he might lash out harshly at their disrespect.

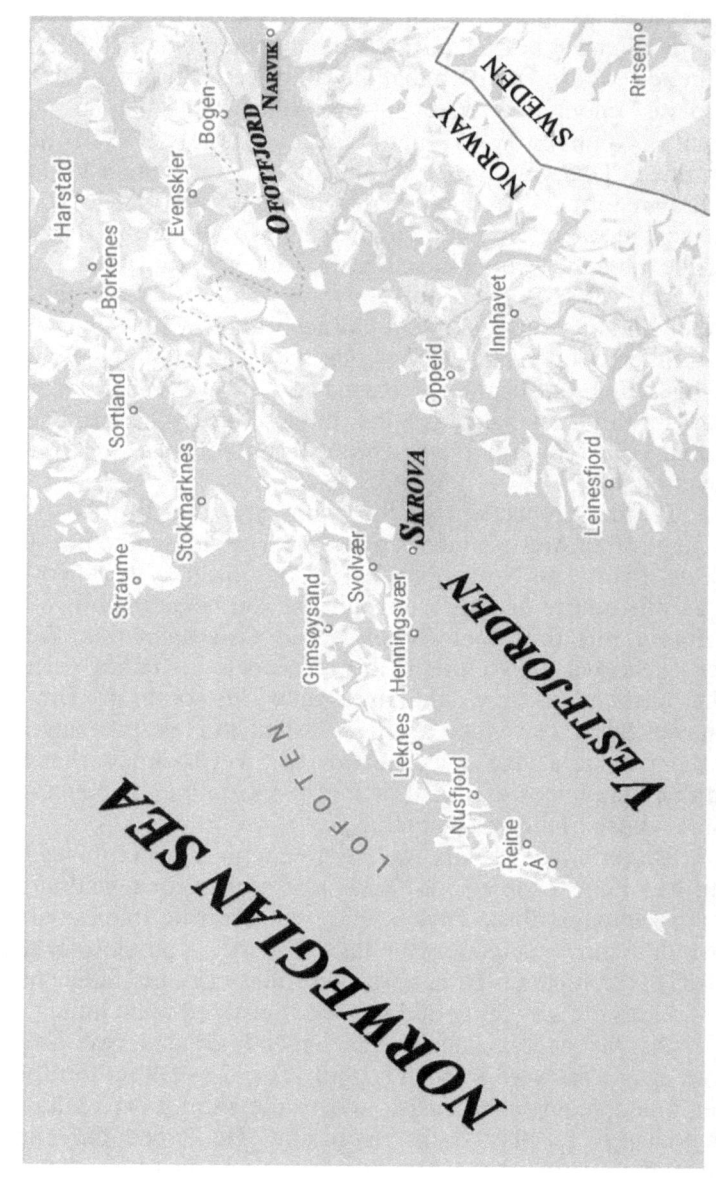

FIGURE 4: SKROVA IN THE VESTFJORDEN, NARVIK IN THE OFOTFJORD

As soon as Birger had come upon the deck of his father's ship, the frigid bite of the Arctic wrapped around him like the chilled clinging fingers of death itself. Birger pulled on his anorak over his seaman's sweater that had been woven on the shores of this very island. The sky was slowly but relentlessly digesting the weak and shortening span of diffused light during this cycle of the season. It would continue to do so until the winter equinox in December, when the day was completely swallowed whole. Then, and only then, would the cycle reverse until the summer brought back all the stolen rays of light.

Birger could then hear the sloshing rhythmic oars of the skiff carrying his cousins to his anchored vessel. He could clearly see the wooden boat which approached the fishing vessel, *Nordlys,* the only belonging his father had left to him other than their home. In the skiff, amidst the sea's morning mist, were two young men, his cousins, Hakron and Erik.

"*Velkommen hjem,* Birger," cried out Hakron, the older of the two brothers, in their native Norwegian tongue. "Come down, and we shall take you ashore to Skrova. Mother was excited when we ran back home to tell her your ship was anchored offshore. She prepares a meal for you now! Come, we shall take you to her."

Birger then turned to the Scotsman acting as first mate. "You and the others stay aboard today and rest. There is nothing on this island to entertain any of you. These islanders are very suspicious of foreigners. Rest for our long days of fishing on these seas starting tomorrow."

His Scottish crew would indeed rest at anchor that day and after their arduous sea transit, the inactivity was welcome. In the days that followed, they would all fish these seas for as many days as it took to fill the ship's holds. After the holds were iced, they would depart for Edinburgh fully laden. There, the Norwegian bounty would demand a small fortune.

This had been the twice yearly ritual that Birger's father had ingrained as sacred in his son. The funds from these excursions, even after paying the Edinburgh sea hands, would provide for them for the next six months until the next Norwegian run. Birger had made this run for years, and despite the loss of his beloved father, still intended to continue this family tradition.

A blast of icy wind on deck snapped his mind back to the present. Birger yelled out for his cousins to watch out below.

Birger then threw the boarding net over the side of *Nordlys*, and climbed down. Hakron assisted him into the skiff. Birger embraced them both, affecting the emotion for his cousins that he truly did not possess. He did not dislike them, he just never really felt close to either Hakron or Erik. Yet, even Birger had to admit that there was a certain comfort in the repetition of seeing them twice each year.

Erik rowed them back to the village pier, while the glow of a lantern held by Hakron embraced the three young men in the warmth of this fragile camaraderie. The lantern cast only a weak glow in the Arctic morning, and was almost unnecessary save that the pre-dawn light reflected off the hanging sea mist in silvery gray wisps. The lantern's rays cast a warmer hue upon the closest shreds of this haze which were already beginning to part and lift. All knew that any illumination provided during the Arctic night could be elusive and easily vanquished by the ever threatening night of winter.

"We are overjoyed to see you again, my cousin," exclaimed the courteous Hakron, "although the news of the loss of your father deeply saddened not only our family, but the entire village."

"We were shocked and distraught," added the more emotional Erik, through the labored breaths of his rowing. "Mother was consumed for days with grief, and only now seems to come to peace with the loss of her brother."

The statements of his cousins touched Birger in a way he could not have anticipated.

"*Takk, mine fettere,*" Birger said, thanking his cousins. "You'll both be happy to know that father was given a Nordic funeral. His ashes were scattered late last night on the wings of these very winds, on the gentle waves of this fjord he called home."

"You must tell Mother," said Hakron, "it will delight her so."

"You came alone?" inquired Erik. "That is terribly dangerous."

Birger grinned broadly. The friendship of his cousins, and their concern for him, began to lift his spirits. "No, I was not alone. Father was with me, guiding me, to his ancestral home. Also, there is a small crew from Edinburgh. All will rest today, starting tomorrow we will fish until the holds of the *Nordlys* are full, and only after that will I embark on my return voyage."

"And Hakron and I will fish with you!" said Eric. "We will fill your holds with fish from theses waters, and you shall pay us, yes? As our uncle always did?"

"Yes, as my father always had, so too shall I," confirmed Birger.

"Your Norwegian is still very good, cousin," said Hakron to Birger. They had been speaking in the native tongue his father had preferred around the house.

"Well, let us see if it remains so," answered Birger, "now that I have no one with which to practice. I fear I may lose it in Scotland, all alone."

Then Hakron cast a glance at his brother, Erik, as if to say, *No, don't say it...*

"You have not seen your Tulla yet?" asked Erik.

"Erik, that is enough!" said Hakron, chastising his brother by his tone. "Birger, please forgive my impetuous brother. Whatever is in his head is instantly out of his mouth."

"No, it is fine, my cousins," replied Birger. "Of course, I have not yet seen her, as I have only arrived in the night. I look forward to seeing her so very much."

It was then that the mist had dispersed and Birger saw, across the *Vestfjorden* from Skrova, the jagged peaks of the Lofoten Mountains clearly. The Lofoten Islands formed an archipelago that jutted out from the mainland into the Norwegian Sea. This chain of islands was so tightly connected that it imitated a peninsula. Yet, as close as each isle was from the next, between them were the nearly impassible currents of the fjords. Each island bore the sharply vertical mountains that rose from the volcanoes that formed them. They plummeted into the sea, leaving barely enough level land to support the few thousand fishermen and their families that lived along the water's edge.

Birger's father used to tell him these were the teeth of the monstrous *Ymir*, which the god Odin had slain. The boy used to argue no, they must be dragon's teeth, for they are so sharp as they cut into the sky. Yet, for all the emotion that was missing from his reunion with his cousins, the sight of this wall of jagged peaks brought forth a flood of memories, deeply imbued with the remembrance of his father. Each memory brought forth a reaction from deep within Birger that he had to fight to subdue.

Birger then turned his head away from the mountain peaks to the south as they approached the several small rocky islands that made up the fishing community of Skrova.

Figure 5: View from Hogskrova (above)
Skrova today with Litlmolla in the distance (below)

The gaps between outcroppings formed a natural harbor, forging a respite that sat in the open waters of the *Vestfjorden*. Skrova was a village of fishermen, their families and little else. Skrova had no gigantic peaks of its own, although its backdrop was dominated by the high mountain formations of *Litlmolla*, the island just to the northeast. Skrova itself would prove to be a rocky and boulder strewn land of only a few high, barren bluffs. The two most prominent were the *Tuvene* and the *Hogskrova.*

The vantage point from these highest points also included a panorama of the entire *Vestfjorden* in summer. The rest of the island was made up of the fishing village of less than two-hundred souls scattered among the rocky outcroppings, grassy trails and a few sandy beaches at the edge of turquoise shallow pools.

They skiff came upon the main pier, where the hands of his cousins lifted Birger effortlessly up to its planks. His cousins scampered up after him, carrying the light that would lead them past the rows of *rorbu,* the red fishing huts that jutted out over the waters that sustained this island village.

They soon entered the *rorbu* that was home to his aunt and uncle. Aunt Eydis was preparing the food until she saw her nephew, for whom she left the stove to embrace. Her arms wrapped around Birger, as the warmth of her soul penetrated him. Her concerns for the then parentless young man, whom she had known for each of the twenty-four years of his life, were but ripples in her cascading torrent of happiness that then washed over her as she held him tightly.

"I am so sorry for the loss of your father," she whispered in his ear, "but I am so delighted to wrap my arms around you again!"

"I am home when I am with you, Aunt Eydis," he whispered in her ear, knowing he was exaggerating his feelings, "as is my father also. Last night I scattered his remains over the *Vestfjorden.*"

He felt a wave of emotion tremble within her, and tears welled in her eyes, but she refused to allow them to fall. She smiled at him tenderly and whispered back as she wiped her eyes, "As it should be."

"Come, eat, Birger," she then said aloud, as her arms pulled back from around him, then sluiced down his own, not unlike the waters of the melting snows diving from the rocks to the sea. She grasped his hands and took him to the small wooden table. A breakfast feast was spread out for him.

They all spoke in the native Norwegian tongue. It was a comfort to Birger, as his father had always demanded they do so in their home in Scotland. It was a tradition that Birger would love to continue, yet he would have no one with which to do so.

At the table sat the brooding figure that was her husband, Ørjan. Birger instantly felt, more than remembered, the dislike his father had for his sister's husband. He was a negative man, and his father never understood how his sister could be attracted to such a beast.

"How long are you here, young Birger?" asked Ørjan flatly, offering no welcoming embrace, nor hand extended to shake.

"Just a few hours, Uncle. I need to press into Narvik, I have business there before I can put to sea again."

"Not in hours, boy," the uncle corrected him sharply. "How many days are you here?"

"Ørjan, be polite, please," interceded his Aunt Eydis. "Birger, I have prepared my *laks og eggerøre* especially for you. Enjoy them along with everything else before you."

"This is wonderful, Aunt Eydis," said Birger. He loved her native dish of smoked salmon and scrambled eggs, as only she could prepare them. On the table, between he and his uncle were large chunks of *brunost*, a flavorful brown cheese unlike any other he had tasted elsewhere. Next to it was freshly prepared *Nøkkelost* cheese, flavored with cumin, semi-hard, almost like a soft French quiche. And no Scandinavian breakfast would be complete without their local whole-grain breads. For Norwegians, this means *kneippbrød*, the most popular bread in Norway. Also, his aunt had prepared *lefserull*, a soft flatbread made from potatoes and cream that is then rolled around a mixture of eggs, fish and local herbs and garden vegetables.

"Boys, go and prepare a boat to take your cousin to Narvik," said Aunt Eydis, "for he certainly does not need to take his own ship on such a short journey. My boys will accompany you today, Nephew."

"*Takk*, Aunt Eydis," he thanked her, "and tomorrow with them both we shall fish these seas until my holds are full and iced." Birger then ate heartily of the tastes of his homeland. His aunt watched with joy as he nourished himself.

"My, Birger, what a man you have become even since your last visit with my brother," she said. "Your father was so heavy of heart then since your mother had died. It had cast a certain darkness over him, the loneliness, you know. He tried to pull himself from its hold, but he was unable to do so."

"He might as well hold an eel by its tail," scoffed Ørjan, quoting an old Nordic proverb.

"Well, Aunt Eydis, now he rests within the eternal light of God," Birger replied.

"You mean *'of the gods'*, that is what you meant to say," insisted his Uncle Ørjan, the Norse traditionalist.

"No, Uncle Ørjan, father believed in only one God," replied Birger, who was surprised by the outburst.

"Then tell me why does this boy who sits before me incinerate his father's body and bring back his ashes to the *Vestfjorden* to scatter on the winds? Where will his God find him on the day of judgement? Surely your Lord could have found him in Scotland, no?" taunted the uncle.

"Ørjan, stop this instant," demanded Eydis. "I should think of all people you would be happy that Birger would see to follow the traditions of our land, and it warms me to know that my brother rests here amongst us."

"My father is home," answered Birger to them both. "Here he shall rest until Our Lord, Jesus Christ, raises us all for judgement. Until then, father will rest on the wings of these winds, on the crests of these waves, and in the shadows of these mountains."

"When your father is judged," replied Ørjan, "your Lord may be harsh upon him, given the nature of his death. For no sailor of his skills drowns upon a such a calm sea as that in which they found him."

"Ørjan, that is enough!" scolded the aunt angrily. "Hold your tongue. Birger is our guest. Be away from here, lest I should release my full anger upon you."

Yet her display of furor could not stem the bitter tide of his words. Ørjan continued, "And the gods that I worship will always judge him even more harsher for defiling that village girl who would later become his wife. He could not stand the condemning looks of the village folk for this sin against them. Your father was never one to respect tradition, and was always in search of only what pleased him. He asked for her hand, her father said no! Your father knew that she was forbidden to him, and he took her innocence anyway. So he was then forced to take her away from these shores! Had they stayed here, no heartless machine would have run your mother down, my nephew, that is for sure."

Birger had taken enough from his critical uncle. The man only taunted him, or anyone who had the nerve to acknowledge that there was a much larger world beyond these shores.

"Perhaps then, instead of a heartless motorcar machine taking my mother's life," Birger replied angrily, "it would have been the cold vacant stares of the people of this village that would have run her down. So my father loved a village woman whose own father objected, does that make him anything other than human? And my mother loved him always, did she not? Does that make either of them, or for that matter me, less than fully Nordic, Uncle?"

Ørjan was unaccustomed to being spoken to in this way, especially in his own home. He looked with an intense agitation at Birger. Yet, he felt a satisfaction that he had driven the boy to the display of contempt shown to him.

"Calm yourself, nephew," he seethed sternly. "All I am saying is that he should have stayed here among his own people, and stood up to their judgement, not run from it. Instead your mother is dead, and your father's own life fell prey to his idle hands. Had he only kept those hands off of her body in the first place, none of this would have come to pass. *And as the old cock crows, so crows the young.*"

"Ørjan, you shame yourself," said his angered Aunt Eydis. "Now leave us."

"Tell me, boy," Ørjan ignored his wife, "did the *Nordlys* dance in the sky as you scattered your father's ashes, or did it merely statically arch from behind the jagged crests of the Lofoten Mountains. Did *Heimdall* allow your father's soul to cross the *Bifrost* to *Asgard*? Does he rest this very hour in *Valhalla*?"

"Ørjan," screamed Eydis, "enough of your Rainbow Bridges and Halls of Valkyres. This boy has enough to deal with, let him alone today as well as in the future. Leave us, or you will never again find pleasure in my company."

Birger watched as his uncle weighed the measure of the implied threat from his aunt. He seemed to wrestle with the idea of the frigid winter's cold extending to inside their home. Extending to inside their bed.

His uncle finally heeded his aunt and rose to leave the room, but not before saying coldly to Birger, "Nephew, fear not the depths of the sea you tread, fear only the depths of your own soul. I pray the dark waters never claim you as they have so many others. But at least you will never again be alone." Ørjan turned his back and walked away from them both.

Uncle Ørjan's last statement confused Birger, as he feared most exactly the opposite, of living out his life in solitude. With the passing of the last phrase from his uncle through the room, Birger thought he detected a flash of discomfort skirt across his aunt's face. It was brief, she hid it well, but not so well that he had not caught its sting upon her.

Birger asked his aunt, "What does he mean I will never be alone?"

Eydis turned uncomfortably away from her nephew as she busily began to clear plates from the table. "Please ignore my husband, Birger. He is a simple man, who knows not when to suppress whatever thoughts his ill-tempered mind conjures up. He somehow thinks it is not Nordic to do so."

Birger thought on the harsh words of his uncle. There was no solace in them, only a vile bitterness that was but a small pull from the deep wells of it stored within the man.

"My father's body was pulled from a calm sea, it is true. It is not for me to guess how he drowned, accident or otherwise. Everyone thinks that when a man of the sea dies in anything but angry waters, that he has taken his own life. I will let them think that, if they should care to. For my father's God will judge him, not I. He is my father, who I still dearly love. I have come to bring him home to rest. That is done. He was a good man. This day, his tortured spirit rests."

He lowered his head, ashamed at the thought that his father may have died at his own hand. They all knew he was a man prone to dark moods, but Birger prayed for his father's sake that this was not true.

His Aunt Eydis then draped herself over his chair, embracing him from behind.

"Birger, my brother was a good man. This is true. Indeed, you should judge him, but not by the depths of his loneliness, but rather by the fullness of his life. By the bounty of the smile that he always had for you and I both. Reward him by living your own life as he had lived his. Learn from his life. Another of our Nordic proverbs says, *A fool learns from his own mistakes, while a wise man learns from others.* My brother took his wife away from Skrova, an act which many here did not understand. They isolated him for this. After her tragic accident, the same people never forgave him for the death of a woman that they say he should never have wed. But you see, he forgave himself even less for losing her. Do not allow the heaviness of his heart to impart itself within yours. For I know one thing is eternally true, that my brother, after the loss of his love, was kept alive only by his love for you."

"If only that love was strong enough to have kept him safe from his own hands," Birger replied, giving in to his own self-doubts.

Birger settled himself. Despite his anguish, he forced himself to eat heartily, for even their discussion had not driven off his appetite.

Later, having finished his meal, he stood and once again caressed his aunt. It was the embrace of two souls who shared unspeakable thoughts about the man they both loved. Birger had never before felt totally comfortable around her. This was the first time, in this very instant, that he truly felt such a closeness to her. It was more than a merely intimate moment, it was as if their souls had washed together in the shallow waters of a common tidal pool, together protected from the sea's fiercest storm.

They were interrupted by the return of Hakron and Erik, who had prepared a boat to take him upon the interconnected fjords to the port of Narvik. There, in Narvik, Birger Alvorsen would pick up the mantle of his father's secret life.

Playing the Mark

"The chain of destiny can only be grasped one link at a time."

Winston Spencer Churchill

What a glorious day for a long walk, Sophie thought. She had been told time and time again by Diane that there was no other city in the world that was more inviting and hospitable for a long walk than London. The city's interconnected network of parks and hidden green spaces breathed a vibrancy into the metropolis that few other world capitals could boast.

The air had a slight nip, not enough for an overcoat, Sophie thought. Her sweater was just right. It was unusually sunny for what she knew of London. This was only her third trip to the capital, all since leaving the CIA at her friend Diane's behest. The day's bright, nearly cloudless skies seemed be a positive omen for this day's promenade, taken at Diane's urging, before her stressful engagement with Miss Anna Barrett.

Diane had recommended a route to her over the phone. "*Zosia,* just walk north from the flat along Buckingham Gate, cross over the parks to Piccadilly and follow it until the Circus where it transitions into Shaftesbury Avenue. Follow Shaftesbury until New Oxford Street, where you will then travel east until you take Museum Street a short block north to Great Russell Street. The British Museum will be right before you."

Sophie began her walk along Buckingham Gate, as her boss and friend had suggested. She had been staying in Diane's flat which was in, perhaps, the most expensive part of the city, in the heart of Westminster. It was just a few blocks to Buckingham Palace and the magnificent parks that surround it. As Sophie walked away from Diane's building, she very quickly came upon the corner of Buckingham Gate and the Birdcage Walk.

There, Sophie deviated from Diane's directions. She wished to stroll along the waterfowl pond of Saint James Park, even if only for a few minutes. She especially enjoyed viewing the pelicans with their awkward grace as they plodded along the pond's grassy banks.

As Sophie walked along the pond's banks, she continued to think of her friend, turned employer, Diane Sterling. Diane was always in Sophie's thoughts, for the young Pole feared for her friend. Sophie felt that although Diane had the skills, business acumen and drive to always succeed in her undertakings, she lacked any faith in her life in anything higher than her own abilities.

In the CIA Diane had been a legend, revered by all who knew her and glorified even more by those who did not. She was simply *"The Huntress*," the woman who unearthed spies, revealed corruption, and ever so nearly paid with her life for doing so. Sophie did not expect to become her friend once she met her, that just seemed to grow organically. It was as if Diane was drawn to the thing in Sophie that was missing most in her own life, and that was faith.

Now Sophie's colleague and friend had become her boss. Diane had also become absorbed with growing her business dealings in America. It seemed to consume her. As if should she somehow fail in her post-Agency life as an investigator, it would wipe out all that she had accomplished within the stealthy world of the CIA.

Diane had bought a second condominium in New York City, which was adjacent to the Sterling Investigations International offices there. She had been spending most of her time there, absent from the UK. When this case arose, Diane had asked Sophie to go to London to lead this investigation there.

Sophie had been to London before. When Diane was attempting to lure Sophie to her new firm, she had invited her Polish friend to come stay with her for a week. That first trip had been little more than a sightseeing junket for Sophie, with the restive moments over meals or drinks providing an opportunity for Diane's intoxicating recruiting pitch.

"*Zosia*," she had said then, "eighteen months ago, you and Emory and I were being hunted by the very firm for which we worked. They wanted to kill all three of us, not because of anything we did, but only because of what we *might* know. Because of what my old friend Stanley *might* have passed on to me before they silenced him forever. Now we have an opportunity to set our own course, to start an enterprise that will help people who are in terrible need. *Zosia*, I find myself in terrible need. I need you and Emory to join me on this undertaking. I cannot do it alone. Think of all the good that we can do, all over Europe and America. Who knows? Possibly all over the world. Think of how many people are in need of our special investigative skills."

Sophie had been lured in. She had asked for a Warsaw office, but Emory demanded an office in Berlin or he would not join them. "*Zosia*, you can work from your home in Poznań," Diane had said, "think of how convenient that will be for you."

And so Sophie had agreed to join Diane and Emory. However, it was the idea of helping those that needed it most that drew Sophie Czystkowska into Diane's enterprise, never a thought of enriching herself. She thought only of helping those in dire need, those who could benefit from the chemistry that the three of them - Diane, Emory, and herself - had forged.

That had been nearly three years ago. What followed was a great disappointment for Sophie. Diane's business ascended quickly on the wings of the publicity she received as being the woman who took on both the CIA and MI6 in the courts and won. With the windfall that followed, Diane established *Sterling Investigations International*.

Initially, the work was mostly of a nature of supporting global business enterprises: finding hijacked flatbeds of very expensive equipment for multi-media shows in Germany, tracking a missing accountant who had been embezzling funds from a Liechtenstein investment house, uncovering a ring of forgers who had been pilfering considerable funds from a pension fund in New York City. There was no helping of the needy, thought Sophie, only helping the rich stay as rich as possible. Sophie had made her mind up, this Conley investigation would be her last assignment from Diane. When it was complete, she would resign and would return to seek more rewarding work within her native Poland.

She had spoken to Diane about her concerns, of course. "All of our clients seem to be either the incredibly wealthy or the faceless companies and corporations that they own. When do we get to help people who are actually in true need, Diane? Those who can't afford the services that they also direly require? This is what I came to SII to do…"

Sophie remembered Diane as always having an explanation barely good enough to keep the Polish young woman with her.

"*Zosia*, we are a new entity. We need to establish ourselves. Yes, our clients are people of considerable means, but they are the ones paying our start-up costs. Let us lay down our roots, and then we will help the less fortunate that need our services once we are established."

As I see it, Sophie thought to herself, *Diane cannot let go of the materialism in which she has always lived.*

It was true that Diane Sterling had grown up in great wealth, in one of America's wealthiest counties - Bucks County, Pennsylvania. She had watched her father so carelessly fall prey to greed, divorcing her mom when she was young. She had watched as her mother, under the stress of a divorce that she had never seen coming, become totally destabilized in life. Her mother had built her entire existence around her father, the man who no longer needed nor wanted her.

It was also true that when her father passed on, he left Diane what can only be considered a not so small fortune. This is how she was able to live in one of London's priciest districts, or to have a second home in New York City. Certainly she had risen on her own abilities within the CIA to among its top ranks, but even these positions could not pay enough for this elaborate lifestyle. Diane had never tasted anything in her life but comfort and privilege, and in doing so, she had displaced any love for God, and to a startling effect, for those less fortunate than herself.

Sophie came to the footbridge that crossed over the pond. She had just passed two pelicans along the banks, and as she reached the mid-span of the footbridge, she searched for the solitary swan that Diane had once spoke of to her. This particular day, it was not to be found.

"After seeing the pain my father imparted upon my mother," Diane had once said to her, "I vowed to live my life like the solitary swan. Never to be dependent on any man."

The difference, thought Sophie, was that even the solitary swan once had a mate. Diane had never tasted love, not from her days as the only child of rich parents, to the present days that found her wealthy in her own right. Diane had admitted to Sophie that over her lifetime she had a multitude of lovers, but also that she had never opened herself up to any man's love.

Sophie rested upon the apex of the footbridge and looked at the wonderful greenery of the park surrounding her. The city was like Diane, she thought. All business, cemented in its own vitality, its arteries coursing with energy. The green spaces were its soul.

Unlike the city though, Sophie thought, Diane had no soul. Diane did not have London's expansive, regenerative, green spaces to revive her. For even in a city as energetic as London, one needed to refresh their spirit.

The parks were one such space to do so. The other was the city's cathedrals and churches. And that was Diane's greatest downfall, thought Sophie, that she had neither love nor God in her life. And life's most precious gift, being the love of God, would forever elude her. Diane had displaced His love, instead, with the love of earthly things, including power and self-importance. These were indeed the fingers of the evil one, thought Sophie, and Diane was firmly in their clutches.

It was then that a majestic bird with a massive wingspan, Sophie thought it possibly a Great Heron, glided gracefully to a landing along the banks of the pond in front of her. It came to stand upright in the shallows, and appeared to be nearly four feet tall. It waded proudly in the serene waters of the pond, away from the collection of other birds that floated sedately upon its calm surface.

Its slender tapered belly was dusted in hues of a mottled and tawny light brown coloration that slowly blended into tucked wings of a steely gray, elegantly speckled with streaks of indigo blue. Its neck and crest featured a bluish array of elegant feathers. Adjacent to its eyes a pale white streak emblazoned laterally as if windswept amongst the rich blue plumage.

Sophie thought the resplendent visitor to have all the traits of her friend Diane. A bedazzling appearance, a commanding presence, but beneath all this finery, it led a solitary, lonely existence. She wondered if it had fled from the aviary of some country manor house, for she had never before seen it on prior visits. After a few minutes, it was driven off by the approach of a leashed dog nearby. It lurched forward, with an awkward thrust, before expanding its wings to their full span. Then, with each stroke of those feathered appendages, its true beauty was revealed. Having appeared a steely blue when tucked, the wings of the bird had, on their unfurling, exhibited a most beautiful display of plumage. As each wing fanned, the blue colorations seemed to drain from the gray and collected in the tips of the wings in vibrant hues of the deepest, most robust cobalt blues. Sophie watched as it flew across the pond to an opposite shore.

Sophie looked at her watch, and feared she may have lingered too long in her walk through the park. It was time to move on, to venture onward and engage in the business of the day.

Sophie then left the pond, walked across St. James Park, and soon found herself upon Charing Cross Road. This she travelled north until it intersected with Shaftesbury Avenue. Not long afterward, having gotten back onto Diane's directions, she found herself walking east on New Oxford Street and then north on Museum Street.

The narrow lane that was Museum Street looked as though it was not much more than an alley or court brought alive with foot traffic. This faux pedestrian promenade was interrupted every so often by the brave navigation of the occasional automobile, which by law, if not by convenience, was still allowed upon the street. It thickened and swarmed with vibrant foot traffic as Sophie came upon the T intersection with Great Russell Street. She stopped to gawk at the black wrought iron fence surrounding the British Museum which had just closed for the day.

The British Museum had surprised the young Polish woman. Whereas other major museums in London were on expansive boulevards, this, the most renowned of London's museums, was tucked away, almost on a back street. It appeared surrounded by a thick growth of the old city's buildings, insulating it, to a point, from the world outside. Yet inside its walls were all the most valued relics of the world from which it appeared to be sequestered.

Sophie took in the sight of the museum and thought to herself that she must return to sample its treasures, but today would not be that day. She looked at her wristwatch, realized her time had come to meet Miss Anna Barrett. She found the narrow doorway that seemed pinned like an afterthought onto the backside of the tourist shop selling miniatures of Buckingham Palace and Saint Paul's Cathedral, coasters of nearly every kind, and various other souvenirs for the world's traveling elite. Sophie turned to press the button marked "Mr. & Mrs. R. Barrett". She instantly realized the doorway reeked of urine.

"And just 'ow may I help you?" came an aged but singsong British female voice.

"Mrs. Barrett, my name is Sophie Czystowska. We spoke on the telephone. I am here on behalf of the Polish International Ancestry Survivor's Trust."

"Yes, yes, the Polish girl who has five hundred quid for me. Come up, darling, please do come up."

Suddenly an electronic latch clicked and Sophie pushed in the red painted door. It opened onto a small hall, barely large enough to accommodate the inward swing of the door before offering the visitor the sole option of climbing a steep set of stairs. Having climbed these, which no longer smelled of bodily relief, only of a deep musk of indifference, did Sophie come upon a door which opened after she had presented herself to a peephole.

In front of her stood an elderly woman, warm and matronly in appearance. In that instant Sophie decided the hardship of many unkind years had thickened her. Fate can be unkind that way.

"Come in, come in, my little Polska friend," said the old woman. "My, my, darling, you'll catch your death of the chill with only a jumper on. Come in, come in to my parlor. I have a magnificent view to offer."

"Thank you for seeing me, upon such short notice," answered Sophie as she entered the lovely little flat.

"Of course, my dear," Anna Barrett replied. "Couldn't possibly think of not doing so. With your being Polish and representing their people and all that. Always loved the Poles, myself, I 'ave. I still remember Father telling stories of how 'eroic their pilots were during the Battle of Britain. Poles 'ave been here in London ever since the start of the Second World War, they 'ave. And we were all the better for it, I say."

"Yes," interrupted Sophie, "thank you for that very nice and warm welcome."

Anna Barrett seemed not to hear her and just plowed forward.

"We love 'em. These days, the Poles come, they stay, they work their bottoms off, earn some money, and they generally go back to Poland. Lovely people. Not like the lot of them migrants."

"Them migrants?" repeated Sophie, not understanding. She looked quizzically at Miss Barrett, begging an explanation.

"Yes, dear," said the woman. "London used to be the safest city in the world. Now, I fear walking out on the street. Terrible slaughter just down the lane in the square a few years back. And this dreadful running down of innocent Londoners on bridges. Then again there's the throwing of acid in people's faces. But, that's not you Poles, now is it? No, your kind are quite delightful, dear. How long 'ave you been working in London?"

"I am afraid I was not clear," answered Sophie apologetically, "for I am only here on a business trip. I live in Poznań in Poland."

"Must be a beautiful little town, I'm certain," Anna Barrett mused.

"It is a very large and modern city, about halfway between Berlin and Warsaw," Sophie corrected her gently.

"Sounds absolutely delightful, love," mused Anna, not caring about the particulars of Poznań, "what's this about my five hundred quid?"

Anna Barrett had cut to the chase. Her interest was in her own immediate windfall. Despite this, the young Polish girl felt as if she would be acting out of character if she did not offer the full cover story.

"Yes, well," began Sophie, "the PIAST, that is, the trust I mentioned over the phone, has decided to award you a recognition grant on behalf of your father's actions during World War II. It amounts to close to two thousand pounds, but I am only authorized to give you five hundred pounds until the DNA match confirms that you are indeed Commander Ian Barrett's daughter."

"Well, of course I am, love," Anna Barrett exclaimed, "been so all my life, 'aven't I?"

Sophie then followed her across the flat to the two tall windows which looked out onto the museum itself and the street below. Sophie stood awkwardly, glancing downward on the bustle of the crowds milling about the black cast iron fenced perimeter of the institution.

"Rupert and I call them our ant farm, dear. Always milling about, aren't they?" The Barrett woman nearly pushed Sophie into her overstuffed chair. "Fancy a spot of tea, dear? I only have Earl Grey, but it has a lovely touch to it."

"Yes, thank you, Mrs. Barrett..." answered Sophie. "That would be very nice indeed."

"Well, about that, dear. It is properly Miss Barrett. Just a spinster, I am afraid. I marked the ground floor notice with two initials just to make the hooligans think twice before trying any of their charades. Biscuits with your tea, darling?"

Sophie could hear Emory as he prepared her last night for this visit. "She is likely a lonely soul. Take whatever she offers, it will relax her. Make her ask about the money, she'll get around to it if she thinks you won't. But engage her in conversation about herself first."

"Yes, that would be very nice," Sophie replied, before adding, "I thought the R. might have stood for Richard or Reginald, a husband, perhaps."

"Oh, not a 'usband, dearie," Anna confessed stubbornly, "old Rupert is my soul-mate, now *inn't 'e?*"

As Miss Barrett said this, Sophie felt a sensation brushing across her boot, and looking down discovered a massively overweight tabby cat that decided to come out from hiding under the chair's upholstered skirt.

"Well, right on 'is mark, is old Rupert," said Anna Barrett, spotting the cat as she handed the cup to Sophie. "There you go, my dear, saucered, but not blown, mind you."

"I am afraid I do not understand," said Sophie, unfamiliar with the term.

"That's me merely saying 'beware, it is 'ot, darling" responded the woman. "So please explain again who it is you are with, my dear."

Sophie sipped her tea, without blowing over it, and it nearly scorched her lips. Her face must have shown her discomfort, for Miss Barrett remarked, "I tried to warn you, darling."

"Yes, yes, you did, ma'am," admitted Sophie, running her tongue over her reddened lips.

Sophie knew that the woman had called the false number posted on the internet listing the night before. It rang in Emory's office in Berlin. Emory's assistant with the obscene Polish pronunciation had fielded it, as Emory had later told Sophie. She would try to repeat the explanation again exactly as the German woman had, as the unsuspecting always found trust in repetition.

"I am representing the Polish International Ancestry Survivor's Trust Fund. It is a fund out of Warsaw established by a very generous set of donors to recognize the actions of those who rescued Poles during the Second World War."

"Lovely," said Anna Barrett as she returned with her own cup and biscuits and slowly sank into the chair next to Sophie. "Never too late to reward the 'Good Samaritans' of this world, I always say."

"We have some very wealthy patrons," continued Sophie, "and they know not many of these heroes are still alive, so these meager awards go to their survivors from a fund of these donors that is very well endowed."

"My, my, I don't rather fancy taking anything from well-endowed Poles, now should I? Sounds rather like a gaggle of filthy buggers, does it not, my dear?"

"I am sorry, Miss Barrett. My English is not very good, sometimes I twist my meanings. Sometimes I make stupid sayings," explained Sophie, playing up her accent. "Not very well endowed, I meant having a generous endowment."

"And this very generous endowment includes the five hundred pounds for my merely meeting with you?"

"Yes, of course, if you will just sign this check for our records," said Sophie, "I will give you the cash myself."

"Lovely. Absolutely lovely," chortled Miss Barrett, taking the draft from her guest to sign, whereupon Sophie slowly counted out the five hundred pounds in twenty-pound notes.

Sophie then handed the excessively tall stack of money over to the woman, who very quickly stuffed the notes in the pockets of her slacks. "So, how exactly can I be of assistance, dear?"

"Well, Miss Barrett, we have first-hand witnesses who have verified that your father, Commander Ian Barrett, rescued Polish pilots who were shot down over the English Channel during the war. They wish you to accept their grant of two thousand pounds on his behalf. We tried to track down his sister, Cassandra, but with no luck."

"Oh, my darling, Cassandra's been deceased for twenty years on," Miss Anna professed. "Even were she still living, that woman didn't need to draw from any relief fund, now did she? Richer than blooming King Solomon, 'imself, she was. Or 'er son was, it is properly said. She married into a Texas oil family. Never had so much as a shilling to toss in my direction, mind you. So your clients have come to the right place, they 'ave."

Sophie felt at that moment that she had the woman's fullest attention. *Now was the time to dangle the hook*, as she thought Emory would have said.

"Well, Miss Barrett, we are certainly happy we have. Allow me to present you with this small token of our appreciation," Sophie said as she reached into the depths of her oversized handbag. "We hope you will proudly display this next to a photo of your father."

She handed the old woman a small cast sculpture showing the crossed British and Polish flags. Upon saying this, Sophie noticed the demeanor of the woman before her changed into a truly sentimental state.

"It is quite lovely, isn't it, dear," said Miss Anna. "Has a very smart look about it, it 'as."

Anna Barrett rose to take the keepsake from Sophie. She held it at arms length to appreciate the patina of its cast surfaces, then set it on the nearest tabletop.

"Coming through loud and clear," whispered a tiny electromagnetic voice said inside Sophie's ear. "I'll tell the London techno-boys their rush job is working splendidly."

The voice was Emory Hauptmann's from Berlin. The casting had embedded within it a listening device that was being picked up down the street by two undercover agents. Their device in turn then digitized the signal, converting it into a live internet feed. Given the small dimensions of the Barrett flat, it would pick up most anything said aloud. It also had an embedded GPS locator, just in the off chance that Miss Barrett tossed it or pawned it, they would know where to go to recover it. After all, it was proof of their invading her privacy.

"So what must I do to get the remaining fifteen hundred quid?" asked Anna Barrett.

"Once we confirm your DNA," replied Sophie, "we will deliver the funds to you here. All we need is a sample of your saliva into a small plastic vial. You should have the remaining funds in no more than a week."

"So your benefactors don't believe I am who I say I am?" asked Miss Anna. "To what exactly are they going to match my DNA, by the bye?"

"Tell her Whitehall keeps a DNA database of all armed forces personnel, past and present which we have access to," Emory said in the funneled tinny voice in her ear. The British military did, but it was unlikely to contain Commander Barrett's DNA from World War II. Even if it somehow should, the British High Command would certainly not share it with outside benevolent trusts, imagined or otherwise.

Sophie relayed the lie, and Anna Barrett accepted it. Then, they collected the saliva sample, and soon enough Sophie was preparing to depart Anna Barrett's flat.

"Sophie, dearest," Miss Barrett said to her, "I do have one request as you leave. Please no discussion of the five hundred pounds to the boys in the shoppe below us. They are kind enough to toss a dented tin of biscuits and some tea my way from time to time. I wouldn't wish them to think they need not extend that kindness any longer, if you read my lead, my dear."

"No, Miss Barrett, our discussion is solely between our PIAST Fund and yourself…"

"And Rupert, of course," added the woman, as if playfully apologizing for her request.

"Yes, and Rupert, of course," added Sophie, smiling. "Thank you for allowing me into your lovely home, and congratulations on your grant award."

Sophie turned to the door when the old woman called out to her, "Who do I call if I don't receive the remaining funds by the end of next week."

Certainly, everything that Emory had predicted about this woman had come to pass. Sophie felt somewhat guilty for lying to her so.

"I am quite certain that you will receive the rest of the funds by then, Miss Barrett," said Sophie, "but if for some reason you do not, just call that number I gave you on the phone. Or you can call me directly." Sophie had given her a card bearing another monitored phone number of the fictitious fund.

"I'll call you, Sophie," preferred Anna Barrett, "you are a lot nicer than that woman I talked to last night. I don't even think she was Polish. Sounded more like a German accent to me. Damned Huns, never could trust them, my father always said to his dying day."

Emory's tinny voice laughed in Sophie's ear. "You just can't fool some people at all, can you?"

"I am so sorry, Miss Barrett," said Sophie, ignoring Emory's words, "but the European Union makes us take on employees from outside Poland. I hope that you can understand this. Please, call me instead. I will most certainly enjoy speaking to you again."

"I certainly will," said Miss Anna, "I really don't care for that wicked Hun."

Sophie smiled and soon was out the door and descending the musty steps when the old woman called after her.

"Sophie, darling, you might wish to try the pierogi parlor around the corner. I hear it is very good Polish food. Not that I might know directly, but so I am told. Might taste better to you than what passes for Shepherd's Pie around here these days. Find it near High Holborn and Kingsway. I am told it is worth the effort."

Sophie thanked her once more, then exited and walked down Great Russell Street, past the two *Sterling Investigations International* employees who were surveilling Anna Barrett's flat from their casual position along the British Museum's fence line. Sophie then turned the corner, out of the line of sight from the Barrett flat's windows, and handed the vial of saliva to a waiting motorcycle courier for immediate delivery to a lab on the south side of London.

Her assignment complete, Sophie felt another twinge of remorse for lying to the old woman. Yet, she consoled herself in knowing that the only harm done was to put two thousand pounds into the spinstress's coffers.

Sophie found her way back to New Oxford Street and proceeded east until she found High Holborn and then Kingsway. A few minutes later she found the Polish Bar to which Miss Bartlett had so rudely referred to as a "pierogi parlor".

As Sophie entered the establishment, she keep repeating to herself the same thought as she had since she left the woman's flat: *When will I do something of service for the needy of this world, instead of performing once more like a pet dog for another of Diane's indecently rich clients?*

Figure 6: Norwegian Fjorden Winter Coastline

6

The Fjords of Narvik

November 1912

"It's not enough that we do our best; sometimes we have to do what's required."

Winston Spencer Churchill

The knife edge of the bow of the small sailboat cut like a surgeon's scalpel across the mirror-smooth surface of the inner fjords. Birger rested as Erik manned the helm. Hakron sat silently beside his cousin. The three men were by then making their way back from the port town of Narvik, returning to the small fishing island of Skrova.

The day had already long grown dark, as was typical for late November in the Arctic. The midday sky had nothing more than a faint steely gray glow that barely outlined the mountains. It reflected in a weakly diffused shimmer from the fjord's surface, not as light directly, but only as trace evidence that such a concept as light even existed at all.

Narvik was drifting away ever more distantly behind them, as was Birger's innocence. He looked past Erik in the stern to see the reflection of the port town's lights flicker in the diverging ridges of the vessel's wake. He then turned to face forward beyond the bow, where he was conscious of the widening gate of granite snow-capped mountains on either side of the fjord's shores creating walls that hovered protectively over them. These cliffs opened ever wider alongside the craft as they left the volcanic-nestled inner *Ofotfjord* and re-entered the more expansive waters of *the Vestfjorden*.

"So, you have met the man you came to see?" asked Hakron solemnly. "Did you conclude your business, Birger?"

Birger thought it strange that his cousin would wait so long to ask this question. Would it not have made more sense to do so at Narvik's docks before they began their return to Skrova? It was then that he answered his own thought by assuming Hakron was merely breaking the stillness of the bitterly cold wind that washed like acid over what little of their skin that was exposed.

"Yes, I did," responded Birger stoically, "I needed to close out some old business for Father."

"Yes," Hakron said, "we inherit their responsibilities and little else."

Birger reached into the inside of his parka, and could feel the box containing the maps and papers that the man, unknown previously to him, had passed under the cafe's table. The entire meeting had been over a cup of coffee and had taken less than ten minutes. All that Birger had to do now was carry the materials back to Scotland and hand them over to the strange little man from London.

As *the Vestfjorden* opened before them, and the small cluster of islands that was Skrova came into sight, the winds picked up. It not only bitterly stung on their faces as the ships's forward motion cut into the breeze, but would occasionally gust from their side, forcing them off course, which required Erik to adjust the rudder.

As the darkness of day enshrouded them, Birger thought back to five months earlier. Then, in late June, light had filled the sky, even at midnight. He remembered that night clearly and fondly, so full of light when Tulla had first come to him. It was near nine o'clock in the evening when she knocked upon his aunt's door. He invited her inside, but she preferred to stay outdoors, as if she wished to avoid the judgement of those inside.

"You said someday we could watch the midnight sun together, Birger," she smiled at him. He remembered thinking how beautiful she was in the late evening sunlight. Her streaming blonde locks flickered in the Arctic winds. They not only glistened, but seemed to frame the vibrant skin of her smiling face with the tempting allure of her youth. "Well, I am ready to see it tonight."

"Yes, I did, young Tulla," he had responded, "but I did not expect to do so tonight. Father, my cousins and I have just come back from fishing, and they are all resting now. Perhaps tomorrow evening when we can all go together…"

Her smiling face morphed into a sullen frown of disappointment. "Tonight is my only chance," she said dolefully, "for my father comes back from sea tomorrow night and will certainly not allow me to do so. Mother said it was all right for you to accompany me so long as we did not let Father know. She trusts you."

Her face now broke into that of a frolicsome imp, "Come, Birger, you can tell me all about your travels across the sea, and those Scottish lassies back at home. I want to hear all about your travels. It is so exciting. I fear I will never see anything more of the world than Skrova and the waters of the *Vestfjorden*."

As she spoke in that doorway, an exuberance overcame Tulla. In her eyes rekindled a mischievous fire. She was a girl of only seventeen, yes, but her beauty had already exploded like the first bloom of a spring foliage. Yet, her smile danced with an impish devilry, inviting him but also forewarning him as to where it might lead. It evoked in Birger the competing responses of intrigue and caution.

"Birger," she pleaded, "you have promised me. Please don't disappoint me tonight. I only wish to share the beauty of the midnight sun with you."

Birger gave in to her plea. He agreed to take the girl, despite the weight of his weariness from having been at sea for the past few days. She danced delightedly upon his words of acceptance. She moved about excitedly when he emerged from his aunt's *Rorbu* with his parka. Even in June, the temperature was peaking only in the low 40s Fahrenheit.

They walked through the town with her pressing herself into his shoulder, her arms wrapped around him, pulling him away from the huddled houses of the main fishing village. "I know just the best place, you will love it."

Tulla led him to the east, out of the seaport, and along the paths of the sparsely populated windswept island. After a long while, she led him down a small rocky hill to a beautiful sandy beach at the end of a long finger-like inlet known to the locals as the *Remøyosen*. Its skin was a long but shallow depth of blue turquoise water that lapped gently upon the narrow golden sands of the beach , those which formed the nail of the finger. Around them, gentle grassy hills cut off the view from the scant number of curious eyes amongst the island. They were alone, and this singular fact excited Tulla nearly to a frenzy.

"Isn't this ideal, Birger?" she asked. "Just you and me and the midnight sun!"

"I am afraid that we will not have a very good viewing of the setting sun here," Birger said to her. "We are too low. The wall of the Lofoten Mountain peaks across the *Vestfjorden* will obscure our view."

"That's all right, my dear Birger," she said softly, pulling him down on the sands next to herself. "We both know that the sun never sets at summer solstice here. I have seen the midnight sun many times with my family. I just wanted to be with you before you sailed back to Scotland in a few days. I guarantee you that we will see the midnight sun together when the time is right."

She leaned even harder into him, and wrapped both arms around his chest.

"Tulla, we will stay here for only a few moments longer, and then we will go back. What will everyone think?"

"I don't care what everyone thinks," she exploded at him, before softening her tone and adding, "I just want to be with you. Besides, I have a little naughty surprise for you."

She pulled his hand inside of her parka which she had unbuttoned. He resisted, but she became more forceful. "I am not going to bite you, Birger, trust me."

He relaxed somewhat, and she led his hand under her parka to a flask tucked inside the waist of her slacks. He pulled it out, surprised by its hardness, its cold touch. Perhaps his mind had expected that she led his hand to the soft warmth of her youthful skin. A minor disappointment flashed on his face, prompting Tulla to laugh devilishly at his attempt to hide his obvious regret.

"Father's *Akevitt*! *Skål!*" she toasted before her youthful blossom of a face exploded into a broad, tempting grin. She giggled like the seventeen-year-old she was. Before Birger could object, Tulla had taken the flask from him, uncapped it and took a deep draw of the clear, eighty-proof liquor. Its name meant *"Water of Life"* in Norwegian, and on these fjords it had been just that for the sea-weary fishermen since the fifteenth century.

Tulla's face beamed with the mischief and revery of what was to come. "Try some, Birger," the girl seductively offered, "it will keep you warm."

"Give me that," protested Birger, snatching the flask back from Tulla. From its weight, he could tell it was full.

He sniffed the drink, thinking she might had filled the flask with water, as a joke. He pulled it sharply away from his face as the spirit rushed harshly into his nasal passages.

"Oh, come on, Birger!" she taunted, "You are the great world traveler, man of the sea, surely you have had *Akevitt!* Come, now, join me!"

Of course, Birger had tasted the spirit many times, but usually as part of a festive family gathering for the holidays. He had never thought to drink it just to become drunk.

"If you are going to be so rude to not join me, then give it back to me," she said to him snidely, "I am sorry that I mistook you for a real Nordic man."

"*Skål!*" Birger cried out, as if to defend his virility. He flipped the flask into the air and drank deeply. Once finished, he added, "We drink this small flask, and then we go back."

A salacious grin erupted across Tulla's face, celebrating the first of the evening's simple victories.

"We drink to the pleasure of seeing each other only twice a year! *Skål!*" She had taken the flask back from him and drew deeply from it, before leaning forward to kiss Birger. He leaned back, but she raised herself over him, until he had no recourse but to accept her warm lips. As he did so, she pushed the Akevitt warmed within her own mouth into his.

Tulla laughed, her lips still pressing hard upon his, and her mirth echoed within him. Her scent filled him as the spirit spread like a fire within him. She pulled back from his lips, and whispered sensually in his ear, "Can the Scottish girls raise your spirits like I can?"

Then, she rolled off him, knowing that she had excited him. "Tonight, my Birger, we shall only drink," she teased, "nothing more."

So they did. They laughed heartily and they drank heavily from the flask.

"I am surprised your father does not have his flask at sea," said Birger between pulls of the spirit. The flask was now nearly empty.

"Oh, but he does," said Tulla with a teasing, alluring smile. "He has many flasks," as she produced a second from the pocket of her coat. The drink had ignited something within her, more than just tipsiness, more than just her lewd intent, more of an unchained desire to live life as a reckless adventure. She uncapped the second flask and drank deeply from it.

"No, no, we must go!" protested Birger, attempting to raise himself from the sand. Tulla merely pulled him down upon herself, laughing.

"We are not finished yet," she protested. "Drink! Drink with me, my Scottish Viking of the seas."

She took another deep pull from the flask, inverting it upright to assist her effort.

"We finish this flask, then we will walk back," he said. Although by this point, he had been warding off other thoughts of his own. The *Akevitt* seemed to ignite a taboo desire in him towards Tulla youthful sensuality.

"If we can walk at all," she said, smiling at him, her eyes beaming more brightly than the sun that refused to set.

"I am serious," said Birger, "after this flask we go back."

Tulla laughed, "Yes, after … we will go… "

She offered him the second flask and as he kneeled over her to drink from it, her hands reached inside his parka to probe the hard muscles of his chest.

The warmth generated from her contact with his taut body rippled from her fingers, and spread like a slow burning flame throughout him. It flushed any residual feelings of restraint from within him.

She pulled him down upon her and kissed him deeply. Her tongue probed his mouth. He hesitated awkwardly. After a second he responded, giving in to her invitation, and pressed his lips hard onto hers. He wrapped his arms around her, under her opened parka. Her skin was hot as it pressed onto him. Then his tongue slid over hers. He could feel her purr a contented "Hmmm…" As he felt it reverberate through him, as it seemed to say, *Take me, I am yours, Birger.*

Then, a cold Arctic breeze blew over the coupled young pair. Its sober chill seemed to revive Birger's conscience, which then attempted to pull him back from the brink. He sensed that Tulla was only drawing him to the very edge of desire to then push him teasingly away. She had not done so in any manner, her actions all indicated exactly the opposite, but Birger feared her scolding rejection was soon to come.

Birger pulled himself away. Away from her exploring, sensuous mouth. Away from the warm brush of her curves upon his arms. Away from the multitude of temptations that beckoned him. Away from that taboo line she seemed so destined to get him to cross. So near. So willing. So forbidden.

"No, we can't," he said tentatively, as in his mind he strained his impulses, as if he could somehow separate out his responsibilities from this flooding sea of desire in which they both might drown.

Tulla pouted, and again feigned disappointment. Then she took hold of Birger's hands and led them inside her parka as both their breaths quickened. Her fingers splayed opened his clenched fists, just as the rays of the rising sun opens a morning blossom. His resistance again yielded, his strong hands bloomed, just as she guided them to her torso. Tulla smiled broadly as their sensual touch flowed over her breasts. First, the surprisingly strong landing of the tips of his hesitant fingers. Then, she laid her hands on the back of his, and pressed flat his palms upon her sweater. His hands lingered there, feeling her breaths harden further under his touch, but after a long second, Birger suddenly pulled his hands away and scrambled to the safety of his feet.

"I want to show you something," Tulla teased, as she herself rose energetically to stand next to him. She again took his hands, but this time pulled on them, almost as a rambunctious child would a reluctant, weary parent. When Birger resisted, Tulla turned from him, coyly laughing, and ran from the beach toward the rise of the trail that led to the rocky hill known locally as the *Hogskrova*.

"Damn it," cursed Birger as he began to chase after her. She was undoubtedly drunk, and her climbing the steep trail to the highest point on this, the largest island of those that made up Skrova, was fraught with peril. A fall, even to a girl as spry and lithe as Tulla, could result in serious, and possibly even fatal bodily harm.

Birger knew he had to catch her, to prevent this playful foolishness from turning into an unwanted folly of unexpected consequences. He was responsible for this young girl, and at this point regretted coming along with her this night. Yes, she was beautiful, and her spirit was vivacious, but was it really worth all this nonsense?

Birger called after her, but the result of which was that she only climbed all the harder along the trails she knew by heart. Birger was less acquainted, and in fact, was fighting the combined effects of his weariness and the inebriation of the imbibed spirits. As he chased after the mischievous Tulla, he fought another form of intoxication, one that he wished to drive from his mind.

After their time on the beach together, Birger had a difficult time driving the mischievous smile, the enticing smell and the touch of the supple skin of this beautiful girl from his mind.

The climb seemed to last forever. All the way up, Tulla called back to him, taunting him, mocking him for the slow determined placement of his feet upon the rocky path. She, on the other hand, scampered ever higher in near effortless abandon.

Despite the hour coming upon midnight, the light of the sun that refused to set illuminated their path. It was not the full harsh brightness of day, but rather a strange illumination as dusk transitioned to dawn, refusing to allow the darkness of night to intervene. The lighting was as surreal as the moment Birger found himself living out, chasing the girl who wished only to be caught. His exertions of the climb appeared to drain the last of his proper judgement from him, as he found himself lost in a swirl of the ethereal lighting, the intoxicating *Akevitt,* and the increasingly sexual allure of this young Nordic woman.

As they reached the top of the rocky *Hogskrova* bluff, Tulla sang out, and began to spin in a tight circle, her arms outstretched to the sky. Birger mounted the summit, leaned forward, hands on hips as he caught his breath. He looked at the beautiful twirling girl who proclaimed repeatedly, "We made it!"

It was then that Tulla stopped spinning and stood with her legs apart at shoulders width to steady herself. She removed the heavy down parka she had worn to that point. Casting it aside, she stood before Birger in britches and the heavy woolen sweater that the women in the town below had themselves artfully made by hand. Her smile invited him, in a manner that seemed the doorway to sin itself.

She had lured him there exactly as the lowest tangent of the fiery yellow sun dipped below the sparkling aquamarine ocean off in the distance. As she looked over her shoulder, she saw what he did. The image of the sun appeared to glow less like a well defined orb, but more so like a wavering fiery plume. It whipped like a flag of blazing yellow-reddish plumes far off on the horizon, slowly undulating in and out of a shroud of pink, and reddish-purple haze. This sensual swirl of color and light gave way to a range of pastel blue skies beyond. Tulla saw the fiery colors of the sun as if they were Birger's temptation, while the calm blue skies on which they burned were the resolve she knew he would never heed.

The height of their climb cleared their view. From this particular vantage point, together they could watch as the sun dipped ever so slightly into the sea just beyond the westernmost tip of the Lofoten Islands. The wall of jagged, vertical mountains ended there, and framed this incredible sight. Tulla and Birger knew that the fiery orb would never fully set, but the illusion of it wanting to do so teased them.

"Look at it Birger," Tulla said seductively. "It wants only what it cannot have."

In fact, Birger then turned himself a full three hundred and sixty degrees, taking in the panorama like none other that his eyes had ever seen. *The Vestfjorden*, alight in all her cobalt blue splendor, seemed to radiate away from the Skrova isles like indigo ink gushing forth in every direction from the depths of an unremitting well.

Birger cast a glance far below them, down into the miniature fishing village from which they had set forth. A pang of guilt ran through him as he thought of Tulla's mother and the daughter she had entrusted to him this night.

"Isn't it perfect?" Tulla cried, as her spinning slowly resumed, in only her britches and the heavy island-weave sweater that she wore. Whether it was the imbalance that her spinning had created, or the effects of the *Akevitt*, or a combination of both that overcame her, she crumpled gently to the ground, like a child's spinning top losing its momentum. Birger moved to steady her, but was too late. He then knelt over her. Her face was alight with expectation, her smile stretched wide by her exuberant mood.

"Are you hurt, Tulla?" Birger asked, but she had not stopped laughing as she lay on the flattened earth that was nearly surrounded by a crown of boulders.

"I have never had a better moment in my life, Birger," she let out in a gleeful gasp. Immediately after saying this, she pulled him down on top of her again. Her mouth found his, and this time they kissed even more passionately. Birger no longer pull away from her, even as her tongue probed his mouth. He hungrily responded, only to have her pull away.

"This is how I always wanted this to happen," she said as she guided his right hand to the buttons of her britches. "Take me, Birger."

He saw the raging flame of desire in her eyes. Somehow, it sobered him. "No, Tulla, this cannot happen."

"It is already happening," she replied, "and we are on the highest point of Skrova, no one else can see us, Birger. Come closer…"

She pulled him nearer to her, and as the midnight sun began its climb upward from the sea that it had never fully dropped behind, she slowly wore down his resistance.

Tulla laughed, and then sang softly into his ear a child's song, one that she had long ago created: *"High above, on Hogskrova's rise, we shall be as one, far away from prying eyes."*

Birger kissed her back ever more forcefully. She responded with a fervor that intended to tell him, *This is what I want from you, Birger*. He knew he could no longer resist her, no longer pretend that she had not stoked the passion within him. She softly moaned as his hands traced the features of her curves between the long, sensual kisses. Her body's delicate scent filled his being, leaving him wanting all he knew he should not take.

His hands continued to wander over her clothes, sculpting her form beneath as if it were virgin clay being measured by the artists hand. She grasped his hand, which had been laid on her form atop the woolen top. She guided it with her left hand as her right lifted the bulky garb. She stared into his eyes as she led his hand up under the canopy of wool and across the flatness of her stomach. Her breath increased to a gentle panting as his strong fingers came to rest upon her breast, this time upon its bare tender skin beneath the sweater's bulk. A smile creased her face as she recognized his pleasant surprise.

"So, are you happy now that you came with me tonight?" Tulla teased.

"I am very excited to be here with you," he said slyly.

She kept her hand over his, slowly guiding it along the upper contours of her budding, delicate frame. With her other hand she reached down to verify his last statement.

"You tell no lies," she giggled.

"It is you who has this effect on me," he sighed.

"Yes, I know, Birger. Let's see what other effects I may have on you."

Her hand began to frantically free him from the remnants of his restraint. Her other hand rested upon his atop her breast. His hand then slipped from under hers and soon joined his other at her waist. She kissed him as his fingers hungrily undid her britches.

Then Tulla submissively arched her back as his hands tugged, which allowed her garb to slide free of her otherwise naked bottom.

"Tulla, everything tells me we shouldn't," he said, gasping as she explored him. His sensitivity to her touch rippled through him like tremors before a quake.

"That's exactly why we must," she replied, laughing devilishly. "I wish to experience what it means to be a true woman, Birger. Only you, this night, can release me from being the child everyone in this town takes me for. You, a man of the world, traveler of the seas, will free me from my sheltered life."

As Tulla spoke, the pace of her breathing quickened. She guided Birger to her. His breathing became erratic, uneven, like the teeth along the edge of a saw. Her mouth hungrily found his. The desire she found in him there was by this point ravenous and had abandoned all attempts of restraint.

And then, he melded with her as one. The words ceased, only guttural sounds soon commenced. Their labored breaths shortly then bore a combination of the sounds of delight and expectation. Her gasps quickened, but seemed to be of neither pleasure nor pain. They were uttered only to accentuate the quickening pulsating pace of their combined experience.

For them, time itself became blended with emotion, infused with pleasure, and rippled with an increasingly ratcheted tension. Their joint spirit became imbued with a sweetly sensual sweat. Their collective passive pleasure had given way to the deeper, more active delight paced by their jointly writhing bodies and panting breaths. The climatic moment became a mixture of ecstatic moans building to shuddering release within them both. Not together. It arrived first in her, deeply within her, before it spread throughout her every tensing muscle. It vaulted chasms within her that she before had felt could never be bridged.

For a brief moment, Tulla was overcome by an incomprehensible weakness that washed away her every thought, her every worry. She was adrift upon a wave of her own private solitude of pleasure, in which even Birger no longer existed.

Birger soon followed, although Tulla did not notice, until she felt the weight of his exhausted frame gently collapse upon her. Over the next several minutes, they lay entwined, but motionless. Birger fought to recover his breath. Beneath him, Tulla melted into that blissful stillness that was the center of the spreading wake of her ecstasy.

"Are you all right, Tulla?" he asked.

"I have never felt better in my entire life," she whispered into his ear. "In fact, I have never before felt this way. This is the very feeling that I wish to fill the rest of my life with."

"Did I hurt you?" Birger asked as he hovered, his arms locked like pillars, as he lifted his weight from her. "If so, I am sorry."

She looked into his eyes and laughed, then raised herself to embrace him once more. She pulled him down atop her, his pillars crumbling as his resistance had earlier.

"You are not listening to me. That was wonderful," she replied after she had again kissed him. In a few seconds more, he fought to pull his mouth from hers.

"That was wrong," he said, as his remorse bore down heavily upon him.

"No," Tulla replied, "that was exactly as it should have been. Kiss me, please."

He kissed her, but not quite as vigorously as before they had made love. She then begged him to take her again.

"I will try," Birger said, still attempting to catch his breath, reasoning that he had already violated his convictions, to do so again would do no further harm other than to compound his guilt.

"No," Tulla demanded, "you *will* please me. Again. Here in the light of the rising midnight sun. Who knows when any setting this perfect will ever come along again?"

While he knew what he was doing was wrong, he took her for his lover once more that night. With every physical escalation of excitement, Tulla had become only hungry for more. It was not the carnal engagement itself that she had seemed to desire, as much as it was the adventure of drawing another soul into the very licentious act that they both knew was expressly forbidden.

That bright night, five months ago, Birger thought as he sat on his cousins' craft returning to Skrova in the contrasting darkness of this winter's afternoon, *Tulla had enticed me to such a level of seduction that my reason had abandoned me. This evening I will tell her it was a mistake, and we should never speak of it again.*

As they neared the docks of Skrova, three figures came out from within the warmth of the structure at the dock's end, where they had been patiently waiting. As the craft neared, the three stood in the frigid cold upon the pier.

"Look, Birger, it is Tulla," cried out Erik.

As they came closer to the town in their sailboat, Birger had to work to make out the images of Tulla and her parents. They were all wrapped heavily in warm coats against the harsh November weather. The darkness prevented Birger from seeing their faces clearly, but the stiffness of their silhouetted bodies suggested something other than mere pleasantries awaited.

Hakron secured the craft and Birger scurried up the ladder to see Tulla. As he neared, Tulla's mother broke away from the stillness of the trio to embrace him. She whispered in his ear her sorrow for his father's passing. Instantly, her husband placed a hand on her shoulder, and pulled her away from the young man.

Instinctively, to show respect, Birger removed the glove from his right hand and extended it to Tulla's father. The stern man did not take his hand, but instead grabbed him by the back of his wrist. He forcefully led Birger's hand inside Tulla's coat, pressing it hard against her belly.

As he felt the emerging swell inside the winter coat, Tulla looked accusingly into Birger's eyes. Her mouth uttered not a word, but the silence of her stare screamed, *This is the young man who did this to me, Father*.

The unsaid accusation nonetheless appeared to register with her father. Birger could feel the man's glare grinding into him, penetrating and ripping away any semblance of propriety he had ever possessed.

"Birger, you have dishonored my family," the father rebuked coldly. "You have taken this child, *this child*," his voice now shaking with barely controlled emotion, "forever away from her innocence. When you leave this place, young man, you will take Tulla with you as your wife, and you are never again to bring her back to the waters of the *Vestfjorden*."

Birger looked at Tulla's face, which was still condemning him in a frigid gaze. He did not recognize the girl, as she seemed the polar opposite of the seductively adventurous beauty to whom he had months earlier made such passionate love. He could hear only the caustic silence emanating from her, as it continued to scream out his guilt over this the soft sobbing of Tulla's mother, which was barely perceptible.

Birger did his best not to flinch, or look away from the father's excoriating stare. He had only a single course of action.

"Yes, I will take her away with me to Scotland," he said, hearing the voice of his own father in his head telling him this is what must be done. "But not until I first marry her here, in this land, so that her family can attend."

"Tulla has no family here any longer," answered the irate father. "You have seen to that. She is never to return. You have disgraced our child. Now you must take her away from this land just as your own father had once taken your mother away before you were even born."

It was only then that Birger understood he may have been conceived in similar circumstances. It explained why his father had left these Lofoten Isles, less from a desire to see the modern world beyond, and more from the need to reestablish the veneer of respectability to their own lives.

"Yes, I understand," added Birger, feeling the weight of his father's sins as they intermingled with his own. "I must find a man of the cloth to marry us."

A soft cry of relief had come over the mother's face, as Birger had offered the wedding. Yet, Birger thought it was only a mask that she wore atop her overall state of anxiety. She must be fraught with terror at having only a handful of hours remaining to be in the company of the daughter she so loved. After his ship departed for its return to Scotland, she would likely never see her child again.

"I know such a preacher," offered the mother. "He is not here in Skrova, but in Henningsvær. I will make the necessary arrangements."

On offering these words, Tulla's mother cried again, much more loudly and in much greater distress than before. She was no longer able to harbor within her the fear of never seeing her young daughter again. Tulla was the daughter she had always had to protect against the overbearing will of her husband. Who would protect this daughter after she was forced to leave these isles, and even more troubling, who would protect her grandchild, the one she would never know?

For all too soon, the *Vestfjorden's* winds would carry her precious Tulla away from her arms forever. This Nordic mother loved her only child, Tulla, indeed, despite her daughter's moods which had always shifted precariously like the troubled winds of an advancing storm.

7 The Pierogi Parlor

*"The soul of Poland is indestructible...
she will rise again as a rock, which may
for a spell be submerged by a tidal wave, but
which remains a rock."*

Winston Spencer Churchill

Sophie entered the Polish Restaurant from the arcade that was actually no more than a walkway between two massive London buildings. To call that walkway an arcade was about as accurate as calling this establishment a restaurant. It was a small wedge of a structure and its tables were arranged throughout the room in the shape of a narrowing triangle. Along its walls were beautiful scenes of Warsaw, Krakow and Gdansk.

At the widest base of the triangular room was a serving bar, where patrons were expected to order their food, which was then brought to their tables when ready. Very similar to the food service in the London pubs, Sophie thought.

It was the visuals of the wall's motif that first comforted her, but when the smell of the food reached her nostrils Sophie felt truly at home. She put her things on a table just near the tip of the triangle's apex before walking a dissecting line between the other seating to the bar that formed the triangle's base. The establishment was empty except for two older patrons who appeared to be thoroughly enjoying their meals.

After perusing the menu boards, Sophie walked to the counter and ordered a meal of *gołąbki* (stuffed cabbage) with sauerkraut and a *Żywiec* beer. Behind the counter was an older woman who took her order and behind her in the kitchen, a man, who Sophie assumed to be the cook.

Sophie could hear their dialogue in Polish, as the order was repeated, even though Sophie had ordered the meal in English. After paying, Sophie returned to her table and wondered if the man and woman were the owners of this seemingly successful business in the heart of London. It was not long after this that the woman who Sophie had assumed was the proprietress brought her meal to her table, and placed it before her.

"I am very curious how you find the *gołąbki*," she said in Polish to her new customer, "given that you surely have a taste for it."

Sophie was taken aback a little, and initially said nothing.

"The locals come in and most always order either the pierogi or a plate of kielbasa. Very few ever venture on to the rest of the menu," said the woman, still in Polish.

"It smells delicious," Sophie finally responded in her native tongue, confirming her nationality. "I will let you know what I think of it before I leave."

"Enjoy your meal, my dear," the server/proprietress said, before adding the customary salutation, "*Smacznego!*"

The food was excellent, Sophie thought, and reminiscent of the *gołąbki* her own mother once fed her. The *Żywiec* beer was a taste of home itself. At one point, Sophie looked up to catch the proprietress and the cook looking across the room at her. Sophie knew at that point that they were talking about her, but other than her being a Polish speaking patron, she could not guess why.

It was several minutes later when the woman assumed to be the proprietress returned. "So, what did you think of your meal?" she asked in Polish.

"It was wonderful," replied Sophie, "and certainly a treat from the rest of the food in London. Do you own this establishment?"

The woman smiled broadly at her. "For many years now," she said, "my husband and I have, and we have been very fortunate."

"What brought you here from Poland?" asked Sophie.

"Both my husband, Mierek, and I were born in England," she said. "My mother came here at the end of the war to escape the Russian Communists overtaking her homeland. Mierek's family came here during the war also."

It was then that the woman said to Sophie something that truly caught her off guard. "It was Mierek that recognized you, by the bye. I knew you looked familiar, but Mierek placed you straightaway."

They conversed in Polish, but Henia had seamlessly included the British phrase "by the bye".

"Recognized me?" The look of stunned surprise on Sophie's face caused Henia to smile broadly.

"You are Sophie Czystowska, are you not?" the woman asked. "You are the young Polish woman who was with that American Diane Sterling that sued both the CIA and the British Secret Service a few years ago, no? It was all over the news here in the UK. Mierek recognized your face immediately, and pulled up the old stories up on his phone, my dear. I don't mean to embarrass you. It is only that this is such a great honor to have you here in our establishment."

Sophie was indeed blushing from the embarrassment of being recognized. "Yes, that was several years ago, I'm afraid."

"I am sorry to be so forward," said the woman, before adding, "and please forgive my rudeness. I am Henryka, but please call me *Henia*. May I call you *Zosia*?"

Sophie felt smothered by the attention she was receiving from the woman. She smiled demurely and said simply, "Of course."

"What brings you to London, young *Zosia*? Do you live here now? Are you still working with that woman, Diane? The one they called *'The Huntress'*?"

Sophie was sure that the last comment must have just been something she read off of Mierek's mobile phone.

"Yes, I am helping Diane with one last case," she blurted out to *Henia*, and immediately regretted it. "Of course, I am not at liberty to discuss any of that in particular."

"Certainly not!" interjected *Henia*. "I would never think to ask as much. It is only a shame that my mother is not alive to meet you. Her family was from Zakopane, in the south, in the Tatra Mountains."

"Yes, I know Zakopane very well," admitted Sophie. "I have been skiing there several times. It is one of Poland's most beautiful treasures."

"I, myself have been there many times with my mother," said *Henia*, "when we would visit family as she tried to find out what had happened to her uncle who disappeared during the war. My *matka* was consumed by it. She loved her Uncle Bogdan so."

Sophie could feel the sting of Henia's old wound as it reopened in the woman's voice.

"Your great uncle disappeared in the war?" she asked.

Henia looked away, uncomfortably, as if to hide her forming tears.

"Yes, I am afraid so. My mother hoped to find out something of his fate here in England when she relocated to London in 1945. She even researched all the available military records, but with no luck. She died heartbroken and to this day no one knows what became of him."

"I see," said Sophie, "that must have been very hard for you and your family, *Henia*."

"Not really so much for me," *Henia* said, "as I had never met him. He was much older than my mother, and she had me somewhat late in life, years after the war. Many Polish men perished during that war and there are many whose families never knew what became of them. But it was the sensational claims made against her uncle Bogdan that my poor mother never got over."

"And what were these claims?" asked Sophie.

"I am sorry. I did not mean to pull you into this. It is ancient family history. It truly was a pleasure to meet you," said *Henia* as she turned to walk away.

"But I am truly intrigued, *Henia*," said Sophie, "what were the claims that were made against your Great Uncle Bogdan?"

Henia stopped in her steps, and then turned back to Sophie. "My mother's uncle was a pilot assigned to General Władysław Sikorski. Do you know of him, *Zosia*?"

"Of course," she responded, "every child in Poland is taught of his courage and sacrifice. He was the head of the Polish Government-in-Exile here in London during World War II..."

"... until he died in a plane crash taking off from Gibraltar in 1943," said *Henia*. "My mother's Uncle Bogdan was no longer his pilot at that point, but was visiting with him that day. After General Sikorski's plane crashed, Great Uncle Bogdan was never heard of again. Many accused him of sabotaging the General's aircraft at the airfield on Gibraltar. Some of the cruelest souls of her countrymen went so far as to suggest that Bogdan was secretly murdered for this crime by the Polish underground!"

Sophie looked at her with a great deal of empathy. "Why would anyone suspect a Polish pilot of killing the head of his country's military during the war?"

"That is what broke my mother's heart the most," said *Henia*, "the accusation was that her beloved uncle had been a German spy all along. Can you imagine the shame it brought upon her?"

The words made Sophie cringe. An icy pain flashed down her spine. What *Henia* had shared was more than a stinging memory. It was an open wound, passed to the next generation. Shame salted the wound.

Sophie then said, "Perhaps I can look into this a little for you…"

"I could not possibly ask you to do that," said *Henia* adamantly, "besides I would have no way to pay you. No, *Zosia*, as the English love to say, let sleeping dogs lie."

Sophie could read the emotions swirling so visibly in *Henia's* eyes. The proprietress' ears had heard Sophie's offer and these words had delighted her soul, but *Henia* was too modest to accept so generous a gift. The proprietress had clearly spoken the words that disavowed what her heart desired most.

"It would be my honor to find the answer to what tormented your mother's heart," Sophie said. "Clearly it weighs heavily still on you also, or it would never have come up in the conversation. I will do this, on my own, for no fee, not just for you, but to clear the accusation that any Pole would have intentionally played a role in taking General Sikorski's life."

"I don't know what to say," said the stunned *Henia*, "I am humbled by your offering to look into this."

"Say nothing," Sophie said to her. "Just write down whatever information you have about your mother and her Uncle Bogdan. If you have any photographs that would help too. I will stop back in two days to collect the information."

"*Dziekuje, Zosia*," said *Henia*, thanking her with tears running from her eyes.

"*Nie ma za co*," responded Sophie. The phrase was one that Poles often used for *You're welcome*, and literally meant *it is nothing*, or as the English might say, *Think nothing of it at all.*

"I can promise nothing other than I will research this to the best of my ability," added Sophie.

Figure 7: Sandbotnen Beach, Lofoten, Norway

8 The Homecoming

December 1912

*"A man does what he must - in spite of
personal consequences, in spite of
obstacles and dangers and pressures -
and that is the basis of human morality."*

Winston Spencer Churchill

Tulla and Birger were to be married on their last evening in the Lofoten Islands on the beach at *Sandbotnen*. It was a somewhat lengthy and difficult journey from the island village of Skrova, and required navigating the narrow fjord passages separating the soaring mountain isles. The ship which would carry them to this site was the sailing vessel which had recently transported Birger to Narvik and belonged to his cousin Hakron.

As they set sail early to catch the waning Arctic daylight, Hakron skillfully maneuvered the waters of the fjords that ran between the massive volcanic peaks making up the Lofoten archipelago like rivulets amongst a riverbed of unending but massive stones. They docked briefly in the town of Henningsvær, to board the Lutheran minister who had agreed, reluctantly, to marry the young parents-to-be.

The vessel then proceeded to sail further westward down along the peninsula, which was in actuality, a chain of closely packed volcanically formed islands. Hakron sailed past the coastal town of Ballstad, before navigating the vessel to his starboard, northwards through the channel that bisected the islands of *Vestvågøya* and *Flakstadøya*. This channel was a fjord-flooded valley between the vertical mountain slopes that rose menacingly on either side of them.

As they cleared these imposing heights behind them, the Norwegian Sea spread unendingly before them in all its majesty. Beyond the edge of these shores, another world awaited.

This day the sea was calm and blue, it invited and sparkled with the few hours of light they had. The return sail, like the ceremony itself, would be shrouded in near total darkness.

Hakron banked the vessel to port, rounding a point beyond which lay the towns of Flakstad and Ramberg, each possessing their own impressive beaches. Across another fjord's inlet, was the crown jewel. *Sandbotnen* was a wide arc of fine granular sands disappearing into the clear teal shallows of the sea. It lived up to its name with one of the finest sand bottoms in all the Lofoten Islands. It was oriented due north, and as the plunging mountainous coastline was behind them, the view of the Northern Lights would be unobstructed, as Tulla had desired.

Aboard the small sailboat were Tulla and Birger, dressed in traditional Norwegian *Bunad* outfits borrowed from her parents. Birger's fit well to his muscular frame, but Tulla's hung from her like a colorful shadow. Tulla's mother was there, of course, but her father had refused to attend "the disgraceful event".

Tulla's disgrace had kept her from having the traditional wedding procession of which every Norwegian bride dreams. Typically, two violinists would precede the bride and groom, behind which bridesmaids, a flower girl and ring bearer, and then family would follow. She forfeited these traditions, as well as that of the *Kransekake*, or the Tower Cake, most usually made by the family of the bride. Also, her dishonored condition would preclude any carver from preparing the traditional wedding spoon - the ornately detailed wooden chain with spoons at either end, carved from a single piece of local white birch. With this, the typical Norwegian bride and groom would eat together their first bites as man and wife. But Birger and Tulla were not typical.

By the time they reached the beach, the thief that was the winter Arctic night was rapidly stealing back the silvery rays of daylight. Night befell them, as had been Tulla's wish. The ship was grounded upon the soft white beach of *Sandbotnen,* but only after the passengers had been taken ashore. Birger stood in the ankle-high icy waters and carried his bride to the sanctuary that was the dry beach. The minister was carried ashore by Hakron and Erik, their arms joined, forming a chair to support his weight for the few steps to the sand. After which they returned to carry ashore the girl's distraught mother.

Having forfeited all else, Tulla had insisted on this night wedding on the beach at *Sandbotnen*. Its white sand was rimmed by a teal, nearly phosphorescent pool of the sea that would soon dance with the reflections of the *Nordlys* - not Birger's ship, which was still moored just off the shores of Skrova - but the Northern Lights themselves.

As the darkness claimed the firmament above them, there first appeared a speckle of pinpoint lights that slowly with the advancing fullness of night transformed into the multitude of stars that penetrated the very depths of the heavens. Their numbers were as vast as the sands of the beach, and to stare into the luminous array of their profusion was to look into the eyes of God Himself.

Then the lights of the *Nordlys* slowly formed over the starlit darkness overhead. Pale at first, serpentine arcs in the heavens moved and reformed as the infinite night further blackened until it achieved a crystalline clarity that could never be matched by the day-lit sky. Having become awash in greenish-blue hues, these ribbons crawled lazily through the pure onyx of the Arctic winter night, which by then dazzled with an immeasurable backdrop of pinpoint stars scattered in the night sky above them. All attending could clearly see the densely speckled starlight blanket through the colorful but transparent ribbons of the *Nordlys*. It was as if the angels themselves had decorated the celestial celebration of the proposed union.

Despite the magnificence of the setting, Tulla was no longer the same buoyant spirit of a girl that Birger had remembered. In the five month interval, she had passed into her eighteenth year. Her pregnant body was fuller, more like a woman than the playful girl he recalled. But it was her temperament that had the most dramatic transition. She had become sullen and morose, and her looks scraped upon him with enmity in the few minutes that they had been permitted alone together. On this, the night of their nuptial ceremony, she failed to display the playful mirth and joy that Birger had so excitedly relived in his memory from their time together atop the *Hogskrova*.

Tulla was a young girl still mourning the loss of her childhood. The loss not of her innocence as much as her ability to further enjoy the pleasures of the vast world beyond these waters that she would discover upon her forced exile. She had told Birger that the intrusion of his manhood had disfigured her.

Tulla felt as if the joy of her youth had been sacrificed to burden her body with forever caring for the pending life which even then grew within her.

Birger had told her how marvelous it was that they were to bring another life into the world, another Norwegian life. That he hoped the child would be a boy that Birger would teach to sail, to harvest food from the sea and to keep alive the traditions of his father. It then occurred to Birger that the life that was so evident in the belly of young Tulla was itself a regeneration of the spirit of his own father so recently lost.

Birger thought that life was a continual search for perfection. And as each individual life failed to find this, God thus recreated more opportunities. Each child born was perfect, even those not physically born so. It was the exposure to the imperfect world that corrupted them.

Tulla's mother had stroked and braided her daughter's blonde hair as they stood on the otherwise deserted beach. Her mother's tears were profuse, and their sense of loss only added to the dark mood of the young bride. She would lose her child, her mother thought, as well as the grandchild that she would never know. Her own child, Tulla, would forever be unwelcome in the very town and surrounding lands that had always been her home. Tulla would never again see these volcanic peaks soaring like the anger of the gods above the mirrored calm waters of the fjords. She would stand under the *Nordlys* no more after this day.

Her daughter's heart would break a thousand times more in her life, like the thousand times her own had broken since Tulla had shamed them with this undesired pregnancy. Yet, even given this, her mother would without a moment's hesitation have loved the child within her child, and would have raised it herself, but her husband would not hear of it. He would accept no other answer to the curse of her shame than to banish his daughter from the land of his ancestors.

The preparations were complete and the hour of the ceremony had come. The couple came together at the center of the beach as the minister began the service. They faced north, looking out upon the vastness of the Norwegian Sea. On their left, beyond the expansive crescent of *Sandbotnen* beach rose an impenetrable Nordic mountain wall. At first, that wall of peaks blocked the winds coming in from the west. But as the ceremony progressed, a strong breeze seemed to have curled around the mountain and was blasting in directly from the sea.

The thick symbolic candle brought to represent the couple's union was snuffed out, and would not relight given the uninvited breath of the sea. The minister was forced to recite the litany from memory due to the lack of light. All attending, even the bride and groom themselves, could not miss the symbolism of this couple being wed in near total darkness.

As the service further progressed, the winds seemed to pick up, and the lights of Tulla's precious *Nordlys* were driven from the sky. Gray clouds crept in like predators, waiting to snatch the unprotected sacrifices of Birger and Tulla's freedom. As the skies became thick with moisture and obscured the hopeful visage of the starlit heavens, the winds began to calm. In a raw, shivering cold, they were married man and wife.

Tulla's mother had become increasingly less in control of herself. Her tears begat a hysteria as the seconds of time with her child came ever closer to an end. Tonight, her daughter would be with her new husband aboard his vessel. Tomorrow morning, with its holds full of the bounty of the seas surrounding Lofoten, that vessel would carry her away forever, along with the grandchild that she would never be allowed to know.

It was then that the skies themselves began to cry. Not in tears of the moment, but in fine white snows that seemed sent to replenish the lost purity of grace and innocence sacrificed upon this frigid beach. As the party, including Birger and Tulla - by then transformed to become man and wife - sailed back to Skrova, the snows fell heavily across the fjord, absorbing all sound within its damning stillness.

The minister was dropped at the docks of Henningsvær, and the craft then plied the quiet waters of the *Vestfjorden* as the snowfall picked up in its intensity. As they approached the vessel '*Nordlys*', Tulla turned one last time to embrace her mother. Tears streamed down the mother's face, as she knew this would be the last moments with her daughter, most likely forever. Through her tears she kissed the cheeks of the newlywed.

"My lovely Tulla," she said through her tears, "how I have failed you. If only I had never allowed you to be alone with Birger, then perhaps…"

At that point her tears turned into an unending cascade of sorrows. Tulla's mother began to heave forcibly, as she was desperate to catch one last breath before she released her daughter forever from her embrace.

It was then than Tulla's mother collapsed onto her daughter's frame, and slid down her body, like an avalanche of snow that even the mountains could no longer hold back.

Erik rushed forward to assist the woman, but Birger held him back. He knew this moment had to transpire of its own doing. The woman on her knees would have to raise herself to her feet, they would not interfere and steal away any of these bittersweet seconds from mother and child.

"Mother, come, come," said Tulla, as she stroked the hair of her mother's sobbing head, its face buried in Tulla's abdomen. "This is not of your doing. Allow me to look in your eyes before I depart from you."

The woman on her knees then responded by grasping her daughter's ceremonial Bunad clothing at its waist and began kissing the belly beneath it.

"Tell your child how much I loved you, Tulla," she begged. Her tears still fell, but subsided enough for her to regain her composure. "Always know how much I loved you, my child, and please, I beg of you, don't ever forget me."

With these words the woman slowly rose to her feet and took her daughter's face within her palms and kissed her cheeks tenderly, before finally kissing her firmly on her lips.

"I could never forget you, Mother," Tulla said, "no more than I could ever forget these mountains and fjords. You were always the one who knew what I needed. You were always the one to give those things to me."

The two women then parted, and then Birger and Tulla departed Hakron's vessel to board *the Nordlys*. It was as Hakron's vessel pulled away to head to the nearby piers of Skrova that Birger wrapped his arms around his pregnant wife. She immediately pulled away from his embrace.

"What is wrong, my wife?" Birger said to her. "Tomorrow, we begin the journey of which you have always dreamt. For then you will see the world beyond *the Vestfjorden*."

The look on her face was racked with angles of contempt. "I no longer hunger to see the world beyond my homelands. The opportunity is ruined by this *thing* you have planted within me. All I have ever wanted was to enjoy the pleasures of those distant lands, which is no longer possible so long as I am tethered by your offspring. The girl who I was lives no longer. She's been enslaved by the seeds of your desires, and no slave takes pleasure in cruising to her indentured destination."

Birger could not respond to such bitterness and acrimony. He wanted only to tell her that this was of her own doing, as she had tempted him under the midnight sun. Then he realized he was dealing not in the realities of their recent history, but more so in his bride's distorted perception of it. Instead he quietly lead her to his cabin, where she turned in the doorway.

"You are not welcome here with me," she said stoically. "Not tonight."

He was shocked, but recognized that his wife was struggling in her mind to accept all that was transpiring so quickly.

"I am sorry to hear that," said Birger, "but strangely enough, I understand. Sleep well, my wife."

Tulla said nothing in response. She merely closed the cabin door and Birger could hear her setting the latch.

How different was this woman, Birger thought, *who draped herself in her own prison of darkness from that exuberant girl who had shared herself with me under the midnight sun.*

Birger stood and stared at the locked door before him. He knew at any point that he could easily burst in on her with a simple throw of his shoulders, but instead decided to allow Tulla her solitude. Perhaps she would find her way within it this night.

Birger went to the helm where the first mate was on watch. The snows continued to enshroud the vessel and the Arctic night air had an even more sinister silence than to which they were accustomed.

"We will stay moored here tonight," Birger said sharply to the mate, with no small talk or salutation. "Wake me as soon as you spot the Arctic light in the sky behind those mountains in the east. We will leave these waters then. My wife has asked to be alone tonight, so I will sleep in your cabin until then."

"Aye, Captain," said the mate. Birger noted that this was the first time that he or any of the crew had addressed him as such. Birger had expected the man to complain about his commandeering his quarters.

"Also, be aware," Birger added, "that my cousins will come alongside our port-side this evening to collect these wedding outfits. I have agreed to hang them there, such that they may retrieve them. Make sure that they are retrieved."

"Aye, Captain," the mate repeated. "I'll see to it."

What prompts this man to freely give the respect which he so stingy withheld only days before, Birger wondered. *A wife?*

Or was it the ability to father a child? Either way, Birger assessed, it had nothing to do with his aptitude upon the seas.

Birger dismissed the thought and then walked to his own cabin to retrieve the ceremonial *Bunad* from Tulla. It was already hung in a scrimshaw bag from the door handle, along with a change of clothes for himself. Birger gently tried the handle, which was locked. He sighed softly, and then took the bag to the mate's quarters where he changed. Thereafter, he carried the *Bunad* folk outfits, the only real remembrances that a wedding had even taken place, other than the marriage license received from the minister, to the port side of *the Nordlys*. There, Birger hung them over the gunnel, in the interminable cold and unrelenting darkness of the Arctic night.

Birger returned to the mate's quarters to rest. He lay on his back for many hours, but sleep evaded his worried mind. *How could this marriage ever work? Who was this woman that would raise our child, and how could she deceive herself to thinking she was the victim of an event that she herself had initiated? That she herself had employed apparently only to steal pleasure and experience from me! Did she not ponder the consequences? Does she not respect our duty?*

Early the next morning began the sea voyage back to Scotland. It was near noon when Tulla first emerged from her quarters. Birger went to her, and though she did not welcome his appearance, neither did she drive him away. They spoke briefly, but only of the weather and the tides. The sea was unexpectedly calm, but with each passing hour Birger's new bride sank deeper into a trough of despondency. After several days at sea, she did not speak at all. And yet, never did she cry a tear after leaving the protective waters of *the Vestfjorden*.

Tulla just wallowed in a dark sorrow, which like a perpetual cloak, wrapped itself around her. She mourned, as a mother mourns a lost child, just as her own mother had wept for her on her wedding night. In fact, aboard ship, Tulla had come to play both parts in this tragedy, for she was the unwanting mother who mourned the loss of the child she had once been. She blamed Birger for stealing her childhood and its freedom of the experimentation of youth. Her innocence and all its accompanying pleasures had been forsaken. Just as she could never go back to being that unburdened and playful spirit, she knew she could also never go home to Norway, the land of her forefathers, and most especially not to Skrova.

On the next to last day, she came to him and stated in a very matter of fact manner, that he could join her in their cabin that evening.

"What changed your mind?" Birger asked.

"You could have come to me these days past," she said, again in an offhand way. "Why didn't you?"

"I was giving you what you wanted," Birger replied.

"A woman will not always tell you what she wants, my husband," Tulla said. "Sometimes a man must simply understand what his woman needs. To be taken, not to merely give herself away."

Birger looked quizzically at her. "That is not my way, Tulla."

"That is because you are not a true man," Tulla replied, "but even so, come back to our cabin this evening."

That evening, as the sun began to dip once more into the sea, Birger spotted the outline of the Shetland Islands. He knew it would not be much longer before they reached the Edinburgh. It was then that Birger went to Tulla and shared the night with her.

The next morning, as they approached the east coast of Scotland, the first rays of daylight filtered through the cold, gray sea fog above the waters of the North Sea known there as the "*Haar*". Birger took Tulla to the bow to show her the hazy outlines of Edinburgh in the distance. He pointed out the opening of the Firth of Forth upon which it was situated and then gestured up the coast to the estuarial waters of the River Tay where they were ultimately headed. She mouthed these unfamiliar sounding names, so foreign to her Norwegian tongue.

"Promise me that you will teach me English," she said stoically to her new husband in Norwegian.

"I thought we would speak our own language in our home," said a surprised Birger, "so that our young child will learn the Norwegian tongue of our homeland."

Tulla would not look at him, but only off into the distant clutter of Edinburgh.

"You would have me tie my tongue with the knotted language of a land that has forsaken me?"

Birger was saddened to hear this, as his own father had always instilled a love of his Nordic homeland and its heritage deep within him as a child. Still, he understood the isolation of exile that bubbled within the cauldron that was his bride's heart. She had been driven away by those who professed to love her.

"If you prefer we speak English in our home," Birger said, suppressing his own desires, "then I will teach you that language."

"Is it difficult?" Despite her voice having carried no emotion whatsoever, he thought he detected a faint spark of interest in her eye.

"At first it can be quite hard," Birger replied, "but you are very clever and will pick it up quickly."

Birger would go on to teach her English over the next couple of years in their home along the River Tay, just past Dundee. However, he decided to start her lesson there upon the ship's deck.

He pointed to his own chest and said, "I", then to hers and said, "You". He then placed his hand over his heart and said, "I love you," just before he went to embrace her.

She pulled away from him, taking two steps back. Her face looked to be in dismay.

"I *not* love you," she said to him in a hard, factual manner, and in doing so displayed the depths of her knowledge of the distant tongue.

Birger was hurt by her response, but ignored it knowing his wife was still in mourning for their homeland. *I will give her time,* he thought, *to absorb all this change.*

Despite his vowing otherwise, deep in his heart, he knew he did not love the girl. He just felt responsible for the situation that they had come to find themselves in. Birger decided he would give himself time, as well as her, for their bond to grow.

"Where are the mountains?" she asked in Norwegian. "You told me Scotland had many mountains."

"It does," Birger replied. "They are inland, in the area called the Highlands. It is not like home, where the mountains thrust forth and rise from the sea."

"You made it sound as if Scotland was the same as Lofoten," she accused him, "on that night you placed this life inside me. You lied to me. This is nothing like the *Vestforden* at all. You burdened me with child, then lie to me about the new land you wish to be my home. I demand that you take me to our dwelling, now, before you go on to Edinburgh."

Birger looked at her with anger in his eyes. *I will not allow her to control me,* he thought. He said nothing for several seconds. *I cannot leave her upon the Tay alone, for she will likely run off on her own in her depressive state.*

"Did you not hear me?" She demanded a response from him. "Take me to our new house first!"

"No! First we will go to Edinburgh," Birger stated in a commanding voice, "and there my men and I will empty the ice holds and I will be paid for my catch. I'll pay and release the crew and then we shall return to our home upon the Firth of Tay."

"No, you will take me to our dwelling first," she demanded, "and then you can go to town and conduct your business."

"I am your husband now," Birger said, "You will obey me when I make a decision."

"Or what?" she exploded. "Will you beat me now that there is no one for me to run to? I will let you know something, Birger, I do not need someone else to fight for me. You will learn that if you anger me, I will always find a way to strike back at you."

Birger had triggered something in her. Something that was trapped. Not trapped within her, as a feeling might be, but more like the response of a cornered, frightened prey, lashing out because it was all it could do. It was trapped.

It seemed that the wrath had boiled over from within her, nearly instantly. She sulked and became very quiet. After a few minutes of *the Nordlys* not changing its course, she settled on another idea.

"Just as well," Tulla then replied, "for I shall get to see this great Scottish city of Edinburgh up close." Birger had thought she had capitulated, when, in fact, she had merely stalled. The first of many battles yet to come had been fought, with Tulla having refused to admit defeat, and Birger having not expected to claim victory.

The Nordlys sailed on to Edinburgh, to the area known as the Leith docks. As they came upon the *Firth of Forth*, the estuary that led into Edinburgh proper, Tulla was amazed at all the docks, wharves and warehouses. There were more people skirting along the river at that hour than all the people she had ever met in her entire life. A single pier held more souls than lived in all of Skrova.

As the gray fog of the *Haar* burned off, the city beyond slowly spread forth from the docks, revealing itself in an unending growth of grayish brown buildings. In the distant hills, these tracts seemed to form hands whose fingers threatened to squeeze the very life from nature itself. Tulla felt in that instant that her own life had likewise been strangled and discarded. She had given up Eden and was cast out onto a harsher and more unforgiving world. All because this man, Birger, had refused to protect her from her own youthful frivolities. Instead, he had taken advantage of her innocence.

Soon their ship came upon the market jetty where Birger would sell his haul. After docking, the holds were emptied and the fish were weighed and sorted. Tulla was amazed at all the activity on and around *the Nordlys*. The sounds of the winches and yells of the stevedores around her were sounds that she had never before experienced. She had been to Narvik a few times, but it was so small compared to this vibrant working harbor. The sounds of the English language, especially as spoken by the Scotsmen, sounded so foreign to her ears. She could not wait until she was fluent in its tongue.

Tulla watched her husband - yes, her husband, she had to keep reminding herself - as he oversaw everything. She watched him collect his earnings from the dockmaster. She watched him, in turn, assume the role as paymaster in paying down his small crew, who greedily took their wages and scampered away from the docks carrying only their duffel sacks full of their soiled seaworthy belongings.

Tulla's view followed Birger as he walked along the dock where he was joined by the figure of a short man in a gray suit, over which he donned a similarly gray overcoat and bowler hat. His shoes were highly polished black wingtips and Tulla had never seen anything like them before. He was most unusually dressed for this setting. She watched as Birger spoke to him as they walked astride along the jetty. As her husband talked, the little gray man seemed to wince intermittently. *Did Birger's words cause him pain,* she wondered? She determined this was not the case, as the wincing intermittently returned, uncontrolled and unwelcome by the man.

Birger handed the man a small wooden box, which he quickly inspected before stuffing inside his massive overcoat. Smoothly, the man withdrew a large envelope from his outerwear and presented it to Birger. Her husband took the envelope and fanned it open to reveal a large wad of banknotes, just before the little gray man placed both his hands over Birger's own. The motion seemed to convey that he should not be doing that there. His actions seemed to say that a certain level of discretion was not only expected, but demanded. That the contents of the wooden box that Birger had supplied to him needed to be kept from prying eyes. The two men parted ways as quickly as they had formed moments before.

Birger came back to the ship and soon enough the two of them, he and Tulla, were alone and at sea for the relatively short journey to Dundee upon the River Tay.

In her native tongue, she told him, "So, now, it is just you and I. All your hands from Edinburgh are gone."

Birger laughed. "Leith," he corrected her. "Those men were all *Leithers.*"

"I thought you said that this was Edinburgh?" Tulla asked.

"The area around these docks is called Leith," he explained as he guided *the Nordlys* out into the River Forth and the sea just beyond. "It is formally a separate town, but is quickly becoming absorbed into the sprawling growth of Edinburgh proper. These men are very proud of their town, and its roots to the sea. *'Once a Leither, always a Leither!'* they say."

"Who was that little man in the gray suit?" Tulla then asked. "Was he a *Leither,* too?"

"God, no, just a friend of my father's from London," replied Birger.

"And the box that you handed him? What was in that?" she pursued.

"Just a Nordic souvenir from Narvik. Something my father promised him once."

"And he paid you what appeared to be more money than you earned for all of the ship's holds full of fish?"

"That was only money he owed my father. Forget it. Quiet now, and allow me to navigate the ship." Birger seemed to her quick to want to change the subject.

"Why did his face contort so when you spoke to him?" she asked.

"The poor fellow has an awful nervous habit. Winces every few minutes or so. Never seen anything like it," he said. "Never you mind, anyhow, as that's bound to be the last we'll ever be seeing of Wincer..."

"Wincer?" she repeated in a questioning form.

"Wincer Wells. Yes. The man was a seaman himself once. His real first name is Graham, but no one calls him that. Everyone just calls him Wincer."

"Sounds as if you know him well," Tulla said flatly, "not that I care."

"He was a friend of my father's," Birger said, "besides that's all done now."

"He seems much younger than I would have expected for someone who knew your father," Tulla said, "even though he tries his best to look much older in that suit and overcoat and those horrible shoes."

"Don't worry yourself," Birger said. "We won't be seeing Wincer Wells again. Now, let's go home, my wife."

The last six words wounded her more deeply than he could ever know. She thought, *I have no home, thanks to you.*

"Here, this is for you," she said. She handed him a fist full of paper she had finely torn while she had watched him upon the jetty. A flame enkindles inside her and lit a wicked smile.

"What is this?" Birger asked.

"Only worthless shreds of paper," Tulla replied.

"I have asked you a question," he said, "so therefore answer me, my wife."

"You cannot control me, Birger. I told you I'll always find a way to fight back. In your hands are the remnants of our marriage license," she explained, "you no longer have proof we were ever even married, so you no longer need call me your wife. Do not expect me to obey you, either. I am my own soul. I will give you your child, after which you will be rid of me."

"My God! What have you done, Tulla?" Birger kept repeating. " What have you done!"

9

Return to Langley

"Study history, study history. In history lies all the secrets of statecraft."

Winston Spencer Churchill

Diane left her hotel in the complex known as National Harbor in Maryland just outside the eastern limits of Washington DC. She drove across the river and past the Pentagon before following the George Washington Parkway that paralleled the Potomac River. This portion of the drive she had always enjoyed, often spotting the Georgetown University crewing teams practicing their rowing on the river's waters. She drove along the tree lined banks before turning into the gate of the George Bush Center for Intelligence, more commonly known as CIA Headquarters in Langley, Virginia. After processing in and parking her rental car, she was escorted to the office of the last supervisor of her CIA career, Carter Norris.

It had been several years since she had left the agency. The Senate had only recently confirmed the first female Director of the Central Intelligence Agency, or DCIA. Carter Norris had become the first African-American Deputy Director of Operations, replacing Jack Trellis, the corrupt thug of a man who had tried twice to have Diane killed. Trellis was now behind bars and Norris had moved over from his Deputy Director of Intelligence position to replace him.

Carter met Diane warmly in the outer office before he escorted her within his inner office. He had forgone the power display of making her wait under his secretary's steadfast gaze. He was genuinely pleased to see her again.

"It is truly wonderful to have you back in the office again, Diane," he said with a broad smile before joking, "but if you've come asking for your old job back, your going to have to prove to us that you still can master the tradecraft."

"Well, Carter," Diane said, smiling herself, "as inviting as that sounds, I have more than a full-time job just keeping my little operation running."

"Not so little, from what I hear," said Norris. "Offices in New York, London and Berlin. Doing very well, I am told. A modern day Pinkerton's. Seriously, I will tell you how much we miss having *'The Huntress'* in these halls."

"It certainly is nice to be greeted so warmly, Carter. You were one of my favorite bosses, always so even-keeled. Not many men could make that jump from DDI to DDO. I am impressed."

"Well, I will share a state secret with you, so long as you promise not to repeat it," Norris said, leaning close to her, "Ops is a hell of a lot more interesting than Intel. And a lot more difficult to handle as well. Now, I am really sorry I can't spend more time with you, but I have to brief the DCI in an hour and I have some last minute prep I need to finish. However, I have asked Jeff McClellan to come up and answer your questions relative to the old OSS days. Have you met Jeff? No, you haven't? Well, you'll love him. He knows all the history inside and out, and nowadays, not many do."

The OSS, or Office of Strategic Services, was the predecessor of the CIA. It was established during World War II under Major General William "Wild Bill" Donovan. At the end of the war, President Truman disbanded the OSS, thinking he no longer needed an intelligence operation. A much reduced intelligence operation was retained within the Joint Chiefs of Staff. However, only a few days shy of two years later, Truman would admit his mistake and create the CIA on September 18, 1947, by signing the National Security Act.

So as Diane finished her pleasantries with Carter Norris, she anticipated that they were about to wheel in a complete fossil who would be familiar with the OSS. When Carter Norris departed, Diane was very much surprised to see a smartly dressed thirty-something of a man walk in.

"Hello, Diane," the young man said excitedly. "It is such an honor to meet with you today. You are quite the legend around Langley, you know. *'The Huntress'*, and all that mayhem that went on under former DDO Trellis. You are an absolute icon here. To be truthful, most agents don't have the guts to take on the Agency. Not in the way that you did…"

As he spoke, he extended his hand to shake Diane's.

Diane had grasped the young man's hand. "And you are Jeff McClellan? OSS expert? I am sorry, but I was expecting someone quite older. Forgive my surprise."

They shook, before the young man awkwardly released his grip.

"No, no, please forgive my lack of manners for not introducing myself. Yes, I am Jeff McClellan. The star-struck Jeff McClellan, you might say, and not so much OSS expert as resident OSS Historian. The OSS began some 77 years ago, under General 'Wild' Bill Donovan, so not many of those fellows are still around these days. Not a one, I'm afraid. So I am the caretaker historian, of sorts. You'll find I am more than capable of answering any questions you may have."

"I am sure you will be able to," Diane assured him.

"Even if the old-timers were still about," McClellan continued, as if justifying his age against his position, "their memories wouldn't be worth accessing. Either details might be long lost to age, or possibly full of embellishments given the years. No, I am the keeper of the files, with no particular interest in reshaping any legacy of those days. Now, I have been instructed to answer any questions that you might have. DDO Norris has validated your T/S Clearance, so I should be able to address just about any query you might have."

Diane could not get over the young man. He was refreshingly matter-of-fact. Carried none of the dust of the old days nor any of the associated need to defend just how good they once were.

They sat at the small conference table in Carter Norris' office. It was quite an honor to Diane to allow her to be briefed in the DDO's office without his being present. She noticed how Jeff McClellan looked about at the photos on the walls as if he had never been there before.

"Well, Jeff, my question is a very simple one. Did the OSS have any operations in Norway during the Second World War? Especially any that may have used a pair of twin agents?"

The man gave a puzzled look in response to her question. "I am afraid you just may have come to the wrong intel agency for that, Diane. The OSS wasn't instituted until June of 1943, and by that point the Norwegian Operations were very firmly the turf of the Brits. OSS didn't really play in that sandbox. Although they probably would have liked to, knowing Wild Bill's taste for adventure. Truth be known, the Brits had their own turf wars going on over Norway. MI6 ran the show from the earliest days, even before the First World War. Churchill himself was very interested in Norway, especially during his second go-round in the Admiralty just before becoming Prime Minister. He was particularly interested in Narvik, as it was being used as a warm water port for shipping Swedish iron ore through on to Germany. Old Winston hatched an operation when he was head of the Admiralty to mine the Norwegian Leads."

Diane was unfamiliar with that term. "The Norwegian Leads?"

"Oh, yes. Forgive me, as I am a great student of Churchill," apologized Jeff McClellan. "I get a little deep into Churchill's nautical vernacular, I'm afraid. Winston was a naval man, through and through. *"The Leads"* was the naval terminology for the protected Norwegian coastal waters. Churchill thought if he could mine these waters, it would disrupt the flow of iron ore to Germany."

"But you just said the iron ore came from Sweden. Why not just ship it from the Swedish ports along the Baltic?" asked Diane.

"Well, they did that also," answered the young man, "but the problem for the Germans was that the Swedish port of Luleå was on the Baltic's Gulf of Bothnia, a waterway that would freeze out solid in the winter months. They could not use it for four or five months a year, depending on the severity of the winter."

"The Norwegian ports wouldn't freeze?" asked Diane. "They are much further north, aren't they?"

"Yes, they most certainly are," answered McClellan, "and Narvik, the main Norwegian port connected by rail lines to the iron ore mines in Sweden, is actually inside the Arctic Circle. Yet, due to the flow of warm ocean currents along the Norwegian coast, residuals of the Gulf Stream, neither Narvik nor the Leads freeze up. So the Nazis would simply carry the ore by rail from Kiruna, the Swedish mining town, over the mountain and down to Narvik. From there, the tankers would carry it down through the Leads, across to Denmark and down the Jutland Peninsula to Germany. In fact, just as Churchill was executing his plans to mine the Norwegian Leads, the Nazis invaded both Denmark and Norway in April 1940. This was, you will remember, in the month before the launch of the attack on the Low Countries and

France. The Brits and the Nazis had a hell of a battle in the fjords and mountains around Narvik. It really was the first major onslaught between the two nations of the entire war. The Brits eventually got the upper hand, until it was clear that France was about to fall. They needed their forces back home to fight off the Nazis who they knew would be coming across the English Channel next. At that point, they had no other option but to pull out and leave Narvik, and all of Norway, to the Germans."

"OK. Got that. Now you said the Brits had turf wars within its own ministries over Norway? How so?" asked Diane.

"Well, it gets back to Old Winston again, doesn't it? As Prime Minister during World War II, he unleashed the commando operation known as the SOE - the Special Operations Executive."

"Of course," Diane echoed, "the SOE. How did I not see that?"

"They were charged during the war with *'setting Europe ablaze,'* to quote Winston's own words," continued McClellan. "Their job was to stand up commando operations to bring mayhem into the operations of the Nazi *Wehrmacht, Kriegsmarine and Luftwaffe*. Also, the SOE was tasked with supporting resistance operations with training, equipment and strategies in occupied countries to counter the Gestapo and SS. Well, the SOE and MI6 ran afoul of each other right out of the gate, and Norway was one of their first areas of contention. Especially later in the war when the SOE was planning and executing the heavy water operations at Vemork."

"I was just reading up on that," Diane replied. "Norway was the only country producing heavy water that the Germans needed for their efforts to build an atomic bomb of their own…"

"Exactly…and the SOE was tasked with making sure the Nazis never got their hands on any of it," offered McClellan. "I can have a technical expert come up and go through just exactly what heavy water is and how it played into the Nazis' experiments, if you like."

"No, don't bother. The head of our Berlin office is a German history expert, especially on World War II," said Diane. "He'll feel cheated if I don't call on him for that. So, I'll focus on the Brits' Battle of Narvik in 1940, and later the SOE ops against the Norwegian heavy water facilities, if needed."

Diane jotted down notes to remind her memory. They seemed to be becoming more necessary with each passing year.

"Do you need a good contact at MI6?" asked Jeff McClellan. "I can make a great connection for you over there. My understanding is that they caretake the old SOE files just as we do those of the OSS."

Diane thought about Malcolm Devereaux, and how much she was looking forward to seeing him once more

"No, Jeff, I think I have just the chap in mind. An old friend of mine who is still in the game. As it is, I am flying over to London tonight. Thank you so much for all you've done for me today."

"No, it was nothing really," said the young man. "but I do have a rather embarrassing request of my own."

"Sure, Jeff, what is it?" asked Diane.

The young man blushed as he forced out the words, "Can I have your autograph, ma'am?"

"Sure," said Diane through a wide smile, "So long as you promise to never, ever call me ma'am ever again!"

10 Return of the Little Gray Man

January 1913

"Craft is common both to skill and deceit."

Winston Spencer Churchill

The note said simply, "I am going to meet Charlie next Tuesday as planned." Birger knew it had been sent by courier directly from London, hand delivered to his modest home on the shores of the River Tay near Dundee. It was unsigned, but Birger recognized the code as being that of "Wincer" Wells. He had never expected to see Wells again. Yet, there was a part of Birger which he had pushed deep within himself, that welcomed the cryptic invitation of the little gray man.

That man had first shown up in Birger's life rather unexpectedly at his home to attend the wake for his father, just before the body was to be cremated. Wells was one of the few people there who was neither a neighbor nor a fisherman from the area. Quite possibly, he was the only one who did not carry the reek of whisky on his breath.

Wells had shown up at Birger's home to very politely extend his condolences for the young man's loss. As Birger received him, he thought the man possibly to be a neighbor from the more posh section of the Esplanade, the road on which his home was located that ran along the Tay riverfront. This man was draped in the finest of tailor's cloth. A bespoke gray suit, wingtip shoes, bowler in hand. His face was taut, but not particularly remorseful. He was the image of proper business itself, he mixed with the others like oil spilt upon the sea.

Commander Graham Ernest Wells had introduced himself as a friend of his father's from when they had sailed together in the Royal Navy. Yet the man was only some ten years older than Birger himself. This made him some fifteen years younger, Birger calculated, than his departed father. It was unlikely, Birger thought, that they had served together at sea.

After the somewhat raucous "ceremony", Wells discretely shadowed Birger, always seeming to linger within earshot. Finally, when the last of the attendees had left, Wells had asked Birger to take a walk with him along the river's shoreline to discuss remembrances of his father.

The home was in a section of the Dundee downriver from the city proper. Here the River Tay widened before delivering its flow into the North Sea. At this point, it became an estuary more than a river, and the locals referred to it as the "Firth of Tay". Here, along the area known as Broughty Ferry, (or as the Scotsmen pronounced it, *"Brochty Ferry"*), began the inverted funneling of its expansive width as it opened like the bell of a horn as it met the sea. With it came the serenity of its waterfowl and wildlife that had drawn his father here.

His father had always loved the sea. He was able to have purchased this land, some of the last undeveloped along the Esplanade. At its far end, closest to Dundee's center, stood the Broughty Castle that dated from 1548. It had at one time protected the entry to the River Tay, and the settlements, like Dundee, that dotted its banks. The seaside section known as "The Esplanade" was strung with the second homes of many of the city's most affluent businessmen and industrialists. Everyone desired access upon the beach there.

Birger's father's home sat at the eastern most section, furthest from the Castle, and the only remaining parcel that had not yet been developed with row-homes or divided Victorian townhomes. His father had the forethought to have purchased the last sandy lot, with its small home, not more than a cottage, really, sitting amidst its grassy expanse.

Birger walked along side the little gray man as they shuffled along the dunes of the Tay's beach. As if in a surreal dream, he watched as Well's wingtips tread upon, then sink slightly into the sand. Golden grains of sand slowly filled the decorative holes in the leather embellishment of its shoe's tips. Wells ignored it all, as if he were a man focused only on his immediate objective. One from which he refused to be swayed.

Wells assured young Birger that his father had been working for someone Wells repeatedly referred to as "the Old Man". When Birger asked who the "Old Man" was, Wells said simply another member, much more senior than himself, mind you, of the Royal Navy.

Wells explained how "the Old Man" had looked after Birger's father. In exchange for his years of sponsorship, Wells had said that Birger's father had agreed to enter into the service of the Old Man on his newest venture. Wells remained cryptic on exactly what that venture entailed. Birger listened attentively to fully understand how this all affected his father, or even possibly himself.

Wells went on to explain to Birger that his father, after having left the Navy, provided a service as a courier of sorts on his regular trips to Lofoten. Wells explained that it was most likely that Birger himself was with his father on many of these voyages.

"You must remember how your father would always make time to travel inland along the fjords, to spend an afternoon each trip in the port of Narvik. These courier trips he did for the Old Man. What your father brought back, he would deliver directly and only to me," said Wells. "I was, thus, trusted by them both to safely deliver that product to the Old Man himself in London."

Wells then explained, in a cold, almost antiseptic manner, that on his next trip to Lofoten, Birger would be expected to fulfill his father's final commitment that had been left so wantonly hanging in the balance by their trusted courier's most unexpected death.

"I don't know you, sir," Birger protested. "Why on earth should I pretend to feel the slightest indebtedness to your cause, whatever exactly it may be?"

Wells looked at the young man with eyes that seemed to peer through him. His little gray face contorted, as if in spasm, before it recovered its air of solemnity.

"It is most unjust that the sins of the fathers should fall onto the shoulders of their sons, now isn't it, my boy? Yet, they certainly do."

Birger detested the man referring to him so callously as "my boy", especially when the man who had earned that right lay lifelessly in the parlor of the modest cottage home they had just left along the Tay.

Birger could not help but feel that Wells, from that point on, tried to affect an artificial air of familiarity with him. This finely clothed gentleman's attempts to express empathy fell flat, as though the innate workings of his personality were not only devoid of the emotion itself, but were also incapable of even mimicking this spirit effectively.

"The 'Old Man' was very fond of your father," Wells confessed, for the first time showing even the slightest glint of feeling. "Your father was one of the first men he called on when he set up shop in 1909. Your father served him well at sea, and he had also served him faithfully since then in the interests of his country. Now, as unfortunate as it may appear, with your father's hand no longer on the tiller, it is time for you to fulfill his service to this country, lad."

The demand, despite the underlying traces of loyalty and patriotism, only produced anger within Birger. *How dare this man, enter my life at this dark moment, and make demands upon me?*

"What country, exactly, might that be, Mr. Wells?"

"Commander Wells, if you please," the little gray man corrected him. "Commander Graham Ernest Wells of the Royal Navy, lad, but do call me 'Wincer'. Everyone else has taken to do so. As to that country, why of course I am speaking of King and Crown, the Realm of England itself."

"Well, Wincer," he said tepidly, "you may have noticed that we are not English, but Scottish. My father may have sailed in the Royal Navy, but he never considered himself an Englishman by any measure."

It was then that Wells again grimaced in a fashion that appeared to distort his face painfully. It was a nervous habit that had earned him his ubiquitous nickname.

"Point of fact, my boy, indeed your father never considered himself anything other than Nordic, did he then? Alvorsen isn't your typical Scottish surname, is it now? Your dearest father lived just about as close to a jumping-off point as Scotland offered for his many return trips to Lofoten, short of living in the Orkney's or Shetland Islands. But he wouldn't sell much fish up there, would he? No, not t'all. Everyone catches their own there. God knows there isn't much else to do on those isles but fish and fuck."

Birger was shocked by the Well's coarseness. He seemed to flash it like a weapon, signaling a change in overall tone.

"But by living just up the coast from Edinburgh," Wells continued, not missing a beat, "he could support his family from his many fishing trips back to his home in Norway. You likely don't realize it, but the 'Old Man' had to pull some strings to get him set up here as he did. Did you never come to ask yourself how a fisherman could have wrangled his way into owning such a choice piece of land as this beachfront parcel? Sure, the Norwegian fishing excursions have been somewhat profitable for your father, but it was his work for the Crown on the side that paid down the bank note on your family home, this stretch of sand along the Tay, and that ship of his. Oh, my apologies, that ship, that home and this beach of *yours*, I should now say."

The words weighed upon him heavily. Of all of father's fishermen friends, none lived upon as nice a spit of sand as they did. One or two even had the nerve to ask Birger earlier this evening if he would be parting with it now that his father had passed.

"Are you suggesting that my father sold out the country of Norway that he so loved to your Crown's government?" Birger asked. "I will never believe that, sir. I've heard enough of this tripe. Thank you for coming to pay your respects to my father, but I am now going to return to my home, so good night, Commander Wells."

Birger turned to retrace his steps home along the grassy dunes. His blood boiled at the audacity of this Londoner, who presented himself almost as having known his father more intimately than Birger himself. Wells' next words would pierce him from behind like an archer's arrow.

"I am afraid your home won't be yours much longer, will it then?" shouted Wincer, stopping Birger in his tracks. "That home and all this land has an outstanding mortgage of seventy-three hundred pounds on it. As it turns out, when your father came into the Old Man's employ, a life insurance policy of ten thousand quid was taken out on him by his new employer. That will do you nicely, putting this lovely home of yours in the clear with a nice tidy sum left over. That is, of course, if your father's death is to be declared an accident and not suicide."

That last word was an assault upon Birger's ears, heart and soul. He wheeled and raced back upon the man, causing Wells to raise a hand placing it squarely in the chest of the oncoming young man, whose momentum had threatened to knock him to the beach.

"How dare you insinuate my father's death was anything but an accident!"

Birger's emotions swelled up inside him, despite having pondered this very point in his own quiet reflections since the death of his father.

Wincer Wells remained nonplussed by the lad's outburst. Birger stared into the flat black discs that were his eyes. A resolute calm, unflappable stillness lie there. Birger's own eyes were raging with a fiery emotion. It seethed out into the muscles of his face, before radiating into his tightening torso and twitching arms. His anger called for these appendages to strike out in rage against this intruding man, who's only real depth of emotion from the overall situation seemed to be an involuntary facial twitch. Wells then lowered his own arm, as if in a gesture to lower the tension of the moment.

"Think through it, lad. A very experienced man of the sea drowns on calm waters. Come now, son, it was well known your father had his black dog days. He surely suffered from a very dark melancholy. I am only saying that if his death is ruled a suicide that policy will be rendered invalid, will it not? Instead, should you complete your father's work and bring back a small parcel for us, then the Old Man has assured me that he will personally see to it that your father's death is officially ruled an accident. I assure you he has both the power and connections to see that through. If you agree, lad, I will be waiting for you at the Leith docks with the cash outlay from the policy upon your return. That would also be the last you will ever see any more of your father's friend Wincer, I should so think."

Birger stared at the cold, odd little man, who had in an instant sprung upon him a trap of circumstances. For the first time, Birger could see this alone was his reason for coming to the wake. He thought, *Had it not been for entrapping the son, would Wells have even shown to pay respects to this father?*

"Not much of a choice that you are offering me," said Birger, as he slowly backed away from the man in the suit.

"T'wasn't intended to be so," said Wincer, as he smoothed the lay of his suit. "that's merely how the world works. Everyone takes away your choices until your only option is to do what they desired all along. So, my young man, just agree to finish your father's endeavor and we will all be the better off for it. We get our package, you get your family's house in the clear, and your Father goes home one last time."

How did this intrusive little man in the gray suit know he intended to scatter his father's ashes in Norway as he had always promised? Exactly how much did he know about his father? How did he know about his father's pendulous mood swings, or even that the man had referred to his own depressive thoughts as 'black dogs' that seemed to threaten him in increasingly more frequent interludes? Especially since Birger's mother had been so suddenly taken from them both.

Birger feared exactly what else this man Wells, and by extension "the Old Man" for whom he worked, knew. Birger had been himself wrestling with great anxiety, not only for the loss of his father, but also in not knowing how he would be able to raise enough funds to retain the house, as well as his father's ship. Birger felt alone in the world and soon feared he would not have a roof under which to lie his head.

Birger agreed, then and there, to courier one last package from Narvik back to Edinburgh on the return from his trip to scatter his father's ashes to the *Vestfjorden*.

"Good Lad!" said Wells. "You've made the right choice, you have. After this next run, you'll be all set. *Bob's your Uncle*, and all that rot. Now, here are a list of eight alphabetical locations in Edinburgh. Memorize them, in case we need to change our meeting site. Also, we will always meet at two bells, or thirteen hundred hours, or one in the afternoon, should you prefer, unless stipulated otherwise. Commit that list to your gray matter, then burn it. If you don't hear from me otherwise, I'll look for you on the Leith docks of Edinburgh upon your return."

"*Bob's my Uncle*?" asked Birger.

"Sorry, lad. It's an English euphemism, a saying, slang, if you will. Means everything has been taken care of. Your as set as if your uncle were in charge of things. From those dodgy days of rampant nepotism," replied Wells, as if those days were not still upon them.

That seems only appropriate, Birger thought. *My own father is laid out in the living room of his home and he still manages to get me a well paying job. Nepotism from the dead - would that more aptly be called Necrotism?*

Still, Birger resented being set upon as he had by this Wincer Wells character. Everything was too convenient. Birger suspected that it would never be as clean as Well's promised. *Just one more trip, lad. You owe it to your father to complete his legacy. Be the good son and do the right thing!*

Figure 8: Circus Lane, Edinburgh

Despite his misgivings, Birger had been recruited that day into the underworld that had been his father's secret pact with an unknown devil. That last trip had since come and gone. Thanks to it, his father rested in the shallow waters that wash upon the base of Lofoten's ragged peaks. The recklessness of the young girl Tulla had ensnarled him, and he had dutifully brought his moody and recalcitrant wife back to Scotland. Birger had delivered that last courier package to Wells on the Leith docks.

Thanks to the insurance money he received in return, his father's house was, by then, his own in the clear. Perhaps all had turned out best that he had decided to accept Wells' offer, as Birger had surely not been expecting to bring home a bride, and especially not one heavy with his own child in her womb.

Now it was only a few months after their return, and despite Birger's telling Tulla she would never have to see Wells again, this note appeared. Birger had once more been summoned to Edinburgh by "the little gray man" as Tulla called Wells.

"I am going to meet Charlie next Tuesday as planned."

It was an innocuous message and on face value meant nothing to him. But he recalled Wells' passion for childishly simplistic encoded theatrics.

Birger remembered the Wells code instantly. The message simply meant meet me at location C (as in Charlie) next Tuesday at the normal time of one in the afternoon. Birger recalled the list of Edinburgh sites that Wells once had him memorize. Location A was Advocate's Close, Location B was the Boy's Brigade Walk and so on up until Location H which was Holyrood Abbey. Very elementary, and designed more to aide Birger's immediate recall than to avoid anyone else's detection. Location C was Circus Lane, just near the top of the hill under the squared tower of St. Stephen's Church.

Tuesday came, and at 2 bells, or 1300 hours or 1 pm, "should you prefer", Birger met the little gray man once more in the shadow of St. Stephen's tower. Together they slowly strolled downhill, through the curving Circus Lane. It had always been one of Birger's favorite spots in the city, so quaint with the cobblestone pavers and the ivy covered fronts of the stone houses, many with well cared for window boxes of some of the most beautiful blooms of flowers to be found in all of Edinburgh.

"I am told you are to be congratulated for the material you brought back to us on the last voyage," Wincer began. "Top rated product, I am told. Details of the project to electrify the train service between the Swedish iron ore mines in Kiruna and the Norwegian port of Narvik. I am telling you this, because I know you didn't bother to look at the take at all. The seal wasn't disturbed, first thing I bothered to check on the dock. The project will allow the iron ore from Kiruna to be shipped more efficiently over the mountains along the Ofoten Railway into the port of Narvik. Then it will be shipped out directly through Norway's warm waters, all year long. Much quicker than shipping it all the way across the countryside of Sweden to the port of Luleå only to have it then sit on the docks as the port freezes solid every winter."

"Wincer," Birger said, "our deal was a one-time affair. I went to Norway, I brought you back your package, and I don't care what was in it. I made no attempt to look. So you can stop with the hard sell. I am through with this business."

Wells seemed not to hear him, as he kept talking in a most dour and pressing tone. "It appears the problem now is that the Huns are looking to get their hands on as much of that Swedish ore as possible. The Kaiser has his heart set on rivaling our navy. Our agents abroad tell us that their military build-up extends to their land weapons as well. Great demand for the Swedish ore in the Fatherland, it would appear. Lord knows when we might be blade-to-blade against the Huns next."

"So, why are we even discussing this? As I told you, I am finished," said Birger. "Why are you even here in Scotland again?"

The little gray man paused and once more affected not to hear Birger. "How is the missus?" Wincer answered Birger's question with his own.

"Round as a whale and irritable as a mad hound. How did you even know about her?" asked Birger, who had been careful to hide Tulla from him. Or so he thought. It was then that Birger suspected that his last encounter with Wells was only an opening act of what was to become a much larger play.

"Our business to know these things, lad, isn't it then? You know the English, and, pray tell, even the Scots don't take kindly to you just hauling in stowaways into their country."

"She's my wife. I have a marriage license. It's all legit, it is!" Birger protested righteously. All was truthful enough, except that the license had been torn to shreds by Tulla in a fit of rage, which Birger had decided not to disclose.

"Then, why haven't you registered her here in Edinburgh, lad?" Wells asked. "Relax, son. The Old Man just wanted me to check up on you, that's all. We've been keeping an eye out for you. And especially her. Big as a house, she is, it's true. Where is she to deliver?"

"Soon," said Birger, "very soon."

"Not when. Where?" Wincer corrected him.

"At home. I've got a mid-wife prepared to attend her," answered Birger.

Wincer Wells then contorted his face not quite so involuntarily, as if the idea of a mid-wife birth at home was not a good idea.

"Risky business that is, Birger. Do you have any idea of exactly how many women die giving birth at home? These are no longer the dark ages, lad. Much safer under a doctor's care. I have been authorized to take you both down to London to see the child delivered properly. Do it in one of those new hospital birthing wards. Got a flat lined up for you as well. Maybe, in return for the Crown's generosity, you could come into the office there and answer some questions that we have about Narvik. Lay of the land, navigational questions, a little Norwegian translation while you are at it. There's even a stipend in it for yourself."

Birger was suspicious, but as it was, Tulla had been in a deep depression ever since she had arrived in Scotland. She felt no excitement about the child's coming. In fact, she dreaded it. She appeared to be still in mourning, having lost her own homeland, her family, and her childhood. She resented Birger.

She detested Scotland. The one thing that she had talked excitedly about was seeing London. It was the only spark of life that he had seen escape from the stingy flint within her. Only this would make her forget about bearing her own child, and how she could never return to the joys of being a child herself.

"I suggest you go and get yourself another Nordic tour guide, Commander Wells," Birger said, as if sensing this may be his last opportunity to escape this man's clutches.

They had come halfway down the lane when Wells paused to kick a small rounded stone with the winged tip of his shoe. Birger noticed not a single grain of the Tay's sand remained entrapped within the decorative features of these highly polished shoes. *Were they even the same pair? Was this whole distraction merely his way of pausing, having not gotten the desired response from me?* Birger wondered.

The kicked stone bounced erratically on the pattern of the cobblestone pavers. It left a small scuff in the shoe's high polish, which seemed to annoy the man, who then bent over to wipe it away with a handkerchief he had quickly drawn. After which he straightened up to renew his assault. However, before continuing the onslaught, he seemed to intentionally wince his face, much different from the random unwelcome spasms, as if the voluntary would somehow preclude the unexpected. Then he resumed with his discourse.

"Most certainly, 'the Old Man' can find someone in London that speaks the tongue, Birger. Perhaps even knows the terrain, and how to navigate the waters surrounding it. But our little family is very much founded on trust. The Old Man's got big things lined up for you with us. You've already passed the first test, and to your father's credit, you are already blood, you are. Kith and kin, all that. *'Thicker than water, sets stronger than mortar,'* the Old Man always says. Fact is, the Old Man feels he can trust you, which only stems from his respect for your father, mind you. He wants to meet you when you're in London. Big honor, lad, that is."

Birger was weary of Wells' hard sell. However, there was a curiosity he held about the one Wincer called "the Old Man." The one who knew and respected his father.

"As much as Tulla would love to go to London, I can't expect her to make that difficult a trip in her condition. She's due in only a matter of days," said Birger, thinking only of what precluded him from accepting Well's proposition.

"Oh, go on, lad, take me up on this offer. For one thing, your little girl isn't so little at the moment. Truer words have never been spoken. However, she will be treated to first class train accommodations, as will you and I and Abigail. Has your Tulla ever even been on a train before? Very posh, indeed."

"And who exactly is Abigail?" asked Birger, "Wincer's got a travel companion, has he? Someone Mrs. Wells doesn't know about?"

"Off the mark, lad, on both counts," exclaimed Wells. "First there is no Mrs. Wells to object to anything I might fancy to do. Secondly, Abigail is the service nurse. Fully capable of delivering your baby should it decide to join the realm somewhere between Edinburgh and London. Abigail is quite skilled, I assure you. She could deliver your little one on top of Hadrian's Wall during a North Sea gale, if need be. Yet, should your Tulla hold out until we get to the London maternity ward, she'll be privileged to receive a fully pain free birth thanks to a new process called 'Twilight Sleep'. Only good thing to come from the Germans lately. They call it *Dammersclaf.* Even better than the ether old Queen Vic used years ago. Of course, the pain is absolutely the same, but the mother has no recollection of it whatsoever using this process. A convenient amnesia, one might say. In any case, it is all set up and awaiting your Tulla."

"That might just work the best for all concerned," admitted Birger, "given her gloomy mental state. Still then, there is her status of questionable citizenship."

Wells sensed he had Birger on the hook and was determined not to allow him to slip away.

"Not to worry, lad, as we will take care of all that for you. Not only will Tulla be as British as Lord Nelson when we are through, so will your child. British to the core," Wells said as he pounded his fist into his chest for emphasis. Wincer then smiled, before involuntarily distorting his face in his trademark tick.

They walked to the bottom of the winding Circus Lane, which led them into the green that was the Royal Circus itself.

"When would we leave?" asked Birger.

"Nurse Abigail and I are prepared to stay on in Edinburgh until you are available to travel. Given Tulla's corpulence, I wouldn't wait very long. You say the word, lad, and I will personally telegraph ahead and see to it that all is made right as rain for you both."

11 Gathering the Team

"Sometimes when Fortune scowls most spitefully, she is preparing her most dazzling gifts."

Winston Spencer Churchill

Diane Sterling had concluded her visit at Langley. She then drove into a nearby Virginia suburb and picked up Flake Ferris at his residence, before continuing on to Dulles International Airport for their evening flight to London. Gone were the days of Diane flying on the Agency's executive jets, but first class airfare, which she then billed on to her wealthy clients, was the next best way to travel.

As they drove to the airport, Diane had a discussion with Flake in the car that recapped all that had transpired to date, summarized as follows:

1. Cassandra Barrett in her later years had claimed to be of Norwegian ancestry and claimed to have had twin sons, who died for their country "during the war" which was interpreted, based upon when the children were likely to have been born, to be World War II.

2. At the time, Cassandra was thought to be confused as she had been diagnosed with Alzheimer's Disease. She had passed away some twenty years ago, and now her son, their client, Jake Conley, wanted to know if there was any truth to her ramblings. He seemed desperate for her tale to be true, to have had half-brothers he never knew.

3. There did not exist any direct DNA evidence from Cassandra, but a secret DNA sample submitted by her son, the client, of his saliva appeared to validate her claim of Nordic heritage. Nothing in the Barrett lineage could account for the high percentage, exactly half, of Norwegian heritage in Jake Conley's DNA. There was even a tinge of the Arctic Lapland *Sámi* nomad within it. Cassandra's direct DNA would never be known, for at her earlier insistence, she had been cremated.

4. Anna Barrett, an elderly niece of Cassandra Barrett, had been quickly located in London, thanks to Flake Ferris' ancestral records research. Anna was the daughter of Cassandra's brother Ian, and her DNA had been sampled and results were at that time pending.

At Diane's direction, Sophie had visited Anna. Diane used her for this interview for a number of reasons. First and foremost, Sophie was a young, reserved blonde young woman who would be viewed by Miss Barrett as very respectful.

Diane knew these traits would resonate with the old woman, and in the process make her feel safe. Diane recalled having seen psychological profiles where blondes were generally viewed as less threatening (and thus more trustworthy) than darker haired persons. Not that this was true in all cases, just a perception that most older persons generally held deep within them.

The next morning, after landing in Heathrow and taking the express train into Paddington, Diane and Flake caught a taxicab to her flat where they met Sophie.

Diane had requested Étienne, her concierge, to have Flake's bags taken around to the St. Ermin Hotel, just a short stroll around the corner. After spending the early afternoon together, the three went their separate ways. Flake walked to St. Ermin's, while Diane spent time with Sophie in her flat. It was then that Sophie first told Diane that she would be leaving the firm as soon as this case was concluded.

It was a desire that had been brewing in her young friend for some time. Only now, the increasing drumbeat of Sophie's desire to leave the firm was reaching a crescendo.

"Please, *Zosia*, not now. I am jet lagged. Please let's have this discussion after I get a few hours sleep and we get a good meal in us tonight."

Diane opened the double doors to her master bedroom suite and expected to find it lived in. It clearly had not been touched while she was away.

"I think I should get a hotel, Diane," said Sophie, surprising her boss. "You have been too kind to allow me to stay here while you have been away."

"Don't be ridiculous, *Zosia*," objected Diane. "You're already in the guest room, apparently, despite my telling you to take my master bedroom. I absolutely will not have you stay elsewhere. Besides, with your staying here, you and I can talk after dinner tonight for as long as we might need to."

And so, Sophie continued to stay in Diane's elegant condominium. She had certainly been comfortable there, but at the same time had found its decor and overall ambiance off-putting. It was a shrine to the most tasteful of art, as well as the finest of materialist possessions. But nowhere in the whole of the condominium was even a single recognition of faith - no crucifix, no rosary, no bible. Diane's home reflected those elements of her personality that Sophie, even though she idolized the woman, found most disturbing - her love of wealth.

For Sophie feared for Diane's soul - her materialism, her secular lifestyle had not only squeezed out God entirely, but Diane went so far as to tell Sophie that she did not necessarily believe there even was a God. This greatly disturbed the young Polish woman.

Later that afternoon, Diane took *Zosia* for a drive to Heathrow to meet Emory Hauptmann, who had flown in from Berlin. They went straight from the airport to a very trendy Italian restaurant in Chelsea on Fulham Road, where Flake Ferris had agreed to meet them. It was only a few doors down from one of Diane's favorite decorating haunts, "The Speckled Grouse". As they had to wait the better part of an hour for their table, Diane said, "Come on, I will introduce you to my good friend, Quindon Sprouse."

Flake quickly commented on the name. "Quindon Sprouse's Speckled Grouse, now that's a mouthful. I always thought Flake was an unusual name. How does one get a name like Quindon?"

Flake seemed to be asking no one in particular.

"Most likely he named it 'Speckled Grouse' because it is an expansion of his family name *Sprouse*," guessed Emory.

"He just '*Geckled*' it, you're saying," said Flake, having some wordplay fun with the added letters.

The four of them walked down to the shop, which had been closed for about thirty minutes. Diane pressed the buzzer.

"I know he's most likely still in there, the old goat." Diane said, frustrated for having mistimed the shop's hours. "I should have had us drop by an hour earlier," Diane said.

"Not with my flight arrival time as it was," said Emory. "I'd rather miss your friend than that Italian dinner. The Italian cuisine in Berlin leaves a lot to be desired."

"So, Diane," asked Flake again, "just how did your friend get to be named Quindon?"

Diane turned her head away from the shop window to look at Ferris. Her eyes were alight with joy at being able to tell the tale of her friend's name.

"Oh, his being called Quindon. Well, that's an amusing story. His father was a Donald, his paternal grandfather was a Donald, as was his great and great-great grandfathers. His father insisted that the tradition be extended, and their son be named Donald, as well. His mother was absolutely horrified at the idea and warned her husband that if he forced her to name their son Donald, she would never refer to the child as such for as long as they lived. The father held his ground, and as he was the fifth Don, his mother forever called him by the name Quindon, with *'Quin'* being a prefix for five, like quintuplets. And it stuck."

"I like that story," said Flake Ferris, "sounds like my sort of fella. Flakey in his own way."

Just as Diane was finishing her explanation when there was some activity on the other side of the shop doorway. Soon, the doors flew open and in between the jambs stood a round doughy man of gray hair and mustache, who was donned in a crisp white shirt with a striped bow tie, french cuffs and very elegant silver rhinoceros cufflinks.

"Well, Diane, how wonderful it is to see you again," said Quindon Sprouse emphatically. "You usually set up an appointment for an after-hour visit, but how entirely wonderful to have you here unannounced upon my threshold."

"Nice rhinos," Diane said, flicking his cufflinks with her forefinger.

"Oh, yes, these," muttered Quindon, having forgotten them altogether. "Something of a gift from the proprietor of that store across the street. Sells silver monkey swizzle-sticks, silver elephant desktop statues and the like. I hear he does quite well. All very upscale, and apparently in huge demand. You might like to pop in next time you come by, not that I wish to lose one of my best customers. You might find it very trendy."

"And I have, Quindon," Diane said, "I've bought a few pieces from him, but you will always be my favorite proprietor on Fulham Road."

Diane then moved forward and hugged the man. Despite their ages being roughly similar, he looked more like a favorite uncle than a friend. "We're just waiting for some *cioppino* down the street she laughed, and I wanted to introduce you to some of my friends - Sophie, Emory, and Flake."

"Well, Sophie, *enchanté*," he said in a heavy French accent, taking and kissing Sophie's hand, causing her to blush. "Pleasure to meet you, Emory, as well. And Flake, is it? My, what a distinctive name, but then again, who am I to talk? I am delighted to meet you all. My, my, where are my manners, please do come in, the lot of you."

They walked into the Speckled Grouse. It was an upscale antiquities and decor store, with a very elevated clientele, and very elevated prices to match. Sophie was quick to notice a few pieces that were very similar, if not identical, to those in Diane's residence.

Diane had already strolled in and was perusing his latest acquisitions. It was too high end a store to merely refer to it as merchandise.

"*The Speckled Grouse* is a clearing house for all things collectible," declared Diane. "Along the way dealing with all these collectors comes a great deal of knowledge, doesn't it, Quindon?"

He seemed embarrassed, as if she had assaulted the humble demeanor he had worked for so long to effect.

"Well, I suppose, Diane, it must. These collectors have the ultimate knowledge in everything they collect. They have to, or they will be continually filched by fakes and frauds. So, if you are to be trusted by the collectors, one must know his material, and the products one carries must be legitimate. I agree that one does obtain some very specific knowledge along the way."

"Carry any Norse collectibles, do you, Quindon?" asked Emory. "Anything from Norway, specifically?"

"Well, that generally is not in the greatest of demand, at this time," began the proprietor, as he began heading for a section of the store, "but I do happen to have a Viking carving of Ragnar Lothbrok wrestling a great serpent. Ragnar was perhaps the strongest of the Viking Warrior Myths, and he is credited for the push west to invade the British Islands."

"Myth? I had always thought Ragnar Lothbrok to be a real human, in the flesh," said Emory.

Quindon searched through his inventory, seeking to find the piece in question. He found the eighteen-inch sculpture in bronze soon enough.

"Ragnar Lothbrok really existed, didn't he?" repeated Emory.

"Yes," replied Quindon, finding the piece in question. "He indeed did exist. However, like most men remembered through history, there is always a veneer of myth overlaid upon the man's accomplishments. I have sold some of these pieces to a Scottish gentleman, but generally they are not in high demand."

Then Flake quipped, "I am surprised any Scotsman would purchase anything Nordic. I would think most of the English and Scots would still despise the Vikings for raiding and pillaging their ancestors. '*Damn the Danes*,' I'd expect they'd say."

"Yes, precisely," said Quindon, stroking his beard in deep thought, "although when something is in little demand in that way, it becomes harder for the few truly discriminating collectors to find. Often one finds he or she is willing to pay even more for the few authentic pieces available."

"Danes?" asked Sophie inquisitively. "I thought we were talking about Norwegians."

"Well, back in the day, my dear," answered Quindon Sprouse, "the Scandinavians were all referred to as Danes, whether they be from Denmark, Norway or Sweden. In fact, it wasn't until the early twentieth century that those three states became truly independent of each other. Of course, by the time of Shakespeare, he had begun to separate the lot. He had Hamlet based in Denmark, and in MacBeth, the bard had the Scots battling the invading Norwegians in the opening scenes. But, the Norway we know today wasn't fully independent until 1905."

"Quindon, any Norse mythology about a woman named Cassandra?" asked Diane.

"Oh, my, my," stated the shop-owner, "how I wish my apprentice Devon was here to address that, He's absolutely keen on the Norse mythology, and is a lovely chap to boot. But, I fear his young heart spirited him away right at closing. He had a social event of some sort he was eager to attend. Cassandra? Hum, I think not with the Norse Gods and all that. Not Nordic, no." he finally said definitively.

"But there are other famous myths of Cassandra?" Flake asked, having read the man's thought process.

"Oh, most certainly, forgive me," said Quindon. "I assumed you all to be well versed with the Greek myths of Troy…"

"Some of us perhaps could use a refresher, my friend. Please, go on," coaxed Diane.

Quindon hated being put on the spot among such an unknown audience. He fidgeted with his bowtie, straightening it. He desperately wished to avoid coming off as a know-it-all, or as he might say, a bloody egalitarian erudite.

"Well, Cassandra was the daughter of Priam, King of Troy. It is said that the god Apollo desired Cassandra so very much that he agreed to give her the gift of prophesy in exchange for her virtuous favors. After Apollo bestowed the ability to ascertain the future upon her, Cassandra refused Apollo her feminine charms, let us say, as we are in mixed company. Apollo could not take back the gift of prophesy, so instead, he cursed her such that no one ever hearing her prophetic words would ever believe anything she said. When King Priam's son Paris left Greece with Helen and brought her to Troy, he prompted the Greeks to launch those thousand ships to secure Helen's return. Cassandra foresaw the terrible destruction that was to come upon her family and the citizens of Troy, but no one would listen to her. In the end, she went mad."

The three of them allowed him to finish, before they looked at each other in awe. The story sounded so stunningly familiar.

"Or at least everyone thought she was speaking words of craziness," stated Diane. "Poor, poor Cassandra!"

Diane paused before asking, "Care to come join us for a meal, Quindon?"

"Well, thank you so much, Diane, but I couldn't possibly," responded the proprietor. "I already have an engagement this evening with an old friend. Yet it certainly has been a pleasure to meet each of you this night. You are always welcome here at The Speckled Grouse."

———••———

The team departed The Speckled Grouse and soon converged upon their Italian feast in the restaurant just down Fulham Road. They sat in the plexiglass bubble of a sunroom that was closest to the street. Under its protection from the rain, which began falling heavily just after they had entered, the team sat at the center table as if they were a decorative live window display. Diane ordered two bottles of the house chianti, a large order of calamari and a tray of antipasto as appetizers, all of which were excellent.

As the wine worked its loosening of their inhibitions, along with the joviality of having them all in one place together over a festive meal, the bonds of their business relationships melted away into a convivial camaraderie. Even Sophie seemed to enjoy herself, slackening the usually taut reins of her serious persona. The amity was even extended to the newest member of the team, Flake Ferris, whose personality seemed to fit right in with the group without force.

"This food is excellent," exclaimed Ferris, "and who says London does not have an ample sampling of delicious cuisine!"

"The same people who eat nothing but fish and chips and steak and kidney pie when they visit…" replied Diane. "I love those treats, but it's like tourists going to New York and eating only hot dogs and kebabs from the street, then bitching about the lack of cuisine."

"I never understood people complaining that about the food here," added Emory, "like I said earlier, I can't get pasta this good in Berlin."

The main courses came, at which point Diane ordered more chianti. Diane and Sophie shared a dish of cioppino large enough to feed them all. Despite this, Emory had ordered the chicken marsala over fettuccini, and Flake had ordered the *osso buco*. Clearly their eyes had gotten the better of them, which they were all thinking when the plates were laid before them, but the aromas of the varied dishes and the London rain falling on the plexiglass covering over their head convinced them all that this feast was a blessing of good fortune. It was not to be tainted with discussion of even the least pressing of business concerns.

"All right, everyone," said Diane, noticing no one wanted to be the first to engorge themselves on their entrees, "before we eat, I want to share a Polish word that *Zosia* has taught me. Before we eat, instead of the customary '*Bon Appétit*', we will now be celebrating with the simple Polish word *Smacznego*."

"*Smach - Nay - Go*," said Flake, sounding it out slowly. "Nice. I like this word. It's fun to say, *Smacznego!*"

"The closest equivalent in English is the word 'tasty'," Sophie informed the group, "so it is like saying, 'may your food be very flavorful,' roughly translated."

Then they all repeated the salutation once more and dug into their meals, except Sophie who first bowed her head in quiet prayer. They worked through their meals, and were nearing the point of having had their appetites sated when Diane's mobile phone rang.

"I need to take this call," she said to all as she rose, "this is the watch team on Anna Barrett's flat. Excuse me, everyone."

As Diane stood outside under the awning over the front door, another cell phone chirped at the table. It belonged to Flake Ferris. He had just begun his assault on the *osso buco*. He had been savoring the cross cut beef shanks in front of him that were delicately covered in parsley, garlic and orange zest. The chirping of his phone had reluctantly caused him to take his attention from the delectable meal before him.

Flake lowered his head to read, and then re-read, the text on its screen. "Well, this is disappointing. Very disappointing, indeed."

"What is it?" asked Sophie.

"The DNA results from your Miss Anna Barrett," he said, as he stared off.

"You know no one at this table is going to breathe until you tell us what that message says," Emory said, breaking the silence.

"I am waiting for the boss lady," said Flake, "here she comes now."

Diane approached the table, noticing the looks of suspense on their faces, save Flake's. His was branded with a look of deep disappointment.

"What's going on?" asked Diane.

"I am afraid that it's what is not going on," admitted Flake. "I was just sent the results of Anna Barrett's DNA test. No Norwegian hits at all. If she is the daughter of Cassandra's brother, there should be results similar to Jake Conley's. In fact, her DNA doesn't match Jake's at all. As if Cassandra wasn't a Barrett at all."

The mood at the table went from being festive to sullen, despite the nearly untouched remains of the joyous repast that laid half eaten before them. It was as if something once mirthful had turned somber, much like a festive mylar balloon that had lost its helium, with its colorful markings sadly twisted into a warped and deflated distortion.

"Well, it is the night for Anna Barrett news, it appears," said Diane. "The watch team just called to tell me that thanks to the monitoring device embedded in the keepsake that Sophie left behind, they listened in to a call she made."

"I knew we should have just hacked her cell phone," said Emory. His comment drew a glare of rebuke from Diane.

"The British government doesn't take kindly to that over here since those issues a few years back with the hacking of the Prime Minister's mobile," snapped Diane. "As it is, we are taking a big enough risk with that listening device."

"Besides, I don't believe Miss Barrett even had a mobile," added Sophie. "I only saw a land line receiver in her flat."

"What the watchers did hear her say to whoever it was she called," said Diane, "was that she had just come into a windfall and was traveling up to Edinburgh in the morning. They could dine together tomorrow evening."

"Great, I've never been to Scotland," said Emory.

"Nor have I," said Sophie.

"No, *Zosia*, you cannot go, for even if there is only a small chance Anna Barrett recognizes you, this entire operation is in jeopardy. No, you stay with me, as I have business with our British friend from Cheltenham tomorrow. Emory and Flake will cover this, along with the two watchers."

12 Into The Fold

February 1913 - January 1915

"One always measures friendships by how they show up in bad weather."

Winston Spencer Churchill

The gray fields of England rolled by the train's windows as they headed south. Tulla had been in Scotland for only a few weeks before she had been shuffled onto this train like a piece of precious cargo to be handled only by Birger, Wells, as usual dressed all in gray, and the latest addition to the team, the nurse Abigail, costumed in a conveniently contrasting white uniform. The four of them crammed cautiously into the compartment meant for six. Soon they would all come to realize the compartment was indeed full.

The hills of Scotland were well behind them by this point. Tulla listened to the thumping click-clack of the train while she looked out upon the brooding skies looming over water-bogged flat fields. It was unlike any land she had ever seen before, and not for the better. Her homeland had been a vertical landscape of diving rocky cliffs disappearing into deep blue fjords, with all of God's tears draining from the peaks in majestic and massive falls of the turbulent white water. There a child's tears could be readily swept away, and even in the bleakest moments, there was hope that the blue skies would soon return.

Instead, through the vibrating glass that was the train's window, she saw only stagnation and submersion. It depressed her, as if her low-lying emotions had no where to be drained away, and could not be emptied from her head. She spoke virtually none of the tongue of these people like her husband, Birger. He was conversing in words she could not understand with the other two. Mostly after their conversations, the nurse would press the stethoscope to her body, never bothering to ask permission, even if only by her actions. It was as if she had become a product to them all, merely a carrier of a cargo that her husband was somehow leveraging for his own benefit.

My God, she thought, *how could all this be happening so fast? I have a husband, this man I barely know. I am in a dull, flat land in the hands of even duller lifeless people. My own life has been stolen from me!*

Her own unspoken thoughts fell hard upon her consciousness, and like the view out the window, they had no where to go except to feed a pool of sorrows that was gathered within her.

A heaviness had overtaken her, and with each day, each hour and each minute, it seemed to become more and more unbearable. No one cared for her own well being, only for that life which grew within her. She was increasingly becoming less of a person, merely more of a vessel, and she knew that after the birth, she herself would become expendable.

"I have wonderful news," Birger said to her in Norwegian. He had been talking excitedly with the gray one and the white one, those that had continued to loom over her. "Nurse Abigail is confident that she hears the heartbeat of not one, but two babies within you. She thinks you are carrying twins."

The news was the equivalent of having not one but two stakes driven through her young restless heart. Tulla said nothing, and only returned the gaze into Birger's excited eyes. She glanced briefly at Wells and nurse Abigail, both of whom bore polite, if not enthusiastic smiles upon their faces. It was an excitement that Tulla did not share. Her despondency grew as she realized that her troubles were to be mirrored in twin births. She flashed a brief, forced smile to them all before she turned to once more looked out the train's window onto what she felt was a melancholy view of a despondent countryside.

Two hours later they pulled into London's Euston Station, and Tulla's depression seemed to lift somewhat. She was amazed at the metropolitan sprawl that was this capital city. As the train pulled into the station, she was amazed at the thicket of crowds upon the platform. There were likely more people in the station than she thought had ever lived on the isles of Skrova.

As they reached the waiting car, Birger asked her in their native tongue if she wished to have the driver take them on a short tour of the city. Her response was the first enthusiasm she had displayed in weeks.

"Is this possible?" Tulla replied. "I would like that very much."

The driver took them through the city. They came upon Piccadilly Circus, before turning south to Trafalgar Square, then through the Admiralty Arch and on to Buckingham Palace. The sights seemed to lift Tulla's spirits, and as they had become dark and introverted on the train ride, the city's lights seemed to alight a radiance in the eyes of the young mother-to-be.

The driver continued on to Parliament Square, and as if on cue, Big Ben chimed out the hour. Then the driver headed east past Whitehall and out of Westminster on to the City of London, proper.

After a brief glimpse of St. Paul's Cathedral dome, the car turned south to work its way across Blackfriars Bridge. Soon they came to their destination in South London, not terribly far from the river.

Tulla and Birger took up residency there that night. It was a small flat, on the ground level to accommodate Tulla's condition. Nurse Abigail checked Tulla thoroughly before departing.

Although Tulla spoke nearly not a word of English, she did muster up a "Goodbye" as Wincer and the nurse departed together.

The nurse had said something that Tulla did not understand in response to Tulla's goodbye. As the door closed, Birger asked his young bride how she felt. Tulla walked over to the window to take in the street scene of the London evening.

"What did the nurse say as she left?" she asked Birger.

"She said that she will see you tomorrow," he replied.

"Why?" she asked, her eyes still sparkling from the ride through the sprawling cityscape. "I thought you and I would see the city together. Have you ever been here before?"

"Just once," he replied, "about three years ago with my father. He had to see someone on business. He wanted to show me the city."

"Who did he have to see?" she asked. Her eyes began to dim.

"I don't know for sure," answered Birger, "but I suspect it is the same man I am to see tomorrow."

"I thought we were done with Wells," she stated, rather than ask. Her eyes had lost their spark entirely.

"Apparently, Wincer Wells is not done with me," he said, "nor is the 'Old Man' he works for. I should only be gone for a few hours tomorrow while Nurse Abigail stays with you."

"I can't understand anything she, or anyone else says," protested Tulla.

"As I said, it is only for a few hours," said Birger, "and I will be back straightaway. This is what is paying for all this, and our babies' delivery. You didn't think this was all free, now, did you?"

The lonely, isolated feeling that she had lost as the train entered the outskirts of London had again found home within her heart. She then realized she had not been freed by the tour of the city at all, only entrapped by the solitude of her inability to enjoy it. She was merely a prisoner escorted to a different cage. She was nothing more than a clay pot, in which wondrous treasures were carried.

The next day came and Birger was escorted by Wincer Wells to an office at number two Whitehall Court near Charing Cross Station. The massive Whitehall Court complex stood proudly upon the Embankment of the Thames, and was strategically located alongside the Ministry of War and only a few steps walk to either Admiralty House or the Old Admiralty Offices adjacent to Horseguards.

As they sat in a small outer office, Wells turned to Birger, looked him in the eye and spastically effected his namesake wince, before saying, "I don't think you realize just how large a moment this is, my friend. The Old Man rarely meets with those in the field, leaving that to me and a handful of his other inner circle. But as he knew your father, so he wished to meet you in person."

"Who is he?" Birger asked directly.

"Let's see who he tells you he is!" said the cryptic Wells, just as the door opened and they were ushered into the inner office. There stood a tall angular man with a trimmed gray hair wearing a highly tailored wool suit. He became the very first man Birger had ever known to wear a monocle, which seemed to hover over his right eye.

Birger and Wells stood almost at attention, as the man's imposing persona seemed to demand it. He reached his hand out to the younger of the two men.

"Good lad," said the Old Man, "coming all this way just to meet with me." He shook Birger's hand firmly and forcibly, without offering his name.

"I am pleased to meet you, sir," said Birger, who intended to ask his name before being interrupted quickly by the Old Man, as if he wanted to prevent the question altogether.

"And how did your lovely young bride weather the trip?" His eyes seemed to measure the recruit that Wells had brought to him.

"She is fine, sir," replied Birger.

"Well, one cannot be too safe with a woman in that kindly way, now can one?" offered the Old Man.

"Excuse me, sir," Birger clipped off the end of the man's sentence, "but how am I to address you?"

The Old Man looked at Wells, with a surprised demeanor upon his face. "Very straightforward, I like that, Commander Wells."

"Yes, sir," replied Wincer, as if he somehow was taking credit for it.

"Young Birger, you can address me exactly as you father did," the Old Man replied, seeming to have respected that the young man was not afraid to force the obviously unwanted question.

"And how might that be, sir?" asked Birger.

The Old Man coughed, not as if he were sick, but merely annoyed.

"Within these walls, you may refer to me as 'C'. Outside, the 'Old Man' does rather nicely. I would have thought Wells here would have brought you up to speed on all that. As for you, I will address you just as I did your father, Alvorsen."

He smiled as he said this, as if the formal surname somehow suggested informality itself.

"What exactly does 'C' stand for," asked Birger, drawing a look of astonishment from Wincer Wells, but only the flash of a pleasing smile from the Old Man.

"Perhaps many things, my young inquisitive friend," C offered, "but let us just settle on the function of 'Chief'".

"But Chief of what?" demanded Birger.

"That's quite enough, Birger," exploded Wells.

The Old Man raised his hand, saying, "No, Mr. Wells, indeed a man has a right to know into which breech he is being thrust. I can't hold his desire for clarification against him."

C then turned to Birger. "Mr. Alvorsen, I am head of a function for His Majesty's Government that we do not advertise. It is in our benefit not to do so. I am indeed the chief of this function. Normally, I am disposed to meet only a very small circle of those who undertake activities that are ultimately my responsibility. One of those was your late father, who, I am told, Mr. Wells has shared my relationship with you, but for clarity, I'll repeat that we served together in the Royal Navy. In fact, he stood beside me as we both got our blue noses, although he was quick to tell me he had crossed the Arctic Circle many times before. He was an excellent seaman, a fine sailor, and a first rate operative."

Operative? Thought Birger. *My father was an operative? What is that?*

"Sir, I am honored that you provided me this audience," said Birger.

"This meeting is intended not as an honor for yourself," said C, "but more as a show of respect for your father, and his contributions to this new undertaking we together had embarked upon."

For the first time that they had entered the room, Birger became silent, not knowing what to say.

"Your father had spoken of you several times to me, Alvorsen," C continued after a long silence. "He was very proud of your seamanship. I must say that we are all very sad at his loss, but it was somewhat expected after he so tragically lost your mother in that ghastly accident with that damned automobile. I felt for you after losing each of them, as I have a son myself close to your age. I once told your father that something would be set aside for you, should anything happen to him. Of course, in taking his own life, one might say that promise was invalidated."

"My father did not take his own life," Birger said tersely.

"Indeed he did, son, indeed he did," said C. "I wished not to believe it myself, but I had an elite team recover your father's ship and body. There is no question whatsoever."

Birger could feel himself tensing up, but deep within he knew this to be true. He was aware he was being tested, that the death of his father had been raised to stoke his reaction.

"Young man," C said after seeing the lad was able to control himself in a manner few could comport, "your father was making his regular trips to the Lofoten Islands for me. The fishing that he took you along for was only a cover, albeit a somewhat profitable one for your family. His side trips to Narvik were to keep an eye on that damn Ofoten Railroad. The one those Scandinavians are intent to haul even more iron ore from the northern Swedish Mines over the mountains to that port. The reason you are here today is because we need that information to continue to flow. I need a native speaking Norwegian possessing superior seaman's skills. So today, my young friend, before you leave this building, you must agree to take up your father's mantle or we are never to request your aide again. Should you decline our offer, out of respect for your father's services, we will still see to your young bride's birthing of your twins, but after she recovers and you both return home to Dundee, all is over. And my promise to him, with the insurance funds already released to you, I will consider to have been fulfilled."

"And should I agree?" asked Birger.

"Then, I will depart the room," answered C, "and Mr. Wells will walk you through the details of our arrangement. You will sign a few papers, and we shall all welcome you into our little family. It would appear to me that you could use a little family about you now. However, ours is a family you will never be able to acknowledge to anyone, not your wife, nor your children, but you will have the satisfaction of knowing that you are continuing your father's mission. So, then, what will it be?"

In saying this, a consideration had been laid before Birger without his knowing any of the underlaying details. How could he commit to such an unknown?

Birger drew a deep breath. He knew Tulla would object to his accepting this offer, as it would surely require on his part many trips back to her former home, where she was no longer welcome. But he could not resist the opportunity to find out more of what his father had been doing within this secretive organization. It was as if he was being offered one last thread of continuity with his unexpectedly departed parent.

"I have one question," said Birger, looking intently into the Old Man's expressionless eyes. "You said you *expected* my father to take his own life given the burden of the loss of my mother. If you knew the anguish that he was suffering, why didn't you do anything to stop it?"

"C" looked at the chained pocket watch he pulled from his vest. It was as if he was determining if he had time to answer the unexpected inquiry.

"There is this Austrian psychiatrist named Sigmund Freud making quite a name for himself these days," offered "C". "Freud has said that, *'no one who, like me, conjures up the most evil of those half-tamed demons that inhabit the human breast, and seeks to wrestle with them, can expect to come through the struggle unscathed.'* I am afraid that while we recognized your father's near-constant struggling with his own demons, we could not prevent his wrestling them, or the tragic result that seemed to be pre-determined. Nonetheless, we are touched by the severity of its impact on ourselves, and even more so upon yourself, and upon your family to-be, young Alvorsen."

"My family to be?" asked Birger, "What do you mean by that?"

"Only that my staff here has access to many professionals trained in human behavior. I am afraid that they tell me that suicide runs in families much as do twins. Perhaps the depression that feeds this beast is an inherent trait within each generation. My only advice to you, Alvorsen, is that no matter your decision this day, be always aware of your own beast within, and whether it be soon or much further into your future, do whatever you must to avert the struggle with it that lies ahead."

13 Secrets of the Service

"Never hold discussions with the monkey when the organ grinder is in the room."

Winston Spencer Churchill

The morning after their Italian meal, the team parted in different directions. Emory and Flake departed from the St. Ermin Hotel via taxi and headed to Euston Station to assist the two watchers who were actively trailing Miss Barrett. Diane and Sophie left the flat on Buckingham Gate and set out on foot for SIS Headquarters on the south bank of the Thames.

Diane led her friend through a small maze of Westminster streets until they came upon the tree-lined Horseferry Road, which led them onto the Lambeth Bridge. The weather was light, fair and sunny, and their walk was pleasant. As they crossed over the Thames, Diane pointed down river to the Westminster Bridge and the Houses of Parliament alongside the river.

"By coming this way, *Zosia*," Diane said, "we avoided all the tourist traffic in Parliament Square and crossing that bridge. It also is a shorter and more enjoyable walk this way. Probably safer too, as all the terror attacks appear to have been on the high tourist crossings of the Westminster and London Bridges."

Once across the river, they turned right and proceeded upriver along the Jubilee Walkway that then transitioned into the Albert Embankment. The next bridge was the Vauxhall Crossing Bridge, and SIS Headquarters was located there on the foot of the river's south bank.

"We are somewhat early for our appointment, *Zosia*," explained Diane. "I suggest we continue to walk further along the south bank by way of the Riverwalk. I would like to stroll past the US Embassy at Nine Elms, then we can double back to SIS Headquarters here."

Sophie agreed, and they continued on. Diane explained to her friend that despite the Thames snaking back upon itself many times along its route through London, in many places nearly in a north/south orientation, as it was here, this side of the river was always referred to as the South Bank, even though they had crossed the river in an almost pure easterly direction.

"One just has to look at the bigger picture," quipped Diane. As they walked, there had not been a lot of discussion between the two women. The night before, after they had retired to Diane's flat after dinner, they had a heated discussion that nearly became more of a row, as the Brits would say, between them. Except, as Diane became more excited and animated in that engagement, Sophie simply retreated into the quiet shell of her personality. Yet, never did she concede a single inch of ground.

"It is exactly the bigger picture that drives my decision," said Sophie, "if that was the true intent of your last comment." She calmly brushed the long straight locks of her blonde hair from her face that the morning breeze had blown across its placid countenance.

The young Polish woman had made up her mind to leave *Sterling Investigations International, Ltd.* and return to work where she could help her own countrymen. Between the last World War and the forty-four years of Communist oppression, there were many disappeared Poles to investigate. She was tired of catering to the rich, and especially the extravagantly wealthy core of billionaires and multi-millionaires that made up most of Diane's clientele.

It was her own "bigger picture" comment that had re-ignited the fuse of the previous night's conversation between them. Diane could not resist engaging her once more.

"Who exactly do you think you will have to pay your expenses, *Zosia*?" Diane had said in her emotional response. "Where do you think you will find clients?"

"I have already found my first client," Sophie snapped back to her. She had told Diane of her discussions relative to the case of *Henia*, her newfound friend and client, seeking knowledge of her great uncle, Bogdan Bratajewski.

"Yes, so you told me," Diane scoffed. "Do you intend to specialize in clients who cannot afford to pay anything at all? How will you live on that type of business? How will you pay your own personal expenses, your rent, your food?"

Diane searched the unnerved features of her friend's face. What angered Diane most was the fact that Sophie had already made up her mind and would not be moved by even the most compelling arguments of logic.

"You have already paid me so handsomely over the past few years that I have saved much and can live from these savings for many years to come," said Sophie in a soft voice. "I simply need to do something meaningful with my life. I will stay on with you until this case is resolved, so do not worry. I just want you to be aware that I will be working this other case on my own time starting today."

"Do you really think all I care about is the money these investigations bring in?" said the agitated Diane, cutting to what she knew was the underlying issue that Sophie objected to. "You really think this is just my *materialistic* heart at work? You think me greedy by nature?"

"No," protested Sophie, "you are not greedy at all. In fact, you are one of the most generous people I have ever known. You shared your settlement with Emory and I when there was no need to. However, like most Americans, you have been raised only to measure success in terms of dollars and possessions. Materialistic? Yes, most certainly. I only wish you could see that God gave you your talents for so much more than calming the conscience of the dying rich. There are so many people in need of the truth, people who cannot afford to buy it as Jake Conley can."

"*Zosia*, no one can buy the truth," snapped Diane, "no matter how much God damn money they have."

At Diane's utterance of this expletive, Sophie had crossed herself and bowed her head in a brief prayer of forgiveness for her friend.

"Diane, my friend, afford me the courtesy of not taking the Lord's name in vain in my presence, please."

"It is a saying," barked Diane briskly.

"It is a blasphemy," responded Sophie softly but briskly, "that has become a bad habit. Every time you say it, you damn only your own soul."

Diane was by this point livid, "Why do you have to be so difficult? So stuck in your ways?"

Sophie looked at her friend and employer with her passive gaze. "Perhaps when everyone else is sliding down along the incline into the abyss, it is good to be stuck in one's ways."

"I give up!" exclaimed the frustrated Diane. "If you want to end up homeless on the streets of Warsaw…"

"Poznań," interjected Sophie.

"… even better, the modern day Polish metropolis of Poznań."

"Please do not mock either me or my hometown," said Sophie. "Our wealth may not be that of London or New York, but our hearts are true to God. In our parks are massive monuments of the cross honoring those who rose in defiance to the status quo. You will find that neither here nor in New York. The Brits and Americans have come to honor only riches and wealth, instead of the wealth of riches and honor that comes directly from God. You have allowed intellectualism and materialism to drive away faith, tradition and reverence of God's ways."

"You are impossible," cried Diane, throwing her arms in the air in a rare display of frustration. Only Sophie seemed to be able to get under her skin so. Perhaps because there was a suppressed part of her that thought the young woman's arguments contained seeds of truth.

"I have decided not to join you in the SIS meeting unless you absolutely require me to do so," Sophie declared.

"I think, at this point, it would be better if you did not," replied Diane, "can you find your way back?"

"Yes, of course," said Sophie, "I do also have my mobile phone."

"Of course," said Diane. They had looped past the American Embassy and were back at the riverfront walk in front of the headquarters of the Secret Intelligence Service. "We can continue this discussion later."

"There is nothing left for us to discuss." said Sophie, before adding the Polish words for goodbye that she had taught Diane. "*Do widzenia.*"

"Yes," said Diane, refusing to reciprocate, "I will see you later."

Diane then disappeared into the entrance of the building, after which Sophie downloaded walking directions in her phone to the London Polish Institute and Sikorski Museum. She then walked across the Lambeth Bridge to begin her very first investigation of her own. A feeling of independence surged through her like a lightning's arc. Sophie was adamant that in using her skills alone she would uncover the details of exactly what became of her client's great uncle, Bogdan Bratajewski.

Diane processed into the facility where she had herself worked for many years before. She was then escorted to a meeting room behind the secured area of the building, where she was shown into an office in which sat a familiar face. The boyishly charming face of Malcolm Devereaux looked up at her with a beaming smile.

"Diane, darling," he said as he rose to greet her, "it is such a divine pleasure to see you once more."

Diane fought the rush of emotions that surprisingly stirred within her. She reached out her hand to shake Devereaux's own, but he merely grasped her wrist and ever so gently pulled it down as he hugged his long time friend.

"Darling, we have been through too much together for formalities, I am afraid," Devereaux said. His arms slid around her shoulders like a blanket. Diane complied physically, but in her mind she realized the wrap of his arm offered only a false sense of security. After all, it had been Malcolm himself who had lured her into the clutches of his superior, George Chartwell, and ultimately to Jack Trellis.

Yet, the last time she had seen him was as he slid down the bank of the Oder River where she lay concussed on a spit of sand. Devereaux had saved her life, but only from the very danger to which he had delivered it. She still held ambivalent, if not competing feelings towards him, but in this moment, she had to admit it felt wonderful to be in his embrace.

Extracting himself from her, Devereaux said as he stood back, still holding her hands, "I must say you look absolutely stunning. Clearly, the success you have carved out with SII agrees with you." His last comment referred to her firm, *Sterling Investigations International.*

"There you have it," Diane mused, "I have made my mark with SII and you with SIS."

"Well, Diane," he responded, "in truth, the only mark I bear since we last met is the stain of the high water mark. My career has ebbed considerably since then. I only even have a career thanks to your testimony of my assisting you along the way. The same review panel that sacked George Chartwell was somewhat sympathetic to me, thanks to your comments, darling."

Diane had always been ambivalent towards him. Just as their dialogue had long swayed back and forth, often with the underlying tease of sexual innuendo, so too had their careers seem to come in and out of harmony. She knew her remarks to the review board could have damned him permanently, but even then she could not fully conquer the side of herself that was still slightly, if ever so slightly, infatuated with Malcolm Devereaux.

"By the bye," he said as he returned to the desk, waving his arm inviting her to take a seat, "it was so considerate of you to ask for me by name for this query. Your name still carries quite a level of *gravitas* around here. It was able to allow me an overnight down from Cheltenham."

"So, you still are there?" she effected, for she knew this already. "Still with your wife, living as lord of the manor? What was the name of her family estate? Oh yes, Millhaven, isn't it?"

"Precisely," Devereaux replied, "except that along the way, I was busted back to working out of GCHQ..." he started before she interrupted.

"The Doughnut?" Diane referred the British equivalent to the NSA that was housed in the massive ringed headquarters building in the suburbs of Cheltenham. It was the result of the progression of British code breaking organizations that began with Room 40 during The Great War, expanded to become GC&CS (The Government Code and Cypher School) during World War II, and was today known as GCHQ, or the Government Communications Headquarters.

"Yes, *the Doughnut*," he admitted, "but I am sad to say that poor Petula is no longer with me. After her parents died off, she came out straightaway. Well, one fancies it was the socially acceptable thing to do by then. Petula then shed me like a serpent's skin. Got married after our divorce to her long-time lover, Melissa. Lives down here in London with her new wife somewhere along the river. Canary Wharf, I am told. Mind you, I still have not received an invite there. Her 'Lissa resents me for some reason."

"What ever became of the Millhaven Estate?" Diane asked.

"Oh, yes, well I am still living there. Pet wanted it maintained within the family, so she actually pays me a modest stipend to live there and run it. All I have to do is turn a blind eye when she comes up for a long weekend with the latest girl she's just picked up in Soho and wishes to make an impression upon."

"She's cheating on the missus already?" asked Diane. "Well, that didn't take long."

"Just because she has changed teams," Devereaux said as a matter of fact, "doesn't mean she has changed tactics. Pet has apparently an eye as oft wandering as my own, Started when she found out her wife, Lissa, had been running around with their personal trainer behind her back. Apparently, Pet's Lissa won't be spared the rod completely. Pet had me following her, can you imagine? I don't know if the term cuckold applies to a lesbian spouse as it did to me long ago, but Lissa and Old Pet are hell bent on making it so. Nonetheless, I have a bit of good fortune going, so I don't wish for anything to disturb it, which means I don't do anything to antagonize Pet."

Diane laughed. "We'll I am glad to hear you have become so assimilated to your new life as a country gentleman squire. Now, onto the business at hand. I am trying to track down a pair of twins who may have been in the service of MI6, or possibly SOE, during World War II. Family name would be Barrett, but so far there is nothing to be found from our inquiries. Mother's name would be Cassandra Barrett, later becoming Cassandra Conley after she moved to the states in late 1919 and married three years later. I hope all these particulars have been forwarded to you."

Diane felt the draping of camaraderie come over them. Despite the years and all that had transpired between them, their discussion felt warm and familiar.

"Indeed they have, Diane," Malcolm Devereaux answered. "Yet, I regret that we were not able to find anything that met these search criteria. I am afraid you have pulled up a dead end."

"Even with regard to the SOE?" asked Diane. She was disappointed greatly, and within herself wondered if it was for the lack of information, or for the lack of an excuse to see Devereaux again. She concluded it was a mixture of the two, and tried to keep her dissatisfaction from showing on her face.

"Yes, even within the files of *The Bulldog's Filthy Sodders*, I am afraid," he said, referring to the nickname of the Special Operation's Executive Churchill created during the war.

"Who?" asked Diane. "*The Bulldog's Filthy Sodders*?"

"Yes, of course," replied Devereaux without missing a beat. "*The Baker Street Irregulars, Winston's Secret Army*, the Special Operations Executive, all one and the same."

"Why *The Baker Street Irregulars*?" she asked. "Wasn't that a Sherlock Holmes thing?"

"Precisely. The SOE's headquarters were on Baker Street, just down a toss from Sherlock Holmes' office and opium den," laughed Devereaux. "Unfortunately, their files held nothing in response to your request, I am afraid."

"Oh, Malcolm, I am so sorry to hear that," Diane said, "I am running into dead ends everywhere on this, I am afraid."

"Your Texas billionaire is going to be so very disappointed," he said.

"You've been spying on me, you twit," she scoffed.

"Only in order to assist in the search," Devereaux defended his actions. "However, I took some liberties with your search request and I may just have a touch of something for you."

"Please, go on," she said, adding with a smile, "if it's worth its weight, I'll take you out for a nice dinner about town."

"I am holding out for at least that *and* a West End show," he said. "In any case, you may find this interesting. When I went through the MI6 records during the war, there were only a handful of cases where the agents used were twins, and none of those involved Norway. So I ran Norwegian operations using British agents."

"Just exactly what did you find, Malcolm?" Diane asked. She had wanted to call him "my *Mad Mal*" but just couldn't bring herself to do so.

"It appears that MI6 did indeed use a Scotsman of Norwegian heritage ," said Devereaux, "named Einar MacAlvor to scout the Ofoten Railway there just before the opening of the war. No records were in the file of what became of him. In fact, his records appear to have been expunged after the war. If he was killed in action, someone did not want that fact known."

"If his records were expunged," asked Diane, "how were you able to find him at all?"

"Only because whoever sanitized his records, never got around to cleaning up his training records in the Scotland Highlands before the op commenced. All agents were trained there, especially those being sent on to mountainous locales. Can't sell a mountaineer who doesn't know a crampon from a carabiner, can one?"

"That's odd, now, isn't it?" asked the puzzled Diane. "Why would someone go to such great lengths to make it appear this agent never existed, only to fail to expunge the training records leading up to operation itself?"

"Well, not so surprising in that there were no computerized record searches back then. Either the person purging these files missed the training records or got stopped for some reason before he could get to them. Makes sense he would have cleaned up the op files first, though, doesn't it? That's what I would have done."

"This all has a very strange ring to it," Diane mused aloud, "doesn't it, Malcolm?"

"But as the adverts on your American *telly* say, 'But, wait, there's more'. I ran Einar's name through the SOE records. He popped up straightaway. It turns out he was also the SOE liaison on a series of Norwegian operations up until 1944."

"Which operations?" Diane asked.

"*Grouse, Freshman, Gunnerside.*" replied Devereaux.

"The heavy water ops?" asked the stunned Diane.

"Indeed, the famous efforts to deny *Der Führer* the materials needed for making his nuclear bomb." Devereaux smiled a broad grin at her. "Then something irked me and I checked Einar's birth records. He was born as part of a matched set. Twins, identical twins, mind you. His brother was named Gunnar. And this part you will most likely find interesting. Gunnar trained in Scotland with his brother for MI6 assignments abroad. However, Gunnar couldn't carry the weight, or 'cut the mustard' as you might say. So he was forced to ride out the war in a MI6 holding camp in Scotland. I think these might just possibly be your lads, darling."

"Just possibly," agreed Diane. "Now I have just got to figure out whether there is any tie between these MacAlvor boys and Cassandra Barrett."

"There is one other thing, Diane," Devereaux stated. "These lads were run by an MI6 dinosaur known as Wincer Wells. Quite a cheeky bugger in his day. Came up with 'C' himself when they opened up shop way back in 1909."

"You mean the original 'C'?" Diane was stunned.

"Yes, the Old Man himself," answered Devereaux. "Ian Fleming's 'M', John LeCarre's 'Control'. All reportedly based on the one and the same Mansfield Cumming."

Diane seemed stunned by this revelation. In any case, she was thankful that there was indeed some vein of information to mine further.

"I didn't think anyone other than Churchill himself spanned across World War I and World War II," said Diane.

"A few others did. Wincer certainly did so. We are only speaking of a twenty year span between the end of the first and the onset of the latter. It gets more intriguing as Wells had been transitioned out of MI6 and into Winston's SOE once it was stood up during the war. The problem was, when SOE was folded back into MI6 again after the hostilities, Wincer had some housecleaning to do. And likely all the more sorry for doing it."

"Wells would have been sorry he did so in what way, exactly?" Diane asked.

"As I said, Wincer unfortunately got caught doctoring the official records. I couldn't gain access to see what he doctored in detail, but I just wanted you to be aware, in case those files don't quite make sense as you dive more deeply into this. Wells was drummed out of the service in '46 when all this had come to light."

"Thank you, Malcolm," Diane said, "I am once again forever indebted to you."

"Don't forget about that dinner, darling," he said.

"I will cook it myself," she jested.

"In that case, we can consider ourselves *Even-Stevens*"

"OK, OK, I can't cook," she laughed. "That aside, it was so good to see you again, my friend."

"Is there nothing else I can do for you?" Devereaux tempted.

Diane wished for an excuse to see him once more, even if nothing ever was to come of it. "Perhaps, there is. This one is also WWII related. There was a Polish pilot by the name of Bogdan Bratajewski who flew for the Polish Prime Minister in exile during the war. You remember Sophie…"

"How could I forget *Zosia*?" he said, remembering Sophie protectively sitting by Diane's side as *The Huntress* recovered in the Swiss Alp safe house after her having been shot in Paris' Père Lachaise Cemetery.

"She's taken on a pet project, let's say," offered Diane, "and may have promised a family member to find this Bogdan pilot fellow."

"And she asked you to have me check the files?" Devereaux guessed.

"Good God, no," Diane said, "she would have a stroke if she knew that I did so. I am just afraid with her limited investigative experience, she may come up all blanks. The reality of it is that she wants to go out on her own, but she's nowhere near ready."

"And you thought that when she does fail," Malcolm said, "that you can come swooping in to save the day and show her how her best interests lie in staying with you."

"I have to admit," Diane said, "it is something along those lines."

"You are ever the nasty, scheming one, aren't you, darling?" Devereaux teased her.

"You are dangerously close to losing that dinner, Malcolm," Diane said seductively, "however, if you come through on this, maybe I'll throw in a breakfast as well."

"The great leaders always know how to motivate those *under* them," he said, equally seductive in tone.

"I'll think I'll let that remark lie," she quipped in response. Diane then rose to leave.

"It's been absolutely smashing seeing you again, Diane. It feels as if it's been donkey years, darling."

"I guess the American equivalent to that," said Diane, "is, '*Don't be a stranger, you jackass.*' Goodbye for now, Malcolm."

"*A tout a l'heure*, Diane," Malcolm said in French.

———••———

Just as Diane and Devereaux were wrapping up their meeting, Sophie had arrived at her destination. It was across the Kensington Road from Hyde Park, not far from the Royal Albert Hall. It was somewhat recessed in what is known as Prince's Gate, a series of stately townhomes with elegant columned porticos and balustraded first floor window boxes. One of the neighboring structures housed the Iranian Embassy.

Sophie had not been there before and she stood before an enormous oak and glass door which bore a freshly polished bronze plaque bearing its name, *"The Polish Institute and Sikorski Museum"*. Near its knob was a buzzer, set in the doorframe. Sophie pressed it and soon the door was opened by an older woman, who bore the kindest set of eyes Sophie had come across in all of London. The woman looked softly upon her visitor before asking in Polish, "How may I help you?"

"How did you know I was Polish?" Sophie asked in her native tongue.

"It is written in your face, my young one," answered the woman, "you have the beauty of Poland imprinted upon your demeanor, my dear. I am *Pani* Magda Cybulska. Please come inside."

Sophie followed the woman Magda inside only to find an entrance way that overflowed with mementos of Poland's contributions to world history. Sophie stepped further into the receiving hall and immediately noticed the tail-fin of a *Luftwaffe* aircraft bearing its sinister swastika tail flash emblem. Over this was written in carefully printed large bold lettering, "The 178th German Aircraft Destroyed by 303 Polish Sdrn" and was dated as "3.7.42 Kirton-In-Lindsey".

"How may I help you, my dear?" *Pani* Cybulska asked. They conversed in Polish.

"*Bardzo mi milo* (I am pleased to meet you), *Pani* Cybulska," Sophie started, "I am …"

"Call me Magda, *proszę*," pleaded the woman. "We are kindred souls, you and I. So, please make an old woman happy."

"Well, *Pani* Magda," Sophie conceded, "my name is Zofia Czystowska. I am in the employ of an investigative agency and I have come to see if you have any records of General Sikorski's staff during the war." She had given the woman Magda her name in the Polish form which she would recognize.

Sophie handed Magda her business card which bore her name in its English form and her position at *Sterling Investigations International, Ltd.* Sophie did not feel guilty for deceiving the woman into thinking that this inquiry was linked to the firm. She had stated two facts, that she worked for the firm and that she wished to see the General's staff records. She never said the two were related, although she knew Magda would assume they were.

"*Zosia*," Magda said smiling broadly, "of course we have all of the General's records and correspondence in our library. You are most welcome to peruse them. They are all, or nearly all, written in Polish, but for you this will not be a problem. We have many World War II enthusiasts who come here only to be disappointed by this fact. Nonetheless they always love the tour of our facility."

"I would love a tour also, *Pani* Magda," said Sophie.

"It will be my pleasure, *Zosia*," the kindly Magda said. "I have both a niece and a granddaughter named *Zosia*. They both are lovely children, but neither are as pretty as you, my dear. I suppose I should not speak so of my own family, but it is true. Come this way."

For the next two hours Magda led Sophie through five levels of Polish mementos and artifacts from every period of their country's heritage. There were several cases full of captured World War II souvenirs, including those bearing the word "Narvik".

Amongst these were what appeared to be a German sub-machine gun, marked as having been captured by the Polish Independent Podhale Rifle Brigade.

"These are from the Battles in Norway's Arctic Circle," explained Magda. "That German machine gun was captured by our soldiers near Narvik."

"Norway?" exclaimed Sophie. "I was not aware the Poles fought there."

"Yes, *Zosia*," Magda replied, "and very bravely so alongside the British, the French, and, of course, the Norwegians. They pushed the Nazis all the way back to the Swedish border, before the Allies had to evacuate due to the fall of France."

"That was very early in the war, wasn't it," Sophie asked. "How did they escape the Nazis in the fighting in Poland? Did they abandon the homeland?"

"Not at all. Once it was evident that the Nazis could not be stopped, whatever units had not been captured were *ordered* to escape the country. As were the remaining Polish air force pilots. There was a path through Romania, which then bordered Poland in the south, but no longer does so. Back then, the fighting forces that escaped Poland came to France where they would re-assemble as army units under General Sikorski as commander-in-chief."

"Yes, I was aware of the Polish Army in France," Sophie said, "where they fought the Germans before boarding the ships which took them to the United Kingdom."

"But before that they fought at Narvik. These Polish forces, known as the Polish Independent Podhale Rifle Brigade, you will see, fought ever so gallantly in those Norwegian mountains. So much so, in fact, that they were recognized by

General Sikorski himself at a later date with the *Virtuti Militari*, Poland's highest military honor."

"And this Brigade is the same as the Polish Independent Highland Brigade?"

"Yes, it is the same. The English call it that because they were later sent to the Scottish Highlands. These are just both different names for the same Brigade."

There were cases full of every imaginable type of artifact from World War II. Even an Enigma device, the encrypting instrument used by the Nazis and thought to be unbreakable.

"Do you know what this is, my dear?" asked Magda.

"Of course," replied Sophie, "as I am from Poznań."

"But *Zosia*, the British will proudly tell you that it was Alan Turing and the team at Bletchley Park that broke the Enigma code during the war."

"Yes," said Sophie, "but we Poles know that Rejewski, Różycki and Zygalski cracked it several years before the war had even began. Had it not been for the efforts of these three mathematicians from the University of Poznań, the British might never have cracked the enhanced code after the Germans added complexity to the machines just before the war started."

Magda smiled with a deep, beaming pride. "You are very knowledgable, *Zosia*. I should sign you up to give these tours."

"You are too kind, *Pani* Magda," the young Pole said while blushing. "This is such a wonderful collection of Poland's history. I wish I had come here on my earlier trips to London."

The tour continued and transitioned in reverse from World War II to just after World War I and the Polish - Soviet War of 1919-1920. Then, the tour reached back to the time of General Dąbrowski's Polish Lancers under Napoleon, and still further back to the elaborate paintings capturing the valor of the Poles fighting against Russia and Prussia in the times of the Partitions of Poland. Everywhere were portraits, flags, swords, banners and insignia. The higher they climbed along the central staircase, the deeper in Polish history they seemed to be pulled.

Finally, Sophie was led to a small reading room. Here Magda sat her before a desk and asked her specifically what she would like to see from the records of General Sikorski, the head of the Polish Government in exile until his tragic death on July 4, 1943. He and his daughter, who also was named Zofia and served as his secretary, did not survive the crash that night as their plane left Gibraltar.

"Do you have any materials regarding one of the General's pilots named Bogdan Bratajewski?" asked Sophie. Once this name had been spoken, the demeanor of Magda changed immediately.

"What an interesting name you dredge up from the past, *Zosia,*" Magda said. "Are you aware that many in the British Government suspected *Pan* Bratajewski to have been an agent for the Nazis? He was with General Sikorski the day of his death, even inspected his plane before leaving Gibraltar himself in another aircraft. The British started a whisper campaign of rumors that perhaps Bratajewski sabotaged the General's plane. One thing is sure, he was never heard from again."

"So I have been told," Sophie said, "and that is why I am here today. To see what facts might lie hidden in your archives of the General's records."

"*Zosia,*" Magda then said, "do you seek to prove that Bratajewski was a traitor, or do you seek to disprove this accusation?"

"I will follow the facts, *Pani* Magda," Sophie then said, "but I certainly hope that they will remove this stain from our countryman."

"Then I will bring you all I have on him in our files," Magda replied.

"And if I had said I was here to prove *Pan* Bogdan was indeed a spy?"

"Then I would have brought to you only each document you were wise enough to specifically ask for," Magda replied with a sly grin, "those and not a single page more."

Soon Magda had brought every archived file containing information on Sikorski's pilot, Bogdan Bratajewski. The files were so voluminous they had to be stacked in a half dozen piles to keep them from toppling over. That afternoon, Sophie began her investigative effort plowing through these documents and taking many pages of detailed notes. It was a labor that would consume her for a week.

__Figure 9: Sir Mansfield Cumming,__
__First Chief of the British Secret Service__

14 The Great War

1914

"There is no time for ease and comfort. It is time to dare and endure."

Winston Spencer Churchill

Birger Alvorsen did indeed join the ranks of the secret organization at the behest of "C". This eccentric fellow, also known as "the Old Man", had once served with his father upon the open seas in the Royal Navy. Strange as it may sound, Birger envisioned "C" as the last connection he had with either of his deceased parents. Out of sheer respect for his deceased father, Birger had decided that he would continue in the surreptitious work of spying for Great Britain.

Although not disclosed to Birger, "the Old Man" was none other than Captain Mansfield Smith-Cumming. A retired naval officer, he had been offered in 1909 the position of heading up what would become known as the British Secret Intelligence Service, or SIS. Later, it would adopt the title MI6, short for the sixth directorate of military intelligence, even though only five directorates were ever confirmed to exist.

Ever since the Prussians defeated the French in 1871 in the Franco-Prussian war, England had become increasingly consumed with the idea of German spies penetrating their society. Shortly after that war, Germany had unified as a nation. Under Kaiser Wilhelm it had begun modernizing and enlarging its navy in order to compete with Britain for rule of the high seas. By the end of the first decade of the new century, the British obsession with German spies had reached a fever pitch. It was fed by bestselling novels with stories based upon the Kaiser's operatives having been assimilated among the British population and into its government offices.

Even though the Kaiser was the eldest grandchild of Queen Victoria, which made him first cousin to England's King George V, the British and their leaders saw in him a potential enemy. Kaiser Wilhelm had increasingly become transfixed on increasing Germany's offensive capabilities. The British greatly feared the threat of aggression from the modernized German war machine.

Within the secretive halls of government, by 1909, it was decided to create an organization dedicated to not only halting the penetration of foreign spies into the Empire, but also to coordinate the efforts of placing Britain's spies in the most secure functions of sovereign states across the globe.

Prime Minister Herbert Asquith organized a search committee headed by the Director of Naval Intelligence, Admiral Alexander Bethell. It was he who had famously sent a letter to Cumming inviting him to discuss an opportunity which he cryptically promised to be "*something good*".

Initially, two men were considered for the head of this secret organization. They were Mansfield Smith-Cumming, nominated by the Admiralty, and Vernon Kell, nominated by the War Department. Kell held a long list of qualifications, for not only had he garnered significant intelligence *bonafides* through his military experience, he was also a linguist having mastered multiple languages including French, German, Russian and some Chinese. Yet despite Kell's overwhelming qualifications, he lacked what was resident in his opponent - charisma.

Mansfield Smith had no intelligence experience of which to speak. He had trained at the Royal Naval College, Dartmouth, since the age of twelve, and served in the Royal Navy in Egypt, as well as against the Malay pirates. However, by the time he was 26 years of age in 1885, Smith retired from the Royal Navy after reaching the rank of captain. It was rumored that he suffered from extensive bouts of seasickness, which was not conducive to a career on the high seas. He continued to work for the Navy (on half-pay) overseeing the installation of boom-defenses at the port of Southhampton. In 1889, he added the name Cumming by his marriage to the independently wealthy Leslie Marian Valiant-Cumming.

Having access to his wife's fortune, Mansfield Cumming (he effectively dropped the use of his Smith surname) unleashed perhaps his greatest qualification for becoming the head of the British Secret Service - his insatiable quest for adventure.

Mansfield Cumming had become an aficionado of motor sports, in both automobiles and power yachts, as they became *de rigueur* for the aristocracy after the turn of the century. He was also interested in all things mechanical, and was attracted to the latest inventions of the time.

After a few years of infantile organizational squabbling, by 1911 Kell and Cumming had both settled into roles as the respective heads for what would ultimately become the British domestic (MI5) and foreign (MI6) secret services.

Mansfield Cumming would go on to be immortalized as founding father of MI6. From nothing he crafted the basic imprint of what would go on to become the world's greatest intelligence service. He fought for its independence even then, as the British Army, the Royal Navy and the Foreign Office all hoped to consume it within their bloated organizations. Mansfield Cumming would become larger than life and it was World War I that made him so.

The Great War for "C" meant sacrifice, loss, myth, legend, and an increasing budget which solidified his consolidated control of all of the Empire's overseas spying operations.

Cumming had been only five years in his role when the Austrian Archduke and heir to the Austro-Hungarian empire, Franz Ferdinand, was assassinated. The June 1914 murder by a Serbian anarchist was the match to the tinderbox that had increasingly become Europe since the turn of the century. Soon, the sides had settled out into the Triple Entente (Britain, France and Russia) up against the Central Axis (Germany, Austro-Hungary and the Ottoman Empire), and "The Great War" was underway. The United States stubbornly adhered to an isolationist position and was determined not to be dragged into "Europe's War".

In August of 1914, the guns of war exploded across the continent. Mansfield Cumming, like so many others, was drawn by the excitement and the incendiary glow of the battle front. In a December trip to Paris that year with his son, who also functioned as his driver, C motored dangerously close to the front. He and his son found themselves between the German and French lines. Having realized their error, the "Old Man" and his son raced recklessly back toward the forward line of the French soldiers, who promptly mistook them for a German scout car and fired upon them. Under fire, his son crashed their motorcar.

Mansfield Cumming survived the wreck, but was himself pinned against a tree. His son was thrown from the car and lay dying in the road. The "Old Man's" foot and a good portion of his leg would have to be amputated. Later, it would become service lore that "C" had cut off his own foot with a pocket knife he carried in order to drag himself over and attend to his dying son. His son did indeed die on that country road, but there is no doubt that the first part of that tale was nothing more than a tall story. However, it would not keep many from promulgating it as a legend. Others would go so far as having accused Mansfield himself of retelling the tale as fact. It was shortly after his recovery from this event that the "Old Man" summoned Birger Alvorsen to London from his Tay River home in Dundee for a second meeting.

Tulla had given birth to the twins. Birger had insisted they be given Nordic names. He seemed surprised when Tulla did not fight him on this. It was not that she agreed with her husband, she was simply indifferent. So, the elder twin was named Gunnar, and the younger Einar, even though mere minutes separated their births. Soon it was apparent that Tulla's indifference extended to her care of the infants.

After a few days, Tulla was released from the hospital back to the Blackfriars Bridge flat. After her London recuperation, they returned to their Scottish home. Birger thought the modest dwelling along a long sandy stretch of beach near Broughty Castle would please his wife, but having the sea at her front door only reminded her more of the home from which she was forever banished. From her indifference she sunk into a much deeper depression, even to the point of ignoring the needs of the twin boys. Birger was forced to bring on help in the form of a young woman to care for the twins.

The nanny came on the recommendation of Wincer Wells. She was of British descent, the daughter of an army colonel who had recently taken a posting at Edinburgh's Royal Castle. Her father's *forté* was teaching military history, Wells had said, although he had been forced to take a much less dignified assignment in Edinburgh Castle.

Birger was not aware that her father had sacrificed and relocated to Edinburgh just to spare his family the shame of a pregnant unwed daughter. Yet, he was so very proud of her when she refused to even discuss not having the child, and watched through the months as she lovingly prepared to become a mother.

When she tragically suffered a stillbirth, her father could easily have called off the transfer. Instead, he felt the utter torment and trauma of the loss his daughter could not shake. The colonel thought the change of scenery in Scotland might help his daughter's overcome her obvious heartache and grief.

His daughter, the prospective nanny, had that year earlier completed her preparatory schooling in London. Despite the twelve month gap in her *Curriculum Vitae*, the young woman had hoped to major in European Languages at the University of Edinburgh. As it happened, she arrived too late to make the start of the semester. She was idle and desperately in need of something to consume her time. Of something to salve her emotional wound.

When Birger interviewed the prospective nanny, Tulla could not even muster enough interest to join him. The young woman was beautiful and in the flower of her youth. Her smile was enchanting, although Birger thought he detected a slight sadness in her eyes. Despite this, she was hired on the condition that she move in with the family. After getting her father's acceptance, the girl took up residence in the beach house.

The nanny took to the children as if they were her own. She loved them instantly and the children loved her in return. Why would they not? She was within a couple years of their own mother's age and even resembled her in general terms. Both were young, blonde and their bodies ripely shaped by recent pregnancies. The only difference was while Tulla was prone to scowl at the infants, the nanny smiled upon them beamingly. Caring for the twins seemed to be just the tonic for what ailed her, that which Birger had always felt was beyond being gentlemanly for him to inquire upon. Birger sensed she was the perfect fit to their family, and came as close as anyone could in filling the gaping chasm left by the moody, despondent Tulla.

The nanny instantly began expanding her linguistic skills to the Norwegian language, and soon gained a rudimentary control of the tongue. Even for someone who possessed a natural gift in languages as she did, Norwegian was a difficult tongue to master. It was a necessity, however, in that she needed to converse with Tulla, if even only simplistically, as Birger's wife had stalled in learning English. The only real connection shared between the nanny and Tulla was in teaching each other their native languages. Sadly, even caring for the infant twins was not shared between them, as Tulla had already ceded this job to her.

As the initial days of her service passed by, the nanny's spirits seemed to be renewed by looking after the children. Nothing, however, seemed to rescue Tulla from her own doldrums of despair. If not for the nanny, Birger began to wonder if the children themselves would have even survived.

So in the months to follow, Tulla and the nanny continued to teach each other their languages. For this reason, Tulla tolerated her. She was content in allowing the nanny to look after the boys. Tulla only seemed focused on one thing, learning English. It was as though that objective was the key to Tulla's future and trumped all else.

Tulla's despondency was only ever alleviated by two things - fighting with Birger, and more often than not, followed by disappearing for hours on end. When she returned she was always in a seemingly dreamlike state of mind. When Birger demanded her to account for herself, her words were nearly incomprehensible. Her thoughts seemed muddled and this drove Birger into an even greater frenzy. To this she would simply say, "Leave me alone, allow me to enjoy this feeling. You have stolen my childhood, and now you wish to take away what little pleasure I have found for myself!"

This drove Birger wild. He followed her room to room, demanding she tell him where she'd been. She ignored him, until she simply walked out of the house again after having grabbed a bottle of his whisky. Birger wanted to chase after her, but then reconsidered given his pulsing anger. He needed to calm down.

He went looking for her when dusk came ashore from the sea, but was unable to find his Tulla. All that night he worried deeply about her, fearing she would harm herself, even drowning herself in the sea under the mixed effect of her stupor intensifying with the effect of the alcohol.

Tulla returned the next day in mid-afternoon, reeking to the high heavens of whisky before she collapsed on the bed. She again ignored every demand of Birger's to know where she had spent the night. Even after she sobered she never told him, it was her way of torturing the man who she felt had ruined her life.

From that point on there were several constants in the dynamics of the beach house. The nanny's care of the children was the most obvious, followed by Tulla's frequent disappearances, often overnight. During this time, the nanny would watch as Birger fell more deeply into his own depression over the dysfunctional state of his marriage.

During November of 1914, "C" demanded another trip to Narvik. A most epic battle then ensued between Birger and Tulla. *The Nordlys* was but a short walk away, moored along the piers in the small harbor on the other side of Broughty Castle. As Birger loaded provisions onto the ship for his trip, Tulla had followed and cursed him in their Nordic tongue for abandoning her. He knew it was his ability to return to Skrova on his way to Narvik that she detested, and she threatened to stow away on *the Nordlys*, leaving behind both the twins and the nanny.

It was just after this threat that the infuriated Tulla left the ship quayside and disappeared once more. He would not see her for three more days, and was forced to delay his departure. Wincer Wells interceded on his behalf with the Old Man.

She returned home reeking of whisky, although Birger had since forsaken the drink in his home in order not to tempt her. Tulla's eyes were as glazed over as he had never seen, and she appeared completely out of control. All he could do was ask the nanny to care for the children and ashamedly for his wife while he was gone.

"I will attempt to help her, Mr. Alvorsen," said the nanny, "but if she leaves the house there is nothing I can do. I cannot abandon the children."

Birger departed with a small crew by a route his father had often taken, up the Scottish coast and past the outlying Shetland Islands, and then across the Norwegian Sea to the Lofoten Islands and Skrova. Once more their cover was to fish the rich Norwegian territorial waters, but his true primary mission was to meet with the agent who had pilfered more data on the Ofoten Railway.

Birger only knew the man by the code name *"Skaði,"* the Norse Mountain goddess associated with skiing and hunting. To him, Birger would only be known by the code name *"Rán"*, the goddess of sea storms and death. This was done for each man's safety, should the other be caught and interrogated.

The two spies would meet briefly in a cafe in the port town of Narvik, just long enough to pass each other the "safe word" for that particular meeting which assured that the mission had not been compromised. The theory was if they had been intercepted by the enemy intelligence group, they would refuse to usher the safe word, and at that point, the exchange was off. Conversely, if the safe words were exchanged then the information was passed.

Birger returned to Scotland, ready to hand deliver to Wincer Wells detailed accounts of all the iron ore shipments from the Swedish mines in Kiruna shipped through Narvik via the Ofoten Railway. Also included were the names and dates of all vessels carrying that ore south through the "leads" of Norway. Finally, the names of the captains of those vessels that sailed under the German flag were included.

Most important, perhaps, to the British Intelligence community were the detailed plans for electrification of the rail line that were passed from "*Skaði*" to Birger. The project was at that point beyond the conceptual phase and had entered detailed planning. This project was of great interest to British Intelligence, given the potential for increased ore deliveries to the Kaiser.

Since the mid-18th century, reindeer had been used to transport iron ore across the border mountains from the great mine in Kiruna, Sweden. When the railway had opened in 1902, the amount of ore that could be moved through Narvik greatly increased. When the electrification of the line was to be completed, the port's handling of the ore would increase dramatically once more. Given all the hydroelectric sources provided by the mountain's unending supply of melting snow, the power supply to the line was plentiful. It was the engineering needed to electrify this line, and the Norwegians progress over the next dozen years that was of primary importance to MI6.

Birger returned home from that trip to Norway only to discover his wife Tulla missing once more. The nanny would only say that she had been gone sporadically while he was at sea. He thanked her for the time and care she had given to the twins, knowing their development would have withered had it not been for her. Birger apologized to this godsend of a caretaker who witnessed all the shortcomings of Tulla as a mother. Birger thanked her profusely for her discretion. She in turn told Birger she would never speak to anyone of what occurred in their home.

Tulla eventually returned to the house on the Tay two days after Birger had returned. She slept off her high, after which they fought viciously for another two days. Even during this time, Tulla appeared to be rambling and at times nearly incoherent. There was always great drama in the house, as Tulla refused to ever tell Birger where she went during her disappearances. Or for that matter, what she had been consuming that rendered her so disoriented and discursive upon her return.

It was in late March of 1915 when Birger was summoned in person a second time to C's office at 2 Whitehall Court in London. As usual, he was joined by Wincer Wells. They both waited in the outer office, until they were cleared to enter.

"Before we see the Old Man," said Wells with a trademark involuntary wince, "I just wanted to let you know that the last tranche of material you brought back from Narvik was indeed top shelf. Really was the dog's bollocks, it was. Damn Huns are getting almost all of their iron ore for the war from Kiruna through Narvik."

"Well, I am unsure of how often I will be able to continue making that run," Birger confessed, "as Tulla is becoming impossible to deal with. Every time I try to come to terms with her, she simply vanishes, sometimes for days."

"Yes, we are quite aware of that, actually," Wells said. "We've been keeping somewhat of an eye on her for you."

He reached inside the interior pocket of his suit coat, and passed a small folded piece of paper to his spy.

"What is this?" asked Birger. He looked at the note as if it were a death warrant.

"This," answered Wells, "is where your Tulla disappears to. Go on, take it. It's only a bloody name and address."

Birger took the note and unfolded it to see a familiar name on it, a young man who lived not far from his own home in the area known as Broughty Ferry. It read:

Keithen MacDonald, 11 Rugby Terrace,
Broughty Terrace, Dundee, Scotland

Birger recognized the street name, as it was just up the beach from his own dwelling. He had walked it many times, a line of cottage homes that were across from a beautiful hedgerow that seemed to delineate this outer suburb of Dundee from the wild beauty of the Scottish countryside beyond.

"It appears your Tulla takes solace there," said Wells. "Most of the time, in fact, while you were away in the Arctic Circle during this past mission. She seems to be in a bartering relationship with Mr. MacDonald. He provides her hard drink, for sure, and we think even some opiates, although that is still not fully confirmed. She recompenses him with …"

"Stop," snapped Birger, "you need not become graphic, Wells. My mind's eye can readily fill in the picture."

"Picture?" laughed Wells, "If it's pictures you fancy, we've got plenty of bloody photographs. Damn clear ones, for when you're ready to man up to them."

Birger felt his own darkness descending over him. He had thought knowing the truth of Tulla's indiscretions would somehow settle the despondency that lately seemed to always dwell within him, yet the truth only laid him more feebly at the sharpened claws of his fears. Birger had always known that he had that a dark beast lurking inside him, and ever since learning of his own father's suicide, he feared giving in to its demonic temptation.

"Now don't do anything rash, lad," said Wincer, with a fetid smile that choked into one of his facial spasms.

It was then that the light above the baize padded door transitioned from red to green. The transition was accompanied by a slight, but audible click, which caught the attention of C's secretary.

"Gentlemen, the Chief is ready to receive you now," said the woman behind the desk. "You may enter straightaway."

She opened the door toward them, only to reveal a second door that opened inward into the inner office. The double doors themselves seemed to be a carry over from a naval vessel's architecture. Birger had even on his earlier visit thought it seemed like a compartmental hatch, but instead of arresting the intrusion of the waves, its function was to prevent the leakage of highly classified information.

They entered to find "C" behind his desk in a large ornately carved wooden wheelchair. "Come in, gentlemen. Forgive my not rising to greet you. Bit of nasty business along the front line, I'm afraid. Shan't be long before I am on my feet again, even if one is to be carved of wood."

"Yes, so many of us have heard," said Wells quickly. "We were quite dismayed to hear of the loss of your son, sir."

"Yes, Wells, thank you," said the Chief matter of factly. "Stiff upper lip, all that rot, you know. Life indeed goes on. Take a seat, please."

Birger thought a tear might have formed in the Chief's eyes. If it had, there was not a chance that "C" would wipe it away. It was not proper of the British ruling class to show their emotions outright, if at all. Better to have one think they spotted the feeling of loss in his demeanor than to confirm their thoughts with a gesture. It was entirely a British trait.

Both men settled into a tufted leather Chesterfield couch that faced the desk. However, it was placed further away from the desk than during previous visit. In fact, there seemed to be a more generous spacing of all the furniture to accommodate C's wheelchair.

"Gentlemen," said Cumming, rolling himself from behind the desk to a position just between, but facing the two men. A tartan plaid blanket covered his lap and legs. "I take it you've heard of the naval disaster in the Dardanelles last week?"

"Of course, sir," replied Wells, "in our circles it is nearly impossible to have avoided this grim news."

"And you, Alvorsen?" asked "C".

"Somewhat," he replied, "I have been somewhat distracted recently."

"Ah, yes," replied "C", "all that tripe with your young wife. One hears she is struggling with the twins, no? And running astray every chance she gets? Well, listen to me, lad, you have to put all that out of your mind and focus on the business at hand. Remember, man, there's a bloody war on."

"Yes, sir," said Birger.

"Now, be a useful chap and fetch me that map and letter opener from my desktop." Birger did so before returning to his place on the Chesterfield sofa.

"It's all bloody Winston's doing, I'm afraid," said "C". "The man's far too young at forty to be running the Admiralty, my opinion, mind you. Fancies himself a sea faring man. He doesn't know a boom from a brass monkey, if you ask me."

"C" held up the map that was pasted on a backing board.

"This is the Dardanelles Strait, just past where the ancient Greeks laid siege to Troy for ten years on the Asian side," he said, pointing with the letter opener. Then he turned to Birger, "Years ago, I had sailed these very waters myself with your father, Alvorsen, on our last visit to Constantinople. Absolutely tricky waters, maddening currents, all that."

"What was the objective of this most recent Dardanelles mission?" inquired Birger, interrupting the Old Man.

"The objective, Alvorsen," boomed Cumming, obviously irked, "was to win the bloody war. Last time I read the intercepts, Russia was still our ally. The only way to get supplies to her was through the Black Sea to Crimea. Don't be daft, son."

Birger felt embarrassed, but decided to ask the obvious question, "Why not supply them through the Baltic Sea?"

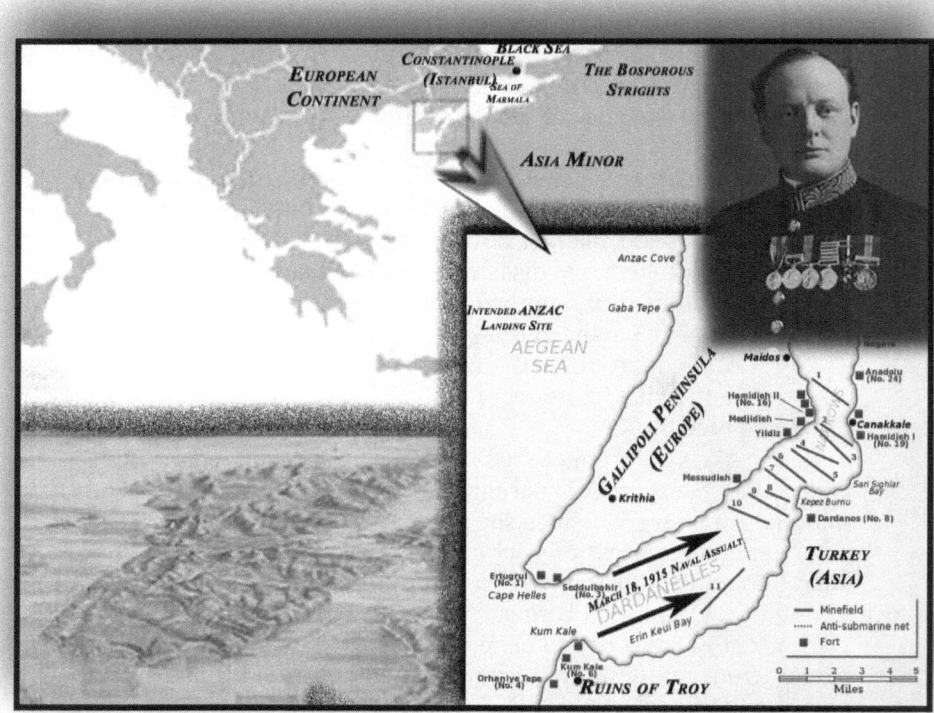

Figure 10: Churchill's Disastrous Dardanelles Naval Assault

An icy stare fell from the old man upon Birger. He was not accustomed to being interrupted, and certainly less so to be questioned by a subordinate, and most certainly not from a raw recruit such as Alvorsen's son.

"Because when portions of it aren't frozen solid, it's full of German U-boats just waiting to take pot shots at our navy with their torpedos," answered Cumming deliberately, but still with a sharp-edged glance. "Now that we have the geography lesson behind us, I will continue. That is, if it should happen to suit you, Alvorsen?"

"Yes, certainly, sir." Birger took no shame in his being reprimanded. He had a question to be asked, and there was no shame in its asking. He had learned the sin was not in the reprimand, only in the failure to ask what needed to be known.

"Lord of the Admiralty Churchill," the man known as "C" continued, "was feeling that his poor old Royal Navy was being left out of this war, so he drew up plans to send a flotilla of dreadnoughts up that asininely narrow strait. "

He thought the Turks in those old earthen forts on both the Asian and European sides would run like the dickens once the battleships lobbed a few shells over their heads. The French were so impressed with his plan they put up four battleships of their own to join the Royal Navy's dozen. They didn't want to be left out of all the glory, now did they? How'd it play out, you might ask?"

The old man looked at them both with hard penetrating stares. First Wells, then Birger. They said nothing, just waiting for the rest of the presentation. Wells certainly already knew the facts, but stayed out of the way of Captain Cumming's re-telling.

"Yes sir," said Wells finally, "Indeed, how, exactly, did it turn out?" Wincer asked, but already knew the answer. He had played his role as the Chief's foil.

"Catastrophe, pure and simple," the chief blared in response. "Winston figured he was dealing with the Old Ottomans, but instead these shores were defended by the Young Turks. Nasty bunch, these sods. The Huns have trained them up something proper." He then laid the map face down in his lap, resting the letter opener on it, its sharp tip dug into the backing board so it would not roll free.

"The navy never properly cleared the minefields. Mind you, the Turks had ten rows of mines across those straits. The results were dreadful," continued C. "Sixteen battleships sailed into that strait and shelled the living daylights out of the forts on both continents. The Turks merely hunkered down, before returning fire. There are even reports that one Turk bastard was carrying shells on his back when his position's loading mechanism failed. Those shells weigh twenty stone or more. Can you imagine?"

Birger did the math in his head. Twenty stone was four hundred pounds. He then pondered the position the Royal Navy must have found itself in. All those massive battleships bottled up in that narrow strait with the path forward blocked by ten rows of mines. Instead of the Turks abandoning their forts, they soon realized that rounds from the ship's big guns sailed clear overhead. Once the Turks returned to their own guns, it must have been like shooting fish in a barrel.

"The real problem," restarted C, "was that the big guns on those dreadnoughts were too close to the forts they were trying to hit. The trajectories were flatter than the chest of a prepubescent lass. Most of the shells sailed straight over the top of them. Only a handful of their guns were taken out by either the ships or by the raiding parties they put ashore. As it was, the fort guns were not the most serious problem, it was those damn howitzers that the Huns had given to the Turks."

"Why would they be worse than the big shore guns of the forts?" asked Birger.

"That's the first good question you've asked, Alvorsen," bellowed C. "First of all, the bloody things are mobile. Get a few rounds off, then drag it away with a mule to a new position. Besides that, those Howitzers lob their rounds onto the ships at a much higher trajectory. Better odds at hitting a target when they fall like rain, you see. We believe that one of those struck the French battleship *Bouvet,* setting her ablaze and taking out her rudder. She drifted then into a line of mines the Turks had laid parallel to the Asian shoreline a few nights before."

"She went down, did she, sir?" asked Wells, again playing his role.

"Like a bloody lead zeppelin, taking over six hundred sailors with her. Then, all hell's handmaids came out, with the *HMS Irresistible* having taken hits and ramming a mine as well. She went down. Then, the *HMS Ocean* struck a mine and went down. *HMS Inflexible* was badly damaged and had to be towed under fire. The fleet retreated with their proverbial rudders between their legs."

"Horrific, sir," said Wells, "absolutely horrific. How can we be of service?"

"Winston's made a dog's breakfast of this, entirely," answered "C". He plucked the letter opener from the backing board of the map. He raised the map and pointed to the peninsula on the European side of the strait. "This, gentlemen, is the Gallipoli Peninsula. The powers that be in Whitehall will never allow our Empire to run away from the disaster in the Dardanelles."

"Another naval incursion, sir?" asked Wells.

"Absolutely not," barked Cumming, "one of Winston's cockeyed blunders is enough. It's high time for the Army to come in and clean up the situation. Next month there will be a full-blown invasion of this peninsula, then the British Army, along with the ANZACs will land, subdue the Turks, and then fight their way up the peninsula to Constantinople."

"Where do we come in, sir?" Wells asked, already knowing the answer.

"I plan to take advantage of that invasion," responded C, "to run a secret operation all the way up here at the thinnest part of the Peninsula near Karalik. If we can reconnoiter this strip of land, we can assess if it is possible to cut off the entire peninsula's enemy supply lines. Wells, you are going to lead this operation for me, and Alvorsen, the Navy appears to be all tied up putting the Army ashore this day. You'll be trusted to put Wells and his team ashore."

"But, sir," objected Birger, "I don't have any knowledge of these waters."

"You can read a nautical map, can't you?" retorted Cumming.

"Of course, but, not knowing the local currents or shifting shoals, it could prove a bit tricky."

"Well, then, 'a bit tricky' is exactly why we retain your services, Alvorsen," Cumming sternly replied. "You're a bloody navigational specialist, isn't that why we keep you on, son?"

"But sir, we could be under enemy fire," quipped Birger. "I'm bound to run ashore and leave us pinned down. Besides, I've got two small sons to raise."

The skirmish that was Birger's assault upon the "Old Man" was washed away by a full frontal counter-assault of immense proportions.

"ENOUGH!" screamed "C", while he raised the letter opener high in his fist and then jammed its razor-edged point into his leg. As he released his grip on it, the blade and handle twanged back and forth from the force of the impact. "IS IT ONLY I WHO AM FIT TO SACRIFICE FOR THE EMPIRE? YOU HAVE TWO MORE SONS THAN DO I, ALVORSEN. UNDERSTOOD?"

"My God," said Birger, still staring at the still undulating letter opener protruding from Cumming's leg. Although Birger knew this to be the wood prosthetic device of his amputated limb, the overall effect was mind-shattering.

"I will take no further questions," announced C after collecting himself. "Either you will accept this mission or offer your immediate resignation from His Majesty's Secret Service. Am I clear?"

"Immensely so, sir," said Wells.

"Alvorsen?" demanded Cumming.

"My wife, sir," Birger stuttered, "I need to discuss this with her."

"You either accept this mission," C bullied, "before you leave this office, or you will resign here and now. We will then ship your wife back to whatever Arctic ice flow from which she thawed. I understand even they don't want her. Accept this instant, and we'll move her, your twin boys and the nanny to the London flat off Blackfriars Bridge until you return. Keep in mind, should anything dire occur to either of you, you have my word that your families will be looked after in exchange for your service. Now, Alvorsen, do you accept this mission?"

A silence echoed loudly through the room while Birger hesitated. "I accept, sir," he finally said, withholding his regrets.

"Now off with you both," answered Cumming.

As the two men stood from the Chesterfield sofa, the letter opener still protruded from "C"'s leg. Birger and Wincer left the room and after the interior and exterior doors were closed the light above them transitioned back to red.

The secretary had gone into the inner office, leaving Wincer with Birger alone in the outer waiting area.

"What was that?" asked Birger.

"That was the Old Man getting his way," answered Wells.

"Driving that blade into his leg?" Birger said. "It was ghastly, and you didn't even flinch."

Wincer Wells looked at the rattled Birger and almost smirked. "Third time I've seen him do that," he said matter of factly. "He enjoys springing it on the unexpected to gauge their reactions, the cheeky bastard. His secretary is most likely in there extracting it right now from his wooden leg. I hear his suit pants looks like Swiss cheese under that blanket."

"What am I going to tell Tulla?" Birger asked aloud.

"Just tell her that she gets another all-expense paid trip to Old London Town," said Wincer. "Tell her the nanny is coming with her, as well. I'll arrange it all."

"Yes, of course," stuttered Birger, "I suppose you'll need the girl's name."

"Already know it, lad," said Wells, "Barrett. Cassandra Barrett. Remember that I'm the one who found her for you in the first place."

15 The Chase

"A lie gets halfway around the world before the truth has a chance to get its pants on."

Winston Spencer Churchill

"So, you've been to Edinburgh before?" Emory asked.

Flake Ferris looked him, as the train began decelerating as it smoothly approached the city.

"Yes, a handful of times," responded Flake. "It tends to be a favorite locale for genealogy conferences. But mostly only in Edinburgh itself. Although, I must admit I have taken a journey once up to St. Andrews. However, I never went to where I wanted to most: the Scottish Highlands."

"Well, who knows where Miss Barrett will lead us," said Emory, "perhaps eventually to the Highlands. One never knows."

"I've never done anything like this before," Flake Ferris admitted. "Do we trail the old lady?"

"The old lady?" repeated Emory in mock surprise. "Come on, Flake, let's keep the target's dignity in mind. Refer to her as the target, or even Miss Barrett, but we don't need to be so pejorative."

"What?" said a surprised Ferris, who had at least twenty years on Emory Hauptmann. "Is she not old? Is she not a lady? Oh, that's right, God forbid I should offend any one of any age to a member of your generation. Those of your ilk weened on *'participation trophies'* and nestled in university *'safe spaces'*. How dare I bring the coarse barbarism of the real world into your life. Forgive me."

Emory had been putting his laptop back into the nylon Sierra Club backpack. He did not bother to look up at Ferris, just zippered up the backpack and then rose to grab his overnight bag from the shelf above his head. His ignoring Ferris only outraged the older man even further.

"Say something, damn it," demanded Ferris.

"The *real world* is not so real at all, it is just an excuse," Emory finally said after sitting again, "for your generation has not bothered to try and change it at all. '*Always been this way, and thus it shall always stay, little ones.*' So condescending. So then, as long as you are working in the field with me, mind your manners and your words. And no, the watchers will follow her. We just need to hang tight until dinner tonight."

Flake took off his glasses and rubbed his brow as if he had just been beaten with the blunt force of incoherent logic.

"So, to you, it is perfectly permissible that we lie outright to an elderly woman - I am still allowed to use those factual words, aren't I? - an elderly woman to whom we throw unearned money just to invade the privacy of her DNA? Then, we leave her a bugged artifact to listen in on her talking to her cat and, God may it please, anyone else. Then we stake out her home and follow her on a trip across Britain, just for the fun of it. Who knows who she's seeing, perhaps a favorite friend? Nonetheless we are on her tail as if she had stolen the crown jewels from the tower. Yet, and I cannot stress this enough, to call her an '*old lady*' is too offensive for your delicate ears."

The train had pulled into Edinburgh's central station. The doors to the train opened and a wave of humanity poured out onto the platform. Emory led the way even as he seemed totally transfixed on the screen of his cell phone.

"I guess I hit a nerve. C'mon, Flake, I've got a book shop I want to hit before we walk back to our hotel, which is in the other direction. The watchers will tell us when Miss Barrett checks into her hotel. We just have to be ready to cover her and whoever she is seeing over dinner. Then we will give them a well deserved break. We will watch over and hopefully listen in on Miss Barrett and her dinner companion. It will be perfect as she hasn't seen either of us before. If she did somehow spot us on the train, she'll just assume it is a coincidence."

"At least you didn't say, '*C'mon Boomer*'. That would have pissed me off to no end," said Flake Ferris as he rose from his seat. "A bookstore, really?"

"Hey, what can I say?" replied Emory. "Edinburgh is a great literary town. This place birthed Sherlock Holmes and Harry Potter, not to mention Sir Walter Scott's characters. I can't wait to see the Scott Monument. Tallest monument to a writer in all of Britain, and that, my friend, is saying something."

The two men walked through the station nestled nestled within the gardens that lay at the base of Castle Hill. Above it, hovered the great hill upon which that fortress and the Royal Mile were elevated.

At one point, Emory and Flake had to walk past Miss Barrett, who had been in a train car closer to the front. She was in the protective visual custody of the pair of watchers, one of whom Emory noticed was walking ahead of her. The other watcher, he assumed, was trailing the snail-paced target.

Emory observed as the first watcher, a beautiful dark-haired Irish girl he knew to be named Erin Anne, stalled herself at a newsstand waiting for Miss Barrett to get closer to her. *These two are real pros, no need to worry,* thought Emory, who hoped to get to know Erin Anne a little better on this trip.

The two men then spilled out onto the main thoroughfare, Princes Street, that ran north and south paralleling the Royal Mile, although at much less of an elevation being at the foot of the great hill. They walked out into a beautiful sunshine and around them bustled all the denizens and visitors of this historic northern capital.

"*Well, laddie,*" Flake said in an embarrassing attempt at the local dialect, "*it is a wee bit soonny tooday, almoost as I huv nivver sin here or anywhaur in Scootland. Aye, I huv bin to this toon miny tims, huv I, always in weather no mair invitin' than a pile of Viking's shyte, soo this is moost unexpected. Now, whair be mah shades?*"

"That's so over the top," Emory said. "Please don't caricaturize these people with your shameful imitation of their brogue, Flake." He hoped no one had overheard the insulting mimicking of the local dialect flowing forth from Mr. Ferris.

"You're the one embarrassing yourself, youngster," Flake said. "The Irish are proud of their *brogue*, but the locals here recognize each other by the lilt of their Scottish *burr*. They physically cringe when tourists tell them how much they adore their brogue."

"Burr, brogue, whatever," Emory reluctantly conceded as he reached into his backpack and pulled out a copy of *"Book Lovers' Edinburgh"* by Allan Foster.

"Well, your '*whatever*' makes all the difference in the world to these Scots," said Flake.

Emory punched an address from the guide book into his cell phone and ignored the scolding from his traveling partner.

"What are you doing?" Flake asked. "Put your phone away, Emory. We don't need directions. I can get us to the hotel. Just a nice walk down this way. See that castle hanging there in the sky above us on that rock off in the distance? The *'Callie'* is just below it, just off this boulevard - Princes Street."

"The Callie?" repeated Emory, "I thought we are staying at the Waldorf Astoria. Don't you even bother to read the itineraries I send you?"

Flake just looked at the young man and shook his head.

"How about you listen to me," replied Flake, "the Waldorf and the *'Callie'* are the same hotel. I've stayed there before. In fact, long before the Waldorf Astoria group hung their prestigious name on the frontage, the hotel was The Caledonian. Locals still call it the *'Callie'*. Look that up on the internet."

He already had. "Looks like your right, Flake, but for now we are heading off in the exact other direction."

"Just where exactly are you dragging my decrepit baby boomer ass to?" Inquired Flake.

"McNaughtan's Bookshop. Been there too? They sell antiquarian volumes, Flake. That means these books are even older than your creakin' bones."

"I love bookshops," confessed Ferris, "especially those that have volumes whose hides are better cared for than my own."

The two men strolled down Princes Street, in the opposite direction from the hotel. They crossed over to Leigh Street, which soon became Haddington Place, where the bookshop was found below street level down a short flight of steps in a ground floor arcade carved out of the space between two large ascending staircases. Huge gold lettering over a black field announced McNAUGHTAN'S, over the curved green sectioned window on the left, and BOOKSHOP over the equally curved and equally sectioned window on the right. A wrought-iron fountain motif railing enclosed the shop from both ascending staircases and the upper floor, as if protecting those who entered its premises from all the distraction's of modern life.

Stepping inside, one was immediately transported to another time altogether, when the art of writing permeated every aspect of life and books were indeed cherished commodities. It was ironic, somewhat, that young Mr. Hauptmann, who was so much of a technical junkie, would equally be enticed by these bound volumes. It was Flake Ferris who was more of the age of the average patron of the shop, that had nearly no interest in the leather clad Quarto's, Octo's and matching volumes that lined the shelves.

Emory browsed about but kept drifting back to a collection of Dickens' works bound in beautiful burnished red leather. He picked up the volume containing *Great Expectations*, and delicately thumbed its pages.

"Aye, that's an excellent choice, sir," said the proprietress of the shop. *"Can't goo wrong with Dickens in red leather, ah huv oolways said. Only problem is that they sell soo much mair quickly than ah kin ever kip them in stoock. And that's the nahcest coolliction ah huv seen in soom tim, mind yeh."*

Flake Ferris cleared his throat, as if to remind young Emory that his impersonation of the local burr was perhaps not so over the top, after all.

"It truly is," replied Emory, cradling the book in his hands as tenderly as he might a small child. He could barely understand the woman. He had to concentrate on every word she said, as if interpreting on the fly. Emory shot back a glance at Flake that said, *OK, you were right about the accents here.*

"If the gentleman maight be intairrested in soomthing from a writer native to this toon," she continued, *"Ah also huv soom beyooteful binding's of Sir Arthur Conan Doyle or Sir Walter Scott's works, but noot in the red, mind yah. Ah even huv a moost beyootefully signed Harry Potter set, shood that maight tackle yah fahncy."*

Emory checked the price pencilled lightly on the first inside cover of the twenty volumes of Charles Dickens' works. It was expensive, but not exorbitant.

"I've been itching to get just such a set, and it's a little hard to find Dickens in Berlin, after all," he said. "Perhaps, I'll sleep on it."

"Yah prerogative, sir," the proprietress said respectfully, *"oolways the coostoomer's prerogative."*

Emory then picked up the volume that contained "A Tale of Two Cities". He looked through it, glancing at the engravings within its covers. Flake Ferris, becoming impatient with the time that Emory was taking, walked behind him and whispered in his ear.

"Come now, my young friend. Putting a book on the shelves may impress the many *Fraulein* you set your sights upon, but merely having shelves full of leather-clad tomes doesn't mean you'll gain their contents by osmosis."

Emory softly closed the book and returned it to the shelf.

"I'll have you know, Flake, that I have read three-quarters of all the books on my shelves. OK, I don't have that many, but what I purchase I do indeed read. The only thing keeping me from buying these on the spot is how on earth would I get these back to Berlin."

"Get them shipped," said Flake. "They'll take care of all that. Do so quickly and let's work our way back to the hotel. I need to wash up."

"Need to wash the dust of civilization from your skin?" Emory scoffed. "For someone so into genealogy, I am surprised you do not have more respect for the writings in these antiquarian books."

"What is the oldest volume you have in this shop, m'am?" Flake yelled out to the proprietress.

"*Will, coorrently, ah believe that would be 'Paradise Lost' by Milton - 1640 or so,*" she replied.

"One thing you learn from genealogy is humility," Ferris said. "Here we have a book that is not even four hundred years old. That, my young friend, is only a small fraction of humanity. When you consider that Homer's *Iliad* and *Odyssey* likely date back to 800 BC, and the *Meditations of Marcus Aurelius* being from the second century, one can get a feel for the staggering loss of how much of the history of humankind has slipped forever through our collective fingers. So much is lost to the tide of time itself. Most people can't trace their families back beyond three generations. It is sad, so very sad."

"And yet, all of those writings you use as examples are still available in print today," Emory replied, "are they not? So, time doesn't actually destroy the works of man, so much as filters it. The passing of time determines which works are worth keeping. That's all."

"The passing of time," Flake Ferris replied, "is exactly what we should be concerning ourselves with, currently."

Emory then said thank you to the proprietress and that he might return the next day.

The two men left the premises, still carrying their overnight bags. Relying on his phone, Emory began to navigate them back to Princes Street, when Flake once again told him to put his phone away. Ferris then led him down the sidewalks of

York Place, past the great mason's works of cathedrals and churches in the area's signature brownish-gray sandstone.

Just before York Place transitioned into Queens Street, Flake led them left onto North Saint Andrews Street, then crossed it and walked the path through the square past the imposing Melville Memorial. The darkened column was named not for the American writer, but the first Viscount Melville from the eighteenth century, a tyrannical figure in Scottish history.

"Where the hell are you taking me, Flake" asked Emory.

"The scenic tour," answered Ferris. "Don't worry, no extra charge."

Egressing St. Andrew Square, Flake Ferris then led them down George Street, in the direction of Charlotte Square off in the distance, past the Commercial Bank of Scotland, and then past a collection of merchant shops before turning left once more to access, one block over, the pedestrian section of Rose Street.

They had made their way through this promenade until Flake ducked into a table of a sidewalk cafe. Emory followed, just in time to hear Flake ordering two Glenmorangie on the rocks.

"I thought you were in such a rush to wash up?" Emory asked.

"Oh, did I say wash up?" Flake answered. "I meant to say wash down. I make it a custom to come here every time I am in Edinburgh and wash down at least one Scotch, or as they say here, simply whisky. So let's wash down a few."

"How did you know I didn't like mine neat?" asked Emory.

"I didn't … " Ferris began to answer.

"Well, I do," Emory interrupted.

"No, you didn't let me finish," Flake replied. "I didn't order yours. Those are both for me."

The waitress returned with the two glasses and placed one before each man.

"My young friend here will have a sarsaparilla," Ferris said to her as he reached for the drink in front of Emory. She smiled, just before Emory asked her for a Laphroaig 10 year, neat.

"You like the peat, I'm impressed," Flake said. "Too much for me, tastes like I'm drinking a bonfire. Far too smokey."

"You're not man enough to handle a little flavor?" quipped Emory. "I thought you would be."

Then Ferris gulped the first Glenmorangie before cupping his fist around the second. Emory's rock glass of the smokey Laphroaig Islay whisky appeared and they toasted each other. Flake Ferris, one round ahead, offered, "Here's to the benefits of traveling on an expense account. Cheers."

Emory sipped his rock glass of potent liquid smoke, before saying, "That was a nice stroll over here. I liked the sights. Still I would have liked to have seen Princes Street."

"I am quite sure you'll see it tonight," Ferris said. "Miss Barrett is likely to want to dine at one of the nice restaurants up on the Royal Mile. We can walk to it from the hotel along Princes Street."

"How can you be so sure?" Emory asked.

Emory was still unsure of what to make of this man. He enjoyed teasing barbs with him, especially the trans-generational ones, he had to admit.

"She just came into a hefty pile of quid," Flake reasoned. "You don't make a trip out of it, coming by first class train, staying at the one of the finest hotels, only to dine at a fish and chip stand, do you? Besides, even if she doesn't go up on the Rock, we'll likely have to walk along Princes Street when we leave to get back to the train station."

"So, Flake, you've just got everything figured out, don't you?"

"That's just the difference between your generation and mine," the older of the two men said. "Your generation demands access to information, and mine values knowledge itself."

"Like I said," Emory went on, "you've got everything all figured out, except, that is, for the main reason you were brought on-board. Why doesn't Anna Barrett have any Norwegian DNA? Her cousin Jake Conley sure does. Means his mother Cassandra must have, too, cause he sure didn't get it from his Texan father. Now, I am not a genealogist, but if Jake's Mom had Norwegian genes in her DNA sample, wouldn't one assume her brother Ian, Anna's father, did too. That would give Miss Anna Barrett a very high expectation of having Norwegian ancestry, would it not?"

Flake looked at his traveling partner, wondering why this young man was so enjoying his inability to explain this dilemma. Ferris decided to try a few explanations on Emory that even Flake himself did not wholeheartedly believe.

"Not if either Ian or Anna were adopted or were illegitimate," Ferris offered, having been through this argument a thousand times in his mind. "But it is very insightful of you to have noticed that this is bugging the hell out of me. Yet I think you are enjoying this altogether too much, my friend. If we can't explain this soon, it will not make or boss or her Texas client very happy at all."

Emory let out a large smile of satisfaction at that last Flake had openly admitted to his frustration.

"Well," Emory continued, "we already checked the adoption route. Both Ian and Cassandra were born naturally to their parents. I suppose it is possible that Cassandra's mother, on the sly, screwed a Norwegian fisherman somewhere in London's East End docks. Now, that could explain Cassandra's having Nordic DNA while her brother does not. After all, it is *possible*."

Emory laughed aloud, just before finishing his Laphroaig. He waited a long second or two, as if he wished to enjoy the warm, smokey flavor of the whisky spreading throughout him. Perhaps it was watching the discomfort of Flake across the table as he squirmed while trying to offer explanations that Emory enjoyed even more. Flake Ferris, despite all his training in genealogy, could not explain why these DNA test results did not support a logical answer, and Emory delighted in watching him writhe in his frustration.

"You'll find as you mature with age, my young friend, that *possible* rarely means *probable*," Flake said. "Everything we have researched says that the Barretts were a proper British family. Besides, even if Cassandra's mother had taken a Scandinavian lover that would have made Jake's mom only half Nordic. We know from Jake's tests that she had to be fully Norwegian for Jake to show up as half. Yet even with this being so, I am confident that something will come to light explaining this situation. Something that even though it may appear rather unlikely, will be the only feasible solution to this puzzle. Whatever it is, I am sure we will find it. I am also sure, it will be something quite out of the ordinary."

"You mean like Cassandra's mom screwing a Norwegian fisherman..." repeated Emory.

"Even more extraordinary than that," Flake said after another deep pull of whisky, "my young friend."

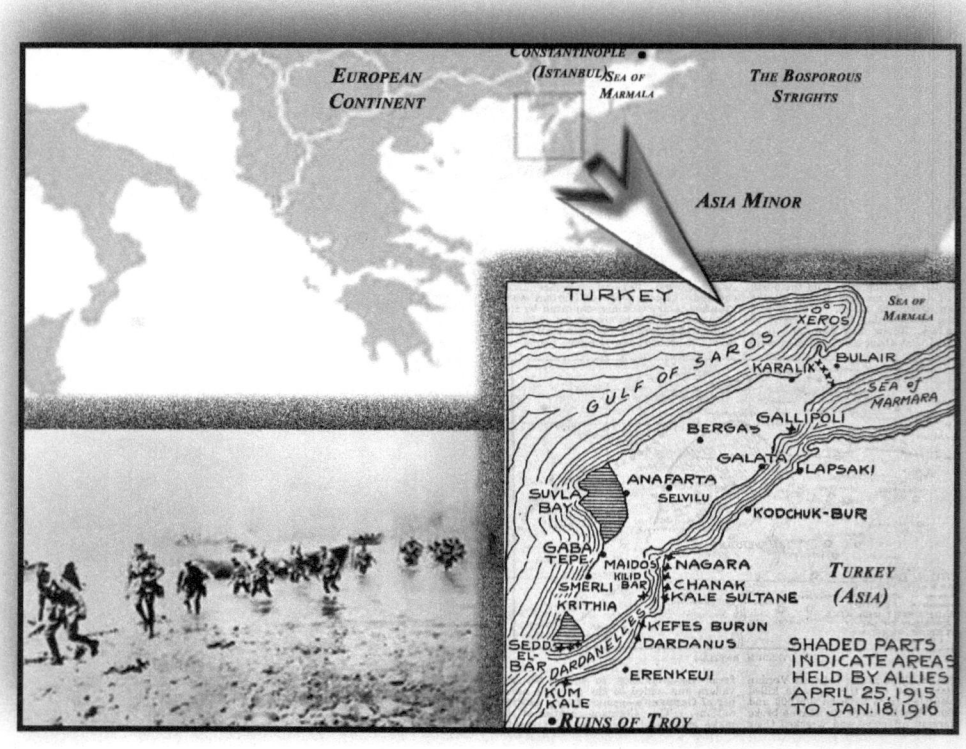

__Figure 11: The Gallipoli Landings__

16 The Dardanelles & Gallipoli

1915

"War is mainly a catalogue of blunders."

Winston Spencer Churchill

One redeeming quality of the English persona is perseverance. Their military leaders refuse to allow an early defeat to stand, so they are compelled to press on until the defeat is rectified with an even more glorious victory. One fatal flaw of the English people is arrogance. Their leaders refuse to admit when a grievous error in strategy has occurred and they double-down their bad judgement in the hopes of washing away the original stain of miscalculation. The line between redemption and damnation resulting from either of these qualities is quite fine, and to borrow from the author (and British spy) Somerset Maugham, indeed it dances upon a razor's edge. To which side falls the fate of British leaders is perhaps defined only by the outcome of any particular event.

The First Lord of the Admiralty, Winston Churchill, had advocated strongly for the naval incursion into the Strait of the Dardanelles, believing that the Ottomans would flee as soon as the British naval guns began their shelling. The Ottoman Empire, then known as "the sick man of Europe," was surely dying, Churchill assessed, having witnessed their poor military performance in the events leading up to this engagement. He had decided that another front was needed to draw German forces away from the stalemated fighting in the fields of Flanders in northern Europe.

His Dardanelles plan was bold. Churchill foresaw a daring naval incursion that would shift the balance of the war into the allies' favor. By opening up the supply lines to Russia through the Black Sea and Crimea, he would also be aiding perhaps the weakest leg of the Triple Entente - Czar Nicholas II's Russia.

Should the success of this audacious military strike perhaps bring some glory upon his office, Winston was prepared to accept it. Of course, it would not, and the many critics that emerged after its failure were all too ready to blame Winston Churchill for gambling with the lives of the British Empire's bravest in an ill-planned scheme to bring praise upon himself.

Churchill had hoped these moves would wipe out an earlier miscalculation on his part. As the war began, the still neutral Ottomans had two battleships under construction and nearing delivery from British shipyards. It was Churchill's decision to seize these vessels that drove the Ottomans to the side of the Central Powers alongside Germany and the Austro-Hungarian Empire.

The Germans quickly recommissioned two of their own battleships to the Ottomans, who most effectively employed them to block the Bosphorus Strait and bottle up the entire Russian fleet on the Black Sea, keeping them from the war.

Having already made one strategic error, Churchill then pressed for a quick victory to clean his slate. It would instead become the singular mistake that would nearly end his career in politics altogether.

With the land war on the Western Front bogging down in trench warfare, he advocated a bold plan upon the seas to reopen the passage to the Black Sea, free the Russian fleet, and secure a path to resupply the Tsar's Russian Army via the Crimean port of Sevastopol.

On March 18, 1915, Churchill sent a force of sixteen battleships, twelve British and four French, into the Dardanelles in four lines, one behind the other, along with other supporting ships of war. The sight of these massive ships, most of which were outdated, but several being of the latest Dreadnaught class, surely must have been intimidating to the Turkish soldiers on both shorelines of the strait.

Yet, what Churchill had not counted on was the steadfast fortitude of the "Young Turks" as they were then known, defending their homeland. One of those leaders was none other than Mustafa Kemal, who would later lead the post war movement for a modern Turkish Republic under the moniker "Atatürk". He and the other young Turks proved to be the steel skeleton that would remain long after the rotting flesh of the Ottoman Empire withered away.

Churchill assumed that the massive presence of the Allied Fleet in the Dardanelles would easily drive the Ottomans from their fortifications on the European and Asian sides of the strait. Of course, that did not come to pass.

Churchill foresaw the flotilla sailing through the strait and onto the Sea of Marmara's remaining one hundred plus miles up to Constantinople. Once there, he foresaw his fleets driving the Ottoman Empire from the war altogether.

That was not to be, as the combined British and French Fleet was badly razed by the Turkish guns and mines. A quarter of the battleships were sunk or put out of action altogether. Even the latest Dreadnaught, the *HMS Queen Elizabeth*, the pride of the British fleet, was struck three times by the shore guns, although she would survive the battle.

The humiliation of the twelve remaining battleships retreating from the strait was a sour taste that the British leadership could not allow to stand. Its acrid taste of failure would go on to follow Churchill throughout his career.

Five weeks later, the high command under the leadership of Lord Kitchener made the decision to land troops in large numbers on the Gallipoli Peninsula outside the Dardanelles. Attempting to capture the benefit of the element of surprise, these landings were attempted in early hours on the southern beaches of *Cape Helles*. Another landing party was to go ashore further north at the specifically selected beach area of *Gabe Tepe*. Here were to be deployed the newly formed Australian and New Zealand Army Corps, forever to be immortalized as the ANZAC troops, fighting for the empire for the first time ever in battle. They would soon become not only a credit to the British forces overall, but also a source of inspiration for their soon-to-emerge independent nations.

Like the Dardanelles incursion itself, this invasion plan would prove to be ill-prepared and doomed to disaster. That morning, the troops on all the southern landing sites came under extensive shore fire from the Turks. The *River Clyde*, a steamer converted into service as a troop carrier, was intentionally run aground to place the troops in close proximity to the beach.

However, due to the failure to prepare with adequate knowledge of the local tides, the *River Clyde* was grounded in water too deep for the soldiers to disembark. Plans to arrange a boating bridge to the shore was abandoned due to the harassment of Turkish automatic fire. By the time a ferry of small craft was devised, the *River Clyde* had come under blistering machine gun fire. The only options available to the soldiers aboard were to jump overboard and drown due to the weight of their gear, or to scurry onto one of the rowboats to be carried ashore. Even in doing so, they remained exposed to the Turkish gunners.

Those that did survive this deadly disembarking soon found themselves pinned down on the beach behind whatever natural cover they could find. They were likely amazed at the number of their brothers that sat still in their deck-top benches aboard the *River Clyde*, who they must have imagined were immobilized by fear. In reality, they would come to learn those troops still seated had died in place to Turkish gunfire, with the weight of their packs and weapons keeping their corpses ghoulishly upright.

At another landing site there was a short expanse of beach surrounded by cliffs. The sweeping machine gun fire from the Turkish manned high-points proved to be just as deadly.

The art of beach landings had not yet been advanced, and the men were ferried ashore by small rowboats, exceedingly primitive by comparison to the specifically designed landing craft employed in later wars. Those who survived the enemy guns during these ferry landings soon found themselves pinned down on beaches, but under a deadly crossfire of Turkish machine gun fire.

The other Cape Helles beach landings were equally brutal, but the British did manage to secure a toe-hold at these sites. Eventually, some 40,000 British and French troops put ashore across this southern tip of the peninsula. The British troops were mostly manned by English and Irish regiments.

That same day, the ANZAC troops were to come ashore further north at the smooth beaches of Gaba Tepe. Instead, having mis-navigated due to the cover of darkness in the early morning hours and the unfamiliar currents, they came ashore several miles even further north, upon a rather unforgiving shoreline. They were met by immediate Turkish resistance. Like their fellow troops further down the peninsula, they found themselves scrambling for cover.

The ANZAC troops had come ashore only to find themselves at the base of a series of imposing mountainous ridges from where blistering enemy fire rained down upon them. To this day that beach is known around the world as ANZAC Cove. These soldiers from the farthest reaches of the empire would cement that name in history through their heroic actions that day.

The only way up those ridges was to climb and fight through a series of deeply set ravines. Twenty-five thousand ANZAC troops came ashore and fought their way onto those rises and displayed exceptional bravery to hold off the Turkish troops and maintain Britain's second (after Cape Helles) toe-hold on the Gallipoli Peninsula. Months later, in August, more troops would be landed in nearby Silva Bay, but even these would not be enough to break out of the ensuing stalemate.

It was during the chaos of all this invasion activity, that Birger Alvorsen navigated a small craft deployed from a British cruiser much further north into the Gulf of Saros. His assignment was to put Wincer Wells and his team of fifteen commandos ashore. They planned to wait until nightfall and deploy under the cover of darkness. Throughout that day, as all hell was breaking loose lower down on the peninsula, their commando interpreter picked up Turkish radio chatter indicating that the Turkish 7th Reserve Division was moving south to reinforce the troops resisting the invasions. What they did not know was that the Turkish 5th Reserve Division still held the coast defending the encampment at Bulair.

That night, under a blanket of darkness, Birger navigated his craft through unfamiliar waters and hazardous currents. He had earlier familiarized himself only with an outdated navigational map of the waters around the upper peninsula shore line. Despite this, he was able to navigate to the beach of Yenikli Bay near Bulair, where the Gallipoli Peninsula necks to its thinnest point. The plan was for Wincer Wells' unit to put ashore, emplace spotters in the highest passes and report via encoded radio traffic on all the enemy's troop movements down the peninsula.

As their vessel came closer ashore, having picked up a head of steam before cutting its engines, Birger engaged a quiet running battery powered propellor, specifically designed for this mission. In this nearly silent mode of operation, one of Wells' commandos sounded the depths.

Just a little bit further and Birger would drop the team on the beach and then return to the British cruiser and the relatively safe waters of the open Aegean. The commando sounded the depths and to maintain the silence, would indicate only by hand gesture when they had reached a safe level to disembark.

The commando stood just aside the helm, and, even in the darkness, Birger's eyes had adjusted to recognize his hand signal. He turned the vessel parallel to the shoreline so as not to ground it. Every man was maintaining operational silence when they heard a metallic sound from the shore, like the slide rack of a weapon being engaged.

It was then when the chain rattle of the machine gun pierced the still night and opened up on the vessel. The first to fall was the commando aside Birger, his upper torso ripped apart, its blood splattering upon Birger's face. After he fell, the next spray of bullets found Birger himself. He was hit broadside in the leg and hip. He fell to the deck, landing upon the commando who he knew already to be dead.

The pain was excruciating, and despite Birger's immediate thought to navigate them back out to sea, he could not raise himself from the deck. He saw two other commandos fall in the next hail of the automatic weapon's fire. His worst fears for this operation had come to pass.

It was then that he felt the power of the engines kick in, churning up the shallow water and sand into a blinding spray of gritty slurry. The bow of the vessel instantly pivoted back out to sea. Birger looked up to see Wincer Wells at the helm, as sparks of wood exploded around him from the fanning machine gun fire. He stood resolute, unflinching, and his actions surely saved the lives of the rest of the crew that night. Their mission was now as damned as the overall Gallipoli Peninsula invasion would prove to be.

Wells managed to navigate them back to the Allies' cruiser off the Gulf of Saros. He had radioed ahead so that the ship would not think it was coming under attack. The living and the dead were transferred quickly aboard. That night, one more commando would succumb to his wounds while another man on board that landing craft began his own long journey of recovery. For in the middle of the Aegean Sea that night, Birger Alvorsen would have his left leg amputated.

17 Winston's WWI Legacy

Historical Reference

"There are a terrible lot of lies going about the world, and the worst of it is that half of them are true."

Winston Spencer Churchill

The Dardanelles Incursion and Gallipoli Campaign would end up costing so much more than just Birger Alvorsen's leg. The loss of over one hundred thousand lives of some soldiers and seamen amidst total casualties of a half million men (a quarter million on each side) to fighting and disease. Not to mention the sinking of the British Navy's prestige upon the waves along with the four sunken battleships. The intended swift moving invasion, fighting its way up the peninsula and on to Constantinople, never materialized. Instead it bogged down into the same static trench warfare as on the Western Front. The heat of summer combined with the rotting corpses of both sides brought forth pestilence carried by flies, despite periodic temporary truces to allow the dead of both sides to be removed. Those who survived to fight from the trenches would often view the dead as the lucky ones, given the hell they found themselves entrapped in.

The stalemate on the peninsula would go on until the first weeks of January 1916, when the last of the Allied forces were withdrawn. Churchill, however, did not last that long. He would be forced to resign from his beloved position as First Lord of the Admiralty in May of 1915, only a little more than two months after the initial Dardanelles disaster. He would go on to volunteer to serve on the continent during the war as a lieutenant colonel in a demonstration of self-imposed penance. It was not his first time in wartime military service, although it would be his last. For the remainder of his life he would draw upon these experiences, especially as the political leader of the last bastion of European democracy during World War II.

What had been devised as a bold use of the British tactical advantage in sea power at Gallipoli and the Dardanelles was wasted due to the twin failures of inadequate planning and underestimating the Turk's desire to defend their lands. These were lessons that Churchill would learn greatly from, but the scar tissue of the Dardanelles would forever brand his leadership as impetuously overreaching to assure the glory of victory.

The shameful associated spectacle of Gallipoli would also, along with the stalemated Western Front, contribute to Herbert Asquith, the liberal Prime Minister, losing his leadership position. In December 1916, his administration, so unprepared for war and the rapid decision processes it demanded, was replaced by the coalition government of David Lloyd George. Asquith would be replaced by the very man he had selected to effect the war on his behalf. While Lloyd George's strengths in planning and organization would immediately be brought to bear, he would have to wait until mid-1917 before Winston Churchill could be brought back into government in the much lesser position of Minister of Munitions.

Churchill would later go on to serve as Secretary of State for War and Air immediately after the Great War under Lloyd George. Combined with his time in leading the Admiralty, Churchill had personally overseen the expansion of the British Navy, the development of the tank, and the fledgling birth of the Royal Air Force - all weapons which would become indispensable in preserving the sovereignty of the British during the Second World War.

Another very significant contribution that was implemented during Churchill's reign as First Lord of the Admiralty was in the secretive world of Naval Intelligence. For in October of 1914, in the Old Building of the Admiralty, a group of academics were assembled for no other purpose than to break the German cypher codes used by its military throughout the war. The group was stood up under the leadership of Alastair Denniston, and became known within Whitehall for the room in the Admiralty in which they resided - Room 40.

Denniston brought structure and order to the group of egocentric college professors, each wishing to prove his intellectual prowess over his peers. His adept ability to gently coddle these types while still thrusting them forward toward their goal was exactly what was needed. He understood them, even to the point that he later married a member of his Room 40 team.

Perhaps, no one of his assembled team needed his soft-handed leadership more than the scholar from Kings College in Cambridge - Alfred Dillwyn Knox. "Dilly" Knox was, within his own mind, an unmatched intellect and was always out to prove this fact to the world. His field of study had been the ancient classics, and the world of cryptography called out to him as a daunting intellectual challenge.

To say Dilly Knox was an eccentric personality was an understatement. He did his best thinking in the bath, or so he claimed, and so much so that a bath tub was installed within the Admiralty for his personal use. If Alastair Denniston was the guiding hand in the velvet glove, then Dilly Knox was the personification of the empowered intellect that lit the sparks of the group's imagination.

The greatest accomplishment of Room 40 was the intercept of *The Zimmermann Telegram* in January 1917. The encoded communication from the German Foreign Minister Arthur Zimmermann to the German Ambassador to Mexico authorized the ambassador to offer the Mexican Government concessions should America enter the war. The telegram empowered the German Ambassador to communicate that if Mexico would open up a battle front with the Americans, they would be allowed to annex as spoils of war any lands from Texas, New Mexico and Arizona that they conquered. Room 40 not only intercepted the message, but it was then leaked to nearly every major American newspaper on whose front pages blared headlines condemning the German deceit.

The result was that the American isolationist policies of Woodrow Wilson, who had just been elected to a second term, melted away in the heat of public anger. In April of the same year, America entered The Great War on the side of the Allies. With her unending supply of soldiers, airmen and munitions, the stalemate of trench warfare was soon overcome, and the fighting ended in November of the following year.

So, Winston Churchill as First Lord of the Admiralty made enormous contributions in the weapons of war, perhaps the most important being the weaponizing of intelligence and crypto-analysis. Even still, the failure of his strategy in the Dardanelles would haunt Churchill's career for over twenty years until he once again clawed his way through sheer persistence to return to leading the Admiralty. This accomplishment came only two days after Hitler invaded Poland initiating World War II.

Yet, even still, the stain of the Dardanelles nearly derailed him from ascending to the position of Prime Minister that he, like his father before him, so craved. The Dardanelles and Gallipoli catastrophes nearly denied the British people Churchill's inspirational leadership, which alone would stabilize the last nation to stand alone in the fight against the Nazi war machine. During the ensuing period, the entire world would become engulfed in the seemingly unquenchable fires of war.

World War I's Room 40 experience had demonstrated the need for the Government Communication & Cypher School, or GC&CS, which was birthed in 1919. Even later, GC&CS would evolve into the Government Communication Headquarters (GCHQ), that to which Malcolm Devereaux was currently assigned. To this day, Alastair Denniston is considered to be the first Director of GCHQ. Both Denniston and Dilly Knox would go on to reprise their Room 40 roles during the early years of World War II. These men would be key contributors to the establishment of a sprawling enterprise which would later become known as Bletchley Park. Denniston and Knox would, in the course of this endeavor, make a fateful trip to Warsaw just six weeks before Hitler's invasion of Poland. The results of this secret trip very well may have turned the tide of the entire conflict.

18 Dinner At The Witchery

"I may be drunk, Miss, but in the morning I will be sober and you will still be ugly."

Winston Spencer Churchill

They were to meet that day at four in the afternoon, as agreed, at the first floor landing of the grand staircase in the Caledonian Hotel. The same staircase that Roy Rogers once rode upon with his horse, Trigger. This was a known fact, as the hotel had enshrined that moment in history from 1954 with a photographic display below the staircase on the ground floor. Emory was struck by this image as he climbed the steps to the floor above. He could not help but think, *With all the famous people who once most surely had tread these flights, this is the most celebrated moment the owners of this establishment chose to commemorate?*

"Trigger? Really?" He said to Flake, "They could not have a photo of a more prestigious dignitary on display? No famous politicians, writers or more famous celebrities?"

Flake Ferris, refreshed after an hour long nap in his room, stood aside Emory as they both waited for one of the watchers to appear. The landing was massive and opened into a ballroom which was not in use at that moment. Emory checked the ballroom doors which were unlocked. After the watcher showed, they would step inside to avoid the echo of their voices being carried up or down the open staircase.

"Replace Roy and Trigger," said Ferris. "surely not. The people of Edinburgh loved the time that Roy and Dale Evans spent here. They were real heroes, and not just because of his movies and radio exploits."

"Ok," Emory quipped sarcastically, "just because Roy was such a nice guy."

"Mr. Scourer of All Things Internet," Flake addressed him, "if you would bother to research as to why Roy, Dale and Trigger were here in the first place, you'll find that in addition to their 'Wild West Show,' they did free shows for the war orphans. They also waited for the paperwork to come through."

"What paperwork?" Emory asked.

"The paperwork for them to adopt one of these children, a young girl from a North Edinburgh children's home. They took her back as their daughter, and raised her in California."

"Imagine that, real humanitarians," Emory said. "They couldn't have their own kids, so they came here to hand pick a near perfect three or four year old?"

"No, as it turns out, they were both just real humans," responded Flake, "with two hearts full of love. They already had several children of their own, and the girl was not nearly as young as you think. She was thirteen. Probably thought she might never have any brothers or sisters to play with by then. Instead, thanks to Roy and Dale, she became a vital member of a loving family."

"You're breaking my heart," Emory replied, but in truth, his spirits had plunged at being corrected once again by Ferris.

It was then that she climbed the staircase and Emory's heart lifted. He had hoped that Erin Anne would show and would have left Fleming, the other watcher, behind at Miss Barrett's hotel to keep an eye on their target. It could very easily have gone the other way, Emory thought, and they would have been briefed by the slightly pudgy, red-haired and freckle-faced Winslow Fleming. To Emory's delight, they had drawn the raven haired Erin Anne, the beauty with the intoxicatingly distinctive Belfast accent. She was slim, fit and for some reason conjured a witch in Emory's mind - a beautifully alluring, young sorceress. How she could be paired with Fleming on any assignment seemed like an error upon which no credibility could be heaped. They were night and day, yet somehow this worked to their advantage. No one would ever see these two distinctly different faces in a crowd and assume they were working in tandem.

"Aye, gents, ya' are all set up, ya' are," said Erin Anne in her delicious Belfast accent, as they slipped into the empty ballroom. *"We were quare lucky, we were. Winnie overhaird the target at the hotel's concierge desk booking a restaurant on the Royal Mile for our target at seven o'clock toonight."*

"That's a little early for dinner, isn't it?" asked Flake.

"Would be a wee bit for me, certainly," she said, *"but the poor lass wanted to eat an hour earlier, but the place was booked solid then. Ya' lads need to be there early to assure yah can secure a nearby table. Ah would suggest ya' take along a nice twenty poond noote or two to influence the Maitre D', or whoever seats you at yah table."*

"What's the name of the restaurant?" Flake asked.

"The Witchery at the Castle," said Erin Anne, *"is the name of the establishment which includes a handful of hotel suites. T'is joost down from the entrance to Edinburgh Castle, close to the place selling whisky to the tourists. Appears to be very posh, so be donning yah best ootfits."*

Emory thought to himself, *The Witchery?* It could not be a coincidence that this named spilled forth from the lips of this lovely sorceress. He took it to be an omen, a talisman.

"Yah booth shoold be waiting ootside the entrance until ya' see Fleming. He will tail the target to the restaurant where he will hand them oof to ya' booth. Ah will pick them up on the way oot of the restaurant. All you need to doo is listen in on their conversation. Here, take this."

She began to hand what appeared to be a cell phone to Ferris, when Emory aggressively reached out to take the device from her hand.

"Best let me manage that," Emory said to Erin Anne, "you know how technologically challenged *they* can be."

"They?" repeated Erin Anne. She looked at Emory with a hint of disgust.

"You know," he stammered, "their generation. Is there a particular reason why I can't just use my own phone?"

She looked at him, pausing, as if she were measuring the young man and not liking what she found.

"Noo, noo," she said, *"soo loong as yah moobile is fitted oot with a high powered directional microphone as this one is. Ah can show you hoo to use it, if it is noot too technologically challenging fer ya'."*

Flake Ferris laughed out loud. He had noticed Emory going far too hard to impress her, only to have her cut him to the quick as she had.

Emory blushed, before saying, "Why don't you run me through on how to use it…"

Erin Anne then took the device back from Emory, who had literally snatched it from her hands.

Erin Anne held the mobile phone at arm's length. Emory pretended not to be able to see its screen, so he brought his face next to hers, almost check-to-cheek. He could smell the intoxicating but delicate scent of her perfume.

"T'is controolled by this app," she began, opening an application on the phone, *"which is preset to auto-ranging up to ten meters, but remember in a crooded environment it can becoome confused as to which discussion to track, so best to put in manual mode and control the distance-to-target here, while the signal strength is shown here. Then ya' will know that ya' are locked on the conversation at the peak signal strength. This on-screen arrow aligns to the directional mic's orientation, but that is preset in the top of the mobile, soo as loong as ya' point the top of the phone in their direction you are certain to get excellent cooverage. Finally, there is a kill switch hard wired onto the case shoold ya' fear you are discovered. Press it and the phone appears to have died, although it is actually still recording. That's aboot it, really."*

She closed the app and handed the device back to Emory. As he took it from her, the skin of his finger made contact with her palm, at which the young woman pulled her hand away abruptly.

"Oother than that, it is a normal moobile phone. It can take photos, text or email. The screensaver password is set to the words 'Target Miss'. Text me if needed, Ah am listed in the contacts as 'Omega'. Certainly text me as they are leaving their table, or if for any reason they appear to be departing the restaurant early."

"If you are listed as *Omega*, then Fleming, let me guess, must be loaded as *Rolex*," he said, smirking. "I mean with you both being *watchers*, and all."

Emory was as pleased with his quip as Erin Anne was infuriated by it.

"Alpha," she corrected him, not finding any humor in his joke at all. *"We take these assignments very serioosly, Mr. Hauptmann. We doon't jooke aboot them, and we never loose a target. Soo, shood ya' remain soomewhat proofessional toonight, Ah wood greetly appraiciate it."*

Emory appeared deflated at this chiding. Her Irish accent had seemed to flare up along with her temper. Once again Flake Ferris laughed, after which he assured the young woman that they would certainly be as professional as she required.

"Where will you and Fleming be during all this?" he asked.

"Ah am going too grab a wee few hours rest," she said, putting her hand out for the room key she knew they had for her, as they were to check all four of them in. Emory placed it gently in her palm. *"Good, leave Winnie's at the desk. Don't want to risk being spotted dooing a handooff whilst he is tracking the target ootside the restaurant. He'll go ooff service at that point, and Ah will be back on as yah coome oot ooff the restaurant."*

"Remember," said Flake, "we need to seize any opportunity we get to gather information as to this other woman's identity."

"Aye," Erin Anne said, *"we booth have been briefed on that. Noow, unless either of you gents have any further questions, Ah need a wee few hours in bed."*

You certainly do, thought Emory, *as do I beside you.*

━━━ • ❖ • ━━━

A short while later, Emory and Flake strolled along Princes Street, aside the public gardens that ran parallel the avenue at the base of the rock cliff upon which rested Old Town Edinburgh, including the Royal Mile.

"See, Emory," Flake Ferris jabbed, "I told you you'd get to experience Princes Street."

"You never fail on keeping a promise, do you, Flake?"

"No, I do not. There ahead is your Sir Walter Scott Monument," Ferris answered. "We've got a little time, yet. Let's walk up to it so you can get your fill, Laddie."

By six-thirty, Emory and Flake waited on a section of the Royal Mile known as Castlehill. They stood on the corner where Ramsay Lane climbed up to meet it. The castle gates having been closed for the evening gave this final stretch of the Royal Mile a very tight and imposing feel. At its other end, The Old Town's Royal Mile began as the Abbey Strand near the Palace of Holyroodhouse, before it widened to Canongate, changed its name to High Street, and then again to Lawnmarket. After the road climbed past the octagonal spires of the *Tolbooth Kirk*, it became known as Castlehill and the road narrowed considerably.

Figure 12: The Royal Mile at Castlehill, Edinburgh

The shops around Flake and Emory there tended to be oriented to tourists. The most obvious of these was the Scottish Whisky Experience. Even at this hour, there was a steady stream of foot traffic in and out of this clearinghouse for nearly all Scottish Whisky products, be they of the single malt or blended varieties. Just below, tightly packed between it and the decommissioned *Tolbooth Kirk,* was the building that contained the Witchery at the Castle Gate.

Flake and Emory watched the tourists mill about the street as they waited for their target and Winslow Fleming to appear. A small cluster of Australian tourists trailed behind a guide who stopped briefly in front of the Witchery to explain its significance.

"This building is called the *Witchery at Castle Gate* for it was here on Castlehill that more witches, women and men both, mind you, were burned at the stake than anywhere else in Scotland. The structure was built in 1595 by the merchant Thomas Lowthian. His initials and motto, '*O Lord in Thee is all my traist,*' are still seen legibly carved in the doorframe here."

The tour guide made a rapid pointing gesture then added, "This entire row of buildings on this side of the Castlehill was almost demolished for no better reason than to make room for more admirers of King James VI as he processed to the Castle. Let's all be thankful that never came to pass. Now, this next church is no longer a church at all. Originally constructed in 1848, it was known as *Tolbooth Kirk* and today serves as...."

The group moved on down Castlehill, shuffling after the guide like a gaggle of newborn goslings.

"You do realize that the German word for church is *Kirche*, don't you?" said Emory as they waited.

"Knock off the linguistics lesson," answered Flake, "here they come."

It was then that they saw the two women slowly climb the hill past the tour group, whose members craned their necks to take in the spires of the former church. Miss Barrett and her much younger dinner guest bantered as one might expect old friends to do as they walked slowly toward the small painted sign marking 'Bothwell Court' at the beginning of the *close* leading to the restaurant.

Flake had assumed they would have taken a taxicab to avoid the climb, but the old gal seemed to be enjoying the walk. As she and her companion negotiated the alley like *close* entranceway to the dining establishment, Fleming appeared out of nowhere. Emory and Flake had not noticed him trailing the target. Fleming then signaled by swiping his finger to his nose, professing, *you're on, lads.* This linking signal between watchers would never be permitted tracking a more professional target, but seeing as this was only a senior and her younger dinner partner, it was deemed not to be a substantial risk.

The restaurant entrance was through a stone masonry arched alley of sorts, known to the locals as a "*close*". This one had been finished off smartly with panelling, and adorned with signs announcing *"Reception"* with a directional encouragement that pointed to the rear. The *close* then opened near the back of the building onto a quaint courtyard garden, complete with gas flame lamps. Flake and Emory had emerged from this short tunnel, and paused while they gawked at the masonry and ambience of the restaurant's outer courtyard, as if they had just been transported through time.

As they passed through the restaurant's doors they saw the two women ahead of them being led off to be seated.

Flake asked the young girl selecting tables for all parties to place them at a table nearby the two women who were just seated. She seemed perplexed, until Flake said that the women were friends who they had been surprised to see just enter ahead of them. And he added, not to worry, they only wished to be close enough to say hello. At this point Flake passed a twenty pound note to her. The hostess then handed two menus and whispered an instruction to another young lass who would seat them.

They were taken to a descending L-shaped staircase that led down along two walls to a large open dining area that was already filling at this hour. As the restaurant was built onto the fall of Castle Hill, there were many windows and as much ambient light as the hour could afford.

Then Flake and Emory were led back away from the dining areas at the stairs' landing, back under an impressive oak beamed ceiling in the direction to the front of the building which ran along, but now below High Street. They passed through several other dining rooms that were lined with fine tapestries and magnificently detailed wooden paneling, and decorated with the most luxurious of country indulgences, recalling the days of the Scottish-French *"Auld Alliance"*. One room was more opulent than the next, although as they walked, the availability of windows and their ambient light was progressively lost.

"The oaken walls behind these tapestries were rescued from a fire in St. Giles Cathedral just down the Royal Mile," explained their hostess as they walked. "The panelling on these walls was recovered from a Burgundian Chateau."

The dining room they had just entered still bore evidence of having been chiseled-out of the rocky strata that lie just below the street level of Castlehill. They had been shown into the original dining room that had all the earmarks of a festively gilded, wooden Renaissance refractory befitting any aristocrat, if not the Royal family themselves.

This dining room was long and linear, and ran parallel to the street front. It was done up in a gothic style, with its rough hewn stone walls covered in fine hand fashioned panelling which climbed to support an intricately carved and warmly stained oaken ceiling. The front wall featured three highly located window boxes, all dressed in the same hand carved panelling which spied out onto the well-trodden expanse of Castlehill's cobblestones.

The ceiling's large exposed oaken beams segmented overhead spans of delicately hand-carved woodwork detailing the skills of artisans long since thought to have forever perished.

The wall facing the street was covered below its lower two-thirds by red leather tufted bench seating. The lighting was candlelit throughout, but instead of large chandeliers that would have competed with the intricate ceiling for attention, the lamps were crystal wall sconces that resembled the small elaborate shaded candles of yesteryear.

They were seated at a table two down from Miss Anna Barrett and her guest. Flake took the bench seating against the wall, Emory the chair in the matching red tufted leather styling. They ordered drinks, and then Emory pulled out the phone and began recording the conversation at the Barrett table, despite easily being within earshot of their targets.

"I hope you ladies don't mind our crowding you a bit," said Flake, "but this is the very table where we both met a few years ago. We could not pass up the opportunity to take it once again."

"No, no, my friend," said Anna Barrett, "enjoy your anniversary," she said to them, trying hard not to show her true emotions.

"Yes, our anniversary," Flake repeated, "of sorts…"

Neither man would hear what Anna Barrett said next under her breath, although the directional mic picked it up clearly.

"Dirty buggers," she scowled in a hushed tone, "an old goat with a young stud like that and showing not a shred of regret. What have the times come to?"

"Just relax and enjoy your meal, Aunt Anna," the other woman could be later heard whispering on the recording to the target. "Forget the Americans, darling."

At that moment, Flake and Emory began to speak loud enough to be clearly overheard. "You know," Emory said to Flake, "this room reminds me very much of that room in Bayeux where we ate lunch."

They began discussing that famous town's tapestry, and this soon enough this led to a long and ranging conversation regarding European history, ranging from the Norman Invasion of England to the Thirty Years' War and onto the Napoleonic timeframe. It was all for show only to cover the fact that they eavesdropped electronically on the conversation of the women.

As their meals came, Emory politely asked Anna Barrett and her guest if they would mind taking a photo of he and Flake with their beautifully presented plates. Anna Barrett demurred, saying that she could never quite handle these modern cell phones, and wouldn't have one herself.

It was then that the mystery woman said, in an agitated voice, exasperated with her Aunt, "Don't be ridiculous, Aunt Anna. Of course, I will take your photo for you gentlemen".

She reached out her hand for Emory's phone. As he began to hand it to her, he ran his small finger over the kill switch, sending the phone's screen to black.

"Can you believe that," Emory affronted, "the damn thing died on me just when I wanted a picture of the two of us! Damn it."

"No worries. Do you have your phone?" she asked of Flake.

"Me? No. I'm sorry to say I left mine at the hotel," he responded, although it was in the pocket of his trousers.

"Given that, then, I will just use mine and send it off to one of you," the woman said, taking her own mobile from the tabletop. "Come now, lads. Cheers it is!"

Emory and Flake leaned over their plates, smiled in unison and the photograph instantly emerged upon the screen of the mystery woman's mobile.

"Just give me a number to text it to and the problem is solved," she said.

Emory gave her the cell number of his own personal cell phone, and she texted the photo to that number.

"I am very appreciative of your doing that, Miss _____ ?" Flake fished. Being closer to her age, he thought she might identify herself. She did not bite.

"As I said," she went on, "it's the least I should do being this is such a special day for you both. What sites in Edinburgh did you take in today?"

"Actually," said Emory, "I dragged my companion here to McNaughtan's Book Store."

"I love that shop," she said sweetly, correcting him in her mind. *Book Shop not Book Store, darling.*

"I am thinking about getting a set of Dickens' Works from there…" Emory added, "bound in beautiful, bold red leather. Almost the same shade as the upholstery of these chairs and benches."

"I love Dickens," claimed Anna Barrett, suddenly rejoining the conversation. "You must tell me which is your favorite novel of his?"

"Well, I really like *Great Expectations*," Emory said slyly, "but, given my druthers, my favorite is *A Tale of Two Cities*. Best of times, worst of times and all that."

"Cracking good story, that is," said Miss Barrett. "My favorite scene is the end when Sydney Carton changes places with Charles Darnay in his Parisian prison cell. *'Tis a far, far better thing I do than I have ever done ...'* I love that bit."

At this point of the discussion, Flake watched the other woman's face. A look of terror suddenly flashed over it, much as the shadow of a hawk instantly terrorizes small prey in the fields as it is cast over them.

"Anna," interrupted the mystery woman with some urgency, "We should let these gentlemen eat before their food becomes cold as stones."

"Sorry," said Anna Barrett, "one just gets so few chances to discuss the classics any more. *Bon appétit*, gentlemen."

The rest of the dinner went off with no further conversation between the two tables other than a polite, "Goodnight, gentlemen, and best wishes" as the two ladies left the dining room.

Emory then picked up the phone with the direction mic, reactivated it, and texted "Omega" that the targets were being passed on to her.

"I certainly hope we picked up some good chatter. I couldn't hear a bit of what they said, could you?" Emory asked.

"Not at all," answered Flake, "they were whispering so much, but at least we now have that other woman's cell number."

Erin Anne had waited on High Street for them, knowing they were heading back to the target's hotel only a few blocks away. She hung back and gave them a lot of distance.

Erin Anne came up to the hotel just after Miss Barrett had gone inside and as the mystery woman was pulling away in a taxi. The watcher from Belfast walked up to the doorman.

"Can ya' tell me where that taxi was heading, sir?"

The doorman's eyes washed his measuring eye over her. "What's it to ya', lass?"

Yet, Erin Anne was not deterred for one second. She raised her arm toward him in response to his question. In her palm was an something instantly recognizable to the doorman.

"More importantly," she replied, pressing the twenty pound note into his palm, "is what it ts to you."

The doorman looked down at the note in his hand. "Could be anywhere, now, couldn't it, darlin'?" Erin Anne then pressed two more twenty pound notes into his palm.

"Dundee," he then answered briskly. "The Esplanade, Broughty Ferry, Dundee East." His pronunciation was that of the truest of Scotsmen, as Broughty Ferry came out more as "Brochty" Ferry.

Not far away, Flake and Emory walked down the incline from the Old Town. They took the route past the Royal Scottish Academy in an area known to the locals as *"the Mound"*.

"You are a damn genius, Emory," said Flake, "all that crap about Dickens!"

"I don't get it," Emory responded. "I just answered the woman's question."

"You don't get it?" said Flake, "You just solved our riddle, is what you've done. You have explained why Anna Barrett has no Nordic DNA."

"Sorry, still not getting get it, I'm afraid, " Emory said.

"You missed the look of instant terror on our mystery woman's face when her Aunt Anna was going off on the two characters trading places in '*A Tale of Two Cities*', just before she cut off the old woman."

"Third time, Flake, I'll say it slower. I don't get it."

"Emory, you may be as dense as the walls of that fortress up there," Flake said pointing up to Edinburgh Castle which by that time hung all illuminated in the night's darkness high above them, "but I love you anyway. Cassandra, Jake's mother, is not Cassandra Barrett. She is someone of Norwegian descent who traded places with Cassandra Barrett. Now, we just have to figure out who she was before she stole Cassandra Barrett's identity."

"OK. Now you're really grasping at straws, Flake," Emory said.

"I don't think so," Flake replied, "and our mystery woman is the key. I'll bet good ol' American Dollars to doughnuts that she is a descendant of the real, British born Cassandra Barrett. We just have got to figure out where that original Cassandra Barrett crossed paths with this Norwegian woman who ended up stealing her identity."

19 Tulla and Birger

1915 - 1919

"Nothing in life is so exhilarating as to be shot at without result."

Winston Spencer Churchill

At Gallipoli, Birger Alvorsen, the proud son of a Norwegian émigré to the shores of Scotland, had made what he thought was to have been his life's greatest sacrifice. He would never again walk, unless assisted by the naggingly remindful pain of a wooden prosthetic leg. He had been transferred to a Royal Navy hospital ship not long after his surgery for recuperation. When he finally was sent "home" from the hospital ship to the city of London, he was moved to a hospital in Chelsea, not far at all from the call of the Thames and the sea beyond.

What Birger did not know, was that this medical stay was on the command of the "Old Man" Mansfield Cumming, but not for physical treatment or observation. "C" was concerned for the heavy burden of depression that would accompany this life altering wound, a state of mind which he had known firsthand. And given that Birger's father had taken his own life, "C" felt he owed it to his old friend that his son not be allowed to follow in his father's self-destructive error.

A parade of visitors soon flooded Birger during his hospital stay. The doctors felt that this would hopefully lift the spirits of the young Nordic-Scotsman. First was the man who had saved his and the rest of the operation's lives - Wincer Wells. Had he not immediately and heroically taken the helm of that vessel, all surely would have died in those sandy shoals off the Gallipoli Peninsula. Wincer came every day, once a day, and Birger soon realized he stayed for exactly one hour each visit. To the minute, oddly enough.

The precision of the visit's length became something of an agitation to Birger. Was he fulfilling an order from on high? Or was it merely the meticulous nature of the man? Either way, it irked Birger to no end.

The second visitor was the "Old Man" himself, although only for a singular visit. "C" did almost all the speaking, a non-stop rambling discourse about the vagaries of war and its demands on the unsuspecting. Duty and sacrifice were his sacred themes, and he rammed then on as if he were a knight of old crashing in a fortress' gate.

"C" railed against Churchill, who by then had been sacked from his position as First Lord of the Admiralty. He spoke of the futility of the current government, in general. However, it was when Cumming began to compare Birger's injuries to his own that Birger became most resentful of his visit.

"No one knows how great your sacrifice really is, other than me, mind you, Alvorsen," he had said toward the end of their "talk", if one could really call it that, exactly. "Both of us have given so much more than could be expected in the service of our country, our empire. We have given our very mobility, now only to attain the rank of those of restricted ambulation. To others we are merely oddities, those who have been fired upon and came out less than whole. Spectacles, we are, to be viewed from afar and pitied from within. Well, damn it man, I will not be pitied! I will not be thought less capable than that which I am so confidently aware that I am. I have eschewed the wheelchair, Alvorsen, as you must. Work through the physical exercises, embrace your prosthetic, let every screaming nerve in the stump that was once your leg remind you that you are a living, feeling man, damn it. Do not give in to the black dog of depression as your father had, Alvorsen, for surely I best know that it is always lurking in the shadows. Be the man he expected you to be. Not his equal, but his better, lad. Follow my example, and remember, if I can not only survive my loss, but thrive in its wake, then you shall also. Do not forget, son, I would never ask anything of you that I have not endured myself! And not only have I lost a leg, but a legacy as well. For I have had forever taken from me my own son, mind you, a sacrifice I would never ask even of you."

"Yes, of course," answered Birger, as he then thanked the head of His Majesty's Secret Intelligence Service for the visit and the rousing words, but unfortunately he was tired and needed to rest.

The visit that Birger awaited the most never came to pass. Tulla would not come to the hospital at all, and on the third day, when Birger was advised a woman was waiting to see him, he allowed his hopes to soar. But as the woman entered the stark room, he was crestfallen when he recognized she was not Tulla at all, but the nanny, Cassandra.

She walked over to his bedside, and gently took his hand in hers. This was something he could not ever imagine Tulla doing. Although the two women resembled each other in appearance - both of moderate build and height, with blonde hair and blue eyes - they could not be any more different in demeanor. Tulla was self-centered, indifferent and wholly absorbed in the things she desired. Cassandra was caring and affectionate, and deeply felt the pain of others. Often she felt this to the point it afflicted her even more than those that bore its burden. And it was clear she was herself bearing Birger's loss. She was pure empathy.

Certainly that had been the case with the children. Tulla had birthed the twins, Gunnar and Einar. Yet she had no real interest in raising them. To her they were stones weighing down her flighty aspirations. Yet, when Cassandra came to their household, she could feel the pain of inattention in the unloved children, even though they themselves were too young to understand it. She cradled them to her bosom, instinctively and lovingly, to draw out their suffering.

"How are you, Mr. Alvorsen?" Cassandra asked. Her eyes were heavy, as if they had absorbed all that he must be feeling and thinking.

"They are taking excellent care of me here," he said, before blurting out, "but do not be offended when I tell you that I was hopeful my visitor would have been Tulla."

Her demeanor stiffened and registered the impact of his statement. She looked upon him in what he took to be pity

"So, no one has told you?" she asked. Her eyes lowered to look upon his hand in hers. She then caressed it tenderly with her other hand. "Mrs. Alvorsen is gone."

"Gone," he said, jerking his hand free from hers, "whatever do you mean? She's dead? My God."

He watched as her eyes became swollen with compassion. It appeared to him that the nanny Cassandra could no longer contain her emotions and she began to cry. Large tears like the first drops of a gale rolled onto her cheeks.

His pain had overwhelmed her sensitivity, he thought.

"I am so sorry. No, of course, she is not dead," Cassandra sobbed, as her tears fell from her cheeks onto his chest. "She left, voluntarily. She said that she could not take all that has been happening, most of all you now returning as …"

Cassandra stopped herself. She had let her emotions lead her words down a trail that ended only in an abrupt cliff.

"… a cripple?" Birger completed the nanny's sentence. "Yes, I can hear her saying exactly that. Come now, my girl, come now. Stop your crying. It was unfair for the others to leave you to tell me this pathetic news."

Birger raised himself in his bed, sending a searing jolt from what he was sure was his missing shin. Another phantom pain. To accompany his now phantom wife.

Birger pulled Cassandra close to him, wrapping his arms around her to console her. She continued to cry. He pulled her closer yet. So close that he could feel the shudders of her own torso on his. Her head then came to rest upon his chest. He could smell the scent of her, not of soaps or oils or any artificial fragrance, but of the natural freshness that infused her. Birger could taste the saltiness of her tears that continued to fall on him, even though not a single one had reached his lips. Birger realized that he had never had this intimate of a moment before. Certainly not with his own wife.

"Come now, my dear," Birger said in a soft tone, "don't let this affect you so. What of the children? Did Tulla take the boys with her?"

The mention of the children seemed to stabilize the nanny. She collected herself, but still rested her head upon his chest.

"No, of course not," Cassandra said, as if they both knew the answer before the question had ever been asked. "They are with nurse Abigail. The service sent her along just to free me to visit you. Tulla told me when she left to take good care of the boys. That I would always be more of a mother to them than she ever possibly could."

"Where did she go, Cassandra?" he asked.

"Into the night," she answered. "I swear it is all I can tell you. It is all I know."

"Into the night," he said again, needing it to come from his own lips. "That was always where she was most comfortable."

Cassandra came every day after that. Wincer Wells had already provided nurse Abigail to look after the twins each day for several hours to allow these visits. The very next day, Birger did not ask again about Tulla. He welcomed Cassandra, who then held his hand for the entire visit. Birger asked her about the twins, her favorite subject to discuss.

"How are the boys, Cassandra?" Birger inquired.

"Very healthy, Mr. Alvorsen," she said.

"Birger," he replied, "Call me Birger."

And she did. Thereafter, she would call him Birger. At least until the change came.

"Can you tell them apart easily?" he asked. "I am afraid I will not be able to. It scares me, being their own father."

"You will see, Birger," she answered, "that they have two very different personalities. It is amazing that after only two years, one can so easily see this. Gunnar is quiet and reflective, Einar is adventurous. They are like two sides of a coin, and they hate to be apart, even for only a few minutes. Quite the ruckus they'll raise, like they will never be made whole again."

"I can't wait to see them," Birger said, "but I am afraid as to what they will think of this…" he said, washing his free hand over where his leg had once been.

"They are only two years old," Cassandra said, "they will not notice. They love you, they will accept you as their father."

"Eventually, they will notice," he said, his thoughts off in the distance. "Eventually, they will ask. About me. About their mother. What will I tell them?"

Cassandra looked hurt at the phrasing of his last question. "What will we tell them?" she said. "I am certainly not leaving you with these children alone, Birger. I have invested too much of myself in them. They are a part of me. And whether their mother should return or not, I am staying on to care for them."

"After this injury," he said, "I am unsure if I will be able to pay you to stay on."

"You have already paid me a lifetime of wages," Cassandra said, "in the looks of love in those two children's eyes each and every day. I may not be as wise as King Solomon, but I am certainly already as rich as he ever was."

It was her nature, Birger thought, for this young woman to be more thankful for her blessings than desirous of her want.

"You are an incredible woman, Cassie," it was the first time that he had called her this. "I am so looking forward to coming home to you."

"As am I, Birger," she said, just then she brushed his hair with her fingers. "The twins need their father."

They talked and took comfort in each other's company. Birger, who had indeed wrestled internally with his path forward in life, then saw a glimpse of it.

At the same time, Birger felt incredibly guilty for having brought Tulla this far from her home, and to what end? To have his wife abandon not only him, but her own children, as well?

Later that afternoon, Wincer Wells dropped in for his precise sixty minute visit.

"Fancy a spot of company, chap?" he always began from the doorway.

Wincer would speak of the war, and the pathetic stalemate it had become. He spoke of trenches and machine guns, gas attacks and aerodromes, of courage and sacrifice. He would drone on for the entire hour, if Birger would allow him so.

"Where is she, Wincer?" Birger finally interjected.

"To whom are you referring, Alvorsen?" Wells answered.

"You know precisely of whom I am referring," Birger snapped, "Tulla! Where in blazes is she?"

"Are you quite sure you wish to know?" Wells replied. "She's become quite the odd duck, you know."

"She's always *been* quite the odd duck," said Birger. "You've got access to the entire Secret Service, including the domestic units. Where the blast is she? She could be anywhere in the country…"

"She could be anywhere in the world," Wincer corrected him, "because she pinched Cassandra's passport. Little good that will do her while the war is on, though. Like teats on a bull while all the international travel is verboten. But actually, we did find her just the other day."

"So you have been looking for her…" Birger said, realizing his thoughts were actually true.

"Let's just say that with your being inside the club," Wells explained, "that anytime a club member's wife takes a country stroll, the club fathers get a little nervous. She might be meeting a lover, who could blackmail her, after all. Or she might be working for the other side. So we keep close tabs on the club members' wives, for their good and our own. Especially when that member is away."

"Where is she, Wincer?"

"Of all places, Liverpool," he replied, "in a hell-hole down by the Albert Docks. Been there ever since the day after she was notified of your injury. Do you want me to tag Cassandra's passport?"

"No, not now," Birger said. "I'll give her some time, and then I'll take a train up and collect her. What is she doing?"

"You really don't want to know, Alvorsen," said Wells.

"How dare you tell me what I want?" snapped Birger. "I didn't want to go to Gallipoli, yet here I am. I didn't want to take up my father's role in your *club*, yet here I am. Now, what the devil is she doing?"

"Apparently, not what but who," Wells said, "as she is working in a dance hall. You surely can imagine all the tasks that entails."

"Damn it, Tulla," Birger muttered aloud. "I suppose it was my being wounded that set her off."

"Quite possibly, Alvorsen," Wells confided, "but that business with her friend Keithen MacDonald seemed to have been the tipping point."

"That bugger in Broughty Ferry? The one she would run off to into the night? What business are you referring to?"

"The Old Man had him picked up," Wells said. "Tossed his home. Put him in the clink on suspicion of being a spy for the Hun."

"When did this occur?" Birger asked.

"Whilst we were away on holiday, it would appear." Wells face flinched.

"Why didn't he tell me so?" asked Birger, "He rambled on about everything else. That bastard just wanted to have me out of the way for this."

"Entirely so, I am afraid," Wells confessed. "The Old Man will never talk shop out of the office. Not as I am now. Yet, I think you deserve to know."

"Was he…?" asked Birger.

"Was he what?" inquired Wells, not understanding.

"Was MacDonald working for the Huns? What kind of mess did Tulla get herself into?"

"Not to worry," consoled Wells. "She and you are both in the clear. That MacDonald chap was nothing more than an opium addict, it proved out. Just to be safe he'll be kept in confinement until the war's won. Tulla was notified by a telegram from a third member of their little den of iniquity. Thanks to her, we rounded up the sender of that telegram also."

"He suspected me?" Birger was incredulous. "The Old Man suspected me?"

"He suspects us all, Birger," deadpanned Wells. "You, me, the whole damned lot of us. It's his job to suspect everybody. He's agreed to allow Tulla to run free, so long as you attest she knows nothing."

"That little peg-legged ferret," said Birger in frustration.

"Pot calling the kettle black, that is. There is something else," added Wells. "The Old Man says it is time to have her, and you, change your names."

"What?" Birger screamed. "Is he totally blind to all I am going through?"

Birger was becoming increasingly exasperated. The blood had rushed to his face. He thought of Tulla, and the predicament she was in thanks only to his involvement in Wincer Wells and the Old Man's club.

Wincer looked closely at Birger, patiently waiting for him to compose himself. When the younger man refused to do so, Wincer Wells spoke plainly and without any hint of emotion.

"It's the war, I'm afraid," offered Wells. "Lots of this going on just now. Saint Petersburg was too German, so it's now Petrograd. Rumor has it even the Royal Monarchy's House of Saxe-Coburg and Gotha is considering changing its name. In any case, I am afraid that the names Birger and Tulla are just a little too Nordic for the Old Man's tastes."

"What on earth does that matter?" said the agitated Birger. "What are we to be called, then?"

"Well, we actually have a recommendation on that matter," Wells said.

"I was sure you would," answered Birger.

"Good tradecraft suggests it be something that feels familiar to you." Wells explained. "Then why not Brandon and Tilly instead of Birger and Tulla?"

"I will not be called Brandon," said Birger, "not in this life."

"Brigham?" suggested Wells.

"Brigand," stated Birger.

"That's not a name, it's a bloody highwayman."

"So am I not a thief?" asked Birger. "Did I not steal Tulla from her family. Do I not steal for the club?"

"I'll have to clear it with the Old Man," said Wells.

"Either it's Brigand or I will not agree, said Birger. "Brigand and Tilly Alvorsen, has a nice ring to it."

"Alvorsen also has to go, not British enough," Wells stated. "We suggest MacAlvor, with it being the Scottish equivalent."

"Brigand and Tilly MacAlvor, then" Birger said, satisfied. "Now I just have to get Tilly back from Liverpool."

"I can arrange to have her picked up for prostitution and delivered to your door," Wells offered.

"That will never work," Birger said, "It would only be all the more reason for her to find another place to which she could escape later. Let's leave her there where we can keep an eye on her. As soon as I can, I'll go up there and face her down."

———•·•———

It was only two days after this conversation that Birger Alvorsen, the soon-to-be Brigand MacAlvor returned to the house at the south end of the Blackfriars Bridge. There he was reunited with his two-year-old twin sons who were delighted to have him back.

The four of them, including Cassandra, stayed in this house for many months, as Birger completed his physical recovery and was later fitted for and became accustomed to the prosthetic limb.

Cassandra assisted him in every way possible. She continued to look after the children whom she had long ago come to love. She cared for Birger, also, and came to adore the man for how devoted he was to his sons. It was in her nature to care for others, even if they could never fully be her own.

She slowly added the role of replacement wife to that of adopted mother of the twins. She had soon mastered both. She would lovingly bathe all of them, as Birger required her assistance entering and exiting the tub. His infirmity first came as a shock to her, but soon even this subsided.

———•·•———

Slowly over time, Cassandra's respect for Birger morphed onto a deep love. She came to realize that crippled or not, he was the most complete man would ever know.

Several months after this, during the late fall of 1916, Birger took the train to Liverpool. He went to the address that Wells had provided him near the Albert Docks.

There he found Tulla working in a dance hall under the name of Cassandra Barrett. Birger spied on her from afar for two days, before he eventually got up the nerve to confront her on the sidewalk one day as she went out for a stroll.

"Hello, Tulla," he said in English, wanting instead to speak to her in the Norwegian tongue, but was afraid anyone overhearing them might report them as spies. It was an obsession in wartime England, and while he would, of course, have been cleared, it would only have tied him up for days, if not weeks.

"What are you doing here, Birger?" she asked, and then not waiting for an answer said, "I am not going back to Scotland with you."

"Then come back to London…"

"Nor to London," she said, "my God, how I hate that Blackfriars flat."

Her English had become better, but she still spoke with a heavy Norwegian accent. He knew the locals must be asking if she was German, and giving her slanted stares of suspicion.

"Your children miss you," he said, "come home for them, if no one else."

"My children? The twins you adore so much that you have to go off and play soldier and have your leg blown off? So, I am expected to come back and take care of them and you as well?"

"I miss you, Tulla," he said, softening his tone, "for God's sake, we are man and wife."

"Not in the eyes of this country," she said, an angry flame of denial threatening to set alight every memory they had. "You took me from my land and my family, so it is only just that I abandon you and yours."

"But what of the twins? Don't they mean anything to you?" Birger had decided to try to leverage any remnants of guilt within her.

"They have her," she said, "they have their Cassandra who wants nothing more than to lead the life that I am all too willing to discard."

Birger lowered his head. It had gone exactly as he feared it might. Then he decided to use his last available weapon.

"You realize they will have you arrested for impersonating Cassandra. They might lay a case for your being a spy, pretending to be the daughter of a British military officer. They will imprison you for sure."

"I would rather be trapped in their prison of terror than being imprisoned in your trap of perpetual boredom," Tulla spat at him in response. Then she lowered her voice and spoke in Norwegian to him. "You took my childhood from me. You took my home from me. You brought me to this dreadful place. You had the only man I ever truly loved arrested and imprisoned. And now you wish that I should place my future in your hands, these that only know how to strangle the life from me?"

"You loved him, Tulla?" he replied, shocked. "How possibly could you? Even so, I want you to know that I had nothing to do with Keithen MacDonald being arrested. You know I would never intentionally hurt you."

"You have already hurt me, Birger," she answered. "Yes, Keithen breathed life into me. He was a man I could find pleasure with. He gave me enjoyment of every sort. And you have in contrast only strangled the very breath itself from my soul. So, in return, I steal the soul of your precious Cassandra. What? You think I never noticed the way you looked at her? As she took your twins, your beloved Gunnar and Einar, to her bosom. If you wish to call out your British policemen and spies, so be it. I will not come with you. In fact, I wish to never see you again. I would rather to be sent to a British prison. Go ahead, make your life with her, and never give me another thought. I will survive, better far beyond any life I could have beside you."

—— • • ——

The next morning, Birger hobbled to the train station, catching the first train back to London. When he returned, he took a taxicab directly to the office of Wincer Wells at 2 Whitehall Court.

"You asked for the new portraits for our passports, Mr. Wells," Birger said tossing two packets of photographs he had drawn from his jacket's interior pocket. "I had these prepared to your directions. I would prefer for you to use these."

Wincer Wells picked up the packets marked "MacAlvor, Brigand" and "MacAlvor, Matilda". He shuffled the images between his forefinger and thumb.

A look of consternation came upon Wincer Wells' face. He looked up at Birger, soon to become Brigand, looked away briefly, and then re-engaged the man. The look on his face was stern and officious. The weight of his gaze indicated that a tremendous decision lie before them both.

"You are sure you want to do this?" Wells said to him. "It is like a bell, old chap. Once it is rung, It cannot be unrung, now can it?"

The passport photos in Wells' hand were splayed like a gambler's hand after having his bluff called. Except with nothing left to hide - these images were all facing upwards. They contained photo-portraits of Birger, but not of Tulla. Instead, the empty packet that read "MacAlvor, Matilda", the long form Christian name of Tilly, had contained photos of the nanny - Cassandra Barrett.

"Do it," Birger said in a clipped, stiffened voice. "Do it or I am out forever."

"And what of the other Miss Cassandra Barrett roaming the docks of Liverpool?" asked Wells.

"She is to lead her own life, wherever it may take her," Birger answered. "Let her keep Cassandra's name, passport, and identity."

"And the new Tilly MacAlvor," asked Wells, "she knows of this, I am to assume?"

Wells allowed the passport photographs of Birger and the nanny to gently drop from between his fingers onto the leather blotter of his desk.

Birger looked sternly into his eyes. "You wouldn't otherwise have reason to know, Mr. Wells, but I am here to tell you that all this was her bloody idea in the first place."

20 The Contentious Conference

"The greatest lesson in life is to know that even fools are right sometimes."

Winston Spencer Churchill

They sat loosely scattered around the massive glass table in the conference room of the London offices of *Sterling Investigations International*. Their reflections, those of Diane, Sophie, Emory, Flake and Erin Anne, danced off its sparkling reflective surface, yet still transparent enough to see the chrome frame below which supported it. The artistic trail of suspended LED track lighting which serpentined above their heads completed the effect of what was modern London office decor.

It was a Saturday afternoon. Everyone was in the most casual of attire. Emory was in jeans and Liverpool Football Club jersey. He was not a fan of the organization *per se*, he just liked the look of its Cormorant logo, as well as the layout of the design which bore the phrase, *"You'll Never Walk Alone."*

Sophie wore a casual knitted dress, Diane slacks and a stunning sweater, and Flake Ferris an old school combination of a plaid sports coat over a black polo shirt and jeans.

Diane began the proceedings by stating, "So, Flake has informed me that he thinks he has cracked our case wide open. He thinks he understands now why the other two agencies hired by Jake Conley never got to the truth. He began telling me his theory of the mystery woman with Miss Anna Barrett at the restaurant and what he believes to be her critical relationship to this case. I have heard the recording for myself. Still, I called you all here because I'd like your thoughts before we make a collective decision as to how to proceed."

Flake rose from his seat to stand next to the screen, then fidgeted with his glasses, before he pressed the hand-held remote to reveal a title screen, "***The Identity of Cassandra Barrett***".

Diane then interrupted him even before he began. "Flake, can you begin by briefing the team on the insights from the dinner conversation between Miss Anna Barrett and her companion? I think that might be helpful."

"Surely, Diane," Flake said, "Well to start, Emory and I sat next to their table and from what we could hear, we learned very little," he said, "just that her companion repeatedly referred to Miss Anna as her aunt,"

Emory suddenly cut Flake off, "And that sweet, little old '*Aunt Anna*' is a apparently a bit of a homophobe."

Emory's homophobe comment seemed to catch the room by surprise. He was referring to Miss Anna Barrett suggesting she was disgusted with the thought of Flake and himself being lovers. The shock to the room was in the way he had so forcefully presented this, so much that it seemed an affront of its own. Emory noticed the strange looks on his colleague's faces, but decided not to apologize for his outburst. He thought it was humorous, but clearly no one else thought so.

"Well, thank you Emory," Flake said after a few seconds, "for that most insensitive interruption. I will say though that after Erin Anne forwarded the recorded file to me, there were some rather insightful moments between Miss Barrett and her niece."

"Such as what exactly?" prompted Sophie.

"Well, first off, the niece offered up a toast to Miss Barrett's father Ian, saying that if it weren't for him they wouldn't be dining together that night at all. I assumed she meant because according to our fiction, if not for Ian Barrett there would be no reason for her aunt to come to possess her unexpected windfall. But it was what Miss Anna Barrett said in response that really caught my attention."

"And what was that, Mr. Ferris?" asked Sophie.

"Miss Barrett said to her niece, '*We might as well toast that dodgy Cassandra Barrett too, for if not for her you wouldn't even be here to enjoy this delicious meal. And I'd have no good reason for a few nights stay in lovely Edinburgh.*' This was followed by a heavy pause, and I assumed a nasty glare from her niece, who then said, '*Come now, Auntie, I told you we are not to talk about that subject, especially in public.*' So there you have it. The niece has basically laid it out bare."

"Have what, exactly?" Sophie asked. "Laid what out bare, Flake? Who is this niece and how does she fit into this whole situation?"

"Well, Sophie," Flake responded, "I'll answer both questions in a second, but first allow me to recap our case file for the team." Flake then cleared his throat nervously as he advanced to the first chart that read:

Cassandra Barrett (1896-2000), Age 104

- Records confirm Natural Birth in 1896 (London)
- Daughter of Royal Army Warfare Officer (London)
- Sibling: Older Brother Ian, Naval Officer WWII
- Out of Wedlock Stillbirth, 1913 at age 17 (London)
- Family Relocates to Edinburgh, Scotland 1914
- Departed Liverpool, Crossed on *Mauritania* 1919
- Cassandra took up residence in New York in 1919
- Arrested in Speakeasy Raids (2) in 1920
- Married Lucas Conley from Colleyville, Texas (1922)
- Sole Issue: Client Jacob Barrett Conley (b. 1933)

"This is what we have been assuming all along to be factually known about our client's mother," said Ferris.

"What does '*Sole Issue*' mean?" asked Erin Anne, not understanding the verbiage.

"Only child," answered Flake. "That's just the strange term we genealogists use for 'only child'. Now, for the real problem." Ferris twitched his thumb and the next slide appeared:

The Cassandra Conundrum

- Jacob Conley's DNA tested as 50% Norwegian
- Client's other genes matches paternal Conley family DNA
- Therefore, Client's Nordic DNA must be from his Mother
- Client is 0% Match to Tested Barrett Family DNA
- Anna Barrett (Cassandra's Niece) tested 0% Norwegian
- Anna Barrett DNA exhibits full lineage of Barrett Family

"*Therein lies the rub*, as the great bard once penned," said Flake, "if Anna Barrett had the expected Barrett DNA, then you can assume her father did as well. If he did, then so should his sister, Cassandra. So how could Cassandra's son, Jake, not have it as well?"

There was dead quiet. Not only could you have heard a pin drop, you could have counted how many times it bounced.

"There is only one answer," said Flake, breaking his own dramatic pause. "The woman we know as Jake's Mom, our Cassandra Barrett, could not actually have been the real Cassandra Barrett."

"Of course she was," argued Emory, "we have all the records. Who else could she be?"

"Emory, you are the one who put this thought in my head in the first place," Flake responded. "As for who Jake's Mom really was, the answer is that she could be anyone. For the purposes of explaining my theory, I will refer to her as *Madame X* from this point forward. You see, my theory is that somewhere between the stillbirth in 1913 and the transatlantic sailing in 1919, *Madame X* stole Cassandra Barrett's identity."

The ungodly quiet of the room had returned and was pierced by an audible, but delayed gasp that came from Sophie. Diane held up her palms. "I'll remind everyone that this is nothing more than a working theory, and that Flake's proposed *Madame X* doesn't mean such a woman actually exists."

"OK, Flake," Emory said next, "we all get it. *Madame X*. With the X as in crisscross."

"I had really intended a crossover," Flake replied, "of one life laid over the other, but crisscross works just fine."

"Sounds like the plot of a bad made for TV movie, if you ask me," Emory scoffed. *"Switched at Birth: The Case of the Missing Daughter of the Sámi."*

"Keep in mind," Flake said to the room, "Miss Anna's comment at dinner, *'We might as well toast that dodgy Cassandra Barrett, for if not for her you wouldn't even be here to enjoy this delicious meal.'* First of all, why would she refer to Cassandra as *'dodgy'*? Second, why would Cassandra Barrett have anything to do with Miss Anna's niece even being born?"

"Who is this niece?" asked Sophie for the second time.

"Excellent question," Flake Ferris replied. "That is precisely why, I have asked our ever-vigilant Erin Anne to join us today. She has been tracking this very mysterious woman who dined with Miss Anna Barrett. I personally believe that woman , the niece, to be the missing link to understanding exactly who our *Madame X* was. She is the answer to this entire question. So at this point, I will turn the next portion of this presentation over to Erin Anne."

The watcher Erin Anne then stood, unaccustomed to the environment of the conference room as she was far more comfortable in the shadows of the street. Her dress was accommodating of the latter - blue jeans, jack boots, and a black leather jacket. She spoke tentatively at first, with her Belfast accent stabbing through her words like the weapon one might assume she was concealing.

"Fairst oof all, allow me to say," she began, *"Ah have no slides to shoo yah, so if it is what yah fancy, you will be a wee-bit disappointed. Also, what Ah am aboot to share with you is the resoolt oof not oonly mah efforts, but those of mah partner, Mr. Winslow Fleming, as well. He is still in Scootland keeping tabs on our mystery woman, as Mr. Ferris has come to call her. Perhaps, Ah can take the mystery away from her, lift the veil, so to speak, such that all of yah might come to understand her."*

Her accent was so heavy that everyone seemed to perk up in their seats as they concentrated to understand her.

"So, this is the woman that Flake and I, sat next to, along with Anna Barrett, at the dinner in the Witchery that night?" asked Emory in a voice that was far friendlier than the tone with which he had accosted Flake.

Erin Anne then turned to Emory, and before answering, drew in a deep breath. It was as if a child might take one last sip of a sweet drink before taking the castor oil.

"Aye, it is she," said Erin Anne with a confidence that slowly began to overcome her nervousness. *"We, that being Winnie and ah, have been shadooing her for the past several days. This is what we have fund oot, soo far. The subject's name is Mattie MacAlvor and she lives beachfront in Dundee's area known as Broughty Ferry in a two-story cottage home facing the doons and the Firth of Tay estuary just beyond."*

"I know that name MacAlvor from somewhere," Diane said in a side comment, "but I just can't seem to place from where." Diane had been overworked on this case and her wits had been worn down as a result. She would soon enough be forcefully reminded of where she had heard it.

"Sure, listen. Ms. MacAlvor's current age is forty-five years," continued Erin Anne, ignoring the disruption. *"She appears in excellent health, despite her smoking like a chimney pot. She lives alone as best we can tell. She does noot appear to work, yet has a loovly lifestyle, quite comfootable actually. And we know that she has a full one quarter of Norwegian DNA."*

Another gasp from Sophie echoed through the room.

"Just exactly how do we know this?" asked Diane. The snap of her tone seemed to underlie a pending disapproval of Erin Anne's investigative method.

"*Ah am afraid Ah may have violated protocol, somewhat,*" said Erin Anne. "*Ah followed her to an ootdoor cafe one day in Dundee. Protocol states we are to watch and noot interact with her. When Ah saw she was alone, having a wee quiet smoke and an ale, Ah decided to take the table next to her and order a sandwich and a bag of tayto.*"

"Bag of tayto?" asked Sophie, not understanding.

"*Soorry, it's me Irish getting between us. Crisps, dear,*" answered Erin Anne.

"Potato chips," said Emory, interpreting on her behalf, but drawing an unwanted sideways glance from Erin Anne.

"So now, you are known to her," asked Diane, "at least visually?"

"*Aye,*" confessed Erin Anne, "*indeed, now Ah am of limited use in trailing her, that is for sure.*"

"Why would you take such a risk?" Diane asked. "Why make yourself known to her?"

A mischievous smile erupted on Erin Anne's beautiful young face. "*So Ah could get me hands on her loovly butt,*" she said, intending to shock the audience again. The intent hit home, with a nervous murmur coming from around the conference room table.

"Her *cigarette* butt," interjected a nervously laughing Flake Ferris, "from which we were able to extract our mystery woman's DNA. Erin Anne gave herself up such that she could carefully take it from the ashtray after the target left the cafe. Only by Erin Anne's doing this could we ever know the woman's heritage. And this niece, Mattie MacAlvor, our mystery woman tested out as one-quarter Nordic, just as Erin Anne had said."

"You think this may be the woman with whom Cassandra traded identities?" asked Sophie.

"Good heavens, no," replied Flake, "this Mattie is only forty-five years old. Besides, if our *Madame X* were still alive today she would likely be setting a life longevity record. We'd be calling her Madame Methuselah, not *Madame X*. However, I do believe that Ms. Mattie MacAlvor is a descendant of the woman whose identity *Madame X stole.*"

"You mean Cassandra Barrett?" Diane asked.

"I mean the woman who used to be Cassandra Barrett," replied Flake, "before our *Madame X* stole that name and identity from her. Now, I would like to have Erin Anne finish with what we know of Ms. Mattie MacAlvor."

Erin Anne, cleared her throat, then continued to present.

"We doo knoo that she was the oonly daughter of Matthew MacAlvor, a real estate speculator in the Dundee area. He wasn't a millionaire, by any means, but he was proominent enough. However, when the market went arseways on him, he was forced to sell the family land hooldings along the Tay shoorline for the development of a row of townhomes where his daughter still lives today. Matthew and his wife gave birth to Mattie in 1975. Unfortunately, his wife died from complications from Mattie's birth. Matthew MacAlvor passed away in 2005 from suicide, a single gunshot to the head, at the grand young age of sixty-five."

"And what exactly was Matthew MacAlvor's lineage?" asked Diane.

"He was the son of a man named Brigand MacAlvor and his wife Matilda. He was bairn to them in December, 1940. Their marriage certificate states they were married in late 1916. Strange thing is we can noot find bairth records for either of them. It is as if they booth came oot of bloody nowhere."

"Could they both have come from overseas to England?" asked Sophie.

"The wedding license states they were both citizens of the UK," replied Ferris. "If they had come from abroad it would have read *naturalized citizens*. Why we cannot find the birth records remains a mystery."

At that point, Flake Ferris looked to Diane. Her face appeared leery.

"So, to recap," said Diane, "we have three generations of MacAlvor's heritage that is Nordic, and also a client with Nordic DNA. So, what exactly is your theory, Flake?"

Flake said nothing, only darting his eyes toward Erin Anne who was still standing before them.

"Oh yes," Diane said, "thank you Erin A,nne for that recitation of the facts, and especially for your taking the initiative regarding the DNA sample. As well, thanks for all that you and Mr. Fleming are doing for us in the field."

"Aye, Ma'am" she said as she moved to her seat, drawing another quick sharp glance from Diane.

"Nobody told her, I'm afraid," said Flake to Diane. He then said to Erin Anne, "Diane dislikes being called *'Ma'am'*. I am sorry, we should have warned you."

"Flake," said Diane, clearly disturbed at his apologizing for her, "let's get on with this. What is your theory, already?"

"Here it is," Flake began. "The two women, Cassandra Barrett and *Madame X* traded identities some time before 1916 when we know that Matilda and Brigand MacAlvor married. This fits my earlier timeline between 1913 and 1919. Somewhere within the new span between 1913 and 1916, the woman who had been *Madame X* became Cassandra Barrett. And the real Cassandra Barrett became Matilda MacAlvor."

"And your *Madame X* just happens to be a pure blooded Nordic type who has a little *Sámi* swimming amongst her gene pool?" asked Emory sarcastically.

"It would explain our situation, wouldn't it?" responded Flake. "Open your mind to that possibility, my young friend."

"So you propose that this switch took place," Emory asked, "after the *non-existent* twins that we are chasing were born."

"Emory, let's keep this respectful, please," interjected Diane. "Go on, Flake."

"So, my theory is that our client's mother was actually born as the woman we call *Madame X*. Before *Madame X* came to America, she gave birth to a pair of twins. At some point her life crossed paths with a second woman who we know, in fact, born as Cassandra Barrett. Exactly when their lives intersected we do not know, nor for how long. My theory is *Madame X* took Cassandra's name before she came to America, married Lucas and gave birth to Jake. She died in the year 2000. However, we really don't know when or where *Madame X* was born. She could very likely have been born in Norway."

"Very interesting," said Sophie, before Flake continued. "On the other hand, the child born as Cassandra Barrett in London had to go on to become someone else. We know that she was born in 1896, that is true. But now recall Miss Anna Barrett's comment, *'If it wasn't for that dodgy Cassandra Barrett, you would not be here to enjoy this meal.'* She wasn't speaking of the real Cassandra, but of our *Madame X* who had impersonated her in America."

"How exactly would that account for the niece even being there?" Diane pulled at Flake's logic thread.

"Diane," added Flake Ferris, "if my theory stands, then Anna Barrett would indeed be the aunt of Mattie MacAlvor. Since we now have the DNA of both women, we know with great genetic certainty that they are indeed closely related. This came out clearly from the comparison of the two DNA results."

"I thought you said Anna Barrett had no Nordic DNA, and Mattie MacAlvor was one quarter Nordic," blared the frustrated Diane. "How can they possibly be related?"

"They are related because they both show the same Barrett family DNA," said Flake, "in Mattie's case in the non-Nordic portion of her genes."

"When, exactly, did you intend to share that fact with us?" asked Diane. She was growing increasingly tired as it appeared Flake was taking the longest possible route to tell his theory. "So does the Norwegian DNA in both Mattie MacAlvor and Jake Conley's samples match, Flake?"

"No, they do not," he said simply. "Why would they? They are not biologically related."

"Now you are really hurting my head, Flake" Diane said.

"Look, Diane," he replied, "if my theory says anything, it is that *Madame X* must be the mother of the missing twins."

"If they even ever existed," added Emory snidely.

"The real Cassandra Barrett would have had no Norwegian DNA herself, just like Miss Anna," said Flake, ignoring Emory's taunt.

"Then where did Ms. Mattie MacAlvor get her Norwegian DNA?"

"From the man her grandmother married, Brigand MacAlvor. The generational traces says he would have been 100% Nordic. But, just like his granddaughter Mattie, he has no *Sámi* traces. Only our Madame X carried those markers."

"And the twins?" Diane asked. "Would they have had those *Sámi* traces?"

"Yes, just like our client Jake," Ferris said, "except even their Norwegian DNA would have been 100%, not just 50% like Jake."

"Why so pure?" asked Diane.

"Because I believe the twins not only existed, but that they were the offspring of our *Madame X* and Brigand MacAlvor. Then for whatever reason, she then took Cassandra's name, went to America and Brigand married the real Cassandra who became his wife, Matilda."

"So you are suggesting, then," followed Sophie aloud, "that the woman who had been born *Madame X* and Brigand MacAlvor were both 100% Norwegian?"

"Exactly," beamed Flake. "And that Miss Anna's niece Mattie MacAlvor's quarter DNA came from her grandfather Brigand. It all fits."

"And where are the twins when this exchange of personalities took place?" Sophie asked, following the next step of logic. "They were already born, but who were they with?"

"Well, Sophie," answered Ferris, "for this theory to hold water, and for Jake's mother's rantings to be true, they would have had to been born by our *Madame X*, before she left for America in 1919. We have the ship *Mauretania's* manifest and passenger lists. It records Cassandra Barrett, who was really our *Madame X*, traveling alone. No records exist of any twins, children or adults on that ship at all. I am suggesting she left them behind in England."

"But with whom?" snapped Diane.

"Wait a minute," Emory interrupted, "you are wanting us to believe that this woman who became our client's mother, that she had the twins, *if there ever even were any*, in England ..."

"Possibly Scotland," interjected Ferris.

"... and abandoned them to go to America to work in a speakeasy. Seems far fetched to me. What woman would up and abandon her two sons to satisfy her own desires."

"It has been known to occur," said Sophie, in a quiet, understated voice. "During the war, there were many cases of women abandoning their children only to try and escape to save themselves. I cannot condone it, but my family still tells such stories. One does not know how one will act when they feel trapped and their very survival is at risk."

"Come on, Soph," said Emory, "that was World War II in Poland. We are discussing a period during or just after World War I in England, or maybe Scotland, where there was no direct combat to speak of. Why would a mother abandon a set of twins in these conditions?"

"Perhaps she felt trapped for other reasons," said Sophie.

"Does the timing even fit the twins being in World War II?" Diane asked.

"If they were birthed between 1910-1915," replied Flake, "they would have been somewhere between 24 and 29 years old at the start of WWII."

"So you believe," said Emory, "your *Madame X* from Norway came to Scotland sometime before 1916, married Brigand MacAlvor, had twins, divorced him, and then went to America and married Jake's dad in 1922."

"Essentially, yes," Ferris replied, "she certainly married Lucas in 1922. I am suggesting before that, Brigand married or at least impregnated our *Madame X*, fathering the twins."

"Did you find the marriage license for this alleged first wife, or anything else to back this up?" interrogated Emory.

"No," answered Flake.

"Any divorce records from this first wife, Flake?"

"No."

"And you looked really hard for both, didn't you?" Emory pressed.

"Yes. Yes, I did," admitted the increasingly angry Flake. "It doesn't mean they didn't *shack-up* at some point."

"So much for the usefulness of your genealogy profession," snarled Emory, "resorting to having two people *shacked up* to explain why we can't find any *real* facts."

The friction between Emory and Flake had become a distraction to the rest of the team. Diane had enough, and decided she would later take Emory aside to explain that while she appreciated his playing the role of a devil's advocate, he was still expected to treat any presenter with a modicum of respect in their meetings.

Diane had to admit to herself that the idea of two people changing identities sounded quite unlikely, but did indeed provide the only viable answers to every question raised by this case's situation. She thought on it a moment longer, and could see where stealing another's identity was much easier to do back in the day before personal vital records were computerized and cross-referenced. Yet, still there was much more data needed to back up Flake's theory. Otherwise it sounded only, as Emory had already said, like an overused plot line for a bad television series.

"OK," Diane said, "so the fatal flaw in all this is as I see it is that we have no record of either Brigand or Matilda MacAlvor existing before they married in 1916."

"I agree," said Flake sheepishly. "That I cannot explain."

"So, we will keep exploring this as a concept," continued Diane, "but I am not very confident that we are on to something. This appears to answer our little dilemma regarding the DNA tests, but it feels like we're building a house of cards."

Emory made a childish face at Flake, as if to say, *See, I told ya!*

"Nonetheless," said Diane, "let's keep pushing to see if there is anything else to be learned about the MacAlvor family. Certainly, let's keep looking for other alternative explanations. Let's not all run down the same blind alley. Flake, is there anything else we can derive from the DNA tests run to date."

"Not unless we had samples from the twins themselves or Jake's mom, directly," interjected Emory.

"I said 'Flake', not you, Emory," Diane snapped. "You and I need to talk later, Mister, about your disruptions in these conferences. This is going to stop." Flake smirked at Emory as having had the last laugh. "So then, Flake, anything else to be gleaned from testing?"

"Not really," he said, "everything Emory said is correct. Jake is the offspring of Lucas and *Madame X,* who they knew as Cassandra Barrett. Mattie was the granddaughter of Brigand and Matilda, the real Cassandra. If Brigand had fathered the twins with Jake's Mom, whatever her name might have been at the time, then we would need the DNA of the twins themselves to prove that."

"What else can we do to prove or disprove your theory," Diane asked Flake.

"Nothing, really, short of coming up with more DNA samples from Jake's Mom or the twins themselves. I personally think it is time we directed our questions to Miss Mattie MacAlvor up in Dundee," said Flake, in a last desperate attempt to gain the information needed to confirm his hypothesis. "If there is a family secret being kept in all this, it's likely she will know it. It is likely to be the very secret that she and her Aunt Anna Barrett appear to have been sharing for many years now. Remember her saying, *'Come now, Auntie, I told you we are not to talk about that subject, especially in public.'* Miss Mattie may likely be wanting to get it off her chest. We all know how secret's can become a weight of their own."

"I'll consider it, Flake," answered Diane, "but at this point I feel I need something else to more firmly tie Ms. MacAlvor to our case."

"What harm is there in approaching her?" asked the desperate Flake Ferris. "I could be up there tomorrow with Erin Anne and we would at least know what there is to be known."

"I said I will consider your request, Mr. Ferris," barked Diane. Her brisk response, with the unusually formal "Mr. Ferris" suggested Diane was not apt to favor his request.

With that rebuke, the meeting came to an abrupt conclusion. As the room cleared, Emory instantly gravitated over to Erin Anne.

"Erin, can I have a moment with you, please?" he asked.

She looked hard at him, as if he had somewhat run afoul of her. Even given this, Emory persisted. He complimented her on her presentation and her fieldwork. He had been for some time enamored with the young woman, but not in a professional way. He felt she had sensed his interest in her all along.

"I think your astute observations are the key to our solving this case. Perhaps we could share a meal together tonight to discuss your thoughts on Flake's presentation. I know some great restaurants nearby. I would love to hear what you think of Mattie MacAlvor and her grandmother Matilda. It might help me focus my deductions. You see, Erin, sometimes, just having another's insights can spring forth my deepest intuitions - those I might not even consciously realize that I am thinking."

Erin Anne measured him in her mind, so to speak. Then she unloaded. *"Fairst off, laddie, let me shere a wee family story with yah. When I leaned back on a chair mah daddy used too say that a carpenter went ta great lengths to put four legs on it, so please use them all. Well, Mr. Hauptmann, mah mother went to great lengths to name me Erin Anne, so please use both names. Yah want to know what I think of the MacAlvor lass? I already told you. I thought her butt to be quite lovely."*

"The cig-cigarette butt?" stammered Emory,

"So, suddenly yah processes of deduction are a wee bit slow, now are they?" she mocked him. *"Exactly what thoughts are yah havin' that yah didn't even know oof?"*

"You, ahh, you are attracted to Miss MacAlvor?" Emory said, more than asked, as he tried to figure out her meaning.

"Doon't be daft," Erin Anne said, *"Ah merely said the wooman had a nice bum. But, in case your deductive instincts are running slower than those of Sherlock Holmes, let me tell you bluntly that Ah am strongly attracted to other women, Mista' Emory. So don't waste your time and your precious intuitions on me. Now, if you are done acting the maggot..."*

"Sure, sure," said Emory, "sorry to have troubled you..."

———•••———

"*Oh, it's no trooble t'all, mah little man,*" she added, emphasizing the word *little*. Then, as she walked away from him, she murmured under her breath but loud enough for Emory to hear, "*Soo, who's the bloody hoomophobe, now?*"

Diane had headed back to her office, where her assistant was awaiting her with an urgent message. She handed Diane a note bearing Malcolm Devereaux's phone number and a request to ring him straightaway, which she did.

"Malcolm," she said into the handset, "it's Diane. I am returning your call."

"Diane, darling," Devereaux said with enthusiasm. "I just wanted you to know that I was able to dig up that file on those twins you were hunting."

"The twins?" she replied. "Which file exactly are you referring to?"

"Well, remember, the MI6 chaps we discussed with the Norwegian background. I am sending the declassified files to you via courier."

Diane was slow to grasp his meaning. *Which files?*

"I am a little confused, Malcolm. Of course, I remember that, but you said there were no twins that you showed up in your research…"

"Well, darling," Malcolm said, "what I had told you, precisely, was that I'd found a pair of twins, but only one of them had been deployed to Norway. However, once one begins mining the past one never knows what veins of truth one will turn up."

"What exactly did you unearth, Malcolm?"

"You'll be surprised to learn that I came across the damnedest thing in reviewing this," explained Devereaux. "These were the very files that Wincer Wells was caught modifying when he was drummed from the service in late 1945."

"Well, that's interesting," said Diane. "We spoke of Wincer Wells. He was the one you said kept one of the twins sequestered in Scotland during the war."

"That's just it, Diane," Devereaux said, "he didn't. He should have, but he did not. One of the twins couldn't pass the mountaineering tests, couldn't properly negotiate the terrain. Wells doctored his file so he could deploy along with his brother.

Wells got caught trying to clean up both the twins' files after the war and was drummed out of SIS for it."

"How on earth did you ever uncover this, Malcolm?"

"I followed the thread," Devereaux replied, "of the twin Einar through the files, who I initially thought was the only brother to deploy. I came across some referenced notes added after the war warning that these files may have been corrupted by our old friend Wincer Wells."

"That's pretty irregular, isn't it?" Diane asked.

"Exactly what I thought. It turned out old Wincer was trying to hide the fact that Einar had indeed been paired with his brother Gunnar while working for MI6 at the beginning of the war. Both of them were sent together to reconnoitre the Ofoten Railway out of Narvik."

"Why would Wells have risked his career to hide this fact?" asked Diane.

"Because Wells," Devereaux explained, "was the very chap who foolishly forged the documents which signed off on sending Gunnar to Norway along with his brother. He must have thought he could go in after the fact and make everything look pristine. Wells got caught cleaning up the files. Cost him his career and pension."

"Still, Malcolm, that's a hell of a lot to lose..." Diane said before she asked. "...The war was over, wasn't it?"

"Read the file, darling. Everything will be clear, trust me," answered Devereaux.

"Just so I am not kept in total suspense until the files come over, save me from having to go back to my notes. Who exactly were these twins?"

"The MacAlvor twins, of course," he replied, "Einar and Gunnar MacAlvor. Don't you remember? We discussed them when we met alongside the Thames."

"My God!" Diane exclaimed. She was shocked. *That was where I had heard the MacAlvor name,* she thought, *from Malcolm Devereaux, during our meeting at SIS Headquarters on the Thames.*

Figure 13: American Airmen Merian Cooper and Cedric Fauntleroy, the Founders of the Original Kościuszko Squadron of the Polish-Soviet War (1919-1920) and the Restored Memorial in Lviv, Ukraine

21 The Pivotal Year

1920

"Difficulties mastered are opportunities won."

Winston Spencer Churchill

After his confrontation with Tulla in Liverpool, Birger felt a guilt as great as any he had up to that point in his life. He had shamed her, and in the shadow of that shame, he had taken her away from her family and her home. If only he had never succumbed to her youthful energy, that manic frenzy that overpowered his better instincts in that amber illumination that passed for a summer's nightfall on the rocky hillside overlooking Skrova and the seas of the *Vestfjorden*. If anything were to happen to her he would never forgive himself.

Yet, that confrontation near the Albert Docks of Liverpool, he was ashamed to say, lifted his burden of guilt somehow. Tulla clearly wanted nothing more than to be free of him and the twin boys they had created together. She implicitly gave her blessing to have him raise the boys, knowing he would be alongside the nanny Cassandra. All she wanted in return was Cassandra's name, and the freedom to start her life anew.

After that encounter, Birger knew that he had tried his best to have his Nordic wife return to him. She rebuffed his every entreaty. His new guilt was that perhaps, just perhaps, he had wished for her to refuse to return to him. He was free from her deep depressions, from her unspeakable indifference towards their own twin boys and from her unpredictable mood swings that were less like a clock's pendulum and more like the constant resetting of a guillotine's blade after its severing descent. Just like Tulla, Birger had a new start awaiting his own life. Under a new name, with a new mate, who would lovingly look after not only himself even with his newly limited capabilities, but also who would nurture the children as Tulla never possibly could.

So, upon Birger's return to London, with the full blessing of the Old Man himself, Wincer Wells would arrange for two transformations to secretly take place. The Nordic wife who had been Tulla was now allowed to become Cassandra Barrett. She was sent a formal request for a review from the passport office. The only finding, as directed by Wells himself, was that her photo needed to be updated. A new passport was granted to her, and it bore the image of Tulla as well as the name of Cassandra Barrett. Thus, her young life was wiped clean of all past sins of the young Nordic bride and mother, Tulla Alvorsen.

From another chrysalis broke free not one but two beautifully transformed new lives. Its silk was spun by His Majesty's Secret Intelligence Service and cocooned around the forms of Birger Alvorsen and the English-born Cassandra Barrett. When the shroud of the transformation was broken loose, there emerged the new Scottish couple of Brigand MacAlvor and Matilda "Tilly" MacAlvor.

For the next decade and more, Brigand and Tilly split their time between London and Dundee as required by Brigand's continued SIS duties. These consisted mostly of translation of Norwegian documents through the rest of the First World War. Every so often there was talk of his resuming travel to Norway. While these assignments did not come to pass during the conflict, much to the chagrin of Brigand himself, they prepared him for just such a service should it be needed later. His ship, *the Nordlys*, was modified to ease his return to sailing.

Of course, the service supplied him with sure-footed assistants who could man the decks and rigging, as the one-legged captain could no perform these duties. This became a running joke between himself and the SIS supplied crew of three. They would affectionately refer to Brigand as Captain Ahab, and would ask just when they might expect to set off in search of the great white whale.

That joke became a salve to Brigand's war wounds. His spirits lifted each time he was upon *the Nordlys*, even if only for training sailings down the Thames to the estuary at Southend-on-Sea. Deep in his heart he knew that he would never serve the Crown by returning to Norway nor anywhere else under sail on the behalf of the SIS. Even though he was physically strapped in a custom-made pivoting wooden chair affixed to the ship's deck, Brigand loved to be at the helm once more. There was freedom being on the open sea and the promise of its endless waters.

After the war, by early 1920, Brigand, Tilly and the twins - Gunnar and Einar - found themselves living a life of domestic tranquility, mostly in Dundee, beachfront upon the River Tay. *The Nordlys* was docked nearby, just on the other side of the Broughty Castle. The boys were raised addressing Tilly as "Ma'am", which soon enough naturally transitioned to "Mum". For surely she had been the only mother these boys would ever remember, as the nanny had raised them both nearly from birth. From the time that Gunnar and Einar were to turn three she was the only maternal figure in their life.

Tilly loved the boys and she loved to look after their father as well. When she had first come into the family's service, she often would feel sympathy for this man, subjected to his young Nordic wife's mercurial temperament. Their volatile arguments always ended with him conceding to his wife's demands.

All but once. Birger had demanded they keep a Norwegian household. It was his way of keeping his father's ways, of honoring the man. In their home Norwegian was the primary tongue. This outraged Tulla, as she had rejected everything Nordic.

Once Tulla learned the English language, she refused to even speak in Norwegian, or would only when she could not express her frustrations and anger in English.

As this came to pass, Tilly realized just how important the Nordic heritage had become to Brigand. She had specialized in languages in preparatory school, so she applied herself in learning Norwegian. At first she had learned from Tulla in exchange for teaching her English. That was until the young mother had abandoned her twins. After that Tilly learned to speak it from the lips of her new husband, Brigand.

Even with her linguistic capabilities, learning Norwegian proved very slow going. But when she re-started her life as Brigand's wife, Tilly insisted on speaking only Norwegian in front of the children, as had always been Brigand's desire. Thus, the boys were raised from the age of three with Norwegian spoken in the household, albeit a somewhat corrupted version of the language due to Tilly's limited exposure to it beyond the walls of her own household. It had proven to be extremely difficult, but Tilly mastered the tongue. It was the best gift she could have ever have given her new husband. Later still, this gift of language would prove to be a curse cast upon their sons.

Tilly knew she had to also teach the twins English so that they could attend school in Scotland. She taught the children the alphabet and the basics of English by reading to them. Her favorite material to read to them was from one of the few books she had brought along with her - The Complete Shakespeare. The twins were raised on near ritualistic bedtime recanting of Macbeth, Hamlet and all the other classics.

Gunnar and Einar indeed grew up speaking both Norwegian and English. While this pleased their father to no end, it also caught the attention of one Wincer Wells.

━━━ ·•·· ━━━

It was Wincer Wells who visited Brigand and Tilly MacAlvor in mid-1920 at their Dundee home to inform Brigand that his former wife Tulla had travelled to America in late 1919 using the passport of Cassandra Barrett. Earlier that year, Tulla had taken a job as a cleaning woman aboard a steamer that regularly worked the route between Liverpool and Southampton.

"It appears," said Wells, "that she had the full intention of making passage to America as soon as regular liner services commenced again after the conflict was over. Tulla (Wells thought it better not to refer to her as Cassandra, lest he should evoke a response from Mrs. MacAlvor) apparently had salted away rather enough of the monies she had earned in her, *err*, well let us be kind and say '*vocation*'. Let's just leave it there."

Wells shot a slackened glance at Tilly, his face then involuntarily and spastically twitched.

"It appears her only desire all along was to make passage to New York, come hell or high water, as the Americans like to say. When she failed in getting a service position on a transatlantic liner, she booked steerage passage to New York."

"Whatever will she do there?" asked Tilly. "How will she earn her keep?"

"Yes, well," Wincer stalled, "it is abundantly clear from her time on the Albert Docks in Liverpool that this young woman is eminently resourceful. I should think those skills will serve her well in the depravity that is New York."

"And we are just hearing this now?" seethed Brigand. "Man of your word, are you?"

"I promised you that we would keep tabs on her, Brigand," replied Wells, "and so we have. Did we lose her in Southhampton? Most certainly. Did we ferret about for days on end to rediscover her trail? Yes, and we have. Tulla is living in New York City, as she had apparently always intended. Yet I doubt even she expected to find herself in its Bowery, a section that I must say is not noted for its grandeur."

"How lovely," replied Tilly, "a harlot roams the back alleys and seediest byways of the largest city in America bearing my name."

Tilly MacAlvor looked down in a depressive manner. Her husband reached over to take her hands in his.

"Bearing your *former* name, darling," corrected Brigand. "You must let her go. After all, we have the twins, don't we? Isn't that what we really wished for?"

"Your husband is entirely correct, Ma'am" Wells said, "for you must fully take up the mantle of this new persona that we have thrust upon you. You must release yourself from your former existence entirely, for that is a life you no longer possess. No longer your lot in life, you see. You are Matilda MacAlvor, and as far as His Majesty's Government is concerned, you always have been, my dear. Cassandra Barrett has departed our isle, perchance forever. I think it will be easiest for your conscience if you can fully grasp that you no longer have either any ties nor affinities to that name. Total release, that's the ticket. It truly is the only path forward, Tilly."

Brigand waited for a second, before comforting his wife. "I know this must be difficult for you, darling, but a name is but a name. And after all, *'What's in a name? That which we call a rose, By any other name would smell as sweet...'* to quote your revered William Shakespeare."

Small wonders never cease, Tilly thought, *my new husband is quoting the bard to me.*

"Yes, of course," she then demurred, "I know I am being nothing more than a spoiled child. But for all one's life to be so invested in a name, from such a grand family, no less, only to watch it being soiled and besotted..."

"As it turns out, our Tulla," Wells said, intentionally interrupting Tilly's melancholy mood, "has found employment in New York's garment district. She had found work there along with many other immigrant seamstresses."

"Well, now," said Brigand, "that's wonderful."

"That woman could not sew a stitch," snapped Tilly. "Couldn't sew a seed in a garden. Whatever she is doing there, for whomever, is not a wholesome undertaking, I assure you."

Tilly was correct. It would not be until Wincer Wells returned next, nearly some six months later, on Boxing Day, no less, that he updated Brigand and Tilly that Tulla, as Cassandra Barrett, had been arrested in a New York speakeasy.

"What on earth is that?" Tilly asked of Wells.

"Since the puritanical Americans have outlawed alcohol in all its forms, a speakeasy is, in a sense, an illegal enterprise in which one may escape to in order to get pissed," he explained.

"Wincer, language, please," objected Brigand. "My wife does not need to be subjected to such coarseness."

"Apologies, Ma'am," flicked Wells.

"Accepted, but in no way required," said Tilly, "for despite my husband's objection I am not entirely a prude. Tell me, Mr. Wells, was *Cassandra* working in the establishment or just imbibing there when she was arrested?"

"Perhaps a chance of both," Wells replied. "She did not work at that point for the facility directly, but our contacts there have come to believe that she was escorting a gentleman for the evening, if you might come to understand me, Ma'am."

"Oh, I see!" replied Tilly. "What charges were brought?"

"Only illegal consumption of an alcoholic beverage, I am afraid," said Wells, his face once more flinching in a spasm. "Yet, this was not to last for long, for she soon turned up in another arrest following a raid on a second speakeasy. The effect of which was that she lost her job in the garment district."

"How unfortunate," Tilly said, "so, she's destitute?"

"Not at all, for soon enough she found herself employed as a hostess in one of New York City's most frequented speakeasies. It appears she had taken quite naturally to this lifestyle, and has become somewhat of a favorite of the crime bosses in the city. As we said, she's proven quite adaptable."

"Delightful," said Tilly of the woman bearing her former name. "How convenient - a woman of no morals set loose in a land of no values. She takes to it like a stray goose amongst a gaggle of ganders. Yet, all in all, I suppose I am to be relieved that she recognized that she could never be the mother that these boys would need. For what mother labors a child, or in this case two, to birth, only to later abandon their children, unprotected and defenseless?"

22 The 1920 Polish-Soviet War

Historical Reference

*"The war of the giants has ended;
the quarrels of the pygmies have begun."*

Winston Spencer Churchill

Indeed, what parents labor so strenuously to bring birth to a child, only to abandon the infant to the wild wolves of the surrounding and darkened forest? Who lays bare a child of even two years old to defend itself from the rabid predators of the world?

The answer is those remaining members of the victorious Allies of the Triple Entente of the Great War. The Tsar's Russia was forever gone by 1920, torn away from history by the ruthless manipulations and bloodthirsty cravings of the Bolsheviks. The loss of Tsarist Russia left only the Allied victors of Britain, France and the United States. The child that was so strenuously delivered only to be later forsaken to the wolfish, predatory Bolsheviks was the country of Poland that had only two years prior re-emerged from the Great War.

Poland had been partitioned, criminally, mind you, in the last third of the eighteenth century. First, in 1772, Russia, Austria and Prussia feasted on her borderlands. It appeared for some time that there the abuse would end, but when Poland adopted a Constitution on the third of May in 1791, Russia and Prussia would then again exert themselves militarily against the country. This time, however, it was not merely its borderlands that were pilfered. It was the very heart of Poland that was consumed two years later in 1793. For what action of the Polish people was this crime committed against them? Merely for the desire to govern what was left of their own country.

What was left after the Second Partition was not itself sustainable. When Tadeusz Kościuszko announced his uprising against Russia in 1794 to reclaim the lands taken in the first two partitions, the Poles were once more militarily overpowered. In 1795, the remaining Polish Commonwealth was wholly consumed by the vultures that were the empires of Russia, Austria and Prussia. Poland had been picked clean by these ravenous carnivores and her bones were ground to meal and scattered to the winds of time itself.

Then something quite interesting occurred. The Polish people, now without a country of their own, fastidiously collected that dust ground from their commonwealth's bones and savored it. This meal, so rich in the marrow of their heritage, they would use to culture the broth on which they would nourish their children over the next 123 years. The Polish heritage, its language, and the essence of its people, lived on despite all the punitive efforts of the partitioning empires to completely eliminate it.

In actions that predated the words of Winston Churchill himself, they would simply *never, never, never* give up their language, their culture, nor their heritage.

In their hearts and homes, the people who had once been Poles remained so, no matter how risky it was to do so. For the heart is the great incubator of those things most precious and lost. In these hearts, for over a century, Poland would live on, not under a flag, but under a pennant of remembrance. Not under a cannon's flare, but under the steadfast fire of reverence. Not under the orb and scepter of a monarch, but under the will and staff of a God they could never deny. In them, a hunger grew to once more rule themselves, and after many failed rebellions and many lives lost, their rebirth would rise like a Phoenix from the ashes of the Great War.

Poland was reborn on the eleventh hour, of the eleventh day of the eleventh month of 1918. Thanks to American President Woodrow Wilson's thirteenth of his famous "*Fourteen Points*", an independent Poland was re-established. The Second Republic of Poland was cradled in the fallow, desolate fields of World War I's Eastern front, where Germany fought against Russia, and Poles from both empires were forced to take the lives of their former countrymen. Families were ravaged, and as in America's Civil War, there had even cases where brothers had been forced to fight against each other on opposing sides.

The scorched earth of the new republic still smoldered. Poland's people had been decimated, with its croplands turned to killing fields drenched in blood. Food was not only scarce but wholly unavailable. Starvation was rampant. Famine cast the reaper's shadow across the country. If not for future American President Herbert Hoover's Food Relief Program, all might have been lost even before it had been re-found. Yet, the Polish People persisted. Nowhere in Poland was the country more ravaged by war than in its Eastern lands, those on the border with Bolshevik Russia.

The treaty ending the Great War defined in detail Poland's new Western border. It was the Eastern borders with Russia, especially those of the lands of Ukraine that were left ambiguous. Poland wished to re-establish the pre-1772 Commonwealth border, and pressed militarily eastward to Kiev in early 1920 facing little resistance. This move was seen by the radical Russian Bolsheviks as a threat to their territory, and the Soviet-Polish War was soon underway. It was described by Winston Churchill to then Prime Minister David Lloyd George as follows: *"The war of the giants has ended; the quarrels of the pygmies have begun."*

Poland was seen as being a world and a half away from both Washington, DC and London in the global terms of 1920. The two-year-old second republic found itself abandoned by both capitals, and up in arms against the newly named and imposing "Red Army".

The war of 1920 between the Bolsheviks of Russia (it would not formally become the Soviet Union until 1922) and the Poles was seen as nothing more to Vladimir Lenin than a stepping stone on the path to spreading Communism militarily first to Poland, then Germany, and westward to the rest of Europe.

Lenin's intent was to do this by overpowering military force, which he assumed would then ignite rebellions in the working classes of those countries, and foment violent uprisings. First, however, the Red Army under Commissar Leon Trotsky had to fight its way through Poland.

Thankfully, two exceptions to Poland's international neglect arose. First was the American aid to the Poles via Herbert Hoover's food relief program. The second came from an individual inspired through his participation in that very program.

During a food relief mission in early 1919 to the besieged Eastern Polish town of Lwów, an American World War I pilot named Merian C. Cooper was impressed by the resilience and fortitude of the Poles besieged within that city by rioting ethnic Ukrainians. Airman Cooper had long been raised on stories of the valor and bravery of the Poles, as his Great-Great-Grandfather, John Cooper, had not only trained under Casimir Pulaski, but rode alongside the Pole during the American War of Independence. During the Charge of Savannah, Pulaski had been mortally wounded by the grapeshot volleys of British cannons. John Cooper took the wounded Pole to the USS Wasp, where he died. John Cooper lived to tell his children and grandchildren stories of Pulaski's heroic bravery, fighting for freedom in a country other than his own.

His descendant Merian C. Cooper had indeed seen the bravery of these people first hand at Lwów. Upon returning to Paris, he and another pilot, Major Cedric Fauntleroy devised a plan to organize a cadre of American airmen who would fly in the service of the Polish Army.

Cooper and Fauntleroy organized this squadron, and in August of 1919, they were hosted to a sendoff dinner at the Parisian Ritz Hotel by none other than Polish Prime Minister Ignacy Paderewski, the world famous pianist.

They later arrived by train in Warsaw, where they established the Original Kościuszko Squadron, composed of American airmen flying the country's primitive Fokker Albatross biplanes in defense of the Polish Army. The squadron was named after Pulaski's compatriot, Tadeusz Kościuszko, who like his countryman had fought for freedom and liberty in both Poland and America.

As an aside, it is here where Britain began to show her true colors in regard to the revived Polish nation. At the peace conference ending World War I, British Prime Minister David Lloyd George was heard to have remarked in a reference to Paderewski representing Poland, "What is one to make of a country that sends a pianist to represent them at a peace conference?"

As the year 1920 progressed, Vladimir Ilyich Lenin ordered a counteroffensive of overwhelming force to be sent against Poland. Two thrusts of the Red Army were unleashed on Poland. The first in response to Poland's push to Kiev was led by none other than Joseph Stalin.

Stalin was accompanied by the Cossack General Semyon Mikhailovich Budyonny who was in charge of the Red Army's highly valued cavalry. The second Red Army thrust was led by General Mikhail Tukhachevsky, only 27 years old at the time, who was famous for having said repeatedly, "Onward to Germany over the corpse of Poland."

Both thrusts of the Red Army were successful. Stalin and Budyonny drove the Poles not only out of Kiev, but also out of the Ukrainian lands altogether. They drove westward back to Lwów. Tukhachevsky drove westward directly towards the capital of Warsaw. By early August, it appeared that the Bolshevik victory over Poland was all but secured. The Red Army was at the gates of the capital, just east of the Vistula.

The Bolsheviks offered punishing terms for surrender, none of which were acceptable to the Poles. The Polish Head of State, its military commander, was General Józef Piłsudski. Ironically, Piłsudski had once been an anarchist on the streets of Saint Petersburg, fighting alongside Vladimir Lenin's own brother Sasha. Sasha was later executed for participating in a plot to assassinate Tsar Alexander III.

Piłsudski went on to a career in the Austrian Army, achieving the rank of colonel. When World War I ended and Poland was re-established as an independent nation, he accepted the country's military command. In March of 1920, Piłsudski was named the First Marshal of Poland. By August 1920, the Polish people faced annihilation at the hands of the Bolsheviks.

Once again, the British Prime Minister David Lloyd George weighed in on the situation. Regarding the impending attack on Warsaw, on the tenth of August, Lloyd George wrote, "If Poland does not accept the Soviet conditions, the Allies will not interfere." It was clear that Piłsudski and the Polish people were on their own once again.

What happened a mere five days later is known thereafter as the "Miracle at the Vistula". For it was recorded that the Poles, facing imminent destruction at the hands of the Bolsheviks, not only prayed to their country's Queen and Protectress, the Blessed Virgin Mary, but also reportedly brought the revered image of the Black Madonna of Częstochowa from the *Jasna Gora Monastery* to the front lines of the oncoming attack alongside the Vistula River in Warsaw.

If there was any divine intercession, then it was effected through the person of none other than Joseph Stalin.

Lenin had ordered Stalin to release troops from his army at Lwów to move north to aide in the attack on Warsaw. Stalin had refused, acting as if he had not received Lenin's order. Even Budyonny's Cossack cavalry was held in reserve by Stalin.

On the fifteenth of August, without reserves from Stalin, the young Red General Tukhachevsky pressed in on Warsaw. The Poles by this time had the Kościuszko Squadron (and its later companion Pulaski squadron) in the skies over the front, which gave Piłsudski eyes on the Bolshevik troop movements.

Piłsudski also had another secret weapon. Poland had not only listened in on Russian radio exchanges, but had developed the capability to decipher the simplistic codes in which they were encrypted. Like the Brits during The Great War with Whitehall's fabled Room 40 focused on breaking enemy codes, Poland had a dedicated, albeit small, codebreaking function. It was imperative for the survival of this resuscitated, fledgling country to listen in on its belligerent Russian neighbors to the east, as well as to the fearsome German State to the west.

Given the information from the broken Russian radio intercepts, which could then be confirmed by aerial reconnaissance of the American air squadrons, Marshal Piłsudski knew that indeed no reserve troops were on the move and a huge gap existed between Tukhachevsky's troops in the north and Stalin's troops in the south. Józef Piłsudski then mustered every available Polish soldier within the city of Warsaw, effectively leaving the capital undefended, and slipped this makeshift army through the Bolshevik gap. The Poles then enjoined with other Polish forces brought north from the River Wieprz, who together then encircled Tukhachevsky's troops.

The Poles attacked the Bolsheviks from the rear from the east. The Russians were caught up between the attacking poles and against the Vistula in the west. The Russians attempted a counterattack, but they were routed and their troops crumbled to a chaotic retreat.

The Bolsheviks managed to re-form and re-engage the Poles further east at the Niemen River, the once traditional border of the two countries, but to no avail. The Poles defeated the Bolsheviks on the Niemen, as they had on the Vistula. In fact, the Poles had prevailed against overwhelming odds thanks to Marshal Piłsudski's decisive action. In doing so, the Poles may well have saved Western Europe from the Red Army's forced spread of Communism.

Nearly two weeks later, Stalin did release General Budyonny and his Cossack calvary. However, given Józef Piłsudski's situational awareness thanks to his intercepted military messages and the airborne squadrons, the Poles were able to release their cavalry to intercept the Cossack's forces near the town of Zamość. What resulted came to be known as the Battle of Komarów, or the Zamość Ring, and took place from September 29 to October 2. It was the last great cavalry battle of the twentieth century, with the Poles not only defeating, but decimating the Russian Cossack forces.

The events at Warsaw are known forever in Poland as the *Miracle at the Vistula*. It is of interest to note that every airman of the Kościuszko and Pulaski squadrons were awarded Poland's highest military honor, *the Virtuti Militari*.

Merian C. Cooper had to wait to receive his honor, as he was shot down and spent time in a Russian Prisoner-of-War camp under an assumed name. The Russians had a generous bounty allotted for his capture or killing. He later escaped and made his way to Riga, Latvia, where he was later rescued.

After the war, Cooper returned to America, where he wrote and published the story of his exploits as the book "Things Men Die For" in 1927. He would even go on to a career in the world of American cinema. He earned a star on the Hollywood Walk of Fame for his producer contributions to RKO Studios, including a blockbuster he created in 1933 entitled "King Kong". Yet, in Poland, he will always be remembered as the co-founder of the American Kościuszko Squadron.

Another man came to recognition for his leadership of the Fifth Polish Army during this war in 1920. He was instrumental in the victories known as the Miracle at the Vistula, The Zamość Ring, and the battles at the Niemen River. This freshly minted Brigadier General was named Władysław Sikorski, and he would go on to lead the forces of the Polish Government-in-Exile during World War Two.

At the same time, in the small town of Zakopane in the mountainous south of Poland, on the second day of October 1920, just as the Zamość Ring closed on the Russians, an infant son was born to a poor but proud family. His name was Bogdan Bratajewski. Having been raised on the stories of bravery and daring of the Kościuszko Squadron, Bogdan would grow dreaming of no other calling in life than to become a pilot fighting the enemies of his country.

__Figure 14: Broughty Ferry Castle and the View From Its Tower__

23 The Rough Wooing

"All the great things are simple,
and many can be expressed in a single word:
freedom, justice, honour, duty, mercy, hope."

Winston Spencer Churchill

Diane had decided this was an assignment that she could not possibly ask anyone but herself to undertake. She waited in that afternoon's "golden hour", just before dusk, leaning against the massive stone walls of the Broughty Castle. She was swallowed in the long blowback shadows of the rampart wall, which for centuries had held back the earthworks behind her. She stood just where the castle complex's outer lawn edged down to the sand of the beachfront of the River Tay. Its cold wet spray pelted her. That was typical for the area - brisk air blowing in from the river estuary on a breeze that was more penetrating than refreshing.

Diane knew she was where she needed to be, at the time that her target, Ms. Mattie MacAlvor would be expected. The watchers, Erin Anne and Winslow Fleming, had marked the woman's precise routine of walking with her dog, Thor, a full blooded Siberian Husky. After weeks of surveilling Mattie, the watchers knew the route and time that she would take Thor out for their daily walk.

There was little they did not know about Mattie MacAlvor by then. Mattie was forty-five years old. Like her grandmother, her full first name was Matilda. It was a name they had not yet learned that the younger Ms. MacAlvor desperately despised. She thought it was so boringly old fashioned, and became enraged whenever someone would joking reference the tune *"Waltzing Matilda"*.

So instead, she went by Mattie, which she liked because she considered it an honor to share her father's name. She was the daughter of a real estate developer named MacAlvor. Mattie had never known her mother, as her mum had died from a cervical hemorrhage just after giving birth to her. The closest thing to a mother's love that she'd ever had was the care of her grandmother, the first Matilda MacAlvor. Mattie had also never known her grandfather, Brigand, who had died before her father was even born. Her "Grandmama Tilly" had always been the matriarch whose compassion and affection allowed her to survive the family's darkest days.

Mattie had lived in the very house that had once been her father's, on the land that once had been that of her grandparents. She lived alone, yet never seemed to mind doing so. She was quite independent, as noted in the watchers' notes.

Her father had been successful, most notably from selling the family's land holdings, among the last to be developed along the river. His success made them affluent, but not to the point that would have left Mattie independently wealthy. Certainly the inheritance from her father had left her comfortably off, enough to do without a job for some time. It had been fifteen years since his death. Mattie continued to live modestly, free from the worry of work, but what neither the watchers nor Diane knew was that her savings were on the wane.

Her parents and grandparents were buried only a few blocks away on a family plot in the cemetery of a local church. Mattie MacAlvor visited the graves weekly, obsessing over them as one might the tombs of a lost child. When her mother died just after she entered the world, her father, then only thirty-five years old, was beset by a massive depression that he would fight for the rest of his life. He eventually was consumed by his despondency, taking his own life when Mattie was but twenty years old. She was unfortunately left to have been raised by a man who could only mourn the ghost of her mother. Luckily for her, she was effectively raised in the care of her "Grandmama Tilly".

Diane was assured that Mattie and Thor's route would be true, unless an unexpected driving rain arose. That day it did not. The sun's angled rays brought a heavenly radiance to the land outside of the shadows in which she hid. Diane first saw her along the beach. More accurately, Diane recognized the Husky whose name was Thor from the many reconnaissance photos.

True to form, they had left Mattie's house, crossed the lane and into the windswept, grassy dunes that separated the beaches of the Tay from the Esplanade. Through those grasses Thor would meander, taking in every scent available, always toward the castle at the end of the lane. They would then track through the wet sandy beach, until they had passed the building that served as the administrative office for the castle museum. Behind it and before the castle's walls, the outer castle green flowed down to the beach. There each day, Thor would all but drag Mattie upward, encircle the castle upon its green and eventually take its master out onto the breakwater wall. There, at the end of the breakwater jetty was Thor's delight - a modern interpretation of the classic sundial. One that held an unending profusion of canine residues and scents, to which Thor would always, unfailingly, lift his leg and add his own.

It was at that stretch where the castle lawn met the sands of the beach that Diane waited. It was here that she had planned to engage Mattie MacAlvor.

"Oh my," Diane exclaimed from the shadow of the castle's wall, "what a beautiful dog! Such blue eyes! What's her name? May I pet her?"

The exclamations caught Mattie a little bit by surprise. Not quite shock, but she was a little startled by the unexpected voice that seemed to come from nowhere. It had been Diane's intention to catch the woman off guard, but not to startle her outright. She decided the best way to soften her approach was to fuss profusely over the full blooded Siberian Husky.

Diane emerged from the shadows to walk up slowly to the animal, allowing it to sniff her hand, from which she had removed her glove. Thor's tail wagged slowly. Diane knew Thor was a male, but intentionally referred to the husky as "she" in an effort to disarm Mattie.

"Certainly," Mattie answered, having collected herself, "but Thor is quite the male I'm afraid. But don't be alarmed, as he is very affectionate, I assure you."

"You are so lucky," Diane said, "to have such a lovely pet. Whatever possessed you to get a full-bred Husky?"

The woman looked at Diane with a hesitant eye. The stranger was kneeling over Thor, rubbing her hands though its thick black, gray and white tufted coat. Mattie was on guard, but decided against her initial instinct not to answer this unknown woman's question.

"My family has had Huskies for generations. *Thor* is the son of *Odin*, and before *Odin* there was *Ymir*."

"Well, you must be Nordic," Diane said, smiling broadly, "with those names. Wasn't *Ymir* the mythical creature at the beginning of the universe, that *Odin* slew, to become the high god of *Asgaard*? And *Thor* was his son, right?"

"Something like that," Mattie said. After a pause, she added, "As I said, it is a family tradition. You're American, aren't you?"

Diane looked up at her with a broad smile.

"Yes, I am, as a matter of fact. My name is Diane," she said, rising from Thor and extending her hand, "Diane Sterling."

"Imagine that," Mattie said, effecting to dialogue with her pet, "Americans quoting Norse Mythology. We don't see that every day, now do we, Thor? In fact, we don't get many Yanks coming through Dundee, with or without the legends of *Asgaard*. Certainly not any longer. It used to be the occasional carload lost on their way to take divots out of Saint Andrews or Carnoustie, but since the mobile phones all now have direction finding apps, not even that. Could it be that you are lost, my dear?"

Diane looked at the woman, her smile then burst into a broad but telling smile.

"No, Mattie," Diane said, calling her by her name, intending to catch her off guard, "I am certainly not lost."

"How do you know my name, Madame?" Mattie reacted, stepping backward away from Diane as she failed in attempting to pull back on Thor as well. "Who are you? Why do you look so familiar to me?"

Diane drew a business card from the pocket of her slicker. She presented it to Mattie MacAlvor with a respectful level of professionalism. It read "Diane Sterling, *Sterling Investigations International, Ltd,* New York, London, Berlin."

"Forgive me for lying in wait for you, Ms. MacAlvor," Diane said, "but it seems so much easier to start a discussion with someone when there isn't a door to be shut in my face. You might find my face familiar from my court cases against the CIA and your country's MI6 a few years back. It was all over the news."

Diane watched Mattie's face, and could see her slowly recollecting Diane's story. This seemed to ease the tension stored in the woman's tortured brow. The tension that had been there dissolved away and a smile warmly creased her softening face.

"Well, stone the crows!" said Mattie. "You're '*The Huntress*', you are! What, it's been several years back, hasn't it, now? You took on Her Majesty's Secret Intelligence Service and won. I remember following that on the telly. Anyone who comes up roses against them buggers and their lot has my full admiration. After what they've done to my family. Where did you ever find the motivation to take them on, if you don't mind me asking?"

"It generally helps when they try to kill you," said Diane with a laugh.

"No, darling," said Mattie, "that's just it. Do you know how many people they kill and get away with it? Never a word is said, not a dicky bird. No, my dear, you are somewhat of a hero in my book, you are."

Thor was by then strenuously pulling Mattie along the castle green, like the member of a team of sled dogs that he was bred to be.

"Do you mind if I walk with you and Thor?"

"Better than that, after we're through, come back to my flat and I'll put a kettle on. Imagine, Diane *the Huntress* searching for me. *Oh, Gordon Bennett!* Am I ever stunned. What brings *the Huntress* to Broughty Ferry?"

Having worked in London for so many years, Diane was familiar with the British exclamation *"Oh, Gordon Bennett!"* as being one of great surprise. It was English through and through, Diane thought, not Scottish at all. In fact so were *"Stone the crows"* and *"Not a dicky bird."* Diane wondered if she had picked these idioms up from her English Grandmama Tilly as a child. Diane also detected no Scottish burr to speak of in her speech, just the flatter and precise cadence of the English. It appeared that Ms. Mattie MacAlvor, despite living in Broughty Ferry since birth, was clutching onto her Barrett family lineage.

Diane walked with Mattie MacAlvor and Thor around Broughty Castle and out onto the wide smooth surface of the breakwater. Diane explained that they were "researching" some genealogy which had led them to her family. They paused at the sundial as Thor sniffed its upright dorsal fin-like triangular blade.

Then, as if after a thoughtful analysis had been completed, Thor raised his leg to add his own scent to overpower the rest. His mission then completed, the three of them, Mattie, Diane and Thor, walked leisurely back along the breakwater towards the castle.

"Funny how time humbles all things, isn't it, Diane?" said Mattie, "For example, this castle has been here since 1495 and in 1547 was a major battle site with the English in *the War of Rough Wooing*. Now its just a destination for my Husky to piddle about on. I won't come out here when it gets wet, lest it might be slick or icy. I'm afraid Thor will pull me straight off into the river. Oh my, does he hate it when we don't venture out. I'm afraid it makes him as mad as the dickens."

When Mattie said this, Diane saw in her eyes a recognition of seemingly unrelated events as being connected.

"Hold on a minute, Diane," said Mattie, "a few weeks back we met that couple of American men in the Witchery. The cute one was talking to my Aunt Anna about Dickens. They were your people, were they not?"

Diane knew better than to try and lie her way out. She seemed to have struck up a connection with Mattie, and lying would only risk all that.

"Yes, I am afraid it was," she said, "and in reality, they really are not a couple, they were just posing to be."

"Well, thank God," said Mattie, "for that old man to be with such a young lad was about all Aunt Anna could focus on. So, you used my Aunt to lead you to me?"

By that point they had cleared the castle and were walking along the lane that was the Esplanade, parallel to the river once more.

"Yes. The *'little Polish girl'* that visited your Aunt in London works for me also. You see, our client's mother was Cassandra Barrett, your Great-Aunt's Aunt. We have been secured to determine if she was truly Norwegian, as she claimed later in life, or perhaps her words were only the ramblings of a woman suffering from dementia. Your Aunt gave us a DNA sample, which suggests she herself was not Nordic. But her Aunt Cassandra's son, our client, tested to be half-Norwegian, meaning Cassandra must have been 100% Nordic. We were hoping you might help us understand these incongruent facts."

Diane intentionally used the term, little Polish girl, as it was what her "Aunt Anna" had repeatedly used on the tape to describe Sophie.

"I am surprised that you would trick an old woman like my Aunt Anna into giving away her DNA. All that folly about a Polish Institute, what-not, and giving it the name of their Piast dynasty of kings, no less. Then to send your lads about eavesdropping on our dinner conversation. Why not just explain it all to her like you are doing to me, dear? No need to be so cheeky, is there?"

"I am sorry, Ms. MacAlvor," Diane said. "I truly am. It was not necessary, I see that now. How, may I ask, is it that you would even be aware of the Polish Piast line of kings? Also, I would like to ask why you call Miss Barrett 'your Aunt'? Your names and lineage might suggest that you both are unrelated." Diane left out the fact that Mattie's DNA had proven otherwise.

"You'll find I have come to respect the Poles, and have studied their history a bit," Mattie offered, "it was something my Grandmama often spoke of. Come in, Diane, dear. I'll brew us a cup and explain all of it to your heart's content. All that and so much more. If, for the love of all that is good, you'll agree to call me just 'Mattie', as you first did."

"Agreed, Mattie," said Diane as they prepared to enter into her home.

It was then that Mattie turned to look upon the Firth of Tay as the sun settled behind the castle. A breeze rustled the grasses and cattails along the riverside into a gentle sway. The light of the setting sun cast tawny hues of ecru and rye that washed over the scene like a sepia-toned treatment of a photograph. Mattie then uttered the words, "Oh my, will you just look at how lovely that is. Absolutely grand."

"You're very fortunate indeed to live in such a magnificent setting!" Diane added.

"Indeed I am, Diane," Mattie responded. "My grandfather Brigand once owned all this land here along the river, and my father sold it such that this bloody row of townhomes could be built. At least he was smart enough to get the prime townhouse to keep as his own as part of the sale."

As they turned to enter Mattie's home, Diane thought, but did not say, *I know, Mattie. If only you knew how I know.*

They entered through a vestibule with a second door, which then opened into a very lovely sitting room. Mattie swept her hand at the small sofa and chair which were positioned such that they faced the window whose view was looking out upon the Firth of Tay.

"Take a comfortable perch, love," said Mattie, "I'll put the kettle on. Then, I have to fetch something to show you. You'll fancy seeing this item very dearly, of that I am quite sure."

Figure 15: Józef Piłsudski and Władysław Sikorski

24 While Everyone Slept

Historical Reference - The 1920s

"If we open a quarrel between the past and the present, we shall find that we have lost the future."

Winston Spencer Churchill

The repugnant aftertaste of death from the battlefields of the Great War, *"The War To End All Wars,"* lingered for the most part of the next decade. The great aggressor state of Germany was not only stripped of its war-fighting capabilities, but was laden with onerous reparations that crippled its economy. The Weimar Republic that was established in Germany soon came under the crushing yoke of hyper-inflation, with the Deutsche Mark becoming essentially valueless. The entire population of Germany suffered, and as a result chaos ensued. Soon enough, opportunists arose to take advantage of the disorder. The Communist Workers' Movement stoked the blaze of disorder from the left, while fascists would soon enough rise from the right to sinisterly sculpt their own versions of brutal order by way of black-shirted thugs roaming the streets.

It was in this crucible of chaos that a veteran of the Great War arose, sent by his own government to spy upon the socialists. Adolf Hitler would soon discover his own penchant for evoking emotions that would reach the darkest chambers of the hearts of the oppressed. This corporal of the Great War would rise to overthrow the dishonor of World War I for Germany, only to have his country supplant it with an even greater stigma.

In 1923, a year that would become critical for so many reasons, Adolf Hitler would stage his first great offensive launched from a Munich beer hall. The march of he and his fascist Nationalist Socialist Party followers to forcibly overthrow the government was known as *The Beer Hall Putsch.*

During the *Beer Hall Putsch,* Hitler was supported by the Nazi leader Ernst Röhm and 2,000 of his paramilitary *Sturmabteilung, or SA,* Brownshirt thugs. The march was cut off by the authorities and degraded into a melee in which four policemen and sixteen Nazis were killed. The Putsch would fail miserably and send Hitler to prison. Once there, he would codify his tenants of hatred in the book entitled *"Mein Kampf"*, or *"My Struggle"* which would be published in 1925.

It was that very imprisonment that would elevate Hitler to the first steps of an ascendency to take over Germany. First as Chancellor in 1933, and a year later when he was empowered as the country's supreme dictator. It was, ironically, his time behind bars in the 1920s that fully set free the hatred in the heart of Adolf Hitler. This hatred would be coupled with Hitler's knowledge gained from the failed *putsch* that he had within his own personality the addictive allure to other Germans who wallowed in economic and cultural despair. Hitler claimed that he would lead them on to a place of respectability within the world, returning Germany to its rightful standing among all nations. His combination of charisma and hatred would soon release the world's vilest plague while England and the rest of the world slept.

Europe would not only sleep during the 1920s, but it would become lost in dreams of delusion. Having defeated the Kaiser and the other Central Axis Powers, the remaining European Allies of the Triple Entente assumed the world to be a much safer place. France and Britain, no longer fearing the Hun, and wishing to save the vast expenditures of defense, soon voluntarily disarmed themselves.

Also in that critical year of 1923, in the neighboring state of Poland, Marshal Józef Piłsudski, who had been the ruling authority since Poland re-emerged in 1918, retired from politics. Despite having led the Poles for six years, in 1922, the recently elected National Democrats removed Piłsudski from his position as head of state. Piłsudski's retirement was not long lived. In May of 1926, under the same cloud of hyper-inflation that had affected Germany by then also enveloped Poland, Piłsudski led a militarily backed *coup d'état*. He would go on to serve as Prime Minister for the next two years, but more importantly, Marshal Józef Piłsudski would wield near absolute power as the Polish Minister of War until his death in 1935.

It is important to our story to note that not every military officer in Poland welcomed Piłsudski's strong-handed power grab. General Władysław Sikorski, who had served under Piłsudski during the Miracle on the Vistula in 1920 and afterwards, refused to commit the troops under his command to participate with the Piłsudski coup. Even though he had previously been one of Piłsudski's favorite general officers, Sikorski soon found himself relieved of command and marginalized within Polish society. For a brief period, he ran the opposition party to Piłsudski. He would, in the end, spend most of his time in France. This would later prove a tremendous blessing for Poland.

Also by 1923, the head of MI6, Sir Mansfield Cumming was thinking of retirement. He had been knighted by King George V in the quadrangle of Buckingham Palace in 1919 at the age of sixty. Cumming had also been awarded France's Legion of Honor, and was one of the last recipients of the Romanov's Order of Saint Stanislaus among many other recognitions for his services. But the "Chief" suffered from angina, and had grown weary of the stress of the highly taxing position.

Although the First World War had brought him recognition as well as a consolidation of power in the intelligence community, Cumming had been disgraced somewhat in 1920 when he had set up a Special Branch in Dublin to combat the often violent Irish Independence Movement. He had quickly assembled a staff of reportedly over 50 agents, only to have 14 of his agents assassinated on a single day by the IRA under Michael Collins' leadership. Cumming was forced to remove the remainder of his agents and shut down the Irish operation altogether. Despite this setback, Mansfield Cumming pressed on as head of British Intelligence.

Cumming had made known his intention to retire, and in early 1923 a second in command was placed under him in the person of Naval Intelligence Admiral Hugh "Quex" Sinclair. In the summer of that year, after having received a long visit from a close colleague in his home, Mansfield Cumming was found dead, apparently the victim of a heart attack. This man who had so notoriously given the British Secret Service its birth in 1909 was succeeded by Admiral Sinclair, until Quex's own death from cancer in November 1939. Thus for the three decades leading up to World War II the Secret Intelligence Service of Great Britain was led by only two different men, both Naval officers.

Sinclair kept perhaps the most cherished of Cumming's traditions, signing his correspondence and directives with the letter "C" in green naval ink. Perhaps it had been started as short for Cumming, but to this day the green "C" is the irrefutable mark of the Chief of MI6.

If that was perhaps the best known of Cumming's predilections, often he is remembered for his strangest. Early on, having discovered a renewable and unlimited source for invisible ink, he instructed his field agents to use their own semen for their clandestine communications. While the seminal fluid did actually prove effective for this purpose, the practice had to be discontinued for the imposing smell of letters received by his office from all over the world.

1923 also brought about Norway's realization of the Ofoten Railway Electrification Project that MI6 had been so keenly following. The throughput of Swedish iron ore leaving Narvik increased dramatically, which would make the Arctic port more strategic to both sides as World War II approached at the end of the following decade.

There was another very notable development of the decade of the 1920s. In 1923, a German firm brought to market a machine for encrypting commercial radio traffic in Europe. Its name was Enigma. It was freely available to purchase. While its utility in the world of commerce was not greatly appreciated, it was the German army, the *Wehrmacht*, that foresaw the tremendous military utilization of the device.

Finally, in that same year, 1923, Winston Churchill was out of Parliament. He had been a Member of Parliament since 1904, although in 1908 he was voted out of his Manchester seat. He was quickly stood up as a Liberal candidate in the Scottish seat of Dundee and until the end of 1922 would represent the district on the Tay, including Brigand MacAlvor and family, although only briefly. Churchill would loose this seat in the November Election of 1922 and spent the next two years out of Parliament altogether. His banishment ended when he returned in October 1924 in the seat of the constituency of Epping. Once again a Member of Parliament, Churchill was reinstated as the Chancellor of the Exchequer.

Churchill's overall history in Parliament would prove an unpredictable one. It was most fortunate for England, that when the Empire most needed him, Winston Churchill was on the benches, although by then, the back-benches, of Parliament.

25 Tilly's Diary

"Man will occasionally stumble over the truth, but most of the time he will pick himself up and continue on."

Winston Spencer Churchill

Diane sat alone in her London office. Flake and Emory were off doing a follow-up at the DNA laboratory in South London at her request. Diane wanted to make sure everything regarding the DNA of Mattie Barrett was above even the most rigorous of questioning. Mattie had turned up with one quarter Nordic DNA, but without the *Sámi* marker traces that Jake Conley's sample contained, but there was something else that had to be verified. When the two samples were compared, it had been analytically determined that Jake Conley and Mattie MacAlvor did not share any common DNA between them. This still bothered Diane, although Flake had explained it in detail.

"Diane," he had said, "there is no common DNA between them because Jake's mom, after giving birth to the twins with Brigand, left for the States and married Jake's Dad. The twins' father then married Miss Tilly, the real Cassandra Barrett, and they later had their son Matthew together. The only link between Mattie and Jake were that Brigand and Jake's mom had once been married, and this fact alone could not tie together their DNA streams. It was only the twins who would possess the DNA of both Jake's Mom and this Brigand MacAlvor, both of whom were 100% Norwegian. And they would have the *Sámi* traces from Jake's mom."

Diane had to think hard about all this. It was like watching a magician's sleight of hand trick. It had to be slowed down to understand exactly what was going on. With no DNA samples of either twin available, she knew it would be hard to explain all this to her client, no matter how badly he wanted it to be true. Yet, there was one very long shot, but Diane decided she would hold this back in reserve. If Jake wanted to pursue it, he could on his own. She knew it would be an expensive gamble.

Diane had gone looking for Sophie, only to find that she had left immediately after lunch once again. She had been following this pattern for the past several days, when Diane, from her office window overlooking Hyde Park, followed *Sophie* with her eyes as she clipped an angle across the park's open lawns, apparently in the direction toward The Royal Albert Hall. Diane felt guilty for having dispatched Erin Anne to follow her and report back on her wanderings.

Diane was returned to her office and was alone, which allowed her to take her first real dive into the largest single acquisition in the short history of her firm. The previous week while in Dundee, over a cup of tea in the riverside townhouse of Mattie MacAlvor, Diane was introduced to the most incredible document - the diary of her grandmother, Matilda "Tilly" MacAlvor. Diane was allowed to leaf through the leather bound journal, one of several, but Mattie was adamant that she would never sell the journal outright.

It was then that Diane had made a risky proposition to Mattie - sell me *a copy* of the document. Mattie deferred, and felt as though she would be somehow violating her grandmother's secrets. It was then that Diane explained, in detail, the nature of the case in which her firm was engaged. A dying billionaire sought the truth, which she, Mattie appeared to have in her possession.

Diane argued that her grandmother, Tilly, had kept her notes not as secrets to be stored away, but to document an incredible series of events such that someday the world, or at least the extended family, could access these recollections.

It was finally agreed upon, after much back and forth, that in two days time they would drive into Edinburgh. There was a firm in the capital that specialized in the forensic examination of documents. The diary, which in reality consisted of several books covering the period of 1916 until Tilly's death, would first be validated as authentic by examining the chemistry of the ink and composition of the paper to assure they were consistent with samples kept of the times. Then, the documents would be digitized, and all information would be accessed only by members of Diane's firm or by their client and his legal representation. There would be no rights beyond these transferred. No publishing of the digitized document in any form would be permitted. Mattie would retain the physical diary as a family heirloom.

The cost to Diane for this agreement was one hundred and fifty thousand British Pounds. The transaction was documented by a legal contract, with the funds transferred as soon as the complete digitized diary was in the possession of Diane Sterling.

Diane had made the expenditure realizing it was a great risk to her firm. If it turned out to be in any way a fraud, she realized the cost could not then legitimately be passed on to her client. Should it prove useful to documenting the question at hand, however, then Jake Conley would not only pay for this digitized version, but surely would want to possess the original. That would be a negotiation between Mattie and Diane's client directly. Diane assured Mattie that neither she herself nor her firm would be a party to those proceedings.

It had been over tea the previous week at Mattie's home when the very first entry of Tilly's diary that she had read captured Diane's attention. It was short, but read:

November 4, 1916 - Today my life has forever changed. For this day, I married a man, who in all truth, I greatly admire, but do not love. Yet, by this union, I am given that which life has, until now, so cruelly denied me. I have the love of two young boys to whom I am to be mother, twins who are not quite as old as my own dearest Percival would have been, had God not taken him from me at birth for the indiscretion of my ways.

Today I start this new diary, for I have become an entirely new person. This day I become Tilly MacAlvor (a name that still rings foreign to my ears). I was born Cassandra Barrett in the year 1896. I led a happy childhood as daughter of wonderful father, a military officer, and his wife. But whilst living in London, at the age of sixteen, I made the mistake of allowing myself to be taken by the young soldier who I had erringly convinced myself of his love for me. He took an overseas assignment, from which he never bothered to return. My young body soon grew to expose my secret. Father, who loved me so always, soon treated me entirely differently. I became the family's source of public shame and humiliation. When my son, Percival arrived stillborn, I was cast into a depression from which I feared I would never return.

Throughout that winter and into the next year, I was left with a feeling of tremendous loss and of the deepest despair. The doctor had told me, in no uncertain terms, that I would never be able to bear children of my own. The thought of having been abandoned by the man who had professed his unfailing love for me, hollowed me of even the will to live. After which I would not only lose his child, but any hope of ever bearing my own. I had the darkest of thoughts during this time, some so horrific I am ashamed even to profess them here.

When I reached the age of eighteen, my father took a voluntary assignment in Edinburgh Castle, where he was to be stationed. Whether Father did this to restart his career, or to allow me a fresh lease on life, I may never fully know. I only know that my life forever changed by coming to Scotland. We arrived too late for me to restart my academics at University, although in my despair I was secretly relieved. When one evening over dinner Father told me that he knew of a fellow officer who was aware of an immigrant family that needed a nanny to care for two infant twin boys, I was elated. As soon as I could I interviewed for the position, lest it fall into the hands of another. The couple were in desperate need and offered the position to me, but required me to live with them so as to provide care around the clock. I begged father to allow me to take it straightaway.

The couple themselves proved to be very queer. The husband, Birger, was a gentleman whose late father had emigrated to Scotland from Norway. His wife, Tulla, he had just brought back with him after marrying her in Norway. She was about my own age, while he was several years older, although not indecently so.

Oddly enough, Tulla treated their twin boys with indifference, if not disdain. I was only too happy to lavish love on the boys, secretly wishing that somehow they could have been made mine by providence. Tulla took every opportunity she could find to run off from them in order to indulge her basest desires. I quickly bonded with the twins, in a way I came to believe their mother never could. I am ashamed to say that I came to think of the boys as my own, with their mother only an insignificant distraction in their lives.

When the husband, Birger, went off to war in early 1915, his wife Tulla strayed even more frequently, leaving me alone with the twins for days on end. I came to love these periods, as awful as that may sound, as I truly felt as if I were the boys' true mother. Tulla would eventually return dazed and incoherent, only to sleep off whatever she had been ingesting for pleasure. It was so odd how she could only care about satisfying her cravings and ignoring the needs of these docile, innocent children. How could a woman be so vile to her own flesh and blood?

When news was received that Birger was severely wounded and would lose his left leg, Tulla packed her things and rushed to leave. She said that she could no longer deal with this imprisoning life, and that she refused to be married to a cripple. When I pleaded with her not to abandon her boys, she told me to take care of the twins. *"They are better off in your care,"* were her last words as she slipped off into a cab. Only the next day would I realize that she had stolen my passport. She never came back, and today she lives in Liverpool, going about under my given name, I am told.

I have raised Gunnar and Einar as my own ever since. Tulla has been gone for well over a year now. My love for these boys is not that of a nanny or *au pair,* but the deeper care that only a mother can provide her offspring. Of course, this is not what has occurred by nature, but only by the blessed touch of God's providence. He had need in heaven for my Percival, which I could never fully accept or understand. Yet, as reward for my maintaining my belief in Him through that darkest period, I have been blessed with not one, but two angelic faces to nurture.

I have also come to greatly admire their father, Birger. He is the most respectable of men, and despite his own limitations, he cares for the boys with as much love and tenderness as I have ever seen in a father. This quality is his own, it is not effected. He is a good man.

Today, I restart my life. I become, legally, with the help of the British Government, his wife, and the twins' mother. All is well as the government never formally recognized Birger's marriage to Tulla.

The price of this union is for me to forever shed my former life altogether, and Birger his also. For this day, he becomes Brigand MacAlvor, and I his wife, Matilda, although I prefer "Tilly". While the wedding was only the two of us in a government office with an officiant from the registry attending, it was more precious than any other event in my life. I was happy to forego the church wedding, the gowns, the flowers, and even the memories. For on this day I legally have become mother of Einar and Gunnar. And perhaps the best part of all is that I will surely be the only mother they shall ever remember, as Tulla abandoned them so young.

26 That Infernal Machine

Historical Reference

"The empires of the future
are the empires of the mind."

Winston Spencer Churchill

In the 1920s, despite the hyper-inflation of the German Deutsche Mark, or perhaps because of it, international commerce became a more prevalent undertaking in Europe. With that, a need presented itself for businesses to disguise their communications over the open spectrum of wireless radio. So, in 1918, an enterprising German entrepreneur named Arthur Scherbius invented and patented a device to encrypt and de-encrypt messages sent over the wireless. In 1923, the same year as Hitler's *Beer Hall Putsch*, that device was made commercially available by the German firm Scherbius & Ritter. The name of the device was *Enigma*.

The device is conceptually very simple. It did not transmit anything, it was only used to encode the messages which were then to be sent over the open airwaves where anyone could record them. For the receiver to understand the apparent gibberish, that string of random letters needed to be de-coded by another Enigma device on the receiving end. Most important of all, both the encrypting and decrypting devices had to have the same series of settings for the message to be recovered.

Physically, the device appears as a keyboard, but without numbers or other symbols. It had only 26 letter keys, no numeric or punctuation characters. Above these keys was a lampboard of 26 characters. An operator depressed any letter key, and the associated encrypted letter then lit up on the lampboard, which was written down by the operator. This was completed for each letter of the message. When the message was complete, the encoded string of characters was handed over to the radio operator to be sent over the open airwaves.

Figure 16: Kriegsmarine 4-Rotor Enigma Device

Wired between the alphabet keys and the lampboard were three (or sometimes four) electro-mechanical rotors. These were in fact the secret to the encryption algorithm of the device. They appeared just as they sound, round discs having a width of about an inch, with ratcheted serrations flaring from its outer edge. Each of these rotors were individually marked, but each had different internal wiring.

Given that they each rotor had the same externally identical design, the three rotors could be installed in the machine in six different combinations, each having a very different encrypting effect. The four-rotor version of the machine could be set up in 24 unique configurations.

When the operator depressed any alphabet key, an electrical signal generated by that key travelled a very circuitous route through the machine. Upon arriving at the first rotor, its internal wiring would transpose the incoming letter to another before passing it on to the second rotor. The second rotor did the same and passed it onto and through the third. Instead of the signal then traveling directly to the lampboard, it was further encoded by what was called a "reflector" which returned the electric signal to pass once more through all three rotors in reverse, but via a different circuit. Only then was the signal finally output to the lampboard for the operator to record.

What would prove *nearly* unbreakable about the machine were its two discrete functions. First, as described above, at each rotor the character is electronically changed to another. As stated earlier, each of the three rotors had patched edges which were designed to mechanically rotate the disc with each keystroke, much like the odometer in a car. This meant that depressing the same character key multiple times in succession would not yield the same result upon the lampboard. For instance depressing the letter "a" 25 times might possibly yield 25 different output characters. The one flaw of the machine's design was that no letter could ever be encoded as itself. Thus no matter how many times an "a" key would be depressed would an "a" character alight on the lampboard.

Second, each device had to be set identically by sender and receiver. There were three unique rotors which could be installed in any of six combinations. But each rotor also had to be set on a starting letter, one of twenty-six available. Therefore, even if the rotor sequence was known, the number of unique settings of the rotors' starting points was still one of 17,576 possible combinations.

It is this complexity of mechanical and electrical variation that made the Enigma device so impregnable to the crypto-analysis methods of the time. It was not long before the German military would come to realize the utility of this machine. The German Army, or *Wehrmacht*, would go on to use the devise with rotors of its own design, different from those commercially available. Also the complexity would be further increased by adding to its front a plugboard, which could translate any letter to another. Up to thirteen conversion wires, could be plugged in by the operator, adding to the possible number of variations of set-up parameters.

The German Navy, or *Kriegsmarine*, would use its own version of the machine, which had not three rotors but four. Each submarine and surface ship would have such a device onboard. The increased complexity was thought to be required should any vessel ever be captured, and its Enigma device end up in enemy hands. Yet, despite the added rotor, the naval Enigma functioned in a very similar fashion to that of the tri-rotor version.

The Poles had long been listening to the encoded messages coming out of the German and Russian armies almost since the country was reconstituted in 1918. They had become very efficient in breaking these codes. In fact, the breaking of the Russian codes in 1920 allowed them to take the daring moves that resulted in the *"Miracle at the Vistula"*, the defeat of the Bolshevik Armies threatening to devastate Warsaw. "

By the end of the 1920s, the Poles were picking up the Enigma encoded German military traffic that they could not break. It was at this point, that the Poles first put a priority upon being able to crack this new code. It was imperative for the Polish State to understand what the German military, just beyond its western borders, was planning.

Codebreaking was a developed skill even in the 1920s, but the Enigma device proved impregnable to the methods developed to that date. For most codebreaking relied at some level on what is called frequency analysis. In English, for example, the letter E is the most frequently recurring, with the letters T and R not far behind. Therefore, anyone trying to break an English language cypher would assess which encoded character occurred most frequently, for sake of this discussion let's premise it is a "Q" and assign that character to "E". They could then solve next for "T" and then "R" in a similar method. But the Enigma device mechanically advanced the rotors with each input, rendering frequency analysis methods useless.

It was the Poles who first became fixated on solving the Enigma code. They immediately set plans in place to attack the German code. They introduced a course in cryptology at the University of Poznań, although the real intention of the course was to screen candidates for the Polish Cypher Bureau in Warsaw. It was here that three incredibly talented mathematicians were discovered. They were named Marian Rejewski, Jerzy Różycki and Henryk Zygalski. They would go on to live a harrowing journey during World War II that only began with the breaking of the Enigma code. Sadly, one of the three would never complete that journey.

27 The Shifting Reality

Historical Reference 1932 - 1934

"Do not let spacious plans for a new world divert your energies from saving what is left of the old."

Winston Spencer Churchill

In Britain, which by the early 1930s was feeling the effects of the global economic crisis, many came to question whether it was not time to replace capitalism with fascism, socialism, or even outright communism. After all, the Brits viewed the ongoing misery plaguing America and their own cities and towns as being the result of a failed capitalist system. During this low point, in October 1932, the far-right elements of the British political spectrum coalesced into the British Union of Fascists under Oswald Mosley. Ultimately, the party was disallowed during the 1940 elections, when Britain was at war with the fascists Hitler and Mussolini.

It was during this low ebb of history when agents of the Soviet Union clandestinely began recruiting in the colleges of Cambridge in the United Kingdom. This would become an investment that would pay rich dividends for Stalin and his successors for many decades to follow. The most notorious of the Britons to be recruited as Soviet agents would be none other than "Kim" Philby, who would go on to attain prominence among the very highest offices within MI6.

In the Soviet Union itself at this time, there came to exist one of the most severe famines which ultimately killed five to seven million people. The Ukraine was most affected, as well as the Caucasus region. It is unclear if the famine was intentionally caused by Stalin to punish these populations, or was merely the result of the implementation of disastrous Soviet planning. In either case, the resulting pain and death were all too real.

Perhaps the singular most significant event of the year 1932 was the German Reichstag elections. During that year, Hitler ran in the national presidential election. He finished second to the incumbent President Paul von Hindenburg, but managed to garner over thirty-five percent of the votes cast. Even more importantly, he had become the favorite politician of the German industrialist class.

Despite his defeat in the Presidential election, the National Socialist party under Adolf Hitler had been gaining in popularity. In November 1932, the Nazis won nearly a third of all seats in the Reichstag, more than any other party, although not an outright majority. From this base of power, along with the support of the industrialists, President Hindenburg was reluctantly persuaded to appoint Adolf Hitler to the office of Chancellor of Germany in January 1933. Once in office, the deterioration of freedom in Germany would rapidly accelerate.

At the end of the very next month, the Reichstag building was set ablaze. Hermann Göring, as Minister of the Interior, blamed the German communists. Hitler quickly seized the opportunity to have President Hindenburg announce the Reichstag Decree the next day. It revoked many basic privileges and rights to the German populace. Thousands of German Communists were arrested, and the German Communist Party was effectively eliminated as a political entity.

Then, in next month of March, Hitler used strong-arm tactics, and employed his *SA* brownshirt forces (*Sturmabteilung),* to assure the passage of the Enabling Act. In the span of three months, Germany Democracy had devolved into despotism. The Enabling Act allowed the Chancellor to effect new laws without having to submit them to the Reichstag. The act was passed on March 23, and later that same day President Hindenburg signed it into law.

Not surprisingly, Hitler's first actions were against the German Jews. On the first of April, a nationwide boycott against all Jewish owned shops and businesses began. On April 7, Jews were prohibited from being employed in the German Government. Following his playbook as set forth in *Mein Kampf,* the Nazis would later that year attack other minorities and "inferior" groups, including the handicapped and homosexuals.

For Hitler there were two last roadblocks to unfettered power. First, he would need the complete loyalty of the German Military Command. The only real concern the leaders of the German military had by then was Hitler's private *Sturmabteilung* troops. The *SA*, which literally meant *"Storm Detachment,"* was a thuggish, brown-shirted paramilitary force several times larger than the army Germany was allowed to have under the Versailles Treaty. The German Army officers viewed the SA as a threat.

Hitler recognized the military's concerns and determined that the SA had served its purpose. At the urgings of Heinrich Himmler and Hermann Göring, Hitler turned the SS and the Gestapo loose upon the SA on the night of June 30, 1934. Over the next few days, concluding on July 2, the SA leadership were brutally liquidated and Ernst Röhm was arrested and later murdered. This purging of Röhm and his SA leadership is to this day known in German as the *"Nacht der langen Messer,"* which translates as the *"Night of the Long Knives"*.

The last roadblock to Hitler's consolidation of power would fall exactly one month later. President Paul von Hindenburg died in office in August 2, 1934. He was eighty-seven years old, and while he had previously had an indestructible constitution, one must wonder if the stress of residing over the new Nazi regime had not contributed to his quick decline. The Reichstag Fire had taken place the month after Hitler had taken the oath as Chancellor. The public burning of books deemed to be subversive to the new government had begun only weeks later.

The constant intimidation and violent pummeling of the nation's citizens at the hands of the SA in the streets had become commonplace. The terror of the *"Night of Long Knives"* had come only weeks before Hindenburg passed away. The German people soon learned that a law had been passed the previous day by Hitler's cabinet combining the offices of President and Chancellor, leaving Hitler as an effective dictator. He then eliminated the office of President and named himself simply *"Der Führer"* or *"The Leader"*.

Figure 17: Rejewski, Różycki, and Zygalski
First to Break the Enigma Code

28 The Secret of Secrets

"It is wonderful how well men can keep secrets they have not been told."

Winston Spencer Churchill

In 1919, Poland had created the organization which would be known as the *Biuro Szyfrówa* or Cypher Bureau. Throughout the 1920s, they closely monitored the evolution of the Enigma device, sensing its capabilities would be militarized by the German army. It was not until 1930 that the Cypher Bureau drafted three recent graduates from the University of Poznań. Unlike earlier career cryptologists who had been linguists or rhetoricians, the Cypher Bureau began enlisting mathematicians. This was because the rotors of the Enigma posed problems that were based on the mathematical concept of permutations. They reasoned that Enigma presented a problem not of mere codes, but of higher mathematics.

The Poles had purchased a commercial variant of the Enigma machine during the mid-1920s while it was still available on the open market. However, even having this device to inspect proved of little value in decrypting the German military traffic. First of all, the internal wiring of the three rotors and the reflector were completely different in the military versions. In fact, the German naval units of the *Kriegsmarine* employed four rotors instead of three. The *Wehrmacht* and the *Luftwaffe* did indeed utilize the three rotor variant of the device.

In 1932, the city of Poznań was Polish once again and had been since 1918. It had been taken from the Germans and returned to Poland following the Treaty of Versailles, which formally ended World War I. Prior to that, it had been in the German province of Prussia, although most Poles would protest that it had long ago been stolen from Poland during the times of the Partitions of the late eighteenth century.

When the city was Prussian, it was known by its Germanic name Posen. Paul von Hindenburg, the President of Germany, had been a Prussian born in Posen. There were also many Poles who had been raised in the then German city. One of those Poles was the mathematician Marian Rejewski.

By 1932, Rejewski (pronounced Rey-YEV-ski) had been working on breaking the Enigma machine for the past two years. Rejewski was able to completely reproduce the military version of the machine in use by the *Wehrmacht*, including the internal wiring of each rotor, despite never having seen nor had access to any of the military variants of the machine or their uniquely fabricated rotors. His success was an astounding feat of mathematics employing permutation theory.

To be completely accurate, the Polish mathematician was aided by captured German daily settings codes provided by their allies in the *Deuxième Bureau* of French Intelligence. Having an old codebook containing this information was of itself valueless, since these settings were changed so frequently. However, knowing an old code's translation was invaluable, as it then allowed Rejewski to confirm his analytical deductions of the internal wiring of the machine and its rotors.

Marian Rejewski was able to confirm his breakthrough in late 1932. Soon two other Polish codebreakers from Poznań, Jerzy Różycki (YER-zee Ro-ZIT-ski) and Henryk Zygalski (HEN-ryk Zee-GAL-ski) were also assigned to break the German codes along with Rejewski. Zygalski developed a series of perforated cards which would prove useful in physically determining the machine's rotor settings. Their matches represented the possible settings of two rightmost rotors (the third rotor did not change very often, like the third digit in a car's odometer). Overlaid one atop the other above a light source, these sheets, became indispensable in reducing the 17,576 variations of the machine's settings to a much more limited and thus more manageable set of possibilities. The smaller set was identified wherever the light continued to show through the stack. These became known as "Zygalski Sheets".

It was exactly the complexity of the vast number of these daily settings that made the Enigma device so daunting. The trio of mathematicians had come up with a unique idea - *Why not use a machine to crack a machine-generated cypher?*

The thousands of variations of the settings came from the fact that there were three distinct rotors. Each had 26 letters assigned to it. These three rotors were numbered 1, 2 and 3, (actually marked with Roman numerals I, II, and III) and could be installed in the machine in any one of six different sequence orders. Therefore, the daily settings had six times twenty-six cubed possibilities, or 105,456 possible settings.

In order to decode messages on the device, the operator would need to know both the order sequence of the three rotors as well as the letter starting position of each individual rotor. The machine the three Poles developed represented the rotor combinations on six vertical rods, one for each combination of rotor configuration. Each rod had three wheels, each containing 26 possible letters. The wheels represented the possible starting points of the rotors. The machine would mechanically pace through each combination of possible rotor settings until a solution was achieved.

As the settings of each of the six rods were mechanically cycled one after the other, this machine emitted a constant stream of "click, click, click…". The cryptologists could do nothing but wait for it to "go off" with the proposed solution. For this reason, they named the device the *Bomba* - the Polish word for bomb. This bomb proved to be the most important ever developed.

The Poles kept their success secret from the world, even from the French with whom they were most closely aligned. With the Zygalski sheets and the Polish *Bomba* device, the Poles were able to reverse engineer a working copy of the Enigma device and read its codes for the next six years. Right up until December 1938, when so much would drastically change.

In another part of Poland, in the south, the child Bogdan Bratajewski was raised in a small village near the town of Zakopane. Bogdan was the oldest of three children, along with his younger brother Albin, and their still younger sister Justyna. They were raised in near-poverty conditions, but in a family of great love. Their peasant parents always seemed to provide for their needs, although their wants would generally go unfulfilled.

It was in the grim economic state that gripped Poland in the early 1930s, that the two young brothers were sent from their hometown to the German city of Breslau (today's Polish metropolis of Wroclaw). More accurately, Bogdan Bratajewski and his brother Albin, were sent to a German farm, just outside the city, in the province of Silesia. They were employed as summer laborers by a family whose name was the Schennings. Justyna was too young and as such was left behind at home, but her own travails would soon enough follow.

The Schenning family was initially harsh on the boys, but over time as they saw how industrious these children were, the German family proved to be more kindhearted. They paid the boys' wages in produce and meats, and allowed Bogdan and Albin to periodically use one of their wagons and a pair of draft horses to transport the foods to the family home near Zakopane.

The boys continued to labor for their family's food for six summers from 1933 to 1938. These fresh fruits and vegetables were canned by Justyna and her mother, while the meats were smoked by their father. The toils of the boys' summer efforts would thus not only feed the family throughout the summers, but the harsh winters as well. Without this arrangement, it is not clear that the family would have had enough food to survive. With the famine ongoing in nearby Ukraine, starvation was all too real a possibility that the family had grown to fear.

As they grew, the two brothers spent much time in the Tatras Mountains. Albin loved to hike the snow laden trails, to climb, and especially was delighted to rappel from the white capped ragged heights. His older brother, Bogdan, would accompany him but spend his hours seemingly only focused on the eagles that would ride the updrafts and hunt for prey. Bogdan Bratajewski had but a singular desire - to learn to fly. Having been born in the last days of 1920's Polish-Soviet war, he dreamt of nothing other than one day becoming a fighter pilot for his country. His greatest aspiration was to one day fly in the 7th Escadrille, the famed Kościuszko Squadron.

29 The Departure

"We are stripped bare by the curse of plenty."

Winston Spencer Churchill

Diane had become obsessed with her continued reading of Tilly MacAlvor's diary. Each day she became more obsessed to know the full story of the woman and her family. She would stay in her office until late at night, have dinner with Sophie before the two of them would return to her flat, where Diane would continue to read before finally giving in to sleep.

On this particular night, at Sophie's request, they dined in Chinatown, just between Leicester Square and the West End Theatre district. Diane had arrived first and was seated by the proprietor. She awaited Sophie's arrival with trepidation, as the two women had been seemingly unable to talk without their emotions getting in the way of their friendship.

Sophie soon walked up to her table.

"Hello, Diane," Sophie said in her own gentle way, but with an oddly unfeeling, impartial voice.

"Hello, *Zosia*," Diane replied, as the voice triggered the thought in her that this might be the last time she would ever have to address her friend by that intimate form of her name.

This night at dinner an uneasy tension had stretched between them. Much like lovers would, they had become so close, that the unwanted awkwardness they felt on the verge of their separating seemed insurmountable.

"Diane, I have something to tell you," Sophie began after they had ordered. "Tomorrow I am returning to Poland. I have done all I can do for you on the Conley case, and I have completed my investigations in London on my own case."

"Well, certainly, *Zosia*," Diane replied. "I didn't expect you to stay on here forever. You can call into our next telecon from Poznań when you get home."

"I don't think you understand, Diane," said Sophie with a look of remorse that her friend had not been straightforward with her. Diane knew she was intent on leaving the firm. They had quarreled about it continuously ever since they were together in London. Diane refused to acknowledge that this would be their final meal together as superior and subordinate.

"Please, *Zosia*, don't start with the '*I am going out on my own*' routine again. If you need some time off, then I'll give you a leave of absence. Take as much time as you need. It will have to be unpaid, unless you have vacation to draw down. Take a break until your head is right. Then, we will be together once more, you, I and Emory. As it should be."

Sophie reached into her large bag and produced a letter, which she handed to Diane.

"Read this, *proszę*," she said stiffly.

"Later, *Zosia*," Diane said, returning to her meal. "I will read it later, I promise."

Sophie slid the letter alongside Diane's plate.

"There is no putting off this moment any longer," Sophie said, "but if you will not take the time to read this brief letter , then I will be forced to tell you it's contents, verbatim, aloud here in this crowded restaurant."

Diane stopped dining and cast an annoyed glare at Sophie.

"Oh, good God, *Zosia*! Do you have to be so damn dramatic," Diane said as she picked up the envelope and slid her fingernail under its flap. She unfolded the single sheet within, which was hand written on company letterhead. It read as follows:

> *To my dear friend Diane,*
>
> *This letter is to inform you that as of this night I am resigning from my employment at Sterling Investigations International. I have learned much during my stay over these last years at SII and the most important of which I was taught by you, personally. Perhaps the lesson I have come to hold most dear is that this employment, despite being highly interesting and very rewarding materially, is not my calling in life.*
>
> *I feel fortunate that the paths of our lives have crossed. It seemed destined to be, perhaps God's will.*

I thank you for recognizing my skills, but the time has come for me to put them to another use. I am and will be forever indebted to you. I can only hope you will come, with time, to respect my decision.

I have taken the liberty to book a room near Heathrow Airport this evening. Thanks to Étienne, your concierge, my things have already been transferred. Tonight, after our meal, we will depart one last time as colleagues. However, I can only pray that the Lord above forever deigns us to be friends.

Do widzenia,

Zosia

Diane felt as though a dagger had been wedged between the bones of her ribs. She re-read the note several times, and with each re-reading, the dagger was withdrawn only to find fresh skin to pierce.

A million thoughts flooded through Diane's brain - memories, snippets of conversations, and a multitude of feelings. Walking Berlin's *Unter Den Linden* in the bitter cold night. Perusing the flower stands outside Paris' *Le Madeleine* Church. Climbing in the cablecar to the top of the *Pfänder* overlooking the *Bodensee* as they together escaped MI6 in Bregenz. But no memory was more vivid to Diane than that of her having been revived from her coma at the safe house in Switzerland, her eyes slowly coming into focus, only to see first the image of *Zosia* at her side. She remembered the instant feeling of love and belonging that washed over her exhausted body and reawakened soul. It was a feeling that she had rarely before experienced during the hectic professional parade of years that was her life.

"You have read this letter, yes?" the Pole asked, as she brushed aside her long straight stands of golden blonde hair.

"Yes, of course I have," the words raced out of Diane's mouth faster than she had expected. *A thousand times over and it still makes no damn sense to me at all*, she wanted to add. Sophie stared at her, expecting Diane to say more, which she did not. She could not. The empty seconds strained into an eternity of suffering, of loss, of betrayal. It was as if the sting of each word must recede before the flood of emotions within her had the slightest chance of gushing forth.

Yet, despite all this, Diane forced herself to talk. She attempted to take refuge in the jargon of professionalism. "Look, *Zosia,* I cannot legally reject this notice, but I want you to know, that in my heart I will never accept it. I know that …"

Diane noticed people at adjoining tables had already cast their gazes in her direction, just before the first of her large tears which threatened to ribbon her face broke free from her cheeks onto the empty plate before her. She lowered her voice to a whisper.

"… I believe that God has sent you to show me what is missing from my own life. Losing you is like foregoing all hope that I might someday obtain what ever graces He might have in store for me."

Diane's arm stretched across the table, her hand seeking Sophie's own. Instead, Sophie merely gently patted Diane's upraised, open palms for an instant before she withdrew her arms to her side.

Diane felt exposed, as if stripped naked of every mechanism she could hide behind, as she faced Sophie's stoic gaze. It had dawned on her only then that Sophie had asked for this meeting in this nearly always crowded restaurant merely to suppress her responses. She assessed only then that her *Zosia* wished for Diane to be held captive, under a siege of her own emotions.

"Diane, you yourself have told me that you are unsure if there even is a God," Sophie responded, leaning forward and lowering her voice. "I have told you on many occasions that there is and that His presence is exactly what is missing from your life. Yet, my decision to leave is based on knowing that staying and telling you this message many times more will not amplify its meaning. I can only pray that my leaving will do so."

Diane felt rejected, and scolded, as if by one considering herself to be morally superior than herself. *How dare my Zosia to treat me this way!* She swallowed the bitterness of this thought and forced herself to respond cooly, but failed to temper her words.

"I noted, *Zosia,* that you got one last dig in by saying how '*materially rewarding*' this job has been. You had to get that message in the letter, didn't you? Does your God hate my wishing to be successful? Would He prefer I fail? If only so those of you who love Him so could fall to your knees and pray for my *destitute ass*?"

As these words left her lips, Diane feared they were tinged with an unintended sharpness formed from the deeply seated torment that lingered within her. She regretted their release and feared she had greatly hurt her closest friend.

"I am sorry, *Zosia*," Diane then quickly said, "I am very emotional. I don't often feel this way. Forgive my outburst."

Sophie looked at her through the glow of a soft smile. She cautiously took her time before responding. "Emotions are God's greatest gifts, Diane, for it is the devil's time when all men and women are stripped of them. Remember this as you investigate your case. Those who do not feel are most capable of carrying out the most wretched of the fallen angel's intentions. Those who are desensitized by hatred or power or greed are those that he seeks to work through. These are the ones who through justifying their own ambitions will carry out his evil plans. Beware any insensitivity growing within you, for it will hollow out your soul, leaving only an emptiness that no professional success, no attainment of power, and no level of recognition can ever satisfy. These ambitions only fuel one's greed, it will draw you to do the evil one's bidding, even if only unknowingly."

Diane's feelings raged and receded within her. *How dare Zosia to address me as if I were a common criminal!* The temple of her mind was under assault. Within it, her own emotions lashed out harshly and then, just as quickly, were sucked back into a vacuum of despair. This ebb and tide repeated, much like the false attack of an enemy who wished only to measure her response. Diane fought to speak her next words plainly, flatly.

"So, you say that just because I desire to be successful, I am only the unwitting accomplice of evil itself?" Diane's eyes could no longer hide her resentment. The edge of her words sharpened with each syllable uttered. "Why do you insist I can not be both accomplished at what I do and at the same time be a good person as well? What has caused you to hate me so?"

Diane's head pounded. She thought Sophie sat before her with a forbearance of superiority. She sensed her dinner companion was taking her time in carefully sculpting her next statement. After several seconds, finally, *Zosia* spoke.

"Diane, know this - you are a good person and I love you. I always will. However, for your own sake, stop defining your value as a person to your success, to your wealth. You will find happiness only when you stop doing that. When you learn to do otherwise, your life will become enriched in ways that you never imagined. I must leave you now, but with a heart full of gratitude for all you have done for me. Perhaps, you will see that what I am doing is not an act in vengeance against you in any way, but instead I am merely following the intentions of my own heart."

With saying this, Sophie stood, walked over to Diane, kissed her on her tear moistened cheek, and left the restaurant before disappearing into the crowded London night. Diane sat alone, adrift in a sea of glances and glares around her that she refused to acknowledge. She felt the bitter sting of the rejection of a valued friend to whom she had once entrusted her own life.

———•◦•———

Diane took a taxicab home to her condo on Buckingham Gate. It was as quiet as a crypt. In contrast, her emotions were swirling in a volatile, turbulent flow. One moment of extreme sadness would radically shift to anger, only to be displaced by the loneliness that seemed to be the ubiquitous undercurrent. For the first time in a very long period of her life, she really did not know what to do.

She decided to escape into the alternate universe through which she had been living so vicariously. She picked up the electronic diary and began reading the next sequential input by Tilly MacAlvor from where she had left off earlier that afternoon in her office.

March 20, 1932 - My, what a grand and lovely day today was! Einar and Gunnar turned nineteen this day. They are becoming men in every sense of the word, but it is my joy to celebrate the little boys that still resides within them both. Nothing calls out the child from within the man like a birthday cake. It is funny how Brigand and I always refer to them as "Einar and Gunnar" despite the fact that Gunnar is actually a few minutes older. I guess the twins would argue that neither of their births were complete before the other brother joined the world.

The twins have always been inseparable, even though they continue to diverge in their personalities. Einar is the stronger of the two, not only in his physique but also in his love for adventure. He is a *man's man*, as they say, and certainly more of the athlete than his brother. His loves are the outdoors, especially being upon the mountains and the sea.

I am afraid that Gunnar, on the other hand, is more bookish and shares my love for Shakespeare. He loves history as well, and we both love that the bard's writings, themselves, are drenched in it. Brigand is perhaps correct as he always says that Gunnar is more apt to read history, and Einar is more apt to live it in the making.

Often I fear for Gunnar's sensitivity, for he is prone to bouts of being morose and introspective for all but the slightest of reasons. Just last week he shared with me that he felt Einar gets more attention from their father than he. That is perhaps an incorrect perception, as I have heard Brigand many times comment on how proud he is of Gunnar's scholastic achievements. I told Gunnar that if he perceives anything, it is perhaps his father favoring Einar's athleticism perhaps because of his own crippling disabilities from the war. He said he had considered this, but nonetheless felt slighted.

Having told Brigand of the lad's feelings, their father decided to take them both on a Shakespeare inspired trip to Glamis Castle, only a short distance from our home. Gunnar was very, very excited at his prospect as he knows the play Macbeth nearly by heart. They toured the castle, complete with bagpipes upon the welcome and a proper Scottish traditional lunch. When they returned, I asked Gunnar his thoughts. He replied that the castle staff were rather quick to applaud Einar's re-enactment of Macbeth slaying King Duncan at Glamis.

However, he went on to explain in detail, Macbeth is only referenced as the Thane of Glamis in Shakespeare's play. The prophecy of the witches was that Macbeth would also become Thane of Cawdor, and ultimately King of Scotland. It is at Cawdor Castle that Macbeth slays King Duncan, not at Glamis Castle at all.

The fact that his brother was lauded for re-enacting something that was historically inaccurate bothered the dear lad to no end. He could not understand why Einar received so much more attention than he, even when his brother was clearly making a mockery of the play. I assured him that people love them both equally, but then cautioned him that this is a man's world. Even among men it favors men of action. It is more quickly drawn to doers of deeds and under-appreciates deep thinkers such as yourself.

Poor Gunnar had trouble with this explanation, as he said he thought anyone could act if they did not foresee the consequences of their action.

I hugged him dearly, and whispered in his ear, that perhaps it is his brother's world for now, but I was sure that as time passed people would come to appreciate his own wisdom more greatly. For time steals from the surplus of youth, but always increases the holdings of those who seek truth and knowledge.

My Gunnar was in a deep state for many days thereafter. Just today his spirits seemed to rise a bit. He said to me earlier that he knew people were more quickly drawn to Einar, and that perhaps may always be so, but that alone could not keep him from loving his brother. I could never find the words to express just how proud I was to hear him utter these words.

I told him how very much moved I was by his statement. He had clearly thought through his feelings and decided how irrational his emotions were. His response was truly telling. Gunnar said that he and his brother were both minted from the same metal and forged together into a single coin. He said Einar is one side, whilst he was the other. If his brother must be heads and he tails, it matters not. So long as they always lived out their lives together. I told Gunnar that I found his to be a very mature reasoning. I again told him of how proud I was of him, for one finds throughout life that there are many things one can live without, like recognition and fame. His answer was that the only thing he truly could not live without was his twin brother, Einar, and that should he ever be cleaved of him, he did not know how his life could ever possibly go on.

30 The Sinister Revelation

Historical Reference - 1936

*"We shape our dwellings, and afterwards
our dwellings shape us. "*

Winston Spencer Churchill

There comes a time when those who have prepared sinisterly under the cloak of darkness fling it free to reveal the acidity of their convictions and the armory of their strengths. That point for Hitler's National Socialists came in 1936. This was when the world would begin to understand the true intentions of the German dictator and his depraved Nazi Party. Hitler and the Nazi Party desperately desired two things in the mid 1930s: military strength and its recognition by the world. 1936 would become the year that both were achieved.

Having begun a covert rearmament program upon coming to power, Germany thrived economically while other nations were still confronted with the horrors of the international financial disaster. In addition to arms and weapons, Germany invested heavily in infrastructure to facilitate their usage. The German Autobahn system of highways was constructed to facilitate the rapid movement of troops throughout the country. Alfred Speer, Hitler's personal architect, designed massive rallying grounds and other impressive structures. Meanwhile, Joseph Goebbels ran the Ministry of Propaganda which adeptly used the print, radio and cinematic resources to re-educate the populace of the rapidly darkening norms of Germany.

In March of 1936, Nazi Germany was ready to reveal to the world its first glimpse of what would become its war machine. The *Wehrmacht* marched its troops into the Rhineland, which had been demilitarized after the Treaty of Versailles.

The Germans were boldly in defiance of that treaty, as well as the Treaty of Locarno (Switzerland), secured by the League of Nations. Despite protests to Germany's move, France made no military countermove. Was this perhaps because the French had reduced their military capabilities voluntarily, as had the British in the years before? In any case, Hitler won his first objective without so much as a shot fired.

As the winter thawed to spring, the Germans wished to increase their standing in the eyes of the world. With the Rhineland secured, Hitler attempted to impress the international community with the remarkable transformation his country had undergone since the days of the Weimar Republic.

Thus, the Nazis's most audacious undertaking of 1936 was Germany's hosting of the International Olympics. On August 1, Hitler oversaw the opening ceremonies in Berlin, which were carefully stage-managed to highlight the Nazi State that had risen like a Phoenix from the ashes of World War I. The now-standard alphabetical entry parade of the world's athletes was introduced that year, as was the relay of the Olympic Torch from Greece.

When the sole runner, the last in a chain of three thousand, entered the grounds and the Olympic Flame was lit, it was truly a moving moment. Accompanied by music arranged by none other than Richard Strauss, the games became perhaps the greatest propaganda achievement up until that time for Herr Goebbels and the National Socialist State.

Hitler recognized that this would be the world's first real look at his emerging state and eased the crackdowns on Jews and other minorities for the next few weeks. Anti-Jewish slogans had been purged from the cities and towns hosting the events. In Berlin, *Roma* (Gypsies) had been rounded up just before the start of the games. Visitors and athletes alike commented on the civilities shown them. The country was immaculate and its people were charming.

With the sole exception of the four gold medals won by the American Jesse Owens, disrupting Hitler's claims of Aryan supremacy, the games could not have come off better for Germany. Far and away the host nation had won the most medals. Its people and country were portrayed in a positive light. So much so that corespondent William Shirer, who would later pen the authoritative volume on Nazi Germany - *The Rise and Fall of the Third Reich* - wrote in his journal after the games:

"I'm afraid the Nazis have succeeded with their propaganda. First, the Nazis have run the Games on a lavish scale never before experienced, and this has appealed to the athletes. Second, the Nazis have put up a very good front for the general visitors, especially the big businessmen."

Perhaps the most closely held secret during the games was that the Nazis were, even then, providing military assistance to General Francisco Franco in the Spanish Civil War which had started the month before. The *Wehrmacht* and *Luftwaffe* were eager to demonstrate the capabilities they had developed. They entered the fray on the side of Franco's Right-Wing Nationalists, who were attempting to overthrow the left-leaning incumbent government of the Spanish Republic. The war became a proxy for one of class distinction between the communist inspired socialists versus General Franco's desire for a capitalist state. It was also a pitting of Spain's traditional religious culture against Communist atheism.

Göring's *Luftwaffe* was dispatched to the Iberian Peninsula, as were Nazi motorized ground units. They instantly proved themselves lethal. The Nazi killing efficiency was most pitifully demonstrated in the 1937 Stuka dive-bombing attacks on the Republican town of Guernica. The town's population was mostly civilian women and their children. The men were generally away elsewhere at war. The ensuing mass slaughter of innocents inspired Pablo Picasso in Paris to create one of his most moving images by the same name. It captured the mayhem and horror in understated shades of black, grays and white. It was as if the reality of colors of this town's desecration was much too vivid and overpowering for the artist to bear.

That Civil War would rage on until 1939. International mass communications other than newsreels and some radio reporting did not exist. While many journalists, including Ernest Hemingway and his soon to be lover Martha Gellhorn were eager to cover the fighting, they would not arrive until 1937. Throughout the Spanish Civil War, Hitler was quick to note that the United States and European nations failed to intercede.

The general populations of America and other countries were far more concerned with the lingering effects of the Great Depression and world-wide financial crisis that still squeezed their nations with the unrelenting grip of a python's coil.

———•·•———

In England, 1936 had begun with a disruption in the reign of the monarchy and would end in the same way. On January 20, King George V died suddenly, thrusting his eldest son to the throne as King Edward the VIII. As the Duke of Wales, Edward had been a young sportsman and a most charming personality. He had worried many in the Royal Family for his lack of interest in marriage. Then, through his social connections, he had met the American divorcee Wallace Simpson, with whom, over time, he had fallen deeply in love.

After his ascension to the throne, Edward made it known that he intended to marry the American, setting off a monarchial crisis. Members of Parliament threatened to resign their seats in protest should this union take place. A hue and cry from all corners of the Empire rejected the dilution of Britain's independence should an American marry the king. Despite the fact that the Church of England was established to give King Henry VIII a palatable end to his many marriages, by 1936 it steadfastly forbid divorce. So, on December 11 of that same year, King Edward VIII renounced the throne to the British Empire so that he could live out his life in peace with the woman he loved. Edward's brother ascended to the throne as George VI, perhaps to show continuity with the reign of his father. The *"Year of the Three Kings"* was then soon over.

After becoming the first British monarch to voluntarily abdicate, Edward and Wallace married and resided in France. Many have wondered how his rejecting the crown may have forever changed history. For had he reigned through World War II, would England have found the courage to continue fighting after the fall of France? Many suggest not, for the abdicated king was later assumed to be a professed admirer of Adolf Hitler, after he was photographed shaking hands with the dictator as Wallace looked on. Even though this photo was snapped before the war, Britain was sent into an understandable rage.

———•·•———

In Poland, life had improved significantly since its national emergence after World War I. Warsaw had become a lovely, sophisticated city where the *bon vivant* lifestyle was to be enjoyed. So much so, that some called it the Paris of the East. The second Polish Republic was in its prime.

However, in the Kataby Woods near the village of Pyry, south of Warsaw, there was a secretive underground bunker where the Enigma codebreaking initiative continued. Thanks to the mathematicians Rejewski, Różycki and Zygalski, among others, the Polish Cypher Bureau systemically listened in on German Military messaging. They decrypted messages at a rate of approximately 75% of all traffic intercepted. It was more than enough to assess the intentions of the evermore aggressive *Wehrmacht*. They understood that this daunting military would be the tool utilized by Hitler to achieve his declared goal of *"Lebensraum", or "living space"* for the crowded Germanic peoples. The Poles knew that in lying directly to the east of Germany's border, their soil was heavily coveted by the Nazi regime. They also knew that the Nazis considered them to be somewhat less than human, as they were often described by Hitler to be *"Untermensch"*. Like his predecessor, Frederick the Great, Hitler foresaw these lands becoming German, and the Poles upon it to serve them as mere beasts of burden.

31 The Greedy Grasp of Wincer Wells

"We are masters of the unsaid words,
but slaves of those we let slip out"

Winston Spencer Churchill

Diane had resisted the temptation to call Sophie. She did not know what she would have said to her, but she was certainly already missing the pleasure of talking to her friend. She had called Emory, who had since returned to run the Berlin office. Diane asked him if he had perchance spoken to Sophie.

"Give her time, Diane," he said. "She'll come back to us. It's only been a couple of days. You've gone much longer stretches than this without talking to her."

"Sure, but that was different," Diane responded. "At least then I knew I could call her. I am not even sure she will bother to take my calls anymore."

"C'mon, Diane," Emory said, "if there is one thing that Sophie is not, it is spiteful. Give her time to wander. She may not like the new life she finds for herself."

They chatted a bit longer with Emory attempting to console Diane's worries. When they hung up, Diane took refuge in her favorite hiding place - Tilly MacAlvor's diary. She had been marking various day's inputs, and decided to re-read the following days entries:

> January 5, 1937 - I am so very lonely today. I look out upon the water, in the distance where the Tay meets the North Sea. I only think of how the waters draining from the highlands travel past me as they rush to leave these shores, and it seems this same situation applies to the days of the youth of my dearest children.

I am all alone in feeling so, for Brigand has taken the twins to London. Two days have since passed and I still could not be any more angry at my husband. He came home to tell me that he had agreed to allow the service to test the boys' language skills. He had said that Wincer Wells had suggested it.

I was so unkind to Brigand. I exploded at his news. I told him that just because his father had entrapped him in this bloody business, that he had no right to do the same to our boys. I then told him to take a hard look at what his "club" had already cost him, and was this, or worse, what he wished on our twins.

That last comment really seemed to wound him, as if my words had run him through. He became instantly despondent, and this dark mood lasted for the next several days. Only the excited chatter of the boys seemed to lift his spirits.

When they took the train out of Edinburgh that morning, I was left alone here, mired in my own regrets. I feel as if Wincer Wells, as his age rushes past him, somehow wishes to revive his fading career through Einar and Gunnar. I sense this "opportunity" is nothing more than a prelude to calamity.

I know Brigand was only attempting to help the lads. Given the economy, they have no real work to speak of. We had tried to get Gunnar to go to University, as he certainly had the grades and aptitude for it. When Einar could not pass the exams to qualify, Gunnar was adamant that if his brother was not able to go, than neither would he. He could not stand to be separated from Einar for that long, and if that meant sacrificing the opportunity of University, then so be it.

Instead the twins have only been able to take odd lots of work here and there, but nothing steady. Neither was proficient enough of a fisherman to make a go of that, even though they both love piloting *the Nordlys* out to sea every chance they could get, under their father's oversight, of course.

Brigand had said that he only wanted to see if their Norwegian language skills were good enough to get them well paying jobs as interpreters of documents and recordings at the service, which he calls *"my Club"*.

Figure 18: A Return to Norway

He made it all sound so mundane and so safe, but I have come to feel that wherever lurks Wincer Wells, mayhem is not far off. I don't trust that man. If ever a man could be both as shady as an oak, and as flimsy as a willow at the same time, it is he.

The boys were so excited to go back to London. The good Lord knows that they don't get to visit there often. At least they'll spend a lot of time with their father. Brigand has been tasked to be there more and more, residing at the dreaded Blackfriars flat. He spends nearly every waking hour in the companionship of Wincer Wells. I know my husband is a good man, but I fear the old maxim that the good never raise up the bad, the bad only pull the good down to their level.

Brigand encouraged me to go with them, but I was still too angry to do so. Also, it would be as if I was condoning this endeavor, which I certainly am not.

———·•·———

Feb 3, 1937 - Brigand and the boys have just returned home from London. I don't know if I have ever seen them all so excited! The lads have "passed" their language proficiency tests by Brigand's employer, "*the Club*". Later, Brigand explained to me that they had passed "provisionally", with some reservations. It seems that their Norwegian tongues are slightly corrupted, and that, my husband says adamantly, must be corrected.

Although Brigand would never say it outright, I am sure he blames me for these impurities. Surely, my having spoken the Norwegian language only inside our home has introduced some mispronunciations and such that need to be ironed out of the twins' Nordic diction.

I asked Brigand why must their pronunciation be so tediously precise if they will only be interpreting documents and the like. He said I could not understand how demanding Wincer Wells could be and how he will not suffer three-quarter measures. Not from his staff, and most certainly not from himself or our twins. It kills me to hear Brigand speaks as if he is in awe of that bastard!

I next asked him that if their skills were not acceptable, than why are the boys so excited? I would not expect this level of energy from them for passing a test without top marks, most especially from Gunnar.

Brigand's answer shocked me. He said that Wincer is recommending that we all, myself included, spend several months in the Lofoten's this spring and summer to sharpen the twin's language skills. That news hit me with he force of a locomotive. Why is this man Wells taking such an interest in these young men?

At first I objected at the news. I reasoned that Brigand and the boys were in no condition to navigate *the Nordlys* through a thousand miles of the Norwegian Sea. Brigand told me not to worry, as *"the club"* will provide Royal Navy sailors to navigate and man *the Nordlys*.

I next contested that we couldn't possibly afford the cost of such a trip, and Brigand again said that his employer would cover it completely, except that we would be encouraged to stay with Brigand's family so as to maximize the twins' exposure to the local dialect.

As my objections were worn away, one by one, I weighed whether or not to make my next comment, fearing it could spark a bloody row between us. When I found the courage to tell him I did not trust Wells one bit, Brigand consoled me. I told him that Wells was making so heavy an investment in the boys that it scared me senseless.

He told me the "Wincer" was a good chap, a "straight rod" as he called it. He assured me Wells was only looking out for the twins' best interests. After all, they would earn far more as government translators than at anything other career not requiring a University degree.

I could not believe that my husband was standing tall for this man. He's not a 'straight rod' at all, I said, adding that Wells was actually rather dodgy. I told him I was sure that Wells was as crooked as a hound's back legs. He's got something he wants from the boys that he's hiding. I can only wonder if Brigand already knows what that might even be and is playing coy. In either case it scares me stiff.

Brigand had told me that he too was sure Wells wants something, that the man wants linguists. From a source he can trust. He's sure that there's a war coming, and he wants both boys to be at peak proficiency when that time comes in translating all the expected Nordic correspondence.

Birger said Wells was sure that the Huns will be wanting to get their grimy claws on as much of that Swedish iron ore as they can. That means shipping it out through Norway. Best that the boys' linguistic skills be at top strokes when all that comes to pass.

I told him I hoped he was right, and Brigand assured me he was. Why can't I believe my husband? Why do I still fear where this might lead?

I suppose it's only that I fear what the man has already done to Brigand, and that Wells will do so again to Einar and Gunnar. When I said this to Brigand, he became unusually cross with me. He said that had it not been for Wincer Wells, he would have died that night off that "damn Turkish beach."

I replied that had it not been for Wincer Wells he never would have been there in the first place. This only infuriated my husband further.

———•—

May 15, 1937 - This morning we sailed into the *Vestfjorden*, the massive fjord encapsulated by the Lofoten Archipelago. I have never seen either a more rugged or more lovely landscape in all my life. This was after several horrid days at sea, although Brigand said by his experience the seas were behaving themselves quite nicely.

I stood on the deck, just behind Brigand's specially modified chair. I am actually very thankful for this sea voyage, as it has lifted my husband's spirits immensely. He had been in a dark mood for several months before the episode of the boys being tested. I fear when he goes there, into that inner shell of his, for he nearly blocks me out completely. He becomes as quiet as a tomb, and worse perhaps, equally cold.

What does he think when in those moods? Through which blackened shadows does his mind wander? I assume I may never truly know, but when I am truthful with myself, I fear most what I know he does also - his ending his own life, just as his father once had.

Yet, returning to Lofoten has been a blessing. Brigand holds my hand in his, and points to the landscape, explaining its features and its associated lore. He takes the time to share everything with me. There is much snow still in the mountains and the waterfalls are everywhere, cascading like silvery plumes. The air is crisp and clean, and the mountains surround us across the great expanse of this fjord, as blue as colored Italian glass. It felt in that moment when we had reached the *Vestfjorden*, as if we had reached safety itself, as if we were held in the very palm of the hand of God.

Brigand pointed out the islands of Skrova as we approached. The islanders had built a lighthouse just off its outermost shoreline, whose beacon he said he would very much have loved to navigate by on his earlier trips. As we gathered closer to the main island of Skrova, I can make out a multitude of rocky outcroppings jutting from the water, much like that upon which the lighthouse is situated. These must be extremely treacherous waters to navigate in the dark. I cannot believe that my husband, like his father before him, had done so many times.

As we sailed past the Skrova lighthouse another vessel came out to sail aside us. It was much smaller than *the Nordlys,* and had difficulty matching speed with us. Aboard its deck were two men, about Brigand's age.

"Hello, *Birger,*" they yelled together, waving their arms at us. They welcomed him home and said they were so excited at his return. I was very much surprised that I was able to understand them, as they spoke in a Norwegian tongue that was pure and undiluted. Brigand waved back to them with the enthusiasm of a small child, and this made me tremendously happy. He said to me that these were his cousins Hakron and Eric.

Later we met them upon the dock. They had assisted *the Nordlys* crew in winching Brigand and his wheel-about chair ashore, as the ladder was near impossible for him to manage with his false leg. No sense in coming this far only to drown under the dock, my husband said, just before he was delivered onto the dockside like some inanimate, lifeless cargo.

His cousin Hakron had again said that it was so good to have *Birger* there once again. My husband seemed delighted to be called by his former name, never used by myself except under only the most intimate of circumstances. Soon, not only was I standing aside my *Birger,* but so by then were the twins. He told his cousins, that he now went by the name 'Brigand', no longer *Birger.* He then introduced me as his "lovely wife" Tilly, and the boys as his sons Einar and Gunnar.

After all the pleasantries were completed, Erik said something in Norwegian, assuming I did not understand the language. He told Brigand, "At least your children are proud to have Nordic names. You leave here last as *Birger* and return as *Brigand*? You leave with our local *Tulla* only to return with an Englishwoman named *Tilly?* Is it that this woman will not allow you to be the Nordic man your father raised you to be?"

His cousin did not shrink in embarrassment when his brother Hakron said to Erik that he was, as always, being so rude to Skrova's guests. Yet, Eric did so when Brigand laughed with a rolling roar and said Erik might owe his wife an apology, "For you see, she speaks a perfectly functional form of the Norwegian language."

Erik's face turned an instant shade of crimson in his embarrassment, and although his accusations had struck me with great force, I forgave him as Brigand continued to laugh aloud.

In advance of our coming, Brigand had sent a letter in which he said that he had much to explain when he arrived. Brigand then told his cousins that he was very sorry to have read in their return letter that Uncle Ørjan had passed away. He said that was such very tragic of news to receive, and he asked after his Aunt Eydis?

Brigand's uncle had died during a landslide while hiking alone in the hills on a nearby island. I cannot imagine a more terrible way to have perished, crushed under the fallen rocks, his last few moments alive in unbearable pain, only to be slowly suffocated as the accompanying flow of mud strangled out his life.

A perverse sorrow crept over me as they discussed this. All laughter from moments before had been driven off, just as light is driven out by the solemnity of darkness.

Brigand was then told his Aunt Eydis had been very sad for many months and only the news of his coming to stay at Skrova had lifted her spirits somewhat. Erik and Hakron had said their mother was quite old, and had moved in with Hakron and his wife. Given this, her empty *Rorbu* was prepared for where we would spend the next several months.

Brigand then asked as to Tulla's parents, and both cousins looked awkwardly in my direction. I told them that it was perfectly fine, that *"Birger"* and I had discussed this. I had intentionally used his Nordic name, which made both his cousins smile. Hakron said that the Jacobsens, Tulla's parents, were both still very much alive and both still very much residing in Skrova. Then Erik said that he did not believe Mr. Jacobsen wished to see Brigand.

Birger told him he could understand this, but to please tell Mrs. Jacobsen that he would like to meet with her. He had news of her daughter to share with her.

I had been forewarned of this by Brigand, so that I might not be shocked. Yet, it still hurt to hear him say these words. I knew he was intent to meet with Tulla's mother to share the photographs of her daughter, the woman going by my own given name in America. Brigand had shown the photos to me in our cabin during the sail. The photographs were provided by that rogue, Wincer Wells, and were complete with images of Tulla's young son who was coming up on four years old. She had named him Jacob, surely taken from her actual family name of Jacobsen. My heart breaks over and over again every time I think of her child's name. His was another precious gift of life given to a woman who could literally care for no one else but herself. A woman who could not even care for her own infant twin children. So now she raises a son whose name is an intentional shambles of hidden meanings. She still to this day carries my name, and has the gall of using it as a middle name for her son, Jacob Barrett Conley.

32

A Year of Crises

"An Appeaser Is One Who Feeds a Crocodile, Hoping It Will Eat Him Last."

Winston Spencer Churchill

If the Nazi Party had flung aside its cape of secrecy two years earlier in 1936, then in 1938 it was yearning to flex the strength of its military's muscles. The year began with Hitler making outrageous demands on the much smaller state of Austria, hoping that they would not be met, and the Nazi war machine could be released in response.

It would be wrong to suggest this menacing fascist state was attempting to overpower a lesser free democracy, for Austria had already become a fascist state itself. Like elsewhere in Europe in the 1920s and 1930s, Austria was politically fragmented and the major parties were based in either Fascism or Communism. Fascism won out under a leader named Engelbert Dollfuss when he seized the Chancellorship in 1932. He declared himself dictator in 1933, just as Adolf Hitler was coming to power in Germany. Dollfuss quickly strengthened his own grip on power, and soon had his Christian Social Party installed as the only viable political party in Austrian politics. Chancellor Dollfuss had used force to ban the other Austrian fascist party, the National Socialists, and the Social Democrats (aligned with the Austrian Communist Party), as well as other independent parties from physically re-entering the legislature building. Dollfuss then had many Austrian Nazi party members rounded up and imprisoned.

Hitler was outraged by Dollfuss' suppression of his Nazi party within the country of his own birth. The situation came to a head just days before the death of President Hindenburg on August 2, 1934, after which Hitler would go on to become the undisputed German dictator.

Figure 19: Hitler and Chamberlain at Munich (1938)

On July 25, 1934, less than one full month after the *Night of Long Knives*, over one hundred and fifty members of the Austrian Nazi Party, dressed as uniformed Austrian Army personnel, entered the Chancellery Building in Vienna. Dollfuss was shot in the throat and later that day died. Other Nazis had seized a nearby radio station, and broadcast reports that Dollfuss had resigned. Whether the Nazis had only intended to physically force Dollfuss to resign, but ended up shooting him after he refused, is not known. However, the *coup d'état* was foiled when Dr. Kurt von Schuschnigg, Dollfuss' eventual successor as Chancellor, led forces to capture the conspirators. Thirteen of the Nazis' number would later be found guilty of Dollfuss' murder and hanged.

It is clear that this event was done with the knowledge and complicity of Hitler and his government. German troops had been amassed at the Austrian border in advance of the coup, and had it not been for Hitler's fear of Mussolini's army (who was then aligned with Austria), the Nazis likely would have stormed into the country.

Many may find that last statement to be incredible, but Mussolini's army had been not only repeated but *feared* to that point, while Germany's was still mostly untested. Austria had already entered into close relations with Italy, and used this border alliance to keep Hitler at arm's length. When *Il Duce* moved four of his tank divisions into the Brenner Pass on the Austro-Italian border as a result of the attempted coup in 1934, Hitler amazingly backed down.

Over the next two years Hitler worked hard to develop his own direct relationship with Mussolini. By late 1936, after the propaganda success of the Berlin Olympics became apparent, Mussolini had also come to desire a close alliance with *Der Führer*. It was then that the Berlin-Rome Axis was created. Mussolini declared it the axis upon which the continent would turn. When Mussolini agreed to his first visit to Germany during late September 1937, his train was welcomed in Munich by massive cheering crowds as well as by *Der Führer* himself.

Mussolini was given a hero's welcome as he was transported across Germany to tour armament producing factories, review goose-stepping parades of Nazi troops and after nightfall, witness massive torch-lit parades and rallies. On his final stop in Berlin, *Il Duce* was introduced by Hitler to a crowd of over one million Germans as the finest statesman of his day. To the crowd's delight, Mussolini addressed them in excellent German and spoke of the cooperation that was yet to come of their two powerful fascist states.

After this carefully choreographed homage to the Italian leader's ego, no longer would Italy protest any movement by Germany in achieving that which had been desired since the days of the Prussian Leader Bismarck himself - the annexation, or *Anschluss*, of Austria into the German Reich.

Having secured Mussolini's complicit non-interference, it was time to make a second pass at annexing Austria. Throughout the end of 1937, Hitler had the Austrian Nazi Party continue to foment mayhem in the streets of the cities there.

Then, on February 11, 1938, Hitler had invited the Austrian Chancellor Schuschnigg to his Berchtesgaden retreat. His residence, known as the *Berghof*, was actually in the Obersalzberg, the hills which towered above the German town of Berchtesgaden. The *Berghof* was perched high in the Bavarian Alps, and was less than twenty miles from Salzburg, Austria just across the border.

The chalet had an impressive view of the snow-capped Austrian mountains of Hitler's youth. The invitation to this residence of Hitler's was not unprecedented for world leaders, especially those from the recent past. The Duke and Duchess of Windsor (the recently abdicated British King Edward VIII and his new American wife) had visited only months before. As had former British Prime Minister David Lloyd George nearly a year earlier.

Schuschnigg thought he was being invited to a cordial discussion regarding the easing of tensions between Germany and Austria. Upon his arrival, he was surprised and dismayed by the presence of multiple German Generals. Hitler then took several hours to berate his Austrian counterpart, and demanded he sign a list of concessions, which included lifting the ban on the Austrian Nazi Party, the release of imprisoned Austrian Nazis, and the placement of Austrian Nazi party members in key government positions.

The German ultimatum was unacceptable, and the Schuschnigg said he would not sign any such document. This did not dissuade Hitler from continuing his onslaught against the Austrian Chancellor. Hitler even took periodic asides with his Generals outside of Schuschnigg's earshot just to intimidate the man. It was clear the Austrian Chancellor was brought to Hitler's retreat under false pretenses and the entire visit was choreographed to put Schuschnigg under intense pressure.

Dr. Schuschnigg eventually weakened and gave into the relentless brow-beating. Possibly having feared for his own safety, he signed the list of demands, but only after having gained *Der Führer*'s *verbal agreement* on the continued independence of Austria. That verbal commitment did not last for long.

By March of 1938, having had his demands from Austria enacted, Hitler began to pursue his true intentions of taking over the country from within. His jailed Nazi personnel had been released by the Austians. Some were placed in key government positions, including the Minister of the Interior. Through this office, Hitler then expanded his demands to the Chancellor, which included his principal desire, the total annexation of Austria and all of its seven million German speaking peoples into the Third Reich. In German, this annexation was known as the *Anschluss*.

In response to Hitler's new demand for *Anschluss*, Dr. Kurt von Schuschnigg decreed that he would hold a national plebiscite on Sunday, March 13, to settle whether the Austrian people desired to be unified with the German nation. Hitler was infuriated. He feared the potential embarrassment of the Austrian populace voting down by the country's union with Germany. Overcome with rage, Hitler mobilized his troops and amassed them on the Austrian border. Hitler publicly threatened an invasion on Saturday the 12th unless the Austrian plebiscite for Sunday was cancelled.

At the same time, the Austrian Nazi Party took to the streets, creating mayhem through riots and the burning of businesses and government buildings. Austria was clearly in crisis, and Britain and France had signaled that they did not intend to involve themselves in any way. In fact, when the Soviet Union recommended discussions of international intervention, British Prime Minister Neville Chamberlain declined his country's participation.

The threatened invasion and the crisis of unrest in the streets of Vienna left the Austrian Chancellor Schuschnigg no other course of action than to resign. As he did so on Friday evening, he took to the airwaves to tell the Austrian people and the world of Hitler's treachery. The Austrian Minister of the Interior, one of the high placed Nazis quickly claimed the Chancellorship and sent a pre-scripted "telegram" asking for the German Army to enter Austria in order to restore order.

On Saturday morning, the *Wehrmacht* stormed into Austria, crossing a mountain bridge over the River Inn near *Der Führer*'s birthplace town of Braunau-am-Inn. From this very mountainous region would come many of Hitler's alpine commando units that would later prove so deadly and effective.

The Austrian populace welcomed the Nazis, and particularly Hitler, as liberators. Later that very same day (Saturday, March 12) Hitler entered the town of Linz on the Danube River, where he had moved to as a young boy, to rapturous applause. After entering the capital of Vienna a few days later, on March 15, he addressed massive crowds from the balcony of the Imperial Palace. Hitler declared Austria to be a province of the German Reich. Again, the applause was thunderous, and later Hitler would boast that he had never before felt so much love from his subjects.

———·•·———

Beware the Ides of March wrote Shakespeare of another day of treachery, nearly two thousand years earlier, but it equally applied to Hitler's homecoming.

Thus in 1938, Hitler demonstrated to the world his unabashed use of the leveraged threat of the *Wehrmacht* to achieve his political objectives beyond the established borders of Germany. The world quietly watched as Hitler enriched the Third Reich in minerals, manpower and stature.

France, Britain and other European countries did nothing to prevent this second defiance of the terms of the Treaty of Versailles. Nor did Italy, since by then Mussolini had undertaken a close military alliance with Germany. Hitler's letter to *Il Duce* following the *Anschluss* thanked the Italian leader profusely for his non-interference, stating, *"I shall never forget you for this."* The communique was gushing with sentiment, as *Der Führer* thanked *Il Duce* for making possible his conquest of Austrian lands which were undertaken without *Der Führer's* army having had to fire a single shot.

Der Führer sealed the *Anschluss* by holding his own plebiscite in both Austria and Greater Germany in April of that year. Not surprisingly, both were reported by the Nazis to have approved the union by over 99% of the votes cast.

Almost immediately afterwards, the Nazi policing functions began to abuse and humiliate the Jewish citizens of Austria. Many photos and much newsreel footage exists documenting Jews, surrounded by Nazi thugs, forced to scrub the streets of her cities as other citizens watched and jeered.

Austria would soon have the first concentration camp outside Germany at Mauthausen on the Danube. There over 35,000 Jews would be executed, not counting those shipped off to the extermination camps like Auschwitz II - Birkenau, later to be established to the east.

Perhaps fortune intervened in the fate of the ex-Chancellor Dr. Kurt von Schuschnigg and his family. He was kept under house arrest for several months. After this, he was confined at Vienna's Hotel Metropole in a small room and was forced to clean the rooms and latrines of his Nazi captors for nearly a year-and-a-half. He then was shipped to the camps at

Sachsenhausen and Dachau. After being evacuated from Dachau by the Gestapo, away from oncoming Americans at the war's end, he was taken to a Tyrollean alpine village town where Schuschnigg was intended to be executed after having survived nearly seven years in hellish captivity.

On May 4, 1945, he and his family were saved by American troops who liberated them before their death warrants could be carried out. He would go on to document the travails of himself, his family and his country in the highly acclaimed memoire, *"Austrian Requiem"*, first published in 1946.

———·•··——

In Poland, all communications of the Germans, both the open speeches of Hitler and the Enigma-encoded traffic of the *Wehrmacht*, were closely monitored. Thanks to the breaking of the Enigma code years earlier, the Polish had insights that the rest of Germany's neighbors could not possibly understand. It is not known if they could have fully perceived the vulnerability of the Nazis as they moved into the Rhineland in '36, or into Austria in '38. But it is widely accepted that had France or Britain militarily resisted in either case, Hitler would have had no option but to back down at both those points in time. The German war machine had grown fearfully strong, but it was still vulnerable at that point to resistance from any first-tier military.

The Poles could surely foretell that Hitler's constant demand for *Lebensraum*, or living space, in his open speeches would ultimately place their own soil in jeopardy. The Poles began plans to shore up their own military. This created a demand for soldiers, and the Polish youth were eager to sign up.

———·•··——

Germany was again soon on the demand for territorial acquisition. Following the *Anschluss* of Austria, European leaders had grown weary of Hitler's tactics. With the completion of the *Anschluss,* Germany had Czechoslovakia encircled on three sides. Britain and France were now eager to prevent war.

It was then that Hitler raised the issue of the *Sudetenland* - the German speaking territories of Czechoslovakia. These territories along the new German border were some of the most productive of the Czechoslovakian country.

Hitler had ordered his generals to prepare *"Case Green"* for the military invasion of Czechoslovakia even before the *Anschluss*. The Nazi plebiscite, in which the annexation of Austria had been validated, had been held in April. Hitler wasted no time, and in May brought forward the first Czechoslovakian crisis. Again, *Wehrmacht* troops were amassed at their neighbor's borders. Czechoslovakia and its well-trained military was prepared to fight the Nazis. Prague moved significant troops to the border to engage the *Wehrmacht*, should they invade.

The May crisis over the *Sudetenland* was ended when Berlin's military plans were leaked to the public. Hitler declared these documents all to be fabricated, which of course they were not. He declared reports of German divisions being amassed along Czechoslovakia's border as mere fiction. Having to make these public denials only made him all the more intent on annexing the *Sudetenland*, and its three million German speaking subjects. Once more infuriated with having to delay his expansion plans, Hitler ordered his generals to revise their planned invasion for no later than the first of October. His generals argued that to do so on the level *Der Führer* demanded would leave insufficient troops to defend against the expected response from the French in the West. Hitler ignored them.

Over the summer of 1938, Hitler ratcheted up his rhetoric in his public speeches on the deteriorating conditions within Czechoslovakia, and the need to protect the *Sudetenland* Germans. In reality, the disruptions were being instigated by the Czech Nazi Party members themselves, and the German propagandists greatly over-amplified their disruptive efforts as being conducted by anti-Germanic Czech extremists.

Over this period the Nazis became aware of the British Prime Minister Neville Chamberlain's desire to do anything necessary to keep the peace in Europe. Chamberlain and his administration had received great praise for his calm response to the May Czechoslovakian Crisis. Hitler was ecstatic when he came to understand the British Prime Minister was so very anxious to discuss territorial concessions to prevent another war in Europe. Chamberlain became the next world leader to be invited to Hitler's *Berghof* chalet above Berchtesgaden.

On September 15, 1938, at the age of sixty-nine years old, Neville Chamberlain, who had never before flown in an airplane, took off from London. His flight to Bavaria took nearly seven hours. One must wonder what his thoughts were as he peacefully flew over the European continent for the first time.

Hitler did little to accommodate Chamberlain. He could have met the British Prime Minister along the Rhine, shortening the elder politician's trip. Instead *Der Führer* welcomed him to the *Berghof* Chalet, requiring Chamberlain to not only fly seven hours to Munich, but then to transfer to a three hour train ride to Berchtesgaden. Even then, the *Führer* refused to meet Chamberlain at the station, only sending a car for him. Hitler awaited in his chalet set in the Obersalzberg.

Despite the travel indignations inflicted upon the aged British Prime Minister, Hitler received Chamberlain with much more respect than that given the Austrian Chancellor Schuschnigg before him. As the talks progressed, Chamberlain was given a list of demands from the German leader culminating with the incorporation of the *Sudetenland* into the German Reich. Chamberlain agreed to present these demands to the Czechs, who were not invited to the meeting, as well as to the French leadership.

The Czechoslovak leaders initially rejected the German demands. Chamberlain pressured them before he returned to talks with Hitler on the 23rd at the town of Bad Godesburg, this time much closer to Britain on the Rhine River. Chamberlain presented a plan for Germany incorporating the *Sudetenland* after a plebiscite of those regions, but Hitler then demanded the *immediate* annexation of these lands. The Czechoslovaks were relying on their joint defense agreement with France to keep Hitler from invading. Yet, the Czechoslovaks fully intended to fight should the German army cross their border.

Hitler maintained that if the lands were not annexed to Germany by the first day of October, Germany would invade Czechoslovakia and Europe would once again be in a state of war. Neville Chamberlain flew for a third time in just over two weeks to Germany, this time to partake in the Munich Conference of four powers: Germany, Britain, France and Italy. Hitler, Chamberlain, Daladier and Mussolini represented their countries. Incredibly, the Czechs were not even invited to participate in determining the fate of their own country.

Late in the evening of September 30, the four powers reached the agreement that awarded the *Sudetenland* to Germany in exchange for Hitler's agreement not to take any further military action upon the rest of Czechoslovakia. The Czechoslovak dignitaries, staying in a nearby Munich hotel, were forced to consent when Britain and France declared they would not assist the country should Hitler invade.

Once more the military crisis had been averted when Hitler was appeased. He was handed the *Sudetenland* provinces without so much as a skirmish, but the man with the increasingly aggressive military remained frustrated that he had not been able to demonstrate its might. That would come all too soon in 1939.

Neville Chamberlain returned to London, having claimed to have achieved "Peace for our time." He was lauded by the press and politicians alike, with perhaps a single exception. Winston Churchill said in response to Chamberlain's claim, "You were given the choice between war and dishonour. You chose dishonour, and you will have war."

———•———

The last crisis of 1938 occurred on November 7, after a Jewish teenager, Herschel Grynszpan, attempted to assassinate a German diplomat, Ernst vom Rath, in Paris. Rath was severely wounded. By November 9, word had spread that vom Rath had died from his wounds. Nazi propagandists precipitated a pogrom against Jews throughout Germany over November 9 and 10. The Nazis employed paramilitary and Hitler Youth groups to initiate the attack, which was planned to look like a spontaneous uprising of the German people. The windows of shops and residences were smashed throughout the German nation.

The pogrom took place not in nearly every corner of the Reich, including Austria and even the German dominated free city of Danzig. Hundreds of synagogues were burned. Law enforcement made no effort to prevent the rioting, looting and arson that ensued. Some 30,000 jewish men were rounded up and shipped to concentration camps, the bulk of which did nothing but they to defend their shops and families.

In the German language, the pogrom was known as *Kristallnacht*, or the *Night of Broken Glass*. Hundreds of Jews died during it, as well as the tens of thousands that were rounded up immediately afterwards. Unfortunately, *Kristallnacht* would become only a tragic milestone along the increasingly violent path of seething anti-semitism which would lead to the Nazis eventual adoption of the horrific *Final Solution*.

———•·•———

Also during 1938, the Secret Intelligence Service (SIS) procured a picturesque estate roughly fifty miles northeast of London in the Buckinghamshire countryside. It was conveniently located near the main rail line to Euston Station. Despite this, it was quite removed from the hustle and bustle of London itself. Its manor house was done up in a most charming Dutch Baroque style which dated back to the late 1870s. This was set just beyond a large tree-lined pond. Its lands were expansive with gently rolling lawns. This facility would, in just over a year, become the Government Communications and Cypher School (GC&CS). These lands are better known as Bletchley Park.

Figure 20: Zakopane Region of the Polish Tatras Mountains

33 The Brothers Bratajewski

1938

"… it is better to perish than live as slaves."

Winston Spencer Churchill

It was in late 1938 that Bogdan Bratajewski and his brother Albin both finished their summer employment upon the Schenning farm outside Breslau. With Germany's growing territorial acquisitions and her continual demands for more, the people of Breslau had become increasingly antagonistic towards Poles. All throughout the region, it was obvious that Poland would be next in the target countries to provide the Germans the *"Lebensraum", or "Living Space"* that Hitler had promised.

But these two young men would not return to their village in the Tatras Mountains near Zakopane. In the autumn, just after the Munich Conference had awarded the Czech Sudetenland to Hitler, both boys headed off to volunteer for the Polish Military. Albin was accepted into the army, and trained to become a member of Poland's elite mountain forces. Bogdan had always joked that his brother was half goat, as he moved so effortlessly on the rocky terrain of their home region.

Meanwhile Bogdan went to the town of Dęblin to achieve his boyhood dream. Dęblin sits at the at the confluence of the Vistula and Wieprz Rivers, a site famous in Polish history, for near there General Kościuszko had his final engagement with the Russians in 1794. Also nearby, the first air squadron bearing Kościuszko's name was formed by American volunteers in 1919. And from near Dęblin came the reserve Polish troops after the American fliers had spotted the gap in the lines of the Russian Forces that was so critical to *the Miracle at the Vistula* in 1920 .. Bogdan had always desired nothing more than to learn to become a fighter pilot to defend his country. He would train to do so at Dęblin. Neither boy realized just how quickly they would each be thrust into the unforgiving talons of war.

Figure 21: Cairngorm Mountains, Scottish Highlands

34 The Highlands

"Kites rise highest against the wind - not with it."

Winston Spencer Churchill

Diane had become mesmerized in the readings from Tilly MacAlvor's diary. Nearly everything else slipped from her focus. She lived only for the next of Tilly's entries. She had become a time-traveling voyeur, as she spied into the recollections of a woman many decades since deceased.

Sophie had even faded from Diane's thoughts, at least over the past several days. Diane had listened to Emory's advice to give the young Pole her freedom. "She shall return," he had argued, "just focus on the case at hand. Before you know it, Sophie will be ringing you up, Diane."

Diane had progressed through the entirety of Tilly's entries to the very end. She had returned to specific entries that would assist her in telling the incredible tale of Tulla Jacobsen becoming Cassandra, and Cassandra becoming Tilly MacAlvor.

October 5, 1938 - I am infuriated with Brigand. Ever since we returned from Skrova and the waters of the *Vestfjorden*, he has been continuously anxious around me. He was not in one of his dark moods, no, this was totally different. He was edgy, and very much unlike himself, he seemed a bit dodgy. It was as if he had news that he did not know how to break to me. At least that was what I sensed, and today I found that my intuitions were spot on, as usual.

Brigand confessed to me, but only after I had badgered him terribly. He finally admitted that Wincer Wells had signed up both boys for training in the Scottish Highlands. I asked why in heaven's name would translators need training in mountaineering? It was then that Brigand's logjam of secrets broke free and gushed forth.

Apparently, Wincer had been told of how well the twins had blended in during our extended trip to Norway. He now wanted the lads to do some very basic in-country work for him. It was this that Brigand could not bear to share with me, and I was incensed.

It's what Wells wanted all along, I told him. There never was a need for translators. That was simply a cover story for his real intentions. Did he know all along?

Brigand was shocked that I would confront him so. He claimed that Wells was not just playing him, or me, all along. He assured me that there certainly must be a true need for translators for Brigand wished to have Gunnar take up that position only.

I was shocked. So that bastard Wells wished to separate our boys, putting Einar on the ground in Norway whilst his twin brother stayed in London, or God knows where, to translate Norwegian documents. Separate the twins, how absurd! I told my husband that they would never stand for it.

As it were, Brigand had already put it to the boys, but they steadfastly refused to be separated. Either they both went together to Norway or they both would become translators. Brigand said Wells tried again to get him to persuade the boys to split, but my husband told him that they had never in their life been separated by even the smallest distance, and they would never consent to be. He admitted to Wells he did not know if they could even function independently of each other.

He said Wells became extremely frustrated. Brigand said that Wells barked at him that he made them sound like bloody Siamese twins. Brigand said he responded to Wincer that for all practical purposes, they might as well be joined at the hip, that they did everything together.

Wells finally conceded. This is what caused Birger to harbor so much angst over the past several weeks. Both boys have agreed to take their training in the Highlands. Brigand's *club* has a special facility there and they would train over the rest of the winter months. Exactly where in the Highlands, Brigand said he was not free to reveal to me.

He did say that if they both passed their tests, they might ship out to Norway in the spring. That was when my emotions exploded. How could he ever think of sending our lads off into harms way? I could have throttled him, there and then.

Brigand then told me to not put the cart ahead of the horse. They were both now young men, 24 years old apiece. Brigand then said Gunnar would always do fine, so long as he was with Einar. Norway is not exactly in harm's way, he said, besides what harm could possibly befall them so long as they were together?

Yes, of course our twins have grown into strapping young men, but I don't think Gunnar has the adventurous streak in him that Einar has. How could Gunnar ever survive that far away? I know that I see them only through a mother's eyes, but they are my children. Perhaps not by birth, but certainly by the amount of love and worry I have invested in them both through the years.

I am so terribly worried about what is going on in Europe. Only a few days ago, Prime Minister Chamberlain said that he had secured Herr Hitler to a peace treaty, and that Germany would never again be at war with the British Empire. Yet, I don't believe that Hun leader one bit. He promises peace to get what he wants, only to then turn and begin to foment the next crisis. Brigand agrees. He thinks, despite Chamberlain's declarations, that war is coming to Europe.

And still he seems fine to be on a path to place our boys in the field, where they might face the enemy? I asked him this directly.

He answered that they would be in northern Norway in the Lofoten Island Mountains. Made me swear to never reveal I had told him so. Most peaceful place in the world, he went on. There is no way that a European war would ever find them there. Safest place for them to possibly be deployed. Brigand reasoned it was far safer for them than even staying here, once the war breaks out

Yes, he is my husband, and I love him, but I can never forgive him for allowing Wincer Wells to sink his hooks into our dear sweet twins.

The next several months of Tilly's entries were basically a mother's worries over the safety of her children while they trained in Scotland. Birger knew exactly where they were training, but could not share that information with Tilly, so it was not reflected in her diary. However, Diane also had the files that Devereaux had sent her on the twins.

In the eastern Highlands of Scotland, there existed during World War II a camp for the training of overseas operatives. It was based in a massive former Victorian hunting lodge in Scotland's Cairngorm Mountains. It was given the designation Special Training Site 26, or STS-26. It was set among thick forests, beyond which rose some of the highest peaks in the United Kingdom. Also, the lodge was situated in the center of a triangle of extremely rugged terrain between *Loch Morlich, Loch an Eilein*, and *Loch Avon*. The name of the Victorian hunting manor in between them that was the training headquarters was *Drumintoul Lodge*.

In a few years, it would be transferred from MI6 to the Special Operations Executive (SOE), which Churchill would establish in mid-1940. This would create a rivalry between the two organizations that would last throughout the war.

Einar and Gunnar had never been to the Cairngorms before. Diane assumed that they must both have had the same initial thought, that it looked like landscape stolen from above the fjords of Norway. It appeared to be the perfect training ground.

Throughout the winter of 1938, Einar and Gunnar underwent extensive training in self-defense skills, small arms and automatic weapons handling and marksmanship, radio and explosives handling, winter survival skills and especially in mountaineering. The final test in the last category was to rappel nearly four hundred feet down the side of a sheer granite cliff. It was this test that Gunnar could not master. Not only had Einar completed the rappelling test himself, but he then did his best to coach his brother through this trial. However, every time that Gunnar would begin the controlled drop, he would freeze and cling to the granite outcropping in a horrific panic. It was a fear that was not rational, but rather instinctual. While Einar was quick to master his own fear through the confidence he had in his athletic abilities, Gunnar did not have that same confidence, and as a result, never conquered the rappelling requirement.

Gunnar's lack of ability to pass the mountaineering training produced a most immediate problem for Wincer Wells. He had only ever really wanted Einar for the missions in Norway, but the twins had decided that they must go together.

Einar was strong and athletic, with a heart set on adventure. He would not flinch under pressure, or so the psychologists that tested them had deemed.

Gunnar, on the other hand, was bookish and introspective. Not totally uncommon in twins, the psychologists had said, to have this disparity in personalities. Gunnar was intelligent, with excellent problem solving skills. The concern was that as he thought through complex issues, he was quick to see the threats inherent in the situation. Whereas Einar would act immediately, Gunnar would think, and with that thinking the seeds of caution, and ultimately of fear, were sewn.

Gunnar had failed the required testing on the mountain's side. The training officer refused to sign off on his being ready for deployment to Norway, despite extensive prodding from Wells. A most frustrated Wincer then traveled from *Drumintoul Lodge* in the Cairngorm Mountains to Dundee along the coast to seek the help of Brigand MacAlvor.

Wells once again suggested that the twins be given split assignments. Brigand assured him that this would be a futile effort. Even if MI6 would threaten them with imprisonment, the twins would not separate. What if they were threatened with separate imprisonment, one twin separated from the other? Brigand was sure even this they would endure over a voluntary separation.

"Why must you resort to threatening them at all, Wincer?" Birger asked as the two men walked along the River Tay Esplanade.

"Then what precisely do you recommend, Brigand?"

"You still have the full confidence of 'C'," Brigand said. "Have him sign off on the override of the trainer's assessment."

"C" in this case was not Mansfield Cumming, who had died over a decade before. Instead, it was Admiral Hugh "Quex" Sinclair, who had succeeded him.

"I am unsure that he will agree to do that," Wells said. "He is a stickler for protocol, and as such would likely have me find another agent for this effort. I have too much invested in Einar already, and finding another Norwegian speaker who can pass the psychological profiling and the training will cost me another year and a half, at least. The good Lord only knows where Hitler and the Huns will be by that time."

"Look," Brigand responded, "explain to 'C' as you did to me, that this is a mere reconnaissance mission. The boys will be doing nothing more than riding the Ofoten Railway, tracking the Iron Ore traffic, and perhaps identifying potential sabotage options, should the Royal Navy need to send in a commando squad to disrupt the railway. It's not like Gunnar is going to be climbing those damn mountains, or ever need to rappel down their sides. 'C' will come around and see the sense of it all."

Wincer Wells thanked Brigand, and told him he would follow his advice and work on Chief Sinclair to override the training. Brigand drove him to Edinburgh, where Wells caught the train to London. Wells looked out the window as the train rolled through the English northlands, deep in meditation. What he had not told Brigand was that he, as well as his Norwegian operation, had recently been reassigned from Chief Sinclair's personal staff to Section D. This was a new section that had been established by Sinclair in the anticipation of war. Its function was to be focused on sabotage of German operations throughout Europe. Sinclair had told Wells not to take the assignment as a demotion, which he did, but rather that the Norway operation belonged under Section D's charter: *"D for Destruction'*

The problem was that Wells had not yet developed a close relationship with his new section chief, Major Laurence Grand, who had made his bones in the Corps of Royal Engineers. Worse than that, the two just did not gel. Wells had been a career intelligence officer, and Grand was a Military Engineer by training. It soon became apparent that spooks and sappers were not meant to co-exist peacefully.

It was on that train that Wincer Wells decided on his next move. He would never convince Major Grand to approve his plan. He knew this, instinctively. Instead, Wincer would go directly to "C", going over Major Grand's head. He would request Sinclair to sign off on sending Gunnar on the Norway Operation despite his failed training. He hoped that this "C" might possibly be persuaded to do so, but was unsure he would.

Had Mansfield Cumming still been alive, Wells would have had no problem convincing him so. But Sinclair had been "C" for sixteen years, now, and Wells had never been as close to he as he had been to Cumming. He feared the chief might reject his request, but he had no other option than to try his best.

The next day, Wells took the tube to St. James Park Station, where he was only steps away from SIS headquarters building at 54 Broadway. In 1926, just a few years after taking over for the suddenly deceased Mansfield Cumming, Hugh Sinclair as "C" had decided he needed something more befitting the growing intelligence agency, and the location in Westminster was perfectly situated.

Wells went to his office. He passed the duty board, which showed Major Grand to be out of office this day. Perfect, Wells thought, as he would be free to call upon Chief Sinclair with his request. At 10:45 that morning he strode to Sinclair's office complex. He found in the outer office, behind her perfectly organized desk, Sinclair's secretary, the lovely Penny Quidling. She had always been kind to Wells when he was on Sinclair's staff, and even on the last few years of Cumming's staff. She had been secretary to both chiefs.

"Oh, Commander Wells," she said, as she flashed a polite smile at him, "how nice of you to drop by."

"Good morning, Miss Quidling," replied Wincer, as he forced as pleasant a smile as he could in response. "I was hoping to have a few…"

"Isn't it exciting about Section D!" Quidlling interrupted. "You are so lucky, you are."

"I am afraid I don't follow," Wells replied, not understanding her reference.

"Oh, come now, I am sure you of all people are in the know, Wincer" Penny played along. "The hotel…Hmmm?"

"Still lost, I'm afraid," Wells said, his face twitching spastically.

"The St. Ermins, dear," she replied, "Section D is going to be relocating to offices in the St. Ermin's Hotel. I think that building is just lovely. Chief has taken me to tea there on several occasions. My birthday mostly. He likes it because it is just a short walk away, and he knows I adore it there."

"I see," said Wells as he felt the news was just one more pull of his career away from the front office. "I was hoping…"

As he spoke Penny reached up and placed her hands on his suit sleeve.

"Do be a dear and not tell anyone that I let you in on the secret," she interrupted. "I not only thought you knew, but I thought this had your hand all over it. What were you about to ask me, Commander Wells?"

"I was hoping to get a few minutes with 'C' today, actually, if I might, " Wells finally got out.

"That won't be possible I am afraid," Penny replied. "He's been called away on an emergency conference. He won't be in for the rest of the week."

"But the duty board says he's in," replied Wells.

"I fear that is my mistake, Commander, far too much going on at present," answered Quidling just as her phone rang.

She lifted the handset to her ear, and upon hearing the voice already projecting from it, she stiffened from her relaxed posture and answered, "Yes sir."

Penny Quidling then pointed to the handset with her free hand, as if to say that it was "C" himself calling. Then, she picked up a pen and began scribbling down the name of a file that the chief apparently needed.

"You say it is in the safe in your office?" Penny asked the voice in the handset. "Yes, sir, I will retrieve it at once and have the service courier hand deliver it to you at the conference."

Wells next heard the click of "C" hanging up, without any pleasantries whatsoever. Penny looked somewhat flushed.

"Commander Wells," she said, "could you be a dear and do me a great favor by watching over my desk whilst I retrieve a file from the Chief's safe? I shall only be a few minutes, and it shall save me from having to lock up the outer office whilst I am in there."

"Of course, Penny," Wells replied.

She smiled when he used her first name, as she was unaccustomed to the informal greeting. She seemed to have liked it. Very much so.

"Grand! Thank you, Wincer," she said returning his smile. "If you don't mind my calling you that…"

"It's what everyone calls me," replied Wells. "So much so, I am afraid I have forgotten my own given name."

It was then when her eyes became warm as he had never seen them before. "Graham is certainly too lovely a name to ever forget. You are such a darling. I shan't forget this kindness."

As Penny Quidling passed him to enter the inner office, she again touched Wells on the forearm. At the door, she paused, and said, "Don't take it personally when you hear me lock the chief's door. He is a stickler on procedures and would be aghast should anyone walk in whilst I have his safe open. I'll be back in a flash."

She disappeared into Sinclair's office and Wells could hear her turn the lock. He then gazed down at her desktop, which was immaculately organized. She was too well trained to leave any documents upon the desktop, but Wells could see that the top drawer of her desk was slightly ajar. She had trusted him to watch over her desk, which either in her haste, or her trust in him, she had failed to lock.

Wells then reached down and slowly pulled the top drawer open. It contained blank copies of Chief Sinclair's official letterhead. A devious thought entered Well's mind. He heard Penny working the combination lock, and from her frustrated vocalizations, she was having problems getting the tumblers to fall allowing it to open.

Wells reached in the drawer of Penny's desk, and with the tips of his fingers gently took two blank sheets of letterhead. He then closed the top desk drawer and slowly opened the drawer just below it. Inside he saw what he hoped to find, a rubber stamp and an ink pad. He removed them, and on Penny's desk, he inked the stamp and slowly but forcibly pressed it upon the two sheets, leaving the imprint "Most Secret" atop the two blank letterheads.

Wells then returned the stamp and ink pad, carefully putting them back precisely as he had found them. He slowly closed the second drawer with his knee as he folded the two sheets in thirds. He put them in his inner suit coat breast pocket just before he heard Penny Quidling unlocking the door from within Sinclair's office.

"Thank you so much, Commander Wells," Penny said as she re-entered the outer office. "I don't wish to push you along, but I must prepare this file for the service's courier. Can't have you looking over my shoulder, can I? Not with 'need to know', and all that still being in play."

"I most certainly understand, Ms. Quidling," Wells said as he was opening the door to the corridor to let himself out.

She had been going through her top drawer, looking for something, when she called out to stop him from leaving. "Wincer," she cried, "wait just a minute!".

He stopped dead in his tracks, feeling he had been found out. Was something amiss that she had recognized?

"Wincer," she repeated, "I hope you are a very talented actor, dear."

"Meaning?" he asked as his face twitched.

"You can act surprised when they break the news about moving Section D to the St. Ermin's, can't you?" Penny flashed a smile at him.

"Certainly," he said. "your secret is safe, I assure you. But when it is announced, and once we are stationed there, I am going to have you over for tea. Just you and me."

"For whatever occasion?" she asked.

"For no occasion t'all, Penny," he said, smiling warmly.

"You are just too much, Graham," she said, flicking her wrist at him as if to say, *away with you, already*.

That night in the seclusion of his London flat, Wincer Wells typed a directive on the letterhead already stamped "Most Secret". It ordered that the files of Gunnar MacAlvor be stamped as passing, allowing his release for the Norway mission with his brother Einar. Tomorrow, Wells would take the express train back to Scotland and hand deliver it to *Drumintoul Lodge*. No one would question the document, and if they should, they would find that "C" was unavailable to discuss it as he was in a secret conference.

Having re-read the document several times, and being satisfied it met the expectations of such an order in wording and appearance, Wells drew a fresh quill pen and a supply of green naval ink he had purchased at the stationers on the way home. He dipped the quill in the ink and signed the document with a large single letter in green :

35 The Rest of Czechoslovakia

Historical Reference - 1939

"The British nation is unique in this respect. They are the only people who like to be told how bad things are, who like to be told the worst."

Winston Spencer Churchill

Beware the Ides of March! On March 15, 1939, one year to the day after he had announced the Austrian *Anschluss* in Vienna, Hitler invaded the rest of Czechoslovakia. The day before, Hitler had demanded the Czechoslovakian President Hácha meet him at the Reich Chancellery building in Berlin. Hitler then reportedly made him wait several hours until around 2 am in the morning of the 15th, when he told Hácha that the tanks and infantry were preparing to invade his country in a matter of hours. Hermann Göring then threatened President Hácha with the bombing of the country's capital, Prague, into annihilation if the president did not concede. President Hácha was said to have had a heart attack on the spot from the pressure applied by Göring. Hácha was, however, able to continue and eventually conceded. At just after 4 am, he called Prague to instruct the military to stand down and to allow the *Wehrmacht* to enter uncontested into what remained of Czechoslovakia. Shortly thereafter, the *Wehrmacht* rolled unopposed once more.

The very next day, Hitler was in Prague, and from the historic halls of Prague Castle he announced that the citizens of Czechoslovakia were members of the German Protectorate of Bohemia and Moravia. He stated that,"Bohemia and Moravia have for thousands of years belonged to the *Lebensraum* of the German people". The Slovak lands were separated into a puppet state of the Third Reich. It was clear throughout the world that the Munich agreement, so celebrated only months before, was now utterly worthless. Prime Minister Neville Chamberlain was disgraced for having pursued "peace in our time. On this same day, the Ides of March, Nazi troops were amassed at the Slovak-Polish border. Hitler was already planning his next manufactured crisis. He was intent on continuing to gain territory until one country resisted, and would give him the excuse to demonstrate to the world what devastation his war machine could produce. The next point of friction would be over the Baltic Seaport of Danzig.

——— • • • ———

On April 1, 1939, Germany launched their most impressive battleship constructed up until that point. The *Tirpitz* was the sister ship of the Battleship *Bismarck*, she was capable of achieving a top speed of 30 knots, potentially outrunning any ship her size in the Royal Navy. Hitler was on hand at the port of Wilhemshaven to tell the world that he had indisputably strengthened his Reich's navy, the *Kriegsmarine*.

Tirpitz weighed 2,000 tons heavier than the *Bismarck*, and like her sister ship had eight massive 15inch guns beset on four elevating turrets. Her armored plating was thought to be resistant to the rounds of most other naval guns of the time. After her launch, she would undergo fitting-out and sea trials, and would not enter service until February of 1941. She was deemed by Germany to be unsinkable. Winston Churchill declared her "The Beast" and would make over thirty attempts during the coming war to prove the ship was no more unsinkable than the Titanic.

36 The Final Steps to War

1939

"You were given the choice between war and dishonour. You chose dishonour, and you will have war. "

Winston Spencer Churchill

Czechoslovakia was gone from Europe's map, just as Austria had been wiped from it one year earlier. With the movement of Nazi troops amassing along their southern and western borders, the Poles knew they were to be next. They became very, very nervous, but nonetheless prepared for war. They could not have foreseen how ruthless an enemy they faced.

For one thing, they were running blind once more. After having had the ability to read the *Wehrmacht's* messaging since 1932, they found themselves once more completely unable to do so. What had caused this?

In December of 1938, the German military upgraded the capabilities of their Enigma devices. They did this by introducing two new rotors to the three already in service. The Enigma machines still only employed three rotors within the machine, but now there were five distinct rotors from which to draw. In other words, instead of there being six possible configurations of rotors, there were now sixty. The complexity had just increased tenfold. The limited number of Polish *Bomba* devices used to crack the daily codes could not possibly keep up with solving the increased number of possible settings.

As the emboldened Hitler ratcheted up his ranting speeches in the spring and summer of 1939 with inflammatory statements made against Poland, the Poles knew it was only a matter of time until Germany invaded their homeland. France and Britain were by this point through with appeasing Hitler, and had made their positions to protect Poland very public indeed.

What Poland did next, totally unprompted by their Western Allies, may have been one of the most consequential decisions of all of World War II. The Polish Cyber Bureau, *Biuro Szyfrów,* invited their counterparts in France and England to come to Warsaw for a classified cryptanalysis conference. The meeting would take place on July 25 & 26, less than six weeks before the onset of the war.

The representatives for French Intelligence were Major Gustave Bertrand (the man who several years earlier had given the Poles the Enigma codebooks and documentation) and Captain Henri Braquenié. The British delegation came from their GC&CS home at the new Bletchley Park facility. These included World War I Room 40 veterans Alastair Deniston, (by then the head of Bletchley Park) and "Dilly" Knox, that facility's top cryptologist.

At this point, Alan Turing was still employed by Kings College in Cambridge. He had been Knox's man all along, and had reportedly been working secretly even then on Enigma for Knox. Neither Knox nor Turing had made much headway at that point. Turing, himself, however, did not attend the Warsaw crypto-conference.

The foreign intelligence officials arrived in Warsaw and took up residence in that town's pre-eminent lodging: The Hotel Bristol. The next morning they were escorted south near the town of Pyry. Once there, the men were taken to a secret bunker facility, nestled safely underneath the nearby Kabaty Woods.

The cryptanalysis conference had been hosted by the Polish Cipher Bureau's joint chiefs, Lieutenant Colonel Gwido Langer and Major Maksymilian Ciężki. The stars of the conference were the three Poznań University mathematicians: Marian Rejewski, Jerzy Różycki and Henryk Zygalski. As the conference went on, the Poles disclosed all they had done over the past six years. They told of their mathematical processes that had led to reverse engineering of the Enigma device. They demonstrated the fully functional Enigma mock-ups they had devised, taught the usage of the perforated "Zygalski Sheets" for manually breaking the settings, and then demonstrated for the French and British intelligence elites their ultimate achievement - the *Bomba* device they had constructed for the mechanized breaking of the daily Enigma settings. In one day of meetings, every secret the Polish Intelligence Cypher Bureau had held most dear was openly laid bare before their colleagues.

The French and British were *gobsmacked*, to use the British phrase. It was beyond belief that the Poles had been reading the Enigma traffic with 75% effectiveness for the past six years. The Poles had successfully replicated the functions and circuits of the Enigma device, right down to the internal wiring of each of the individual rotors, including those that had been added in late 1938.

Dilly Knox especially found it difficult to accept that the Poles had been able to achieve through mathematical prowess what he himself had not. Knox had always considered himself an unmatched intellect, and here were *bloody foreigners* claiming to have broken the code he himself had found to be unbreakable.

The Poles explained they were sharing all this, because of the impending war. No longer had the resources to expand their *Bomba* approach to the Enigma variant that had begun drawing from five distinct rotors. To make it even worse, the *Kriegsmarine* Naval Enigma device, which employed four rotors, had been upgraded in late 1938 to draw from a pool of eight rotors. The Poles could simply not keep up with the changes. But from what they did know from their intercepts prior to those changes, it would not be long before Hitler attacked.

It was clear that not only were more resources needed to continue the Polish work, but that the products developed to date (such as the reverse-engineered Enigmas, the *Bombas* and the *Zygalski Sheets*) needed to be removed from Poland before the war began. The French and British, once over their shock, were all too happy to aide the Poles.

The conference continued a second day, after which the Poles and French left with an incredibly enriched understanding of Enigma. Knox would return to Bletchley Park to share what he had seen with Alan Turing, the latter having reported once the war had begun. Likewise, the French were amazed, and Bertrand was quick to offer whatever assistance he could to the Poles going forward. This pledge would come to have a significant bearing on our story.

Within days of the Kabaty Woods Conference, the Polish *Bombas,* and other hardware were being shipped out of Poland to their cryptographic colleagues in Paris and at Bletchley Park. It would prove to happen not a moment too soon. The Nazis would commence with *"Case White"*, the invasion of Poland in only 36 days. Had the Poles not shared their secrets, all would surely have been discovered by the invaders.

—— · • · ——

The secrets of Bletchley Park were tightly held until the 1980s. Only then did several books begin to be published on what had gone on there during the Second World War. When they eventually did, and until the present day, the narrative that evolved was that a small group of University *"boffins"*, as the English were apt to call them, broke the Enigma code through sheer intellectual prowess. Little was made of the contributions of the Polish Cypher Bureau, or more specifically of the ground-breaking works of Marian Rejewski, Jerzy Różycki and Henryk Zygalski. Yet, what these three men pioneered in the 1930s is as vital as any other work performed at Bletchley Park in shortening the war.

Indeed, the Polish Cypher Bureau's decision to share their most precious secrets with the West provided the British GC&CS an incredible head start. One that would save innumerable lives. One that to this day remains largely uncredited to this three brilliant mathematicians.

As a testimony to these points, many of those closest to him believe that Alan Turing, the man most personally attributed with breaking Enigma, would have protested against the lack of recognition of the tremendous contributions of the Poles. It was perhaps Turing's homage to the work of Rejewski *et al.* in naming the machines he devised as the *Bombe*, whose design elements very similarly resembled the Polish *Bomba*. While Turing had not met directly with the Poles before coming to Bletchley, Dilly Knox had brought him up to speed on the accomplishments of these foreign mathematicians. Turing would later meet with them in France, as we shall see.

The perforated sheets that were developed by Henryk Zygalski, known today throughout the intelligence world as *"Zygalski Sheets"*, were also utilized at Bletchley Park. Except that they were renamed as *Netz*, from the German word *Netzverfahren*, or *"net method"*. This last reference referred to the visual process of setting the perforated sheets, one atop the other on a light table. The light would shine through in holes in the "net" representing the possible remaining rotor configurations.

The *"Boffins"* at Bletchley would certainly improve upon the *Bomba's* design and scale it to a level that could never have been achieved by the Poles. But there is no denying that they were given a running head start in a race for freedom itself.

———— • • • ————

Less than a month after the Kabaty Woods Conference there was another secret conference in Eastern Europe which would prove equally consequential. On the 21st of August, Adolf Hitler, once more at the Berghof, received a response from a message he had sent to Joseph Stalin. The Soviet leader had agreed to receive Hitler's foreign minister in Moscow.

On the 23rd of August, just eight days before Hitler's invasion of Poland, he sent his Foreign Minister, Joachim von Ribbentrop to Moscow to meet with his Soviet counterpart, Vyacheslav Mikhailovich Molotov, to sign a non-aggression pact. Molotov was one of the true Bolshevik conspirators of the 1917 October Revolution in Russia. It is here where his name became associated with the simple but effective street-devised incendiary device known as the "Molotov cocktail". " Stalin trusted Molotov, as much as Stalin ever trusted anyone at all.

Publicly, Molotov and Ribbentrop signed the non-aggression pact that would in history forever infamously bear their names. In secret, Germany and Russia agreed to the timing of and the particulars of how to divide Poland amongst themselves, wiping it completely, once more, from the world map.

Stalin feared the power of the German War Machine, even though it still had yet been forced to fight. He feared the *Wehrmacht* would not stop at Poland's borders but would press into the Soviet territories as well. Perhaps what motivated Stalin most to sign the treaty was the tepid response of the Western Powers in refusing to stand up to Hitler in Austria and Czechoslovakia. Stalin deemed the non-aggression pact as vital to his interests, with the added benefit of securing half of the Polish lands to act as buffer between Germany and the USSR. Hitler, on the other hand, wished only to invade Poland without triggering a Soviet response. After Poland was crushed, Hitler would deal separately with the Communists he had long loathed.

The MacAlvor twins were to be dispatched to Norway in July of 1939. Just in the weeks before they sailed with their provisions, and about a week before the Polish Crypto-analysis Conference was held in the Kabaty Woods, Einar and Gunnar were briefed by Wincer Wells and a sour-faced bespectacled gentlemen, dressed in tweed, who was only introduced to Einar and Gunnar as "Dilly".

The twins had signed their Official Secrets Act documents long before they were even allowed to access the STS-26 training site in the Scottish Highlands in the autumn of the previous year. On that day in July 1938 just before their deployment, they were forced to sign an additional document that stipulated under penalty of life imprisonment they were not to reveal what they were about to be shown. After they had signed, a wooden box was placed on the table, and opened to reveal what looked like a typewriter without a carriage.

"Please," said Einar, "not more radio training. We are ready. We are more than ready. Gunnar is a complete genius with the wireless sets."

"Relax, lads," said Dilly. "This is no mere wireless set. In fact, this device does not transmit nor receive. Yet, this is the most valued and dangerous device in the hands of our German counterparts. This is *Enigma*."

Dilly looked to Wells, who had examined the twins' bemused faces. They had never heard of this "Enigma", as well they should not have. Then Dilly continued his briefing to them, with the most serious of looks seemingly screwed upon his already tight face.

"Enigma is an encryption device, nothing more. We know from intercepts that a militarized Enigma unit is in use in Narvik. We think it is being used to send encrypted wireless messages to Berlin on the iron ore shipments coming from the Kiruna mines in Sweden for shipping on to German ports."

"You think or do you know all this as fact?" Einar asked.

"We are not yet able to break Enigma's cypher," Dilly admitted.

"Then how can you know what message they are sending?" Einar followed up.

Einar was answered by his brother, "Because they are able to correlate the times of the encrypted intercepts to those associated with either the trains' arrival, or of the departure of the ore freighters."

"Cock on, lad," said Dilly, obviously impressed with Gunnar's quick and perceptive mind. "We just might have a spot for you when this is all over."

The briefing lasted several hours. The twins were trained on the device, its overall encryption function, and especially the functionality of the rotors. The twins were shown how to open the device, access the spindle on which the rotors were set, and how to remove the rotors. Both Einar and Gunnar were given hands-on practice at removing the rotors and reinstalling them.

Dilly instructed them that the unit on which they were practicing was only a non-militarized commercial version, and that the militarized version may appear similar, but not exactly the same in appearance. He then said if they were to come across anything remotely similar to it, that it was to be noted. Even beyond that, if it were ever possible to safely steal such a device, they should certainly attempt to do so. If they could not manage the entire device, then they should take, at the very least, every available rotor. These were small enough that even if all five rotors were taken, they could readily be contained in the pair of pockets of an overcoat, or even in a small cloth bag if necessary.

It was then that Wincer Wells produced just such a small cloth sack. He emptied it carefully on the table in front of the device. Five replica rotors were spread on the table before them. They were numbered in Roman numerals from I to V.

"These are non-functional versions to aid your recognition. Should you come across the Narvik device, you may be ordered to do whatever is possible to steal the device, or if nothing else, the real rotors from the device, replacing with these non-functional replicas."

"What good will that do?" Einar asked. "Won't the operator know that they have been swapped out when he attempts to code or decode the next message?"

It was then that Wincer Wells looked cautiously to Dilly. He then returned his gaze to the twins to answer Einar's question.

"I have perhaps confused you somewhat when I described these replicas as being non-functional. They contain a new explosive developed by our scientists, based on Czech formulations, known as plastic explosive. The French call the stuff *"plastique"*. There is enough in these rotors to thoroughly destroy the Enigma device completely."

Gunnar and Einar exchanged incredulous looks.

"You want us to carry these?" exclaimed Gunnar. "We could blow ourselves to bits."

It was then that Wincer Wells cleared his throat, but before he could respond, his face contorted into his namesake spasm. "This new explosive material is extremely stable," said Wells after recovering his composure, "so long as it does not have an electrical current running through it. It is very safe to handle and transport. You both will be trained tomorrow on its use. You are only to use these replicates if you cannot take the entire unit and have to swap out the rotors."

"Won't the operator report the destroyed unit back to his superiors?" asked Einar.

The comment drew a curious look from Wincer Wells. "We may have misled you somewhat on that also," he said. "There won't be anything left of the operator. There's enough explosive in those rotors to leave only the smallest bits of debris. The idea is to make it appear the operator got taken out by another blast and the device was collateral damage. If this is pulled off properly, there is very little chance the Nazis will shutdown all their networks and redesign Enigma from the ground up. Even if they should, it will take months and cripple their war communications, but we would rather they not do so."

Wells then showed the twins how to prime the replicate rotors, such that they would be set to go off.

"Incredibly enough," Dilly said, "we use the current from Enigma's own batteries to set off the charges. Simply replace the rotors, turn on the Enigma device, which powers up its batteries, and then depress any key. Once that key is pressed, there is no delay. My point being, you don't wish to be present when the operator tries to use the device. It surely will take out anyone in the room, and quite possibly even the next."

Einar looked at Gunnar. Both were dumbstruck. Gunnar then said, "You expect us to pinch that device or its rotors?"

"No," barked Wells, "this is a secondary assignment only. This training is preparation only should the case arise that you come across that Enigma device whilst in Narvik. Most likely you will never even be made aware of it. Whoever is transmitting from Narvik is a highly skilled professional. But if you were to come across anyone having such a device you are to notify me. The bloody rotor bombs are only in case we decide to make a play. I don't want either of you taking their use into your own hands, do you understand? No heroics."

The brothers looked at each other. Einar then spoke for them. "Most certainly. If we come across any opportunity to proceed, we are to contact Wincer Wells. Quite clear. What exactly are we to communicate to you?"

Wincer's face screwed into a spasm, then uncoiled. "You are to engage on the emergency frequency. It will be monitored throughout all the hours of each and every day you are deployed. Simply say that you've found *Thor's Hammer*."

Gunnar said the single word, "*Mjölnir*."

"What?" asked a confused Wincer Wells.

"That is the name of Thor's Hammer," explained Einar.

"Are we to use the English phrase '*Thor's Hammer*' or '*Mjölnir*'? asked Gunnar. "*Thor's Hammer* sounds quite suspicious, doesn't it?"

"Our operators won't understand '*Mjölnir*'," saidWells.

"Father can drill them on it," said Einar, "I think Gunnar is correct. I find '*Mjölnir*' sounds much more natural. Less likely to be noticed."

"Fine," said Wells, exasperated. "*Mjölnir* it is. Then after you make that signal to us, you are to do nothing except monitor that frequency every hour at quarter past until you hear my reply of either the words 'Paris' or 'Athens''. Paris means proceed, Athens means abort. Understood?"

"Completely," agreed Einar. "Paris - Proceed; Athens - Abort."

It was not until hours later when they were alone on a walk around the grounds outside that twins discussed the briefing between themselves. Before them the Cairngorm Mountains rose spectacularly as if models standing in for the peaks of Arctic Norway.

"This is a most highly guarded secret they shared with us today," said Gunnar.'

"No more than all the other secrets to which we have been privy over the last eight months," said Einar.

Gunnar looked at Einar, and understood that his brother had not put together the pieces of information as he had.

"I would disagree, my brother," said Gunnar softly. "First of all, they make us sign another security document. This is so delicate that even the bloody Official Secrets Act is not enough? Second, they don't share this us until two days before we depart. They were keeping this, their greatest secret, for last in case our mission was to be cancelled for any reason at all."

"Their secret is that they are trying to crack the German cypher code?" asked Einar.

"Yes," said Gunnar, "but more so that they are having no success in doing so. They are getting desperate to be even considering this foolishness."

"You make a strong point, my brother," replied Einar.

Gunnar then cleared his throat in such a way as to give Einar notice that a challenge was to follow.

"Diseases desperate grown, By desperate appliance are relieved, Or not at all." Gunnar quoted Shakespeare. It was a game they played. Gunnar quoted the bard and Einar attempted to guess from which play.

"Macbeth," offered Einar.

"Hamlet," corrected Gunnar.

Then Einar reacted playfully with his own quip, "But, my brother, we are leaving the land of the Scottish Thanes only to hidden amongst those once thought to be Danes."

———•·•———

On his return from the Kabaty Woods Conference outside Warsaw, Dilly Knox immediately sought out Wincer Wells. He called on him at the MI6 offices on Broadway in Westminster.

"We need to cancel that Norwegian mission," he said. "Let's get those exploding *faux*-rotors back from those lads."

"Too late, old chap," said Wells, "the boys are already deployed. They arrived in Skrova days ago. Why do you suddenly want to call it all off?"

"Never mind that," said Dilly, "lets just say the landscape has changed over the past several days. No need now to take any silly risks with Enigma."

"Don't worry, Dilly," said Wells, "the lads are instructed to contact me in case they think they have a go. I will just stand them down should they raise the flag."

"I pray your confidence in their following orders is well placed," said Wells. "I should have known better than to engage you Section D chaps in on this."

37 The Final Preparations

"A state of society where men may not speak their minds cannot long endure."

Winston Spencer Churchill

Diane Sterling worked late into the evening. She had fully absorbed every entry in Tilly MacAlvor's diary. She had all the answers to the questions that Jake Conley had posed to her. She was at this hour going over her presentation that she would use to brief her billionaire client.

Tomorrow she would fly from Heathrow to Washington DC. There she would spend the evening in a hotel near Dulles airport before meeting Flake Ferris the next morning and flying on to DFW. After deplaning, they were to be escorted to the Conley encampment on the Brazos by helicopter, getting in just before noon. That evening after dinner, she and Flake would make the presentation to Jake Conley and this assignment would be completed.

As she went through the powerpoint slides, thinking about the exact wording she would employ, right down to the phrasing of each bullet. She jotted in the notes any other salient points to be made verbally to each slide. She found long ago if she prepared this way, more times than often she would feel confident enough to appear natural. At worst, she would come off prepared but stiff. In either case she avoided the ultimate sin, being unprepared to the point of appearing to not have mastered the material.

Diane was taking Flake along to answer any detailed genealogical questions, as well as to show the depth of talent that she had utilized to solve this case. Certainly, she expected Jake's son, Wade, to contest their findings.

Wade Conley had been calling her ever since she had scheduled the meeting. He wanted an advance read out on exactly what they were to present to his father. Diane would not share this with the man, telling him he would soon enough find out along with his father.

"Damn it, Diane," Wade had snapped on their last call, "we are paying you a small fortune for these answers. Now, tell me what you found or I'll have this meeting called off altogether."

"Wade, you've made a mistake threatening me," Diane had said. "You also made a mistake saying 'we'. Jake is putting up the small fortune, not you. Besides, he warned me about your trying to get ahead of him on this, if you recall. If you want to cancel the meeting, go right ahead. I'm sure Jake won't be too pleased with it, though. Now, I will see you in two days time down in DFW. Don't call me again. You'll find out what we have to say along with Jake, presuming he'll still want you in the room after I tell him what a pain in the ass you're being."

Wade Conley did not have an immediate reply. After several seconds of tomb-like silence, Wade finally said, "All right, Diane, have it your way. But if you give me any reason to, I'll make sure my lawyers have you tied up in court for so long that you'll wish you had never taken this case."

"Goodbye, Wade," was all she said before hanging up. That had been two hours ago, so she was startled when her mobile phone once more chirped at her. She dreaded talking to Wade again, but when she looked at the phone's display, she was relieved to not find Wade's name there.

"Malcolm, so nice to hear from you," she had said warmly. "I was actually just thinking of you. Are you here in London or still up in Cheltenham?"

"The latter, I am afraid," Devereaux said. "To be more precise, in the Malverns at Millhaven. So, I am afraid I am far too distant to accept your dinner offer this evening."

Diane laughed before responding. "Well, as it is, I am far too busy to wine and dine you tonight. Beginning my trek back to Texas tomorrow morning, so, I am just going over my material one last time. Seriously, I really do want to thank you for all the material you've dug up for me on this. I would have been lost without it all."

"That's exactly why I am calling, darling," Devereaux said. "I wanted to make sure you saw that last set of documents I had couriered over to you this morning. Remember you had asked me to see if I could find any information on this Bogdan Bratajewski that Sophie was looking into? The files I sent to you pertained to that."

"Yes," Diane replied, "I got your voicemail this morning. I am sorry I had not gotten back to you since then, but it has been a hellish day. I was going to go over those files when I returned from this trip. Then I'd have the time to think through how I would present them to Sophie without stepping all over her case. Tricky stuff, to say the least."

Diane thought he would understand her desire to focus on the material later.

"That's exactly what I was afraid of, love," admitted Devereaux. "Diane, you must look at that file tonight, before you get on that plane tomorrow. It is imperative, my dear."

"OK, OK, Malcolm," she answered, "I guarantee you that I will, but it still won't go to Sophie until I get back."

"Perfect," said the relieved Devereaux, although his voice was still hard with urgency. "Don't be just telling me that only to slosh me off the phone."

"I promise, Malcolm, I promise," she moaned in an exaggerated, stretched-out reply. "I swear that if I don't you can lock me up in the Tower."

He chuckled with a devious tone. "Darling, if I lock you up, it will be in someplace much more comfortable than the Tower, and I'll be in there with you."

"I might well have guessed," Diane replied.

They spoke further for another minute or two, small talk and repartee, before hanging up. Then Diane, true to her word, went through the incoming bin to find Malcolm's package of files. She carefully sliced open the top of the manilla envelope with the bubble wrapped lining - this man spared no expense - to find the files on Bogdan Bratajewski with the markings of the SOE.

The file was thick, and Diane gave it her preliminary review. It covered the time period from 1939 until late 1944. As she scanned the included documents, Diane could immediately sense the importance of what was contained within it. She would rather have spent her remaining time with the Conley presentation, but she had promised Devereaux...

Paper-clipped to the front was a hand-written note from Devereaux, which read,

This Bogdan Bratajewski appears to have been a most interesting fellow. As I had said to you, once one starts burrowing in the past, one never knows what will be found. Particularly note the flagged excerpt. I hope this helps both you and Sophie in both your investigations.

Kind Regards,

Your Malcolm

Diane felt as if she was wasting valuable time until she flipped to the page with an adhesive tab on which Devereaux had drawn an arrow shape. It was entitled, *"Disciplinary Review of Commander Graham Ernest Wells, SOE."* It was dated September 26, 1945. Unlike all the other material he had sent her on the twins which had long ago been declassified, these documents had been marked as having completed a declassification review only in the preceding weeks.

Diane then assessed that the reason this material was so late in coming to her was that Malcolm Devereaux had to undergo an emergency declassification request, which even if it were expedited, could take months. Somehow he had gotten it done in weeks, perhaps only because of the fact that the material was well over seventy years old. She wondered if he employed her name, as the woman who had brought such visibility into SIS' corruption, to expedite the process.

Diane read through the document. Then she read it again. And again. Each time more slowly, as if that would improve her comprehension. Each word seemed to fall in place, like the tumbling images of a slot machine. She found herself in a stupor, not unlike that of drunkenness, or that imparted when re-reading the winning numbers of a lottery ticket.

"Oh my God," she kept repeating, softly, under her breath, although there was no one left in the office to hear her.

She finally snapped out of her delirium and into a mode of action. She copied the file, sealed the replica of the documents in a fresh manilla envelope which she marked with Emory Hauptmann's name.

Diane then texted Emory the following, "Need you in London office ASAP. Document left in your care to be delivered to Sophie immediately. She will be arriving in London in two days time. Most urgent. Call me."

Diane then took the originals and stuffed them into her briefcase. She would take them along to Texas with her. It was only then that she realized that Devereaux had likely been electronically stalking her movements, just as she had been doing to Sophie. That was how he knew she was flying to Texas the next day.

Her phone rang. It was Emory.

"Boy, do I have a most important mission for you," she began.

"I'm listening," he said.

"I'm leaving a copy of a file here in the London office." Diane said. "Get your *Hinterteil* over here and make sure it gets into Sophie's hands before she briefs her client."

"I haven't spoken to Sophie since her *dupa* went AWOL," said Emory. "Clearly she doesn't want us interrupting her with anything just now. Do we even know when she's making her outbrief? How am I supposed to find her?"

"For God's sake," Diane said, thinking to herself Sophie would protest these 'profane' words coming from her lips, "you are a world class detective, Emory. Act like one when I need you to. I'll leave you her travel itinerary here along with the file."

There was silence on the other end of the phone. It was awkwardly heavy. Diane thought at first she had offended her man in Berlin and was preparing to apologize for her forcefulness, when he replied.

"Oh my God! You've been tracking her all along …"

THE END OF "THE TWINS OF NARVIK, PART I"

Author's Apology:

I really hate to leave you dangling from this cliffhanger...

...but, I hope you are enjoying this tale of Birger and Tulla, Brigand and Tilly, Cassandra, Bogdan and Albin, and of course the twins, Einar and Gunnar.

This story is completed in Part II, which, if I am not giving away too much, begins with the arrival of the twins, Einar and Gunnar, to the Lofoten Island area just outside of Narvik. I assure the reader that all questions you may have remaining will be answered in that volume.

As always, I have stayed as true as I possibly could to the historical record in this novel. I always feel somewhat mortally betrayed to read a historical fiction where the writer has introduced factual elements entirely of his own making. I promise not to do that to my readers, and whenever I must bend the arc of time to fit my plot-lines, I will always confess those venial sins to the reader in my endnotes. Those endnotes will follow the conclusion of this tale in Part II.

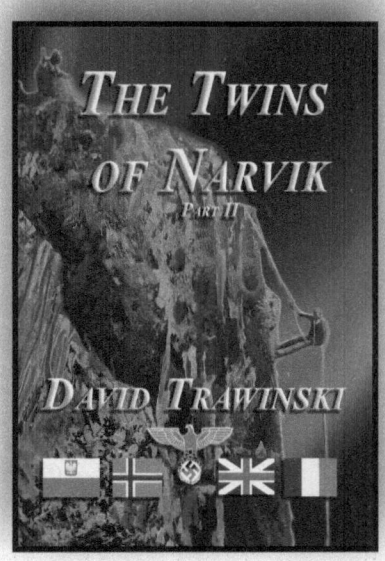

The Twins of Narvik

Is Proudly

Published by

Figure & Image Attributions

Figure 1 *Narvik Image from Wikimedia Commons*
(Public Domain)

Figure 2 *Churchill Montage Arranged by David Trawinski*
rom Wikimedia Commons Elements

Figure 3 *"Nordlys" Travel Map Prepared by David Trawinski*

Figure 4 *Vestfjorden/Ofotfjord Map Prepared by David Trawinski*

Figure 5 *Skrova with Litlmolla*

Licensed Adobe Stock Image 382931381

by "Joerg/stock.adobe.com"

View from Hogskrova

Licensed Adobe Stock Image 216803458

by "Jan BysTri/stock.adobe.com"

Figure 6 *Fjord Photo Copyright 2020 Elizabeth Marie Trawinski*

Figure 7 *Sandbotnen Licensed Adobe Stock Image 175372604*

by "Oleksandr Dibrova/stock.adobe.com"

Figure 8 *Circus Lane Licensed Adobe Stock Image 362574527*

by "Mark/stock.adobe.com"

Figure 9 *Mansfield Cumming Image from Wikipedia Commons*
(Public Domain)

Figure 10 *Dardanelles Montage Arranged by David Trawinski*
from Wikimedia Commons Elements

Figure 11 *Gallipoli Montage Arranged by David Trawinski*
from Wikimedia Commons Elements

Figure 12 *The Royal Mile at Castlehill, Edinburgh*
Licensed from Wikimedia Commons

by Farwestern - Photo by Gregg M. Erickson

Figure & Image Attributions

Figure 13   *American Airmen from Wikimedia Commons Elements*
Cooper/Fauntleroy at Biplane Photo
(Public Domain)
Lviv Memorial
File:To American Heroes….jpg
by Robin from Krakow, Poland

Figure 14   *Broughty Ferry Castle*

Castle - Licensed Adobe Image 401684086

by "Artur/stock.adobe.com"

View - Image Licensed from Wikipedia Commons

Figure 15   *Piłsudski/Sikorski Arranged by David Trawinski from*

Wikipedia Commons Image Elements

Figure 16   *Arranged by David Trawinski from*

Wikipedia Commons Image Elements

Figure 17   *Enigma Device Photograph from Narvik Museum*

Copyright 2020 by Elizabeth Marie Trawinski

inset over Licensed Adobe Stock Image 190381676

by "Paul Robertson/stock.adobe.com"

Figure 18   *Norway Original Photos Copyright 2020*

by Elizabeth Marie Trawinski

Figure 19   *Munich Conference, Flickr, Public Domain*

Figure 20   *Tatras Mountains*

Licensed Adobe Stock Image 112559198

by "Grzegorz_pakula/stock.adobe.com"

Figure 21   *Cairngorm Mountains*

Licensed Adobe Stock Image 198011016

by "mountaintreks/stock.adobe.com"